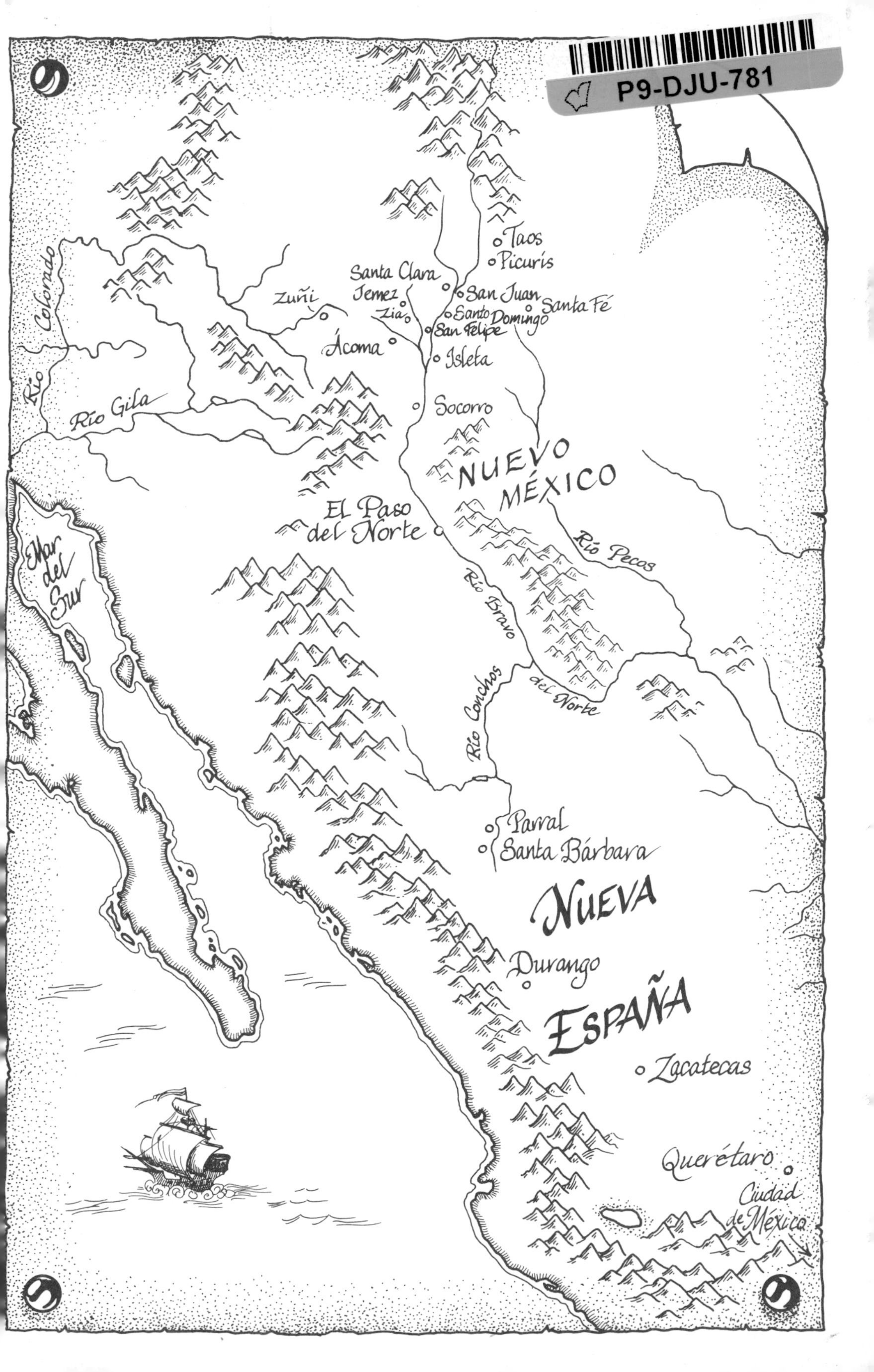

Río Colorado
Río Gila
Zuñi
Santa Clara
Jemez
Zia
Ácoma
Taos
Picurís
San Juan
Santa Fé
Santo Domingo
San Felipe
Isleta
Socorro
NUEVO MÉXICO
El Paso del Norte
Río Pecos
Río Bravo del Norte
Río Conchos
El Mar del Sur
Parral
Santa Bárbara
NUEVA ESPAÑA
Durango
Zacatecas
Querétaro
Ciudad de México

# ÁCOMA

*A Novel of Conquest*

# ÁCOMA

## *A Novel of Conquest*

LANA M. HARRIGAN

A TOM DOHERTY ASSOCIATES BOOK
*New York*

ÁCOMA: A NOVEL OF CONQUEST



This book is printed on acid-free paper.

A Forge Book
Published by Tom Doherty Associates, Inc.
175 Fifth Avenue
New York, NY 10010

Forge® is a registered trademark of Tom Doherty Associates, Inc.

Interior drawings by Gary Moeller

Design by Patrice Sheridan

Library of Congress Cataloging-in-Publication Data

Harrigan, Lana M.
Ácoma : a novel of conquest / Lana M. Harrigan.—1st ed.
p. cm.
"A Tom Doherty Associates book."
ISBN 0-312-85257-6
1. Oñate, Juan de, 1549?-1624—Fiction. 2. New Mexico—History—To 1848—Fiction. I. Title.
PS3558.A6258A64 1997
813'.54—dc21 97-16432
CIP

First Edition: September 1997

Printed in the United States of America

0 9 8 7 6 5 4 3 2 1

*For* R.W., J.F., E.B., and R.H.
*who make it all worthwhile.*

*"¿Agora quem vai preparar o jantar?"*
—Jorge Amado, *Gabriela, Cravo e Canela*

It comes alive
It comes alive, live, live.
In the south mountain
The jaguar comes alive, comes alive.

With this animal of prey
Comes the power,
    comes the deer
        comes the antelope
Comes the power of good fortune
                        in the hunt.

—Ácoma prayer to give power
and spirit to a hunting fetish

# Contents

# Acknowledgments

Any writer of historical fiction owes an enormous debt to the historians, diarists, anthropologists, ethnologists, scribes, storytellers—to anyone who ever recorded or passed down a piece of information or dug out that piece of information and deciphered it. My personal debt to these researchers and common men and women is immeasurable.

No one loves a bureaucrat. They have been loathed or ridiculed for centuries; I, however, must sing a paean for these poor souls who have never garnered an ounce of respect. If it were not for bureaucrats and the bureaucratic government of seventeenth-century Spain and the Catholic Church, little of the knowledge necessary to recreate the colonial history of New Mexico or the southwestern United States would be available to us today. If a document cannot be found in archives in New Mexico, perhaps a copy of it may lie in a dim corner in a musty stack of papers in Mexico City or Guadalajara, or in that treasure trove, the Archives of the Indies in Seville.

From all of these centuries-old documents, historians past and present have labored uncountable hours to bring light and understanding to events obscured by time and often language. I cannot begin to list all the researchers from whose efforts I have so benefited, but in the bedrock for the study of the founding and early colonial history of New Mexico are: George P. Hammond and Agapito Rey, whose two-volume translation of the Oñate documents is a treasure of New Mexican history; France V. Scholes, whose monumental effort published in the *New Mexico Historical Review* brought us the turbulent and troublous history of New Mexico's seventeenth century; Gaspar Pérez de Villagrá, whose twenty-four-canto epic poem, *La Historia de la Nueva México*, published in 1610, gives an eyewitness, albeit prejudiced, account of the battle of Ácoma as well as of the founding in 1598 of Spain's farthest North American capital; Leslie A. White, ethnologist, whose work begun in the 1920s among the Ácomas, along with Matthew W. Stirling's *Origin Myth of Ácoma*, and Dr. Ward Alan Minge's vast research on the history of the Ácoma have all enriched our knowledge of and admiration for the People of the White Rock.

And I am gratefully beholden to the people of Ácoma, whose beauty, strength, and endurance have inspired the imagination of anyone who has ever laid eyes on their magnificent mesa-top home.

I owe a particular debt of gratitude to two dear friends and preeminent scholars, Professor John L. Kessell, noted historian and editor of the De Vargas Project at the University of New Mexico, and Dr. Raymond R. MacCurdy, Professor Emeritus of Spanish at UNM, authority on the Golden Age Drama of Spain. If I ever needed a shred of historical information, John was my source. No matter how insignificant my question, he answered with careful attention and his infectious enthusiasm. Tim MacCurdy, my former professor of Spanish literature and now novel-writing colleague, and I shared many cups of coffee discussing how one transforms an academic orientation into the creative process. I prize his valuable input and help.

I have a special place in my heart for my early readers who were there when I was taking my first baby steps in novel writing—each gave me crucial advice and unstinting support: Elvira Lima, Christina Squire, Sharon Stine, and Carolyn Tuttle.

There is a special category of thanks reserved for two-time Spur Award-winning author, Norman Zollinger, whose generous phone call on my behalf launched this book. *Mil gracias*, Norm.

And it is my great good fortune to have worked with my nonpareil editor, Dale Walker, who with his insightful red pen taught me more about writing than I could have learned from a library of books.

I have received abundant and generous help from many sources, but I must offer a *mea culpa* for any deficiencies in the novel; all errors are mine, and mine alone.

I have saved them for last, but their importance rests at the very top, their gifts to me incalculable. They are my incredibly talented family: my cousin and Professor of Art, Gary Moeller, who captured brilliantly and beautifully in brush strokes what the pen hoped to render in words; my extraordinarily gifted sisters whom I cherish, Linda, without whose affirmative response none of this would have ever begun and on whom I still depend for her consummate insight, and Diana, who has given me invaluable and discerning critiques; my remarkable mother, who is my authority on the English language and grammar as well as the person whose advice I need and treasure most; and my dear father, whom I call when I need a piece of information about animals, weapons, music, physiology, or about a host of subjects among his vast repertoire; my three sons, John,

Erik, and Ryan, whom I respect and admire enormously for their intelligence and wit and who always told everyone their mother was a writer before I believed it myself; and above all my beloved husband, Ray, who always believed in me and gave me the richest gift of all: freedom to pursue a dream.

# Pronunciation Guide

**Ácoma** – AH-koh-mah
**Alegría** – Ah-leh-GREE-ah
**Alejandro** – Ah-leh-HAHN-dro
**cíbola** – SEE-boh-lah
**Dorotea** – Doh-roh-TEH-ah
**Eulate** – Eoo-LAH-teh
**Fabia** – FAH-bee-ah
**Isidro Inojosa** – Ee-SEE-droh Ee-noh-HOH-sah
**K'atsina** – Kaht-SHEE-nah
**Kiva** – KEE-vah
**María Angélica** – Mah-REE-ah Ahn-HEH-lee-kah
**Nuevo México** – NWEH-voh MEH-hee-koh
**Ordóñez** – Or-DOHN-yehs
**Oñate** – Ohn-YAH-teh
**Queres** – KEH-rehs
**Rohona** – ROH-hoh-nah
**Santa Fé** – SAHN-tah FEH
**Vicente** – Vee-SEHN-teh
**Vizcarra** – Vees-KAH-rah
**Zaldívar** – Zahl-DEE-vahr

*Note:* In Spanish, double and initial *r*'s are trilled; single *r* is somewhat like a quickly pronounced *d* in English: the tongue lightly taps the roof of the mouth just behind the front teeth. *B* and *v* are often indistinguishable.

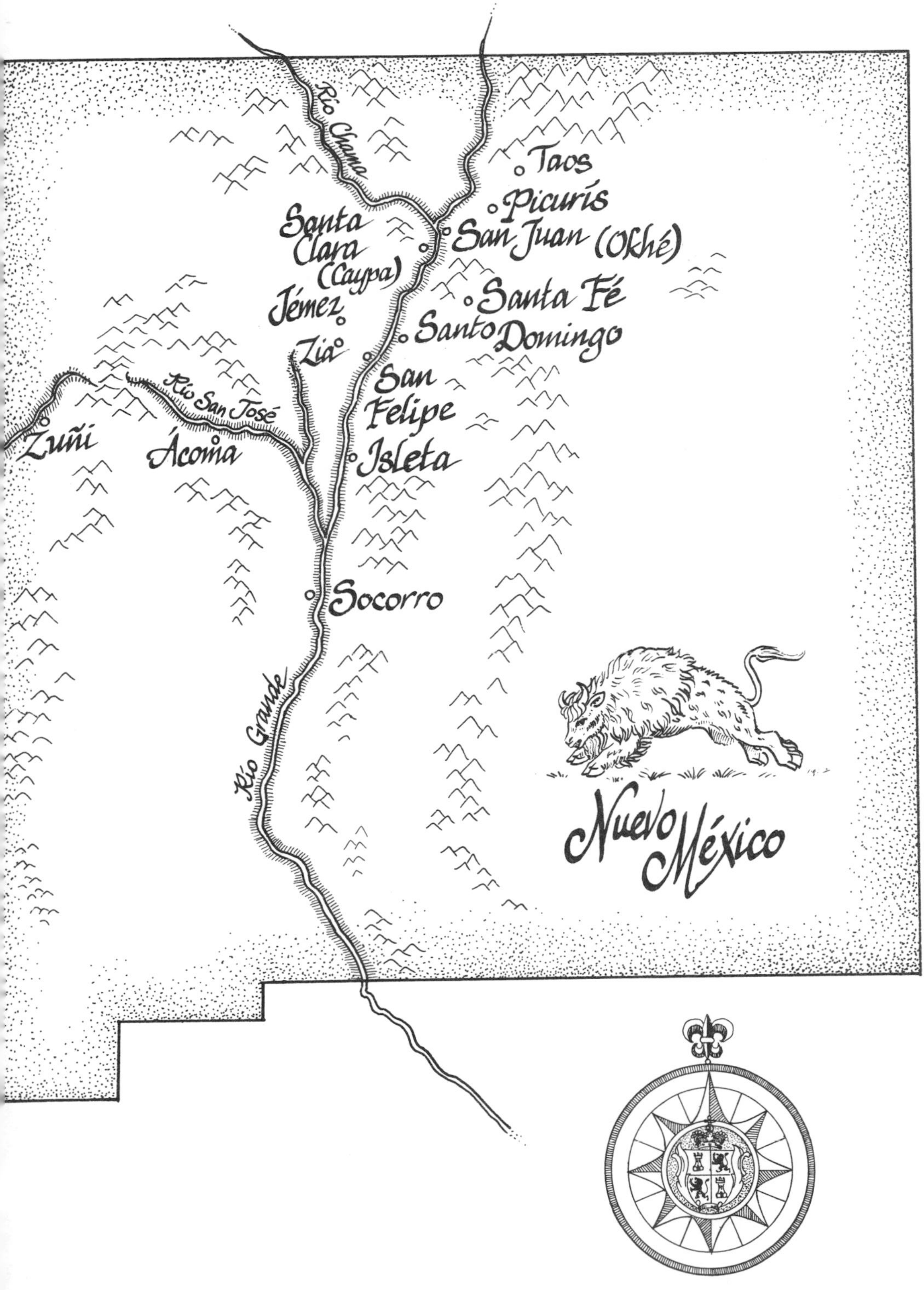

Río Chama
Taos
Picurís
Santa Clara (Caypa)
San Juan (Okhé)
Jémez
Santa Fé
Santo Domingo
Zía
San Felipe
Río San José
Zuñi
Ácoma
Isleta
Socorro
Río Grande
Nuevo México

# Prologue

Suddenly, like the bloody talons of a hawk, the dawn sent its claws over the eastern mesa and stained the escarpment a vivid red. The valley floor lay in darkness as the vertical walls of the rock citadel sprang to prominence, etched deeply in the early light. Silence filled the valley, and the only movement was the dawn as it slowly outlined two figures standing at the edge of the cliff. One held itself erect, arms raised and outstretched toward the east, a bundle in its hands. At that moment the first sliver of the day's brilliance crowned East Mountain.

"Behold, Sun, the new child whose name is Rohona!"

The medicine man gathered the bundle to his breast and chanted a high prayer that rose into the still air like spirals of piñon smoke rose from the houses on winter mornings. He handed the baby to his wife, who stood next to him with a basket of prayer sticks upon which lay the soft *wabani* feather bundles the baby's parents had made.

The *chaianyi* took the basket of prayer sticks, held it out toward the sun, and then hurled it over the sheer cliff edge. "Go with wings to the K'atsina and give this newborn child a long and fortunate life," the medicine man prayed aloud.

He turned toward the baby and gathered armfuls of air. First he gathered from the north, then the west, the south, and east. He blew the air toward the child, giving the newborn the breath of life.

As he turned away from the blinding sun, his wife silently followed him, her moccasins raising puffs of dust that hung in the cold air like miniature *shiwana*. Their steps were quick but measured as they walked down the rows of the tall earth-colored dwellings. At a small stone cistern formed by the rock of the mesa, the man knelt, took the baby, unwrapped it, and dipped it in the frigid water.

A sudden, loud squall rent the brittle air, and the woman leaned forward, quickly swaddling the howling child in its soft woven blanket. They rose and continued on until the *chaianyi* stopped and handed the baby back to his wife as he turned to grasp a pine ladder that leaned against a windowless wall. They ascended and crossed the terrace roof to an open door.

*"K'aiya!"* The medicine man called out as he paused outside the door.

*"Hai yeh!"* a man answered from within.

*"Heh O!"* a woman responded.

The *chaianyi* spoke with the authority of his position. "This child, named Rohona, has come to his home. Here he shall live. He is coming in, bringing crops, game, and a long life into his house. He is coming in."

"Let him come in!" the two voices spoke in unison from within. The medicine man stepped aside and allowed his wife and the newly named child she carried to enter, and inside, the mother of the child made four gathering motions toward the door as if she were gathering in the things of which the medicine man had spoken.

The woman's dark eyes filled with pride as she took the baby into her arms. "Oh, my son," she whispered, clutching the bundle close, "oh, my Rohona."

The scent of piñon smoke pervaded the warm room. The only sound was the murmuring of family members as they gathered around the four-day-old child whom the *chaianyi* had just presented to the sun and given a name that would protect and give him power.

Words of praise and beauty for the new child were spoken as everyone took seats around the carefully crafted sandpainting of a turtle the *chaianyi* had made. At the head of the symbol of long life sat a banded medicine bowl, and three sacred *honani* corn ear fetishes lay on the sand mosaic along with flints and the paw of a brown bear. The background colors of the painting were yellow for north, blue for west, red for south, and white for east because life and power come from all directions, and it was for those things, for the newly named child, that the *chaianyi* now prayed.

When the prayer ended, the baby's grandmothers appeared with steaming bowls of deer and blue corn stew. They served the medicine man first, placing his bowl in front of him at the turtle's head. With eagle plumes, he wafted the steam from the bowl four times over the sandpainting. He dipped a tiny morsel of meat from the bowl and fed the turtle. Then everyone ate.

With care and ceremony the medicine man swept up his painting of colored sands and gathered his things into his deerskin pouch. He chanted a final prayer over the new baby's cradleboard.

Into the fragrant cedarwood of the cradleboard a piece of turquoise had been inlaid with piñon pitch. The sacred stone, the color of the summer sky, would lie under the heart of the baby Rohona to protect him and give him long life.

## Part One

# LA CONQUISTA

## Conquest, January 1599

# Chapter 1

Late in the afternoon on the twenty-first day of January of the year 1599, Sergeant Major Zaldívar, nephew of Don Juan de Oñate and brother of the slain Maese de Campo, rode in full armor astride his caparisoned horse toward the base of the sheer-walled mesa where his brother had met his death seven weeks ago. Along with his brother, the natives had slain two officers, eight soldiers, and two servants while others like Captain Vicente de Vizcarra escaped, though badly wounded, by leaping from the high cliff to the steep dunes of talus and finely ground sandstone that encircled the mesa. The Ácoma would pay for the deaths of Spaniards: *that* Sergeant Major Zaldívar had sworn on the soul of his mother.

As his eyes focused on the top of the *peñol* bathed in the long rays of the setting sun, the Sergeant Major's face flushed with rage. There on the summit he could make out hundreds of natives, some of whom were wearing the armor and brandishing the swords and arquebuses of his slain brother and countrymen.

"By the grace of God I'll see *all* you whore's offal die with your guts spilled on the ground!" he muttered savagely through his teeth. A fleck of spittle caught in his chestnut-colored beard. Abruptly turning in his *estradiota* saddle, he motioned with a gauntleted hand for the men to stop. Had he not had orders from his uncle to first ask the Ácoma to surrender peacefully and hand over their leaders, he would have stormed the rock at once. But he would play out this charade.

"So that the accursed natives of this village can hear the decree our governor signed in our glorious capital of San Juan, the official secretary of this expedition will now proclaim its requirements!" he bellowed. "And Tomás, the translator of this army, shall render it in their language." Zaldívar yanked back on his horse's reins, causing it to rear, punctuating his fury as he shouted, "Let the natives make *no* mistake as to our *purpose*!"

The setting sun decreed, however, that the battle would have to wait until the following day.

Powder had been dried in the sun and sifted before they left San Juan. The soldiers carefully oiled their guns and tightened the springs on the wheellocks, but still there was the checking and double checking that every good soldier did. Nerves were wound as tight as the guns, and it would be difficult for some to sleep. The sentries Zaldívar had posted, however, would find it even more difficult to remain awake as the long night wore on and the biting cold seeped beneath their rough wool cloaks and numbed their bodies.

High on the summit, none of the Ácomas slept. Strident chanting and the accentuated beat of drums reverberated throughout the night, peopling with painted specters the dreams of those Spaniards who might have managed to fall into a restless sleep.

Rohona felt exhilaration as he stood in the cold predawn on the highest rooftop of his earth-colored dwelling, looking out across the faintly illuminated winter landscape of the valley that stretched out around their rock-perched home. When the sun crested the eastern mesa, North Mountain would glisten from the snows the *shiwana* had brought. He welcomed the coming battle. He distrusted the strangers when he first encountered them in the villages along the Big River, but now he knew the terrible killing power of the weapons they possessed.

Many days ago when the fight broke out on their mesa and the Ácoma killed the strangers who tried to steal their food, he had seen the men of his village cut down as if they might have been dry cornstalks. The strangers' weapons killed from a distance, hurling balls of fire, destroying whatever they hit, turning flesh and bone into blood and splinters. But arrows, too, killed from a distance, and they were many, the warriors of Áco, compared with the seven tens of strangers. And they were on the Rock. By throwing stones down on them, even a woman could keep those strangers with killing sticks from scaling the mesa. He knew that Kakuna, her body heavy with child, would be able to protect their home.

Rohona opened his palm and looked at a pale pink bead carved in the shape of a flower. He had found it near the slain body of the leader of the pale ones. He rubbed his fingers over the bead and slipped it back into the deer leather pouch at his waist. From the pouch he took a small bit of cornmeal and sprinkled it in the six cardinal directions: north, west, south, east, the zenith, and the nadir.

"Sustain us, Iyatiku," he prayed aloud, "sustain your children."

* * *

The wait had ended; battle preparations completed. The Franciscan Father heard the confessions of seventy men, and the Mass for victory, said under the bright, cold January sky, assured a place in heaven for those who might die—or so the soldiers fervently believed. At a motion from the grimly smiling Sergeant Major, the bugler blew a loud blast on his trumpet, and the Spaniards with a cacophonous roar of *"¡Santiago!"* began the battle, their armor flashing brilliantly in the afternoon sun.

The first row of infantry, muskets on their rests, blew on the match looped in their hands that would assure enough heat to ignite the powder. With precision they clipped the match into the serpentine device on the lock of the arquebus, took aim at the high mesa top, and fired on command. The long lever-like trigger brought the serpentine and its glowing match into the priming pan, igniting the gunpowder and hurling the arquebuses' lethal lead balls toward the native warriors on their lofty perch. A gray, acrid cloud of smoke obscured the view, but screams of falling, dying men told the soldiers their mark had been successful. Another row stepped forward while the others reloaded. Momentarily the rain of rocks and arrows ceased as the first volley crashed into the summit, but within seconds, great heavy rocks again came pitching down from above. The noise was deafening while smoke from the guns and dust raised by crashing rocks provided the camouflage needed for the Sergeant Major and his twelve picked men as they circled the base of the mesa.

To the south they found more sloping rocks than the sheer cliff face of the north side. They began the rugged ascent, keeping to the crevices in order that they might not be seen, but all wondered apprehensively whether there were sentries posted to watch the rear of the mesa.

As they climbed, they saw that the mesa at Ácoma was two massive rocks separated by a deep, narrow chasm along which ran a narrow pathway. The walls sometimes came as close to each other as twelve paces and were separated by a deep fissure with jagged rocks a hundred feet below. Sawed off halberds made the ascent easier, although the chink and clang of their armor reverberated deafeningly in the sandstone crevasses, and they expected at any moment a hail of stones would send them falling to a gory death below. Although the day was cold, sweat trickled down inside their heavy armor.

"*Santa María* have mercy on us," was whispered again and again as they climbed, winded from the exertion. Occasionally they stopped for a moment to get their breath and looked up at the rocks above them, crossing themselves before continuing their ascent. They climbed on, apprehension mounting with every step, but no rocks fell and suddenly they found themselves on the top of the mesa. They had breached the stone fortress unchallenged.

They sucked in deep breaths of air, smiled, and made fists and silently spoke the word *"¡Santiago!"* They were on the second mesa, and as they looked quickly about, Vicente de Vizcarra motioned to an outcropping of rocks.

"There!"

All saw immediately that from the elevated position they would have a good vantage point from which to fire into the village. They scrambled across the sandstone mesa top, but as they reached the rocks, they were discovered. The Ácoma who spied them across the chasm yelled an alarm. It was obvious to the Sergeant Major and his party that the natives had not expected them, but in a matter of moments several hundred warriors were running toward the second mesa where the Spaniards rushed up the rock outcropping to position themselves.

"Four slugs to the load," the Sergeant Major ordered, and with the expertness born of long practice, the armored men fitted the key of their wheellocks onto the square stem projecting from the center of the wheel. The powerful spring on the inside of the lock plate was wound quickly, bringing it to full compression.

The Sergeant Major ticked off the names and then continued, "First volley. On my order."

The natives heaved long beams across the deep fissure that separated the two massive stones that made up the mesa, and yelling blood-chilling war cries, they came pouring over the rocks toward the armed strangers. Many of the Ácoma carried stone-studded war clubs that with an accurate blow could disable the strangers in spite of their metal shells. Others were armed with flint and obsidian knives or stone missiles, and all carried bows with arrow-filled quivers slung across their backs.

*"Preparen,"* the Sergeant Major barked, *"apunten."* Juan Velarde, Marcos Cortés, Cordero and León Isasti cocked the hammer of their wheellocks. *"¡Fuego!"*

The triggers snapped the flints down on the edge of the wheels as the coil springs were released. With rapidity and force the wheels revolved against the flint, causing a shower of sparks to ignite the powder in the priming pan, and the first volley of four slugs to the load cut through the forward wall of natives, shattering arms, faces, and bodies, dropping them mangled and bleeding. The blast caused the warriors who followed to trip over the writhing wounded and dying who fell at their feet. The force of the blow momentarily halted the onrush, giving the first soldiers time to begin to reload. When the wave of anger-blinded Ácoma rushed the Spaniards again, a second volley rang out as the pyrites of their wheellocks sent sparks to the powder, and that time it was Cristóbal Sánchez, Pablo de Aguilar, Antonio Hernández, and Vicente de Vizcarra who sent many a brave young warrior to an early grave.

Noise, smoke, and confusion enveloped the mesa top. The carnage was terrible, but still the Ácoma came on, blinded by fury at the few strangers who could kill so many of them at once. Those natives less guided by rage, however, spread to the side, running and leaping nimbly across the rocks, intending to approach the Spaniards from behind.

The Sergeant Major saw their purpose and motioned to Captain Vicente. The captain nodded. Both drew their swords and moved quickly down the rocks, and as the first warrior reached them, war club raised, the Sergeant Major's sword flashed, cleanly slicing the native's head from his neck. Blood spewed, splattering the Sergeant Major's chest armor, and as the severed head bounced sickeningly down the rocks, a second native died, his skull cleaved by Vicente, the brains spilling out onto the rough sandstone of the mesa top. In spite of the bloody slaughter, the Ácoma came on, only to be mowed down again and again.

Evening approached and in the fading light, as suddenly as they had begun, the natives stopped their suicidal rushes and began to drag their dead away, leaving a few warriors to keep the strangers at bay with arrows lest they give chase. But the Spaniards had no intention of leaving their position among the rocks that had served them so admirably.

The setting sun turned the rocks of the sandstone gold then dusty rose, and the sky in the west bore streaks of lavender while that to the east was a deepening violet. The Spaniards rested for a moment without speaking, leaning back against the rocks, their guns loaded and cocked.

The Sergeant Major broke the eerie silence that had fallen over the mesa top. "We've got to get more men up here. We'll never be able to gain a victory until we can cross to the main mesa." The fatigued men nodded. "I'm leaving you in charge, Captain Vicente," Zaldívar spoke. "I'm going down to let the others know we're safe and to bring back more men. I'll return at daybreak. However, if the savages begin again, keep your same position here." His voice was hard. "That's an order. Keep the bastards occupied until I can reach the summit with more men."

The Sergeant Major paused and looked toward the shadows that darkened the eastern rim of mountains. "The moon will be full tonight. It'll rise early and set late, so you'll have good light to keep watch by. No savage should be able to approach you unseen." With that he left them and was swallowed by the dusk that dropped quickly over the sandstone pinnacle.

The pale rays of dawn turned the mesa top shadowy gray. Stiff with cold, the handful of Spaniards who had spent the night there quietly stretched their tired, rigid muscles and peered nervously into the deceptive half-light, wondering if at any moment the savages would commence attack. They relieved their bladders there where they waited because no one wished to risk drawing attention to himself with movement and the inevitable sound of jangling armor. They waited and watched for the faintest motion on the opposite side of the mesa, but the fierce pueblo of the previous day appeared deserted. No sounds reached their ears. No sign of life flickered—as if the village had never been inhabited.

"*Jesús*, do you suppose the bastards all managed somehow to escape down off the mesa during the night?" León Isasti whispered nervously.

"Maybe the *hijos de puta* have gone for reinforcements to the other pueblos," Vicente de Vizcarra added.

The Spaniards waited, their impatience and apprehension growing. They cursed under their breaths.

A faint sound of creaking armor floated to the mesa top. The soldiers leaned back and breathed a sigh of visible relief. Reinforcements were on their way.

"I left twenty men below to guard the base of the mesa," Zaldívar spoke when he finally reached them. "I brought forty with me. No native will escape. We are now more than fifty on this goddamned rock."

Zaldívar looked at his men, his eyes intense. "God knows how many warriors we face. We were told this pueblo has more than fifteen hundred inhabitants. How many of those are of fighting age? How many died yesterday?" The men shrugged, and he answered his own question. "Only *Dios* knows, but whatever the case, we know for a fact we're outnumbered many times over." He scanned the faces of his men. "Does that matter?" he demanded.

The men spoke in vehement whispers. "By *Santiago*, no!"

"We are Spaniards," the Sergeant Major continued. "This village falls today!"

"*¡Así sea!*" the men hissed.

The Sergeant Major's face relaxed and he smiled. "I have ordered a beam brought to the top. We'll position it across the crevasse so we can cross into the village itself."

He turned and looked toward the mesa top where the Ácomas' houses stood. Still, there appeared no life on the opposite side. As the sun rose, the bitter cold became less intense, but the men seethed with inaction. The beam arrived, and the Sergeant Major gave the order to throw it across the chasm.

A dozen soldiers quickly crossed onto the other side and were preparing to cover their comrades when, with no warning, five hundred natives rushed out from hiding, their shrill war cries shattering the cold, still air. They sent a rain of arrows so thick the Spaniards who had crossed the chasm fled in disorder back across the beam.

"*¡Jodidos!*" the Sergeant Major cursed viciously. He well knew he could not afford to send a suicidal wave against such numerous foe.

The entire morning passed as Spaniards fired their arquebuses across the gap, and the Ácoma sent hundreds of arrows back. By noon the Sergeant Major was raging.

"*Nothing* has been accomplished! Nothing! The fighting can't go on like this! *¡Hijos de puta!* We *must* bridge the gap! Bring up the two culverin!" he shouted to Pablo de Aguilar. "I don't care how the hell you do it, Captain, just get those fucking things up here!"

Hours passed as they waited for the soldiers to drag the small cannons to the top of the mesa, but it took the Spaniards only minutes to station them, load, and prepare to fire.

"Now, you heathen bastards, you're going to learn who Spaniards *are*," the Sergeant Major said with satisfaction as he motioned to the gunners.

After the wadding was tamped down, two hundred small iron balls were rammed into each muzzle. "Raise the elevation," the *alférez* ordered, and a soldier pushed the quoin-block backward as instructed.

The Ácoma continued sending waves of arrows across the chasm. The fuses on the culverin were lit, and the soldiers stood back. In a deafening roar that rumbled across the mesa and out over the valley in which the enormous rock perched, the two guns belched clouds of smoke and a scything iron destruction. When the smoke began to clear, piles of Ácoma could be seen dead and dying, and wails of terror were heard amidst the cries of anger as the Ácoma retreated. Once more the thundering brass weapons pounded the other side, sending walls of houses crumbling.

"*¡Adelante!*" the Sergeant Major shouted, and with a wave of his gauntleted hand, the Spaniards threw the beam across the chasm again and this time poured unchallenged onto the other side, gaining the first mesa where they pursued the fleeing natives. Swords were drawn for close quarter fighting while the arquebuses and culverins continued to fell the Ácoma who were in full retreat. Houses began to burn, sending smoke billowing into the cold air. The streets of the village were littered with bodies.

At last the fighting ceased. An Ácoma chief, blood trickling down his arm from a shoulder wound, came forth from the houses. Zaldívar motioned for his men to hold their fire. "Get Tomás!" he shouted, and the interpreter was brought forward.

"We ask for peace for our village so that the killing may stop," the Ácoma chief said humbly. "Too many of our people lie lifeless upon our mesa."

Tomás translated the words for Zaldívar and then in Queres spoke the Sergeant Major's reply to the chief. "You will be treated with mercy and justice. Call your warriors to come out without their weapons."

Tomás turned back to the Sergeant Major when the chief replied. "He says he responds with thanks in the name of his people. They will fight no more."

Following Tomás's order to the chief, the plaza began to fill with warriors. Few if any were without wounds. Women poured into the square bringing basket upon basket of corn, stacking them, along with piles of blankets, at the Sergeant Major's feet. They brought the peace offerings in humility, tears streaming down their faces.

The Sergeant Major stood in triumph, his eyes glittering with a fierce, malicious pleasure. With scorn, he surveyed the gifts the women had brought then savagely began to kick the baskets over, spilling the corn onto the ground. He kicked over the piles of blankets.

"Get this *porquería* out of my sight!" he screamed. "Do you think I would take your filthy food and blankets—the same that you denied my brother when he came in peace to your village?" Like frightened animals, the women ran to remove the gifts they had brought.

"Place the men in the *estufa*," the Sergeant Major ordered, turning from the women as he motioned to a large ceremonial *kiva* built side-by-side with the houses. "We will question them about the death of my brother!"

The Ácoma men of fighting age were herded to the *kiva* and down inside into the darkness of the sacred room. Vicente de Vizcarra stationed himself on top of the *kiva* roof at its entrance.

"Bring them out one by one!" the Sergeant Major shouted. The first warrior came up out of the *kiva* and down the outside ladder. Roughly he was prodded toward where the Sergeant Major stood triumphantly.

"Robledo!" he shouted to a soldier, "García and Hernández, on the double. You have the honor to act as the execution squad for these sons of whores!" The three soldiers came forward and unsheathed their swords. "Ask this bastard," the Sergeant Major spoke to the interpreter, "if he knows who killed my brother."

Tomás spoke a few words in the Queres tongue, and the Ácoma shook his head. "He says he does not know," the interpreter replied.

"You die," the Sergeant Major spat. The soldier holding the Ácoma man shoved him forward, and instantly Robledo ran his sword through him. "Throw him off the cliff," Zaldívar ordered viciously. "Next!" he shouted, turning back to the *kiva*.

Had the Sergeant Major or the other soldiers bothered to notice, they would have seen the horror on the women's faces and would have seen them slowly back away as another warrior was brought out to meet the same fate. The soldiers shouted encouragement to the executioners, enjoying their bloody job. Again and again the scene was repeated.

The Sergeant Major watched with satisfaction. "That is for my brother!" he would shout for each sword thrust.

The victors had lost count of the number they had thrown over the edge of the cliff, when suddenly Vicente de Vizcarra yelled down to the Sergeant Major, "No more will come out!" Peering into the chamber, he shouted over his shoulder, "The bastards have broken holes into the adjoining houses!"

Arrows and stones rained down from the rooftops. It was only then that the Sergeant Major saw that the women were gone and that they, too, hurled rocks from above.

"Fire the houses!" he shouted. "We'll smoke the *hijos de puta* out!"

Once more the battle raged. Rather than being taken alive, some of the Ácoma ran and plunged to their deaths off the edge of the cliff while others leaped into the fires that now raged through the houses. It soon became apparent to the Spaniards that the Ácoma were killing each other. The soldiers stared as wives and children knelt in front of their husbands and fathers to have their throats slit for a fast and painless death, and then the father would turn the stone knife upon himself.

Kakuna, her stomach large with his unborn child, knelt in front of Rohona. "Oh my husband," she said plaintively, "I would rather die than be captured by these barbarians." Rohona looked at the flint knife in his hand, looked at his young wife, her obsidian hair lustrous in the sunlight, and his whole body trembled with horror.

"If you love me, use it!" she cried, grasping his arm.

She dropped her hands from his arm and turned her tear-stained face up to him, closing her eyes. Slowly he raised his hand, and a cry of rage exploded from his chest.

"Stop them!" the Sergeant Major thundered. "We want them alive! Round them up! On the double!"

At last the remaining villagers were herded into an open plaza, and when the fighting finally ceased, five hundred and fifty Ácoma, more or less, were captives. Of that number, only fifty were men.

# Chapter 2

Captain Vicente de Vizcarra kneed his gray-white stallion forward and growled angrily at the man who had stumbled and fallen to his knees, "Get up, you heathen savage. We're almost there." The whip in his hand snapped sharply and accurately, raising an ugly welt across the man's high cheekbone.

Blind fury seized Rohona, and he lunged to his feet, straining against the iron fetters that shackled him to the other men. Unfeeling of the pain, he tore at the manacles, no longer able to endure enslavement, and the whip came down across his back, ripping at his flesh, but again he lunged against the chains, and again the whip cut across his back and sent him falling once more to his knees onto the hard, sharp rocks. He raised his head and looked up at the man with red hair growing on his face, and the man was laughing. The horseman held the whip ready in his hands, and his pale, almost colorless eyes were evil like a witch's. Once before Rohona had seen those same evil eyes without color, and a deep, black hatred blazed upward in him. The man saw it, and he laughed.

"What's going on, Captain?" the Sergeant Major asked Vicente as he reined his stallion next to the captain's.

Vicente motioned with his whip toward the Ácoma who pushed himself with obvious pain to a standing position. Blood trickled down the man's hands and feet where the iron of his fetters had bitten into raw flesh. The captain laughed again.

"When will these stupid savages realize we are Spaniards—that we are the army of the King of Spain?"

The Sergeant Major smiled a hard smile and turned in his saddle to look at the rest of the captives. "Yes, it was a glorious battle. My uncle the governor will be pleased. Now there will be *no* doubt in the natives' minds as to who rules this province of *Nuevo México*." He turned back to Vicente de Vizcarra. "Let's get these heathen on the march again. I'm anxious to get back."

The snow-capped peaks of the Sangre de Cristo Mountains loomed in the distance, ruggedly beautiful, but it was cold and blustery when they reached the pueblo of Santo Domingo with the captives from Ácoma, and no one remarked on nature's frigid beauty. It had taken well over two weeks of winter to make the hard march across the rough land, land that even in summer was barren and inhospitable.

Women and children were herded like animals and at night lay huddled together on the frozen ground; the old and infirm who could not keep up were kicked aside and left to die. The men were in chains, their wrists and ankles bleeding sores so that when one man stumbled and fell it was agony for many, for the weight of the falling man pulled on all the manacles, causing the iron to bite painfully into raw flesh. They were not allowed to be unchained to relieve themselves, and their bodies stank with filth. Many of them bore the marks of whips across their backs, and their lips were blue and cracked from the cold and lack of water. The men were kept separate from the women so that the women might not ease the suffering of the few Ácoma warriors who remained from their once proud village.

Rohona looked up at his people. All were barefoot and none had blankets in which to wrap themselves. For himself he did not care; he wished only for death. All their possessions, save what the soldiers took as booty, lay smoldering on top of their deserted mesa. The only inhabitants of their once thriving high-perched home were the gluttonous carrion crow that feasted on the dead. The dwellings the people had lived in for generations without number were put to the torch. Nothing but a pile of rubble remained, and because the soldiers could not carry all the stores of corn—corn that would have fed the Ácoma for three years—what was left also went up in flames.

Vicente de Vizcarra urged his horse forward to ride alongside the Sergeant Major. "*Dios*, am I glad you sent messengers on ahead to tell Don Juan of the glorious victory we won at Ácoma mesa," he snorted. "I've had enough of this ass-freezing weather."

The Sergeant Major nodded in agreement. "Thank God my uncle decided to come south to Santo Domingo to await our return. Now we don't have to push on to San Juan for those last hard leagues." He smiled and stroked his beard. "But I should have known that our new governor and the conqueror of *Nuevo México* couldn't wait to bask in the glory of his troops!"

Vicente de Vizcarra suddenly pointed in front of them. "Look."

"We've been sighted," the Sergeant Major spoke. He turned in his saddle. "Form up, men!" he shouted. "We have a welcoming committee."

The bugler sounded the order and the cavalry reined their horses into formation while the infantry fell into step. Backs were straight and heads lifted high. The army of the King of Spain north of the *Río Bravo del Norte* marched proudly toward its governor.

Don Juan de Oñate as he rode out to meet them was resplendent in his gleaming armor as befitted his position of *Adelantado* and highest civil authority of the new province.

"Well done, Sergeant Major," his voice boomed as he rode forward and stopped in front of his nephew. "You have acquitted yourselves as true soldiers of the King of Spain, and you have made your governor proud."

"The grace of God has smiled upon us and sustained our honor, Uncle. We give you this victory in His name that He, also, may be proud of our efforts on His behalf," the Sergeant Major replied piously.

With the majesty of a king, Oñate wheeled his horse and a short while later led the triumphant soldiers into the plaza of Santo Domingo as thundering shouts of *"¡Santiago y Rey!"* and *"¡Viva! ¡Viva! ¡Viva!"* boomed into the brittle air. The cold sun reflected brightly off the metal armor, and trumpet fanfares sliced through the voices of revelry and rejoicing. The governor lifted his metal-gloved hand, and silence fell over the dusty plaza.

His voice was resonant. "The feats of my nephew will be compared to the greatest heroes of times past!" At that moment a biting wind funneled down the valley of the *Río del Norte,* thinning the rich voice of the gray-haired leader. "The defeat of Ácoma will go down in the history of Spain as one of its most glorious conquests. Men will long remember the valiant heroes who marched forth from our new capital of San Juan to put down insurrection so that Holy Mother Church might be able to save the souls of the savage heathen in this land. When the final roll call is made on high, the deeds of these returning men will wipe away their sins, and God will surely welcome them into his arms as true sons like his own mighty son, *Jesús Cristo.*"

*"¡Viva! ¡Viva!"* rose the shouts again, and armor jangled noisily. The Sergeant Major spurred his stallion forward, and with a proud bow from horseback, presented to his uncle the official documents of the expedition against the pueblo of Ácoma, which the secretary, Juan Velarde, had duly recorded.

"These documents," he shouted for all to hear, his chestnut-bearded face hard, "show that the natives of the pueblo of Ácoma were given three chances to surrender before any punitive action was taken." His voice rose and vibrated with barely controlled anger. "But with villainy and viciousness the heathen refused our offer of peace, thereby forcing us against our desire to take the drastic measures that were taken. These documents show also that the Ácoma claimed to surrender but with treacherous actions renewed the fight, thereby causing the unnecessary death of many more of their kindred. May God have mercy on their souls!"

Oñate grasped the documents in his gauntleted hand. "These will be entered into the legal proceedings against the natives!" he shouted, and his voice reverberated. "I appoint Captain Alonso Gómez de Montesinos as the Ácomas' guardian and defense attorney so that they may have a fair and legal trial according to the laws of our motherland. The heathen of Ácoma stand accused of treason against the King of Spain! Treason!"

A roar of indignant anger rose from the soldiers, and when Oñate's hand silenced them once more, he continued. "I will allow three days for the completion of this trial—three days and no more."

Three days later, no cloud marred the vivid blue sky, but the early morning air was bitingly cold in the deserted plaza. Even the village dogs had not yet left the sheltered spot where they had spent the bitter hours of darkness. Nor did any of the mangy animals suspiciously venture out to sniff the man who entered the plaza from the southwest. He was hunched over trying to keep his warmth within him as he rolled a heavy cottonwood stump into the center of the plaza. The dust raised by the stump hung suspended in the frozen air as the thunk-thunk of the rolling log echoed dully off the walls of the mud-stuccoed houses that surrounded the plaza.

As he began to hammer, several villagers appeared on the rooftops of the three-storied dwellings that clustered around the open area. The people stood like wind-graved sandstone as they peered out from the blankets that were pulled tightly about them. The clang of metal striking metal shattered the frozen air as the man hammered a hinged iron bar onto the tree stump. The blacksmith lifted the curved side of the bar and worked it up and down several times to test the smoothness of its movement. He placed his foot on the block and brought the curved iron bar down over his arch. The iron bar held his foot securely, and he seemed satisfied with his work.

The sun rose higher in the frigid blue sky but did not lessen the intensity of the cold. The deserted plaza began to fill with soldiers, and more villagers appeared on the rooftops. Metal clanked, mixed with the sounds of laughter as the soldiers sought a good vantage point from which to witness the coming spectacle.

*"Abran paso,"* a soldier said roughly. "Let these captives through." A corridor opened among the milling men as soldiers prodded the captives from Ácoma into the center of the plaza.

The sun glinted off the blades of half a dozen sharpened axes that leaned against the large cottonwood tree stump. The soldiers hooted and jeered at the captives but were silenced by a strident trumpet fanfare. Another corridor opened in the crowd, and the governor walked proudly into the center of the plaza. Two blue-robed priests whose tonsured heads gleamed in the sunlight followed him. Behind the friars came an honor guard of armor-clad men, one of whom carried aloft an embroidered red and gold standard that fluttered only slightly in the cold air.

The gray-haired leader lifted his arms and motioned the crowd to back away and leave the center of the plaza free of people. Silence fell over the dusty square, and when Oñate spoke, his voice was loud and unpitying as it carried throughout the plaza.

"In the criminal case between the Royal Court and the Indians of the pueblo and fortress of Ácoma, the heathen are accused of treason, of having wantonly killed Don Juan de Zaldívar, Maese de Campo, general of this expedition, and Captains Felipe de Escalante and Diego Núñez, eight soldiers and two servants. In addition to this, after my Sergeant Major, whom I sent in my place, had repeatedly called upon them to accept our peace, not only did they refuse to do so, instead they received him with savage hostility.

"Wherefore, taking into account the merits of the case and the guilt resulting therefrom, I must and do sentence all of the Indian men and women from the said pueblo under arrest, as follows":

There was not a sound in the crowded plaza as he continued. "The men who are over twenty-five years of age I sentence to lose one foot!" His voice rang out, "In addition, they are sentenced to twenty years of personal servitude!"

The soldiers bellowed their unreserved approval of the punishment. Vicente de Vizcarra smiled. So the Governor decided to use the punishment he suggested. He looked at the captives from Ácoma, but they showed no emotion. They would not know their fate until the translator had rendered the gray-haired man's words into their own language.

Oñate continued, his voice cold and harsh. "The women over twelve years of age I sentence likewise to twenty years of personal servitude!" Again shouts of approval filled the air.

"And the Indians from the province of Moqui who were present at the pueblo of Ácoma and who fought, I sentence to have the right hand cut off and to be set free in order that they may convey to their land the news of this punishment!" The governor lifted his hands for silence as the soldiers again filled the air with their boisterous approbation.

"And all the children under twelve years of age I declare free and innocent of the grave offense for which I punish their parents. And because of my duty to aid, support, and protect both boys and girls under this age, I place the girls under the care of our Father Commissary, Fray Alonso Martínez, in order that he, as a Christian and qualified person, may distribute them in this Kingdom or elsewhere in nunneries or other places where he thinks that they may attain the knowledge of God and the salvation of their souls!

"The boys under twelve years of age I entrust to my Sergeant Major in order that they may attain the same goal!"

Had the Ácoma understood the words that told that their children were going to be taken from them and sent to Mexico, never to be seen again, their grief would have filled the cold February air. As it was, only the voice of Oñate broke the stillness that had fallen over the plaza of Santo Domingo. His last words vibrated.

"This being a definite and final sentence, I so decree and order!"

The interpreter stepped to the governor's side and a sudden, biting wind numbed peoples' faces, making eyes water. The interpreter lifted his voice and spoke in Queres.

It began slowly, but then the wail of grief rose from the dusty plaza and set the dogs of the village to howling as the captives heard in their own language the words the gray-bearded man dressed in metal had spoken.

Rohona did not flinch when he heard the sentence. He had no children. His only child had never been born. Of what difference was a foot, when he had lost everything already? The only thing for which he now wished was death. The carnage of his village was seared in his mind and caused him to writhe and sweat and cry out in his sleep. Why hadn't he died like hundreds of his fellow warriors? Death would have been preferable to the memories that nightly tortured him.

"Kakuna," he whispered. "Kakuna." The sound was no more than a quiet howl that the icy fingers of the February wind stole from his lips, but the sound carried the keening of grief in it. He saw Kakuna kneeling in front of him, her face lifted toward him, and her words returned to him. "I would rather die . . ." He could see the flint knife in his hand poised to do her bidding. Then the burning timber fell, crushing her beneath it.

He knew nothing more until he felt himself dragged along the ground and heavy chains placed on his wrists and ankles. Somewhere he had a vague memory of climbing down the mesa and of the painful lash of a whip across his back. He found himself bound to other men in the open land far from Áco mesa. Above his right ear, he felt a painful lump and he would experience a dull, pounding headache. At times he slipped into a nightmare in which he saw himself trudging along with the other captives of his village. But gradually his head began to clear and the headaches became less frequent, and he knew the nightmare was real.

Dust swirled in the plaza of Santo Domingo, choking prisoners and soldiers alike. When the translator finished speaking, a blue-robed priest stepped forward and intoned a long prayer. The natives of Santo Domingo who had blankets pulled them more closely about them. The captives from Ácoma had no such luxury and stood exposed to the merciless February wind as it swept down from the snow-covered mountains in the north. The priest raised his arm and made the sign of the cross over the condemned and immediately the execution of the sentences began.

Two soldiers grasped a manacled man from the group of captives and dragged him to the center of the plaza. They forced his foot up onto the tree stump and the iron bar was brought down over the arch of his foot and tightened like a vise. The captive struggled violently, but the soldiers held him securely. Quickly the henchman hefted the heavy ax and with one swift, accurate blow severed the foot just in front of the iron bar.

The ax bit through bone and flesh and blood gushed out over the tree stump. A strangled scream ripped from the man's throat and then another as a hot iron was pushed against the wound to sear the severed blood vessels. Another captive was brought forward and another. The tree stump was soon covered with blood that was already beginning to coagulate. Dirt was tossed on the block between amputations to keep the feet from slipping on the bloody surface. Occasionally the man with the ax would scrape off the accumulated gore.

"Ah-a-a-a Ai'!" Shrilly the war cry rose up from the valley floor and shattered the cool, clear air of the mesa top. The sound had not yet died when another just as blood-chilling as the first followed.

Rohona's young eyes widened with terror. Never in his nine years had he heard the signal of danger shouted with such vehement necessity. He wanted to run to his mother and hide his face in her woven skirt as he had done when he was younger and heard the hoot of the owl, terrified it would peck out his eyes as old grandmother told in her stories, but he did not run to his mother. He straightened his back, though his eyes were still wide with fear. He knew he was growing up; he must no longer be a child and flee to his mother when he was afraid. He must be brave, brave like his father who was a member of the proud Opi Warrior Society.

Again the shrill cry of imminent danger sounded, and Rohona became aware of his surroundings. Women and children scurried up the ladders to their houses, quickly lifting the pine logs after the last person had ascended. Farther down the long house row the Opi warriors and the members of the Antelope Clan were pouring down the outside ladder of the ceremonial chambers. With the exception of their faces, which were reddish brown, the bodies of the men of the Antelope Clan were painted pink. Black underlined their eyes. They wore only a long breechclout and a soft eagle feather in their hair, and all they carried for their defense was an ironwood fighting cane called *yabi*.

Just as Masewi, one of the War Twins, the Opi warriors' faces were painted black and white: white below the mouth and black above. From the back of their hair dangled a long feather, and eagle down covered their heads and eyebrows. The Opi were clad in buckskin shirts and long red buckskin leggings that reached from their moccasins to their knees, and above the leggings their legs were painted white. The Opi carried long flints and knives with them for their defense.

A scarcely audible gasp escaped Rohona's lips when he recognized his father standing at the top of the *kiva* ladder ready to descend. What was happening? Why were the warriors pouring out of the *kiva* as if they had been awaiting the alarm? What was the sudden peril in which the village found itself?

"Rohona! Hurry!" He heard his mother shout urgently from the roof of their house. Her hands, face, and arms were yellow, smeared with corn pollen. He turned and darted toward the ladder, but just as he reached it, he stopped, remembering his bow and arrow lying in the dusty street where he had dropped them in surprise at the first sound of the danger cry. He heard his mother shouting for him to leave the bow, to climb the ladder to safety, but he would get his weapons. Silently he called to the eagle to give him wings and to the rabbit to make his feet swift. As he reached the bow and arrow, he grasped quickly at them, scraping his knuckles on the rough sandstone of the street. Unaware of his smarting fingers, he turned and ran for the ladder faster than he had ever run before. He had just grasped the rough pine when he heard them.

They rushed into the village from the west, shouting like demons, brandishing knives and clubs and small trees they had torn from the soil. Swiftly they fell upon the Opi warriors and the men of the Antelope Clan. In his fear they looked ferocious and grotesque to Rohona, and for a moment he stood transfixed, unable to move. There was a peculiar fascination to the horror of the scene that kept his eyes riveted on the intensifying combat. Why had they come? Why were they fighting? Their heads seemed enormous, their mouths looked like snouts, and their painted faces were vicious.

Above the clamor of the battle his mother's voice called out with desperation, "Rohona, Rohona, climb the ladder! Climb the ladder!" Her anguished cry found its way through his frozen fear, and he sped up the ladder as quickly as a jackrabbit flushed from its hiding place beneath a greasewood bush darts to another. As he jumped off onto the roof, his mother yanked at the ladder and quickly pulled it up. "Get inside," she said urgently. "Be quick, my son."

"No, Mother," he whispered, his voice trembling as he crouched behind the parapet and peered over it to the streets below. "I must watch, I know I must watch. I must learn not to fear."

"If you wish," she spoke softly, "but take care to stay very low, my son." With swift strides she crossed the terrace and entered the house, leaving him alone on the roof, crouched behind the parapet.

The hand-to-hand combat in the streets became more fierce by the moment. The fighters lay sprawled in the disarray of death, blood-soaked and lifeless in a carnage that filled him with a terrible fear. Even the ground appeared to bleed. What was happening? He was certain the village had been preparing for an important dance. What was happening?

In horror he suddenly recognized his father in the melee—recognized the buckskin shirt his mother had only recently made. Fighting desperately with a fearsome attacker, his father lunged and parried with innate grace in the fierce contest. Terror clutched at Rohona, and he could scarcely breathe. How agile and strong his father was—and brave. He had never known his father to fear anything. Suddenly the flint knife flicked out toward his father's throat. His father lunged to the side, thrusting also for the attacker's throat, but not in time. Blood spurted out, covering his father's new buckskin shirt and spattering his assailant's as well.

Rohona cried out and ran blindly to his mother. With gulping sobs he told what he had seen. His baby sister toddled to him, her big eyes dark and wide. She, too, began to wail, not knowing, however, the cause for tears.

# Chapter 3

The cries of his memories faded into the wailing of the women that rose from the plaza of Santo Domingo in high keening sounds of grief as they were forced to witness the mutilation of husbands, brothers, sons, and fathers. Rohona tensed the muscles of his jaw and again sought to shut out the strident sound. "I have the promise of Iyatiku," he whispered to himself as he remembered his father and the bloody fight he had witnessed as a child.

That night long ago, muffled voices had awakened him as he lay curled under his rabbit fur robe. Normally he would have turned over and fallen asleep instantly, knowing that it was only his parents talking into the late hours after his father had returned from the ceremonial chamber. But that night he awoke trembling with fear. He peered from under the rabbit fur and his face turned ashen as he saw his mother sitting near the floor hearth, her hand in a light gesture touching the cheek of a man who sat there. Rohona sucked in his breath in terror. The man had the same appearance as his father who had been killed in battle that very afternoon.

The two adults turned toward the sound. "Come here, my son," the man spoke. It sounded like his father, but Rohona lay frozen under his robe unable to move. A second time the man spoke, "Come here, Rohona."

He crawled, trembling, from under the rabbit skin and approached the man who so closely resembled his father. The man reached out and grasped his hand. He was warm, real. "It's me," his father spoke with a soft laugh. "I was not killed. It was the other's blood you saw."

*"Dyáðyá,"* Rohona cried, throwing his arms around his father's neck, but then he stepped back, the worried look once again on his face. "But what about the K'atsina? Why were they angry? Why did they come to

the village to kill? Why, when they have always come at Natyati to give us presents?"

His father smiled gently at him. "Do not ask questions, my son. When you are old enough, you will know the answers."

The answers had come that same year. On a hot summer day the war chief had gone through the village announcing the coming of the K'atsina for the summer dance. Rohona was terrified. Would they come again, angry and fighting, as they had that terrible time in the spring, or would they come bringing presents as they used to? He was filled with shame at having so much fear.

As the day of their appearance in the village approached, Rohona grew more and more apprehensive. "I am not afraid!" he whispered to himself countless times, but it had done no good. Fear ate at him. He could not let his father know his shame. The day before the K'atsina were to arrive he picked up his small bow and a special arrow he had made. He trotted through the dusty street until he came to the edge of the mesa. Climbing across the craggy rocks whose sand-graved surfaces made his moccasins slip as he hurried too quickly, he reached the spot he sought. Across the deep chasm there was a cleft in the façade of a sandstone pinnacle. Inaccessible to man or beast, the rock could have felt only the perch of a taloned claw or perhaps the eight legs of *k'amack*, the spider.

Many were the times he had seen men and older boys shoot arrows into the innumerable cracks and crevices of the mesa on which their village perched. The practice of aiming at a specific crevice was not only an enjoyable way to hone skill with the bow but was also a way to send prayers to the gods. He had lost many arrows to the deep chasm below in his attempts to lodge just one in the cleft of the pale pink sandstone of the pinnacle, but he had never succeeded. With each failure the achievement of that feat had grown in importance in his mind until it now symbolized the ultimate test that would determine that he was no longer a child. "I must learn to be a man," he said with vehemence. "Men have no fear."

His fingers trembled slightly as he took the special arrow from his small quiver. He knew the added weight of the tiny bundle lashed to the shaft would slow the speed of the arrow, but his was an important prayer to make that day. He held the arrow in the palm of his hand. With the other he took cornmeal from the small pouch he wore at his waist and sprinkled it on the arrow as he prayed.

"Give me courage, Iyatiku, mother of us all. Make me brave like the War Twins. Make my arrow reach its mark so I will know that I will never have to be afraid again."

From his pouch he took a small obsidian animal figure. "O Rohona, for whom I am named," he continued to pray, "O Rohona, the cleverest and most courageous hunter of them all, O Rohona, jaguar-of-the-south whom few have ever seen, grant me your courage!"

He rubbed the obsidian fetish along the shaft of the arrow. Carefully he replaced the stone figure in his pouch, inserted the arrow in his bow, took a deep breath, and with all his strength let the arrow-offering fly. As the arrow left his bow, he closed his eyes momentarily, opening them just in time to see the arrow's smooth arc take it into the cleft where it disappeared.

He stood motionless for a moment, unbelieving. Then he leaped into the air and gave a shout of joy and triumph. Again he stood still, his face sober. Once more he took out cornmeal and sprinkled it to the cardinal directions.

"Thank you, Iyatiku," he whispered with reverence. "Thank you, O great Rohona, O mighty hunter. From this day forward I shall fear *nothing*—ever!"

Now, without fear he had awaited the coming of the K'atsina for the Natyati. They came as fierce as ever, large heads painted vividly, dancing in the prescribed order: first on the north side, then on the west, then the south, and then the east. When they had finished, they gave out presents and he received a beautiful new quiver made of lynx fur. And he had not been afraid. Iyatiku had kept her promise.

Another scream registered in Rohona's mind, and he shuddered. As the blood of another warrior gushed out over the tree stump, his memories came rushing back to fill his mind in place of the horror he was witnessing and awaiting.

That winter he was initiated into the secret K'atsina society, and four days later he was startled to see his sponsor at the door. "Come," the man said, "your initiation is not quite over yet." Rohona's face showed surprise but obediently he followed his new father down the ladder and through the village to the southern edge of the mesa. What was this part of the initiation? He had never heard about this before. What more remained before he was a man?

Behind an outcrop of rocks they came upon the Antelope Head Man, and sitting on the ground were K'atsina, their heads resting on the ground in front of them. Rohona's eyes widened. There by one of the heads sat his father dressed in the garb of a K'atsina, and he was smiling. The K'atsina weren't real! They were the men of Áco. It had all been a trick, and he felt a deep sense of betrayal. He clenched his jaws together to keep from shouting his anger at the cruel deception. Why did they make the children believe the K'atsina were real? His face burned with shame, remembering how afraid he had been.

The Antelope Man began to speak, his words soft and soughing. "Oh, my children, it was a time long ago, before we lived on our high mesa of

Áco. It was when we lived in the north at the place called Kacikatcutya. There the real K'atsina visited the village and brought presents, but one day the people made the K'atsina very angry by making fun of their faces. The K'atsina were filled with rage, and they killed almost everyone in the village before they stopped."

The Antelope Head Man's voice rose in emotion. "To keep from repeating such a carnage, the K'atsina no longer visit the people to bring them the gifts of Iyatiku. It is necessary now for men of the village to impersonate the K'atsina, and they impart their power to these men when they are wearing the masks. The men you see here are your fathers and your uncles, but when they put the K'atsina heads on, the K'atsina enter their bodies and they are no longer your father or your uncle, and they must work for the K'atsina so that life may be sustained for us."

The Antelope Man continued, his tone reverent. "You must learn to dance beautifully so that the K'atsina will be gratified and it will please them to send the clouds to bring life-giving rain to our crops.

"Although the real K'atsina remain at Wenimats, their home in the west," the Antelope Man spoke solemnly, "you must always respect and send them your deepest prayers, for they are the ones who sustain us, we, the Ácoma, the children of Iyatiku, the people of the White Rock."

Rohona felt shame wash across him for his feelings of betrayal. He had prayed and those prayers had been answered. *That* he knew with complete certainty because the hated fear no longer dwelt within him as it once had. He listened to the Antelope Man as he swore them to secrecy.

"You must never reveal the secret of the K'atsina lest you anger them and the K'atsina cause calamity to befall you or your family as it once befell the People of the White Rock at Kacikatcutya."

Now he understood the bloody fight that had caused him such great fear. It was the reenactment of the massacre at White Rock. "Is the fight a ceremony used to remind us of Kacikatcutya and to remind us that we must always respect and revere the K'atsina?" he asked his father as they returned to their dwelling.

His father smiled at him. "Yes, my son, and it is a very sacred ceremony for us." He looked down at Rohona and continued. "The blood you saw shed in the battle was that of a deer, slaughtered for the purpose. The blood of the deer's heart is used to fill a length of intestine that is worn at the neck, and it spills its blood when it is pierced by a knife."

His father continued, his voice serious. "For four years following the whipping ceremony, you must undergo the training to become a K'atsina dancer, my son. You must practice your dancing, Rohona. You must strive to make it beautiful in order to please the K'atsina and Iyatiku."

Rohona nodded solemnly, and as they walked on, he spoke to himself, "I *will* learn to dance beautifully for you, Iyatiku. You kept your promise to me. The rhythm of my feet will touch Mother Earth and I will fill you with pride, I promise. So, too, will my mother and father be proud when they hear the voices of the people remark on the beauty of the dancing of the warrior Rohona."

Rohona's face was as immobile as the rock of his mesa when he was brought forth to the chopping block. Hands chained behind his back, he walked forward between two soldiers. It was not necessary to drag him. He seemed impervious to the mutilated feet that lay strewn on the bloody ground. No trace of fear flickered in his eyes as he looked directly at the black-bearded ax wielder. The man averted his eyes, but Rohona, as his foot was placed in the iron vise, continued to look at him. He felt the iron bite into his skin. He looked away toward the west, toward Wenimats. A picture of Áco mesa strewn with real dead flashed through his mind. He would never dance again. Never more would his dancing touch Mother Earth in beauty. Never more could he dance for Iyatiku who had kept her promise to him.

The ax fell, and his foot was gone. His teeth were clenched and the only sound he made was a strangled grunt as the hot iron burned into his skin. The last thing he remembered before he fainted was the acrid, nauseating smell of seared flesh.

He awakened in agony. He lay on the ground with the other moaning men, a crude bandage around his stump. As a light dusting of snow began to fall, the captives were dragged into a dank room and piled on the floor.

Later, one by one a Spanish soldier came in to claim the *zopo*, the cripple who would be his slave for twenty years. Rohona was not aware that the man who came to claim him had coarse red hair growing on his face and pale, almost colorless eyes.

# Chapter 4

The lumbering two-wheeled cart came to a groaning stop in front of the mud-plastered houses.

*"¡Puta madre!"* Captain Vicente de Vizcarra cursed as he dismounted from his horse. The long trip from Santo Domingo to San Juan was cold and miserable, and he vented his anger on the Tlascalan muleteer who had driven the cart up the difficult terrain to the dingy village that was now their home. The muleteer had already started toward the rear of the cart laden with its human cargo, but the captain nevertheless brought his riding crop down across the back of the Indian.

*"¡Ándale!* Get those bastards out of the *carreta*!"

The Tlascalan pulled the Ácoma men out of the cart one by one, dumping them on the ground if they were unconscious or shoving them to the side if they could stand. A number of soldiers stood in a circle looking for the slave allotted to him for twenty years of work. The soldiers laughed and joked as they stamped their feet to warm themselves against the cold, unaffected by the sight of the filthy, wounded men being pulled from the cart. As each saw the slave designated for him, he dragged the man off. Other carts arrived with more Ácoma men while the women who were to be slaves were herded behind.

The Indians of Ohké, as they had called their village before the arrival of the Spaniards, stood on the rooftops of their communal houses and watched as the carts were unloaded. Their faces were cold and hard, half-hidden behind the blankets in which they wrapped themselves.

*"¡Carajo!"* the captain cursed when he saw the muleteer drag out the Indian Oñate had given him, at Vicente's own request. The savage was delirious, his breathing shallow and rapid. Cursing under his breath, the captain seized the man under the arms and dragged him to his house.

With his mud-caked jackboot he kicked open the crude, heavy door. "*¡Bruja!*" he bellowed, pulling the man into the room as a cold blast of air swirled inside.

An old woman, her face dark and wrinkled like aged leather, came scurrying into the *sala*. The scowl on her face disappeared when she saw the native in the captain's grasp. Vicente dropped the senseless man in a heap on the floor and gave him a prod with his dirty boot. "Take care of him, *bruja*!" he commanded. "You better not let him die on me!"

Just as the old woman reached the delirious man, a younger woman stepped into the room pulling her shawl more closely about her against the cold draft of air.

"Fabia, what is it?" María Angélica asked as she saw the old woman kneel beside something on the floor. Her hand went to her mouth in horror.

The old woman looked at the Indian's bandaged stump and made a face at the disgusting sight. Carefully she began to rip away the putrid cloth, muttering to herself.

"Behold your new slave, my dear," Vicente said to the younger woman. "You get to keep him for twenty years."

"Sweet Mother of God, what happened to him?" she asked as she stepped tentatively toward the savage.

"Justice!" Vicente laughed harshly. "We cut off all the bastards' feet," he gloated. "I suggested it, and the governor ordered it. But as you know, Oñate's a practical man—had we cut off the feet at the ankle, the heathen would have been scarcely more than cripples. By merely cutting off the front part of the foot, they will be able to stump along and even carry heavy objects once they become accustomed to keeping their balance again. But with the front of their foot cut off, it'll be more difficult to flee." Vicente looked down at the man and gave him a prod with his boot toe. "I'd like to see the *hijos de puta* climb their mesa now!"

Horror washed across the younger woman's face as she crossed herself. "Forgive us, *Dios*, for our sins," she whispered, and at the sight of the man's blood-blackened stump, she reeled with nausea, unable to continue her prayer.

"Serves the proud bastard right!" Vicente said with satisfaction.

"No one can possibly deserve *this*," she said, revolted by the sight and smell. He laughed again, and she looked up at her husband's cold, pale eyes and saw only cruelty. "We are barbarians," she whispered with anger, "barbarians for what we have done."

"We are Spaniards," he said proudly. "We have only shown justice and redeemed our sacred honor."

"Sacred honor? And what about mercy?" she demanded quietly. "I thought we were supposed to come here to show the heathen the *love* of *Dios*."

"Show this heathen God's love?" Vicente answered with a snort. "I just hope he lives so he can know what *Hell* is like for the next twenty years!" With that he turned on his heel and left the house, commanding once more over his shoulder, "Don't let him die on me, *bruja*!"

The old woman threw a dark, forbidding look at his back, but she spoke gently to the young woman. "Come, Angelita, we must get him to a room. Take one arm, and I'll take the other. We must drag the *pobre indio*. It is the only way." They grasped the native's arms and pulled him haltingly across the floor.

"Stop a moment, Angelita. Let's catch our breath. *Madre mía*, it would be easier to drag a bag of sand upstream than this sack of festering humanity across this dirt floor," she muttered. The young woman nodded mutely, averting her face from the body at their feet.

*"Bueno,"* the old woman sighed with resignation, *"otra vez."* María Angélica pulled her *rebozo* up around her shoulders but it slipped off as she reached down to grasp the Indian's arm again. Her skin crawled when her hands touched the feverish flesh.

"*Jala*, Angelita," the old woman spoke, and they pulled in concert, dragging their burden into a back room of the dwelling and to the edge of a rough-hewn cot.

"Under the arms now," the old woman said. As they heaved to get him up on the cot, the Indian's head rolled to the side, and a string of saliva ran from the corner of his mouth. The man was filthy and his stench made the whole room reek. María Angélica leaned against the wall and gagged. She shoved the back of her hand against her mouth, trying to keep from throwing up.

"Oh, God," she whispered with horror.

Once on the cot, the Indian twitched and began to thrash weakly, grunting and moaning unintelligibly.

"Go, Angelita," the old woman spoke, putting her hand to her nose to guard against the smell, "old Fabia will care for him."

María Angélica looked down at the delirious savage. Was he the one who killed the Maese? Robbed her of the one presence she needed more than any other? A sob caught in her throat. Now that the Maese was dead, how could she endure life in this horrible, desolate place to which they had come? Could she endure knowing that perhaps she was as much the cause of his death as was this savage? She could not hold back her sobs. *"Dios,"* she whispered with anguish, "did you punish the Maese, are you punishing this poor heathen because of *my* sins?"

Her head dropped forward and tears fell onto the folds of the *rebozo* she held limply. "Punish me," she whispered, "I was the one who loved a man who was not my husband. Please," she begged, "punish no one else for my sins."

Fabia grasped her arm and said sternly, "You did not sin, *querida*. *Dios* knows that love from the heart is never a sin."

María Angélica looked at the old woman, her face grim and tear-stained. "The Maese is dead. *Dead*! Now this heathen is mutilated. And my husband is alive. How can you say that *Dios* knows love from the heart is not a sin?"

A black scowl covered the old woman's face. "*Dios* knows the cruelty of the captain your husband, and He will deal with him in His own good time. But do not punish yourself, *querida*, for the Maese or this heathen. The soldiers carry the guilt, not you, Angelita, *not you*."

"Fabia, I know we all must share the guilt for *this*," she said as she motioned toward the Indian with his mutilated foot. She choked at the stench that filled the room. "God in Heaven could not condone this. I know He could not. I thought the heathen were barbaric, Fabia." Her eyes were bleak. "We are no better—we are *all* barbarians! Just as the savages have paid for killing the Maese and his men, so eventually one day must we pay for this hideous deed." Her body trembled slightly as she looked down at the filthy Indian. "I will atone for my sins, Fabia. I swear, I *will* atone."

"Go, Angelita," Fabia said, putting her hand on the young woman's arm, "go rest, now. Pray for this heathen because by the look of the foot, I fear prayer is all that will save him."

"No," María Angélica whispered as she tried to control her nausea. "If *Jesús Cristo* could suffer for us, I ought to have to suffer, too. *Dios* knows I did not want to come here, but there is no job too revolting that I will not do now."

"Angelita," Fabia spoke as she took the younger woman's arm and tried to lead her from the room, "old Fabia will care for him. It is not necessary that you help. Do not be so hard on yourself, Angelita. Besides, it is not a job for the *señora*."

"Oh, but it is," she said with bitterness and resignation, pulling her arm from the old woman's. "You know I am not the same innocent girl who began this journey. You know as well as I the strong dose of reality we have all had. There is no need for you to try to shelter me, Fabia, it is a futile pursuit in this godforsaken land, and you know that." She swallowed, and when she continued, her voice was no more than a hoarse whisper. "But I swear to the Almighty that I will show this poor creature that there is a God and that not all Spaniards are barbarians. I swear it, Fabia, I swear it."

The old woman nodded glumly, saying only, "We must see to the foot. It does not look good. It does not look good at all." She put her hand on the Indian's chest for a moment. "He may have fever in his lungs, too."

"I will find clean linen for bandages," María Angélica said and hurried out, pulling her *rebozo* more tightly around her.

Fabia brought to the dank room an iron kettle with boiling water in addition to small sacks of herbs and pots with ointment. She was known for her curing skills, but the best *curandera* could not cure blood fever if it had gone too far. Carefully the old woman washed the wound and applied to the red, oozing stump a hot, pungent poultice that smelled of pine resin.

María Angélica knelt by her and handed her the bandages. She had never seen or smelled anything quite so horrible. She bit the inside of her cheek until tears came to her eyes and prayed for strength. "*Virgen María*, don't let me be sick, don't."

After Fabia bandaged the foot, she began to remove the tatters of clothes the man wore. "We must bathe this *pobre* and try to get rid of this awful stench."

When the old woman turned and saw the embarrassment and horror on María Angélica's face, she said quickly, "Go, Angelita, old Fabia can take care of things now."

The young woman shook her head but closed her eyes against the sight. "*Nuestro Señor* humbled himself to wash dirty feet, I must do no less." But she could not touch the savage. Instead, she reached down hesitantly, revolt covering her features, and picked up the filthy rags of clothes. "I will burn these," she managed to whisper.

"Hail Mary full of grace the Lord is with thee. Blessed art thou among women and blessed is the fruit of thy womb Jesus," she spoke quietly as she knelt at the side of the low rough cot and prayed the rosary.

"*Querida*," Fabia said softly as the young woman finished the decades and kissed the crucifix, "come away. The *pobre indio* will be all right if you leave him for a moment. You must eat. You must sleep. You cannot stay day and night at his bedside as you have been doing. You must quit this punishing of yourself."

With the back of her hand, María Angélica pushed a strand of hair off her forehead. "I've got to stay," she said wearily. "*Dios* has given this poor heathen into my care. I can't fail, I just can't. You know the *padres* tell us to love our enemies just as *Dios* loved those who cruelly nailed him to the cross."

A look of impatience crossed the old woman's face. "You don't know that this *indio* was the one," Fabia muttered. "But what *Dios* sees fit to do at times is strange, that is certain."

"Yes," María Angélica agreed quietly, "I don't understand why, Fabia, but I believe he has brought this poor heathen to my household for the salvation of my own soul."

Fabia scowled and started to reply, but María Angélica continued, her voice filled with heavy defeat. "*Dios* knows how I hated the natives of this land when I heard that the Maese had been killed at that terrible place they call Ácoma. I felt hate, pure hatred, in my heart, and I wanted them to die. I truly did. I would not have cared if every last one had been wiped from the face of the earth."

She dipped a cloth in a bowl of water and wiped it across the feverish man's forehead. "But when Vicente brought this poor wretch here, I saw how horrible hate can be." She shuddered. "Never could I sanction the cruelty and abomination the soldiers have committed. I know that the Maese would never have permitted such an outrage." She choked back a sob. "And for his sake I must show this heathen that there is a *Dios* in heaven."

"That is all well and good," the old woman said glumly, putting her hand on the young woman's shoulder, "but *Dios* will allow a person to eat and sleep. Get out of the house. Go see your friend Dorotea. Let old Fabia stay by his bedside. Certainly you trust these old hands to care for him."

María Angélica looked up at the old woman and put her hand on hers. "Of course," she answered with a small smile, "of course I do dear, dear, Fabia, but I shall not leave the house until the fever breaks."

The Italian clock that had miraculously survived the long, torturous leagues of travel north chimed two as María Angélica gently shook the old woman who dozed at the bedside of the fever-wracked form. She wondered how old the Indian was. He scarcely looked twenty-five. How had they determined the men's ages in order to decide who would have their foot cut off and who would not?

"Go back to sleep, child," Fabia said as she came awake, "you need more rest."

"No, I am awake now. I will take over. But perhaps in the afternoon I shall nap." The old woman nodded and padded out of the room. María Angélica drew her wool *rebozo* more closely about her. It was cold in the room. She could hear the wind outside, howling down from the snow-covered mountains, and she shivered. She pulled an old blanket snugly up around the Indian, but in his fever he kicked it off.

She had not been out of her house since her husband had dropped the savage on the floor of their *sala* as if he were a side of beef. Days lost their meaning as she cared for the *indio*. She had not been raised to perform the duties she had undertaken in the face of Fabia's protests, but their long, hard journey north had changed her life. She was well aware that nothing would ever be the same again. Ever. She knew *she* would never be the same.

At first it had revolted her to touch the Indian, but no longer. She could now put her hand on him to comfort him when he became delirious and babbled in his strange, unfamiliar language. He said something that sounded like Ka-Ku-Na over and over again. How many other slaves were in the same condition as this poor heathen?

It was early afternoon and she was sitting by the Indian's bedside when the old woman announced Dorotea. María Angélica came quickly to her feet and ran to embrace her friend. "Oh, Doro," she said with anguish, "what they have done to them is *so* horrible."

"I know," the other young woman replied, "the soldiers are brutal beyond words." She walked over to the bedside of the Indian and looked down. "Is he going to live?" she asked.

"I don't know," María Angélica said with a heavy sigh, suddenly feeling insupportably tired. "Fabia is doing everything she can."

Dorotea turned back to face her friend. Her mouth was hard. "Be glad your husband was given a man," she said harshly. "Isidro was given an Ácoma girl as a slave. She can't be more than sixteen or seventeen, if that. My soul shudders at what she and her people are suffering."

Dorotea paused and swallowed before she continued. "God, you would not believe what Isidro has done to her." Her face was stark. "She has marks all over her body from where he has bitten her!"

María Angélica's face showed disbelief, and Dorotea laughed bitterly. "Yes, *bitten*. She has welts all over her thighs and buttocks, and her breasts are covered with ugly purple bruises—you can even see the teeth marks!" Tears welled in her eyes. "It is so horrible."

María Angélica started to speak, but the words died in her throat as Dorotea choked back tears and continued, her voice quavering. "Last night I could stand no more. I heard muffled screams and whimpering and then the whip. Each crack made me jerk, and I could not keep from crying.

" 'Why do you let him do it?' I asked *Dios*. 'Why don't you stop him?' I simply couldn't stand it any longer. I wiped the tears away and walked to the room where they were. He didn't even hear me open the door."

Dorotea's voice was hollow, but she did not stop. Her hands trembled, and her clear brown eyes were focused on nothing. "There he stood, naked, a whip in his hands as that poor girl, naked also, cowered on the floor, covering her head with her arms as he cracked the whip again and again, missing her by only a hair's breadth. Once or twice the whip caught her, and she flinched in pain. 'For God's sake, whip me, Isidro, instead of her!' I screamed. He jerked around abruptly, and when he saw me, do you know what he did? He laughed. He just laughed, and that scar on his cheek made his face the most evil thing I have ever seen."

María Angélica stood motionless, and Dorotea swallowed. "I know you won't believe it," she said, "but I pulled my gown off. I would not back away. 'Whip me instead of her,' I said. I was *insane* with anger, fear, horror. My voice didn't even sound like my own. He laughed and stood there unashamedly—his *picha* hard and erect, poised like a venomous snake. He laughed again. 'So you want to watch, heh?' he said as he walked over to the girl and yanked her to her knees facing him and pushed her face against him and made her . . ."

María Angélica's arms hung limply at her sides. Tears sprang to her eyes and trickled down her cheeks. "What have *we* done?" she asked softly. "I have never harmed another human being that I know of. Why are we being punished?"

"I don't know. I don't know," Dorotea responded. There was a long pause before she turned to look back down at the feverish man who lay on the rough cot. "The real reason I came," she said wearily, "is that the girl has been trying desperately to talk to me. It is so difficult to communicate with her, but she has had such an urgency in her attempts that I finally called Tomás to translate. She had heard talk from some of the other Ácoma slaves, and it seems she thinks your slave may be her brother. So I brought her here to see if he is or not."

For the first time in days, María Angélica smiled. "Oh, Doro, could it be? How I would like to know at least his name."

"Siya," Dorotea called, and a young Indian woman stepped through the door, her eyes downcast. Dorotea walked over to the girl, and taking her hand, led her to the cot where the feverish man lay. María Angélica saw a purple bruise on the girl's neck and shuddered.

The girl fell to her knees and touched the Indian's cheek. "Rohona," she said as she began to cry, "Rohona, Rohona." Presently she rose and pointed to the man. "Rohona," she repeated and pointed to herself saying words neither María Angélica nor Dorotea could understand.

Was the Indian's name Rohona? María Angélica pointed to the delirious man. "Rohona?" she asked.

The girl nodded her head affirmatively and repeated, "Rohona."

"There is a word he says all the time," María Angélica spoke to her, "Ka-Ku-Na." She pointed to Rohona and then to her mouth and repeated the word "Ka-Ku-Na" several times.

At first the girl did not seem to understand, but suddenly she brightened. Again she nodded her head saying, "Rohona, Kakuna," and put two fingers together. The Spanish women did not understand. For a moment the girl thought, and then she took her hand and made a motion as if she had a very large stomach. Next she made a cradle with her arms as if she were rocking a baby.

María Angélica thought she understood. "Kakuna," she said making the motion of the big stomach. She pointed at the man. "Rohona," she said, "Kakuna and Rohona," and she put her two fingers together, "man and wife?"

The girl nodded vigorously.

"Oh, Doro, his name must be Rohona," María Angélica said. Then she turned back to the Indian girl. "And where is Kakuna?" she asked. The girl shook her head sadly, uncomprehending the words the Spanish woman spoke.

"She probably died during the massacre," Dorotea whispered, and tears welled in María Angélica's eyes.

"We won't stay any longer now," Dorotea said as she put her hand on her friend's arm. "But we will return tomorrow and you need to get some rest."

The Indian girl took María Angélica's hand and breathed on it. "I have learned that means 'thank you,' " Dorotea said.

María Angélica looked at the young Indian woman and spoke. "He is in God's hands. All we can do is pray for His mercy." It was obvious the girl did not understand. María Angélica patted her gently on the hand.

Fabia showed the two women to the door and returned to the room. She started to speak, but her mistress interrupted as she tiredly pushed her unkempt hair out of her face. "The captain will expect to have his supper waiting, Fabia. Please see it is ready."

*"Querida,"* the old woman spoke, "go rest now. The *indio* will be all right alone for a short while."

"No," she said softly. Fabia heard the resolution behind the quiet word and nodded with resignation.

The room fell quiet save for the raspy breathing of the Indian. María Angélica stood looking down at the man's face. His eyes were closed and he might have been unconscious, but there was a crease of pain that drew his eyebrows together. His high cheekbones were prominent and his face angular. Her throat constricted in a sob as she looked at him.

"Please don't die. Too many have died already. There has been too much horror. Oh, Maese, why did you have to die?" she spoke with anguish.

She fell to her knees at the bedside of the Indian. "Oh, Maese," she whispered again as she rocked back and forth hugging herself, tears rolling down her cheeks, "why did you have to die? I cannot stand my life now that you are gone. I did not know I had such a need until you showed me."

She ran her hands over her breasts and her body shook with sobs. "I want your hands touching me, Maese. *Dios*, how I ache for you at night. I have never felt like I did that night as you held me against your naked body. You were so warm, and your arms and hands were strong and so very gentle as you cradled me and caressed me. I *never* wanted it to stop, but now the pain tears me apart and my dreams torment me."

She rocked back and forth. "You are with me in my bed and your hands caress me until I am frenzied with desire. I am on fire, and I beg you, 'Oh, Juan, Juan, please, *now*,' but then I awake and my body is trembling with need, and the enormity of your death crashes down upon me, and I do not know how I am going to survive here."

Tears slid down her cheeks and she was choked by sobs. She reached out and placed her hand on the Indian. "Don't die," she pleaded. "I already have one death on my conscience. Please, don't be another," she begged.

Her head slumped forward onto the edge of the cot as she whispered through her tears, "Please don't die. Please don't die."

## Part Two

# LA ENTRADA

## Entry, April 1598

# Chapter 5

The light was blinding. Like a thousand crazy dancers it glinted and flashed into the brilliant, cloudless blue sky. For a hundred miles it shouted their presence, announcing their coming, long before the clanking metal, the screeching cart wheels, or the raucous animal sounds gave evidence of their approach.

They stood in formation under the glaring sun. To the left was the cavalry mounted on beautifully caparisoned horses, draped in silk and damask trimmed with silver tassels or gold embroidery. The suits of armor were highly polished, some embossed with precious metal, and like mirrors the chest plates gleamed, reflecting the sun that beat down from the infinite blue that spread above them. Some wore full suits of armor from the visored armet that hid the identity of the wearer down to the greaves and sabbatons that protected the lower legs and feet. Others were outfitted with lighter three-quarter armor consisting of a coat of plate, thigh armor known as cuisses, heavy jackboots, and a curved morion helmet. Various were the weapons they carried. From the swords, double-edged and single, to lances, arquebuses, and wheellock guns, the invaders were well outfitted, and their high-spirited fighting horses danced and snorted as they were reined tightly in formation. To the right was the infantry, protected by leathern and strongly quilted jackets. They held their halberds, pikes, and poleaxes upright at attention, but the blades gave the impression of movement as the light danced on the sharp spikes and cutting edges.

A makeshift bower of willow branches and leafy cottonwoods occupied the center between the cavalry and the infantry, and although protected to a degree by the dappled shade, its inhabitants suffered from the blinding glare and the rich, heavy clothes they wore. Brocades, silks and satins, velvets and lace were soiled as their owners knelt on the sandy frieze tarpaulin that had been spread on the ground beneath the bower.

Fabia looked to where María Angélica knelt on the frieze in the dappled shade, clutching the silver crucifix of her coral rosary, and she thought the young woman's hands might have trembled. Fabia saw her shift her weight on the velvet cushion and try to adjust the farthingale that held out the voluminous silk of her skirts. With little success the young woman tried to gather the mulberry-colored fabric closer to her, allowing more room for the others who also knelt under the crowded bower. Fabia knew that the carefully starched and fluted lace-edged ruff at María Angélica's neck did not allow her freedom to see if her skirts were molesting anyone, and it was obvious the wide ruff came within a hair's breadth of impeding her movement as she dabbed with her Holland lawn handkerchief at the beads of perspiration on her forehead.

Fabia sighed and tried to smooth the worry that she knew creased her old face. *Oh,* mi angelita, she whispered to herself, *may* Dios *be merciful to us. You have already endured more hardship than I ever dreamed you would have to suffer. I am thankful your* pobre mamá *doesn't have to see it. God grant us a safe journey from here on.*

María Angélica shifted again uncomfortably, but there was nothing that she could do about the perspiration that was sliding down her back. It felt like an insect crawling under her clothes, and she prayed the ceremony would soon be over. She was not sure she could endure much longer because what she wanted to do was scream and assure herself it truly was sweat and not an insect there, but the ceremony was a solemn one and filled with especial emotion for all, and she could not be a disgrace.

It had been an arduous journey and the long uncertainty of the delay they had to endure had left many bitter as the Viceroy, the King, and the Council of the Indies vacilated in their decisions. It had been a grim and prolonged wait for the group at Santa Bárbara. Many of the soldiers and colonists sold everything they had owned in order to finance their journey with Oñate, and all their worldly goods were with them. Food they intended for the march was long since consumed. Seed wheat they hoped to use for their first crops in the new land was ground into flour to feed their families, and much of their livestock had been lost or stolen in the valley. Many people deserted and more wanted to but could not because they no longer had anything, their fortunes long ago exhausted. She and her husband, however, had joined the group late, and had not suffered through the long wait.

They had arrived just as Oñate was given the go ahead to march, and by the time the group finally left the last outpost of civilization and began their long-awaited conquest, Vicente was filled with excitement. It was a hollow jubilation for the others, however, and she was overcome with apprehension and dread. She had been married less than two weeks when she was forced to leave the only home she had ever known, but now at last they were on the sandy, willow-lined banks of the *Río Bravo del Norte*, the wild river of the north, the entrance, the *entrada* to *Nuevo México*, the land they would conquer, pacify, and colonize for the King of Spain. The friars would bring the Gospel to the heathen, and by the grace of God, they would find gold, silver, and other precious metals in abundance, making the rigors of the journey into that wild unknown all worthwhile. They would become rich like the men who had discovered gold and silver at Ixmilquilpan, or San Luís Obispo or in the barren mountains of Zacatecas. Or so was the hope beating in almost every breast.

Toward the front of the bower knelt the friars clothed in blue sackcloth, their tonsured heads bowed, and among them the Father Commissary was distinguished by his elaborately embroidered brocade vestments. Behind the friars she and the other gentlewomen, wives of the officers, along with their children, prayed and clutched their rosaries. The soldiers' wives were behind them, and those who had neither the protection of the bower nor the frieze on which to kneel, servants and slaves and the wives of the Tlascalan Indians who made up the body of the infantry, were obliged to kneel in the rough sand.

She turned and caught Fabia's dark eyes on her and saw the look of worry and apprehension in them before Fabia could hide it. María Angélica smiled at her, but she knew it did not fool old Fabia. She knew her old nursemaid was well aware of her fears for this journey, but a sudden shudder ran through her. Until that moment when she saw Fabia's eyes, she had not realized just *how* grave the old woman's concerns were. She had never seen a look on Fabia's face like that she had just glimpsed. She tried to tell herself that Fabia was simply worrying about the purple silk dress since there were so few good clothes left, but she knew that the look was not concern over the mulberry silk. María Angélica turned back to face the front of the bower and crossed herself quickly.

Kneeling in front of the vast assemblage on one knee, his back to them as he faced the muddy, swiftly moving river, their gray-haired leader dressed in full armor, his helmet under his arm, began to speak.

In a rich and resonant voice the great grandson-in-law of Moctezuma and Hernán Cortez took possession of the land. "In the name of the most holy Trinity, and of the eternal Unity, Deity, and Majesty, God the Father, the Son, and the Holy Ghost, be it known that I, Don Juan de Oñate, Governor, Captain General, and *Adelantado* of *Nuevo México*, by virtue of the authority of Jesus Christ and his servant the most Christian King, our lord Don Felipe, second of that name, hereby declare that I take possession of this land this thirtieth day of April, the feast of the Ascension of our Lord, in the year fifteen hundred and ninety-eight." The voice of their armor-clad leader took on a more determined tone. "Among the reasons for this conquest is the great number of children born among these infidel people who neither recognize nor obey their true God and Father. The salvation of these souls should demand this."

As all witnessed the ceremony of the Act of Possession, emotion rippled through the colonists and the jubilation that had been lacking as they left the mines at Todos Santos began to swell in all hearts. María Angélica's hands trembled as she clutched her rosary. "What do you have in store for us, *Dios*, in this remote corner of your domain?" she whispered and crossed herself again. She lifted her eyes back to the gleaming metal of Don Juan's armor where he knelt in the sand. His sonorous voice filled the silent air, broken only occasionally by the cry of a baby before it could be put to the breast.

"All these objects I shall fulfill even to the point of death, if need be. I command now and will always command that these objects be observed under that severest of penalties." Don Juan's voice carried absolute authority. "Therefore, in virtue of the above, I take possession of these lands. I take possession once, twice, thrice, and all the times I can and must of the lands of this *Río del Norte*, without exception whatsoever. I take all jurisdiction, civil as well as criminal, power of life and death over high and low, from the leaves of the trees of the mountain forests to the stones and sands in the rivers."

Rising, Don Juan handed his helmet to his page, Cristóbal Guillén de Quesada, and took in his hands the wooden cross that the Father Commissary, Fray Alonso, had been holding. The metallic swishing of Don Juan's armor as he walked with the cross to a large spreading cottonwood was the only sound to disturb the silence. His page handed him a hammer and nails, and with his own hands, Don Juan nailed the cross to the tree. He kissed the cross and then knelt, praying with great conviction, "O Holy Cross, divine gate of heaven and altar of the only and essential sacrifice of the blood of the Son of God, open the gates of heaven to these infidels. Give to our King and to me, in his royal name, the peaceful possession of these Kingdoms and Provinces. Amen."

María Angélica clutched her hands together to keep them from shaking. *Could* this conquest be peaceful? Had there ever been a conquest without death and destruction? Cortez's conquest of Mexico itself had been brutal and bloody. "Please, sweet Mother of God," she prayed, "keep us safe and let there be no bloodshed."

At that moment Don Juan raised the royal standard. The trumpeters sounded a fanfare and the arquebusiers fired a deafening salute. The gold-embroidered flag fluttered in the air. On one side the coat of arms of the King of Spain shimmered in the sunlight, and on the other, the imperial coat of arms was no less brilliant.

Having raised the standard aloft, Don Juan stabbed it forcefully into the sandy ground and shouted, "Spaniards! Witness the symbol that I take possession of this land, and swear on your immortal souls that it shall be *forever*!"

Everyone broke into loud cheering, and many faces were wet with tears. María Angélica had a brief moment of difficulty rising, as did many of the other women who had knelt during the solemn Mass and ceremony. She experienced a fleeting pain as she straightened her half-numb legs, and turning to her side, she held out her hand to Dorotea, who was also attempting to rise. Dorotea smiled through tears as she grasped the outstretched hand and rose. Neither spoke as they squeezed the other's fingers.

María Angélica wiped her eyes. "We must pay our respects and offer our congratulations to Don Juan," she said softly.

"Yes," Dorotea said. Her tears ceased, and she laughed quietly. "I am sure our governor will have his own respects to pay to you, María Angélica." Dorotea motioned with her hand toward the silk dress. "You look beautiful today," she whispered, her brown eyes smiling. "Even during the worst of the journey when we were all exhausted and dirty, you were still lovely. I don't know how you do it. When Don Juan sees you now, looking like a princess in your violet silk, his eyes will hunger even more!"

María Angélica's cheeks flamed. "Don't say that," she whispered. "You know that isn't true. Please, you've said that before, and you know I don't like for you to say things like that."

*"Bueno,"* Dorotea answered, looking away, "I shan't say it again."

Fabia touched María Angélica's arm and the young woman started. When she turned, she saw her old *criada* standing there; she had not heard her approach. Had she overheard Dorotea's words? Fabia's dark eyes betrayed nothing—not even the fear for her that María Angélica had glimpsed earlier.

Fabia smiled and patted her cheek, and she turned and patted Dorotea's cheek. *"Las más bellas de todas,"* she said and smiled again.

Dorotea laughed. "I don't consider myself one of the most beautiful, but thank you for saying so, Fabia." She leaned over and kissed the weathered cheek of the old woman.

Fabia squeezed her hand, and her voice was serious. "There is more than one kind of beauty, *Señora* Dorotea. Beauty from within is perhaps the most powerful of all."

"She is right, you know," María Angélica added.

"I guess I'll have to take your word for it, since I am outnumbered."

Fabia chuckled and turned to María Angélica. "Enjoy the festivities, Angelita. I am going to check on the preparations for the banquet tonight, but I will be back to the tent for your *siesta*."

"*Gracias*, Fabia."

"You are lucky," Dorotea said, nodding toward Fabia as the old woman walked away.

"Yes, I know," María Angélica whispered. "I don't know what I would do without her. I don't think I could survive."

"Come," Dorotea said and they turned to follow the others who had crowded around the new governor.

María Angélica's satin slippers filled with sand the moment they stepped off the frieze, and she held the wide skirts of her best dress trying to keep them out of the grit. She felt foolish and out of place in the mulberry silk with its wide, fluted ruff, its puffed and slashed sleeves, and the long ropes of pearls that were knotted around her neck.

She saw a bird of prey circling lazily, high overhead. She thought the impressive array of military armament and courtly fashion that they displayed there in the barren wilds, hundreds of miles from the last outpost of civilization, might have seemed less incongruous in that particularly desolate setting if had there been eyes to witness the spectacle they presented. The *buitre* certainly wasn't impressed as he circled overhead—he only hoped for a meal, perhaps a desert rodent flushed up by their herds of animals or a carcass left by a coyote. An *escalofrío* ran down her back.

She crossed herself quickly and her fingers touched the pearls at her throat. The *buitre* wouldn't care that they were some of the few remaining jewels she possessed. Vicente had sold most of her others to buy mining equipment and the mercury needed for the extraction of silver. She did not begrudge the money spent to buy the livestock because she could understand the need of that for colonizing a new country, but the vast outlay for mining equipment seemed excessive to her. Her husband, however, was convinced that rich veins of ore awaited them, and the person quickest to set mining operations in progress would become the richest colonizer of the new province. She did not share his passion for wealth.

Perhaps it was because she had never had to do without. She had not willingly chosen to undertake this dangerous journey, but she could not defy her husband's decision. Even if she had wanted, she no longer had any say over her inheritance nor her life. God knows she did not want to come to this wild, desolate land to live, but perhaps it was His will. Perhaps He was testing her, perhaps that was why she found her life so difficult to endure. God willing, Vicente would find the gold or silver that he so desired; perhaps then he would not be so unpleasant. Perhaps. Uncertainty gnawed at her continually and left a larger hole than her prayers could fill.

They approached the group surrounding the governor who had just finished signing the long parchment Document of Possession at the small velvet-draped table set up for that purpose. Although she and Dorotea were well back in the crowd, Don Juan spied them and made his way to their side, a broad smile on his face. Sunlight gleamed off the armor of his chest plates.

"Ah, *Señora* de Vizcarra," he spoke warmly to María Angélica, taking her hand and bringing it to his lips in fine courtly style. "You wear the color of Our Lord's Passion, but I aver that it is mortal man's passion that it inspires." He let his lips linger on her hand, and she dropped her eyes in embarrassment at the compliment and its inherent sacrilege. She felt Dorotea's eyes on her when she responded.

"I fear that this color of Lent is inappropriate for today's joyous Feast of the Ascension of our holy Lord, but we were commanded to don our finest attire for this most awaited ceremony of the Act of Possession, and this is the best gown of the few left in my possession." She tried to remove her hand from his, but she felt the pressure of his fingers tighten on hers, and she let her hand go limp.

Don Juan answered, but she could not tell whether there was criticism in his voice. She did not want to meet his eyes. "You were wise to follow my orders, the orders of your temporal lord, and I am sure our Lord in Heaven can only be gratified by the beauty of His creatures."

She made no outward indication of her displeasure, but once again Don Juan had referred to himself as their lord. Was he really assuming the role of a royal sovereign as some of the soldiers and colonists were beginning to whisper among themselves? She was spared his further attentions as he loosed her hand and turned to Dorotea. "*Señora* de Inojosa, I see you, too, followed the admonition of your leader. You look lovely on this glorious day for our King and monarch, Don Felipe, may God protect him."

"Yes, the day is certainly one to be dedicated to our most powerful sovereign without whose wisdom, assistance, and authority we could never have reached this place." María Angélica glanced at Dorotea and heard the edge in her voice and the special emphasis she put on her words. Dorotea's eyes met those of the governor and did not fall.

"Yes, of course," Oñate answered smoothly, but his words were brittle. "Good day, *señoras*," he said with a small bow and then turned to the other people waiting to congratulate the new governor of the province of *Nuevo México*.

María Angélica was relieved to be out of the governor's presence as she and Dorotea strolled, skirts lifted out of the sand, toward the shade of some wide-branching cottonwoods.

"I'm so glad," she said after they had passed out of earshot of the group surrounding Oñate, "so glad, Doro, that you are on this journey. You are my only friend. I feel so alone except for Fabia. If you were not along to talk to, I fear this expedition would be unbearable."

"Are you so sure that it isn't, even with my presence?" Dorotea answered with a bitter laugh. "I will never understand why men pursue wealth above everything, relishing danger all the while." Dorotea glanced with disdain at the men outfitted in their gleaming armor.

"I don't understand it either," María Angélica replied, looking toward where the soldiers were gathering, "but I do understand the desire to bring *Nuestro Señor* to the savage heathen so that they might know salvation."

Dorotea's laughter this time had a cynical edge to it. "How do you know the savages aren't happier and better off the way they are now?"

"Doro, how can you say that? How can you say they are better off without the knowledge of *Dios*?"

"I didn't say it. I merely posed the question. Oh, look!" she said, pointing toward the horsemen, "the battle is about to begin!"

At that moment a horse and armor-clad rider came galloping up to them, reining to a stop so close that the horse's hooves, biting into the sand, sent the grit all over the bottoms of their skirts. With a gauntleted hand, he raised the visor of his armet.

"Ladies, my compliments," Vicente said with a small bow from the waist. "I am going into battle against the Moorish infidel and beg a boon." His red-bearded face smiled as he looked out from his helmet toward them, but his pale eyes were hard. "Please," he continued, using the medieval Galician Portuguese of the *cantigas* of courtly love, "wouldst thou favor me with a small article that I might carry into battle as a remembrance of the one for whom this heart solely beats?"

María Angélica hesitated but tried not to show her distaste as she stepped to the side of the gray-white Arabian stallion. "Take this token," she said tonelessly as she handed him her handkerchief.

Vicente took the scented square and brought it to his lips, waxing poetic in the courtly style of the troubadours as he punned on the religious poems of the *Cantigas* of Santa María.

*"Qual é a que per seu seno liso*
*nos fez aver paraiso?*
*María Angélica, mia senhor.*

*Who is she who by her thighs*
*has brought us paradise?*
*María Angélica, my lover."*

A look of chagrin spread across her face, and Vicente laughed at her discomfort as he tucked the handkerchief in the gorget of his armor, wheeled his horse about, and went to join the other jousters.

Although the Moors had long since been driven from the soil of the motherland with the divine help of the nation's patron saint Santiago, the blood of the mighty Crusaders still coursed through those Spanish veins. It mattered not that many of them there that day had never set a foot on the soil of Spain, as their birthplace was the soil of the New World, the soil of Mexico, the New Spain.

As the "Moors," on horseback armed with lances, and the "Christians," on foot with arquebuses in their hands for their defense, prepared for their "holy" battle, those of the entourage not involved in the fight gathered enthusiastically to watch. Wife, mother, servant, slave—all crowded to the front to get a better view.

María Angélica had lost her enthusiasm for the pageant and protested, "Let them have their sham battle. I'm sick of watching them show off."

"It's just entertainment," Dorotea said as she pulled her by the hand and sought a good vantage point for them. "Let's just enjoy the spectacle."

At that moment there was a shrill blast on the trumpets and the thunderous roar of *"¡Santiago!"* filled the air as the lance carrying Moorish infidel bore down on their chargers toward the armor-clad Christians. The air reverberated with tumultuous noise. Fierce cries of *"Allah!"* and *"Mohammed!"* vied with those of *"¡Santiago!"* Metal clashed against metal in loud bursts like cracks of thunder, and the sand raised by hoof and foot rose in gritty clouds, covering the participants and spectators alike. Horses neighed, and the caravan's dogs howled at the deafening noise. Lances were knocked from infidel hands, and an unlucky Christian here or there fell in a clanking heap as he was unexpectedly knocked to the ground by a charging steed. The faces that were visible were fierce visaged, and as passions ran high, it would have been difficult to determine, had one not known ahead of time, that the battle was a sham.

At last every Moor lay "dead" in the sand, and once again the shout of *"¡Santiago!"* thundered from the throats of the conquering Christians, and then a new shout arose. *"¡Nuevo México y oro!" "¡Nuevo México y oro!"* "New Mexico and gold!"

# Chapter 6

"Fabia," María Angélica called out, "*ven acá*. Can you help me remove my dress, please?"

The old woman lifted aside the flap of the frieze tent and stepped inside where the young woman sat on a carved, tapestry-covered chair that looked out of place in the dusty tent.

"Ah, *mi angelita*, how beautiful my angel looked today," the servant woman spoke with a smile. "How good it was for these old eyes to see you thus, dressed like a princess, like you should always be."

"Fabia," María Angélica spoke softly, taking the wrinkled hand of her maid into her own, "our lives have changed."

*"Sí,"* the old woman answered with a nod, her face unsmiling now, "our lives have changed, and I feel I have broken my solemn promise to your poor *mamá* who is in heaven."

"How can you say that, Fabia?" she asked, as she brought the old woman's hand to her cheek in a caress. "Are you not still with me?—still caring for me as you have done since I was born?"

*"Cómo no,"* the old woman replied, and then she made a gesture toward the frieze tent and its makeshift accommodations, "but your *mamá* never expected to see you like this."

"Things will be better when we have reached *Nuevo México* and have founded a capital worthy of a new province," she said with encouragement.

"You think old Fabia does not see how often you are on your knees praying?" The alert, dark eyes of the old woman looked penetratingly at her.

"Yes, it's true," the younger woman responded, dropping her eyes from the gaze of those that understood her much too well, "I have been praying more than usual, but I am asking *Dios* and the Virgin to take care of us and guide us on this dangerous journey."

"One is wiser at times," the old woman said, "to look to an intelligent, able man who knows the road to guide one on a dangerous journey."

"But may one not ask *Dios* to supply us with such a mortal man?" she asked.

"I suppose it does no harm," the old woman answered without conviction as she turned and smoothed a wisp of the young woman's hair back under the caul that held it. "Do you wish to let down your hair while you rest?"

"I think not. You did such a beautiful job with it this morning." María Angélica patted her hair that was swept over a wire underframe and caught up behind in a net caul made of threads of thin gold wire and seed pearls. "Captain Farfán has written a play that is to be performed this afternoon, and I shall want to attend."

*"Muy bien,"* the old woman said, "then we shall just remove the gown so you may rest before this afternoon's activities."

With her deft old hands she began to remove the puffed and slashed sleeves of the silk dress. Carefully she laid the sleeves aside and began to unfasten the bodice. Next came the heavy skirts and petticoats, followed by the steel-banded farthingale that gave the skirts their voluminous shape. She removed the ribbon straps that held the farthingale suspended at waist height, and the young woman stepped out of the contraption.

When the old woman removed the deeply pointed busk, María Angélica breathed in deeply, free now of the steel-reinforced garment. "I have grown accustomed to the simple clothes of the journey," she sighed. "I am not used to all these restraints."

Fabia chuckled. "So you are becoming a 'loose' woman?"

"Fabia," María Angélica rebuked her, "I am not. It is this journey that makes one change whether one wants to or not."

*"Sí,"* Fabia answered darkly, *"tienes razón.* This journey will change everything. Everything." Her look was masked as she turned to a trunk that sat in one corner and took from it a pale yellow muslin robe. She helped the young woman slip it on and tied the ribbons at the throat and down the front.

"Now," Fabia clucked like an old mother hen, "lie down and rest. I will wake you in plenty of time for Captain Farfán's play." The old woman drew the cloth that partitioned a small sleeping alcove in the tent.

As if she might have been a child in her care, the old woman checked later to see that María Angélica was sleeping. The old *criada* heard the clanking of armor and Vicente's loud laugh. A look of displeasure crossed her wrinkled face. The door flap of the tent was yanked back and the captain entered, his page behind him.

*"Hola, bruja,"* Vicente said, as he addressed the servant lady with his customary term of "witch" and tossed his gauntlets to the side. She mut-

tered something in her native Nahuatl, and although he did not understand, his smile became tight at the corners of his thin lips. "Fetch me some fresh water, old woman," he said harshly as he seated himself on the tapestry-covered chair.

"The *señor* is going to ruin the fine chair if he sits on it with his armor that smells of horses," Fabia said disapprovingly.

With obvious displeasure he rose and availed himself of a wooden carton. "The water," he growled, "fetch me the water."

*"Sí, señor,"* the old woman answered, adding as she stepped out of the tent, "the *señora* is sleeping. She is needing her rest. It would be a kindness to keep your voice low."

"Of course, of course," he answered, rubbing his red beard absently where it had become matted by the helmet. As the old woman let the tent flap drop, he noticed the mulberry-colored silk dress lying carefully folded across a trunk. "Help me off with my armor," he said impatiently to his page. Laying the helmet aside, the young man quickly began to unbuckle the plates of chest armor. He took the rerebraces off Vicente's arms and removed the cuisses that protected his thighs. When the greaves and sabbatons were removed from his calves and feet, Vicente spoke harshly. "Now get out of here." The captain turned his back, but the page still stood there. The look in the slender young man's intense, dark eyes might have been one of distress at his master's apparent displeasure.

"May I polish the *señor's* armor," he asked.

"You don't ask if you may polish it," Vicente answered crossly as he turned around. "It is to be oiled and polished after every encounter in order to be kept free from rust. Now remember that! How long is it going to take to train you, Mateo?" he added with asperity.

"I wish to learn to serve the *señor* well," the young man spoke quietly. "I will try to learn quickly."

"You had better," Vicente said shortly. "Take the armor and go." Mateo scooped up the armor but was unable to secure all the pieces at once. Impatiently Vicente gathered up the rest of the armor and dumped it outside the tent flap. He shoved Mateo out the door and quickly tied the interior straps to secure the door flap in place. He pulled off the quilted *farseto* he wore under his chest plates and sat down on the wooden crate. He glanced again at the mulberry silk lying across the trunk, and a hard smile touched his lips.

"I've been away from this caravan much too much, I think," he muttered to himself. "God, I'm tired. I've been gone for weeks on end on these accursed scouting details. How many nights have I spent in my own tent anyway?—three, four, five?"

He spoke as if he were conversing with a companion with whom he had already discussed what was on his mind. "Now that we're so close, *so close,* I *must* be able to look for gold. I know that. God damn the governor for outlawing personal prospecting—but so be it," he muttered.

"I must do *something! She* is going to have to be my ticket to free access. I see no other way."

He stood up and walked over to the silk dress and picked up one of the sleeves, fingering it absently as he looked at the drape that separated him from his sleeping wife. "Damn her," he whispered. "Damn her pious, religious ways, and to hell with her gentle upbringing. What the hell good is gentle upbringing around here? For my part, I'm sick of acting the gentleman. Her inheritance was of use to me; perhaps she herself can be of use to me also." He dropped the sleeve and looked back at the drape.

"There's no getting around it. She's got to learn the way of the world. She won't be of any use to me the way she is now, that's for damned sure," he muttered as he walked over to the drape and paused.

María Angélica came awake, but she lay behind the drape, her eyes closed trying to fall back to sleep although she knew it was futile. Why didn't Vicente leave the tent and go find his friends for a game of cards as he always did? What was he muttering about with such vehemence? She dreaded the next few days when they would attempt the crossing of the river. She had heard the men talk of the dangers of the swiftly flowing *Río Bravo*. God protect them when they tried to cross it!

After so many hard leagues of travel with no water for drinking, much less for bathing, the bath Fabia had prepared for her the previous day had been wonderful. The governor said they would follow this *Río Bravo del Norte* all the way to the native pueblos, the majority of which were located on the banks of the swift river. How nice it would be to have a constant source of water at their disposal, but would Vicente now be gone again for days at a time on scouting details as he had been for almost the entirety of the journey? She prayed he would. She could scarcely tolerate his presence, and the infrequent nights she had had to endure his attentions were hardly bearable. How could her father have ever married her to him?

She heard the drape snatched back, and her eyes flew open. "What is it?" she asked with alarm as she sat up and clutched the muslin robe. "What is the matter?" she asked with worry. Vicente had never disturbed her rest before.

He laughed. "Why, nothing's the matter, dearest wife."

"Then what is it?" she asked, unbelieving that he would burst in upon her for no reason.

"Ah," he said with amusement, spreading his hands to indicate her attire, "the flower has lost her purple petals, but she is lovelier still in yellow." He took a step toward her and she shrank back, clutching at the throat of her robe.

"Please," she whispered, "I was resting. I fear tomorrow may be a long and difficult day."

"Tomorrow will be a long day for all of us, my dear," Vicente replied with a short laugh as he came closer.

"Please go," she said as she pulled the wrapper tighter and shrank back. "You are embarrassing me. I'm not properly dressed." He snorted. "Please, not now," she whispered, realizing suddenly what he intended, "please, not in the daylight for it would be sinful."

Vicente laughed. "And who told you that?" he asked cynically. "Your beloved blue-robed eunuchs? If they can't see a woman naked, then they don't want other men to either, not even husbands!"

"You should not blaspheme so," she said defensively. "The success of this journey depends upon the good favor of God."

"That's *pura mierda,*" Vicente spat. "You have been sheltered far too long. No longer will your 'duty' be just a few moments at night in the dark while you lie there stiff as a piece of unseasoned leather. I have been thinking for some time now about this, my dear." He looked at her and smiled evilly. "I need to teach you." His hand reached out toward her. Her eyes were filled with dread as she drew back, but the gesture was useless for he grasped the muslin in both hands and pulled it open, tearing the satin ribbons.

"No," she whispered as she moved to the side. "No."

*"Sí, sí, sí,"* he hissed as he yanked her back and pulled the wrapper off.

She pushed at him although the effort was useless. "Not like this, please," she begged. "The tent is so thin, what about the others?"

She tried to jerk free, but her attempts resulted in her undergarments being ripped from her also. Her helplessness was intolerable. She had had no choice in her marriage, but she did not want to accept this. She heard Vicente's obscene laughter as he enjoyed her futile struggles. She was filled with anger and fought back harder, hitting him with her fists. For the first time in her life she knew hatred. She continued to struggle, overcome with impotent rage. *He can't do this. He can't do this,* she cried to herself.

He grasped the gold and pearl-encrusted caul that encased her hair. "Let's get this thing off," he said as he yanked the finely made net of gold from her hair. "I want to see all that dark hair cascading on your naked body!"

"No," she gasped. She felt the net torn from her hair and heard pearls fall to the ground, but her protest was useless, for he was pulling her hair down around her shoulders. She ceased fighting and lay still. Limp and inert, bitter tears trickled from the corners of her eyes. Vicente did not notice or did not care. He swung his leg across her to sit straddling her, his thighs on either side of her hips. Her face flamed with embarrassment while his pale eyes surveyed her.

"*Jesús,* I should have looked at you in the daylight before this. I knew you were a good-looking woman—I could feel that at night, too—but, *Dios,* what beautiful breasts." He squeezed them and flicked the nipples between his thumbs and forefingers, chuckling when they hardened under his touch.

"Please don't," she begged.

"I'll do whatever I like," he laughed harshly, "and I like this." He leaned forward and buried his face in her hair. He reeked of sour sweat, and she thought she might be sick. He bit her earlobes and then her neck and shoulders. His mouth descended to her breasts, and she whimpered with pain.

"For the love of God, you're hurting me," she whispered. He sat up and lifted himself off of her, and she thought he was going to leave, but he had only stood to remove the breeches that had protected him from the metal armor.

"Open your eyes, my dear," he spoke. When she did not do his bidding, he hissed again, "Open your eyes, *mujer*!"

Trembling, she opened them warily as he sat down. He grasped her hand and placed it on himself intimately. She jerked her hand away, filled with revulsion, but he pulled it back and rubbed it over him. Her body shook with sobs. Vicente laughed. He dropped her hand, and she yanked it back.

"No wonder whores have so much business in New Spain," he muttered. "They're the only women who know how to please a man. Now, let's continue with our little lesson, dearest wife. I am telling you now that you're not going to be one of those high-born Spanish wives whose husbands would not shock them with the realities of life. Your 'wifely duty' is not going to be a few moments in the dark. I have plans, big plans. Your beauty is going to serve me well, my dear. Make no mistake."

She jerked involuntarily when his hand touched her. "Don't fight me," he said, as he pinched her breast, and she bit her lip to keep from crying out. His hand slid down her belly and started between her legs, but she squeezed them together. "I said, don't fight me," he spoke as he pinched her viciously again. She cried out that time, unable to keep from it. "Open your legs," he said harshly.

"*Por Dios*, no," she pleaded.

"Open your legs," Vicente commanded and she obeyed, choking back sobs. She felt his hand on her intimately, and she burned with shame at what he did to her, and when she felt his mouth take the place of his hand, she thought she was going to be sick. She clamped her teeth together to keep from screaming. Finally she felt the weight of his body cover her as he thrust into her, and grunts of passion filled his throat.

At last he lay still, his heavy weight pressing her down. The stench of his sweaty body was so strong she wanted to retch. She prayed he would leave, now that he had finished with her, but he did not.

After a few moments, she realized he lay heavy in sleep on top of her. Hate surged through her, and she pushed until she was free. He did not awaken as she pulled away, and she averted her eyes so that she would not have to look at him. She was filled with loathing as she ducked past the cloth drape. Once on the other side, she fell to her knees and could not control her sobs. She tried to pray but could not. She felt filthy and unclean—before in the darkness it had always been over so quickly.

Slowly she became aware of Fabia's voice outside the tent flap. She looked up and, seeing the straps fastened, ran to undo them. The old servant stepped in and María Angélica fell into her arms, tears streaming down her cheeks. Fabia pulled her *rebozo* from her shoulders and wrapped it around her mistress.

"There, there," the old woman comforted her, as she smoothed her tousled hair. The sobs finally stopped and María Angélica wiped the tears from her eyes.

"Let Fabia get you a bath, *querida*," the old woman spoke softly, "it will make you feel better." María Angélica nodded mutely as Fabia went to the door. From outside she retrieved the *tinaja* filled with the water that Vicente had ordered her to fetch. With a scowl, the old woman glanced at the drape that separated the sleeping alcove behind which Vicente snored loudly.

She pulled a brass tub from a corner and poured some of the river water into it. Tying back María Angélica's hair with a ribbon, she helped her in, and from a trunk the old woman took out a bar of scented soap with which she began to lather her young mistress. When she finished, Fabia admonished her to stand and poured the remaining water in the *tinaja* over her to rinse. The young woman shivered. Fabia dried her briskly with a heavy towel that she then wrapped around her.

"Now let's get dressed," the old woman spoke in a hushed tone, obviously wishing not to wake the man who still snored behind the drape.

María Angélica hesitated. "How can I go to Captain Farfán's play now?" she asked, her voice hollow.

"It would be better to go, *querida*," Fabia replied, "otherwise people will inquire of you why you were not there, and you may feel greater embarrassment."

"Oh, Fabia," she spoke. "What he did was so revolting, so sinful. I must go to confession."

Fabia patted her gently. "What a man does with his wife is not necessarily sinful, *querida*."

"But it was daylight, Fabia, and he put his mouth on me," she said, covering her face with her hands as she remembered what he had done.

"That is not a sin, Angelita." Fabia spoke softly but reassuringly. "Perhaps he should have been more gentle, but it is not wicked. It can be a good thing with a man you love, *querida*."

"But *you* of all people know I don't love him," María Angélica said with disgust.

# Chapter 7

Vicente had never been in a better mood as they sat at the long tables set up for the feast. The men had changed from the armor of the morning's spectacle and were clothed in fashionable puffed breeches and colored hose, doublets and short capes. Bonfires built along the river's edge lit up the night sky and odors of roasting meat mingled with the smoke of mesquite wood. Beeves, lambs, and kids broiled with noisy crackling over the fires. Oñate had ordered a fitting banquet to celebrate the Act of Possession. A large cask of hearty Castilian wine was tapped and the celebration became even more animated.

Servant women had spent the entire afternoon preparing stacks of hot tortillas. *Frijoles*, salt pork, and chile had been stewing all day in large *ollas*. Little wooden cartons of quince preserves and fresh goat's milk cheese filled one table. Although provisions for the journey were running dangerously low, there was nothing spared that night to prepare the feast.

Vicente laughed and drank and recounted stories with the other officers, and it appeared he did not notice his quiet and withdrawn wife. She might have been a stone for the attention he paid her. She sat staring at her hands in her lap, anger and shame still seething within her. Fabia had said there was no sin in what he had done, but she would not listen to the old woman. She knew she would have to go to confession before she could feel clean again, but how could she face one of the friars with what had happened? On the march as they were, the anonymity of the confessional was scarcely possible as a makeshift bower or the open air served as a church, and a small screen was the only thing that separated confessor and penitent. How could she tell a saintly *padre* what had happened?

That afternoon Vicente had escorted her to Captain Farfán's play, and her embarrassment made her burn inside. He took her hand and placed it on his arm and covered it with his own in a possessive and intimate gesture. His touch was odious, and she loathed him.

Everyone but she appeared to enjoy the captain's play immensely, dramatizing as it did the joyous reception the friars would receive from the heathen in the new land. She scarcely watched, her shame even greater knowing that others might have been aware of the afternoon's occurrence.

Tents were pitched close to each other and offered scarce privacy. There was little that each person did not know about every other person on that march. People had commented on her different hairstyle from the morning. Where was the beautiful gold caul and the pearls? How could she tell them Vicente had ripped it from her head and that she had spent the afternoon on her knees trying to find the pearls that had fallen from her hair? When she thought about how little she had left of clothes and jewels, she wanted to cry. The muslin robe was ruined now too.

Fabia said she would save the fabric to use for baby clothes because surely they would be blessed with a *niño* one day. María Angélica shuddered. She did not want to think about that. For the love of God, why had her father married her to Vicente?

She knew the answer, although it was a question she continued to ask herself bitterly. She knew her father was dying and wanted to see her taken care of. But why did it have to be Vicente de Vizcarra? He was tall and might have been good-looking, but there was a harsh set to his thin lips and a cruelty in his pale eyes. She had not liked him the moment she first met him, and she tried to tell her father that, but he would not listen. Did he know her husband was going to liquidate her inheritance to join this expedition? She could not believe he did because he spoke of being thankful there would now be a man to take over the land and *hacienda* when he died.

Vicente had never mentioned one word about searching for gold in the far off reaches of *Nuevo México*. It was only after her father's death, two days following her marriage, that her husband impatiently told her to prepare to leave, for he was going to join Don Juan de Oñate in his conquest of *Nuevo México*.

Vicente was afraid the governor had already set out on his expedition, but much to his relief and to her dismay, he found that orders from the Viceroy had delayed Oñate's march.

And so they joined the other colonists at the valley of Santa Bárbara. It was a nightmare, and only Fabia had kept her from total despair. On the march, she hardly saw Vicente and things were somewhat better. He volunteered for every detail to search for water or a good route for the carts so that, to her profound relief, he was scarcely with the main body of the caravan. She had had to perform the wifely duty she hated only infrequently. The marriage night had been painful but quickly over and the other times the same. Little had she known what it could be like until today. Before, he would be gone for days and would return exhausted, demanding only a few brief moments of her body, and she would steel herself to it. Before that last terrible leg of the journey to reach the *Río del Norte* when they had to cross the sand dunes, travelling leagues without water, he was gone for days along with the Sergeant Major and a few other men who were searching for a route to the big river.

*"Los dos Vicentes."* Everyone had begun to call them that now—the two Vicentes—Vicente de Zaldívar, Sergeant Major of the expedition and nephew of Oñate, and Captain Vicente de Vizcarra, her husband. They were birds of a feather who shared the same given name as well as a host of other similarities.

Both had cold eyes in which a scarcely hidden cruelty lurked. Their thin lips curled frequently in contempt and scorn; they drank and gambled to excess. They were overbearing and arrogant, tyrannical and haughty. They courted trouble and danger, and from the moment the two met, they recognized the kindred spirit in the other, or if they did not recognize it as such, there was something in their personalities that drew them together. The others in the group recognized it, too, and when anyone said "the two Vicentes" there might be a touch of admiration or a touch of disapproval in their voices, but whichever, there was always a trace of fear.

What she found so strange was that those two unrelated men could have so many similarities, and yet two blood brothers were entirely different. Juan de Zaldívar, Maese de Campo of the expedition, was Vicente de Zaldívar's elder brother by three years, but he did not resemble his younger brother except in his courage and a familial physical similarity. Both were of good stature with chestnut-colored beards, but there was nothing harsh about Juan de Zaldívar's face nor was cruelty ever evident in his eyes. He was kind, unlike most of the officers, but the soldiers obeyed his orders implicitly.

On some occasions when the Sergeant Major would visit the Vizcarra tent, the Maese de Campo would accompany his younger brother. While *los dos Vicentes* talked, she would chat with Juan de Zaldívar, and to her surprise he was quite well read. She enjoyed his visits immensely; few people in the entourage had even a rudimentary education, including Dorotea, who could read and write only a little. She found a welcome conversationalist in the Maese de Campo, and although Vicente knew nothing of the books she had hidden deep in their carts, she had told Juan de Zaldívar of them.

"Doña María Angélica," a voice spoke warmly to her, "why so quiet on such a happy occasion?"

She gave a start as the voice intruded into her thoughts, and she turned to greet the speaker. "*Señor* Maese, how nice to see you," she said with surprise, smiling up at Juan de Zaldívar, who gave a crisp bow.

There appeared what might have been a bit of concern in his eyes, and she did not want him to pursue his question about her quietness when everyone else seemed so elated, and she added quickly, "I had wanted to congratulate you on the splendid battle this afternoon. It was so vividly portrayed one forgot that one was on the banks of the *Río del Norte* and not on the sands of Arabia."

"Those are kind words, *señora,*" the Maese responded with a smile. "May I?" he asked, nodding toward an empty chair.

*"Cómo no,"* she said, smiling, but her smile slipped without her knowing it, and as she continued to speak, a note of apprehension crept into her voice. "Tell me, *Señor* Maese, do you know when we will be crossing the river? What of the rest of the trip? How much farther do we have to go?"

"Ah, *señora,* would that I could answer all your questions," he responded with a quiet laugh as he crossed his long legs and she saw the muscles outlined by the tight-fitting crimson hose, "but only God knows for sure what lies in store for us. As to crossing the river, though, *señora,* we shall follow it for a few more days, hoping to find some natives who can show us the best place to ford. As a matter of fact," he said, nodding toward her husband and the Sergeant Major who were laughing and joking along with some other officers, "the two Vicentes will go on ahead tomorrow to look for guides. We know from the Espejo expedition of eighty-one that there is a crossing that all the natives use."

"I hope we find it soon!" she said fervently.

"And why is that?" he laughed in response to her show of emotion.

"I, I don't really know," she answered hesitantly, looking at him. "I guess I can't really believe we are in *Nuevo México* until we have crossed the river."

A voice broke into their conversation. *"Señora,"* Don Juan de Oñate interjected, "you mean that even after our most solemn and joyous celebration of the Act of Possession you do not believe that *Nuevo México* is actually ours?"

"Oh, no, *Señor Gobernador,*" she murmured, startled to see the governor standing there. "It's not that. It's just that . . ." she paused, trying to phrase her answer so as not to give or add offense, but Oñate spoke up with a laugh.

"I share your sentiments exactly, *señora*. I, too, am impatient to cross this *Río del Norte*."

"Ah, Governor," Vicente de Vizcarra said, noticing Oñate's presence, "may I offer you some *jerez* in my tent later this evening?"

*"Con mucho gusto,"* the governor replied with a broad smile. "I don't know where you found it, but that is some of the finest *jerez* I have tasted. Do you have anything in those many carts of yours besides wine?" Oñate asked with a laugh as he pulled up a chair and joined the joking men.

"My carts contain only essentials," Vicente replied straight-faced, "of which wine is one of the most essential!" He leaned forward and said with a laughing, conspiratorial tone, "I pray to God that the friars get their vines planted quickly! We would not want to run out of sacramental drink, perish the thought. I assure you, however, if wine becomes scarce, I will be sorely tempted to take the cloth myself and thus assure more ready access to the heavenly beverage!"

All, with the exception of his wife, laughed with appreciation at the captain's sacrilegious joking. The Sergeant Major raised his eyes to heaven and crossed himself in mock fear, whispering, "Lord, deliver us from our necessity. May the soil of *Nuevo México* produce the noble grape in abundance as befits our wants."

"Amen!" the others added fervently in unison. Even the Maese de Campo laughed good-naturedly. Oñate turned to the two Vicentes and began to talk of finding the ford of the river. María Angélica's eyes dropped to her hands. Surely they were going to incur God's wrath if they continued to blaspheme.

As if he had read her thoughts, the Maese leaned toward her and said with confidence, "Do not worry, *señora. Dios* knows we must try to lighten our spirits on such a long, difficult journey."

She tried to smile. "You are a good man, Maese, I pray you are right. It's just that I . . . " she paused as she sought words, "it's just that at times I am very fearful of this journey."

Juan de Zaldívar smiled with reassurance and nodded toward the other men who were engaged in discussion, heedless of them. "You need have no fears, *señora*. With a wise leader like my uncle Don Juan, with the captain your husband, with my brother the Sergeant Major, and with myself concerned for your welfare, no harm shall come to you. We shall see to that."

"I am not worried simply for my sake," she spoke. "I fear for the children, for the whole expedition. We are so far from civilization."

"On my honor, this expedition shall succeed." The Maese's clear brown eyes did as much to dispel her fear as did the conviction of his words.

"That I ask fervently in my prayers," she replied. The Maese smiled at her again, and she was vividly aware that it was a smile so unlike her husband's.

"Certainly, *Dios* cannot fail to answer the prayers of such a child of His as you, *señora*," Juan de Zaldívar spoke. "I'm sure your prayers must reach His ears very quickly." He added softly, "Might I presume to ask to be remembered in one also?"

"I always ask for your safety, Maese." She dropped her eyes when she realized how her words might have sounded.

"Thank you, *señora*," he said sincerely. "With your prayers I am even more confident."

"Well," Vicente said, rising a bit unsteadily, "shall we repair to my humble abode, gentlemen?"

"With pleasure," the others replied.

Oñate stepped in front of his nephew the Maese de Campo to reach for María Angélica's chair to help her rise.

"Captain," he spoke to Vicente, "may I have the honor of escorting your beautiful wife?" María Angélica glanced quickly up at the Maese, but he just smiled and shrugged as if to say, he's the governor.

"Most certainly," Vicente answered. He was well aware that his lovely wife made his access to the governor much easier, and he would take advantage of his good fortune in having an object that pleased Don Juan de Oñate.

As the group started toward the tents, Vicente called out to a lean, hawkish-looking man with a jet-black beard. "Captain Isidro, care to join us for a glass of *jerez* in my tent?"

The man smiled, but the scar on his cheek made the smile appear a grimace. *"Por supuesto,"* he answered with a laugh, "who could refuse that *jerez?*" He turned to his wife standing by his side and said impolitely, "Go to the tent, Dorotea."

María Angélica spoke up. "We would be pleased for Doña Dorotea to accompany you, Captain Inojosa."

"No," he said rudely, "she has work to do."

María Angélica started to protest, but she saw her friend shake her head "no," and so she remained silent. She had never met anyone who seemed quite as malevolent as Isidro Inojosa. Even the two Vicentes seemed less cruel than this man with his black beard and disfiguring facial scar. She wondered how Dorotea could stand to have him touch her, but anger and shame suddenly welled in María Angélica again. She had had no say in her marriage to Vicente. Did Dorotea feel for her husband what she felt for her own? Why couldn't they have someone like the Maese de Campo, someone who was kind? She was sure he would not be rough. She blushed with embarrassment and dropped her eyes. "For my thoughts, forgive me," she prayed silently.

*"Señora,"* Oñate said, startling her, and he laughed, "what must go on behind those beautiful eyes of yours? I have just seen a myriad of emotions cross your lovely face and yet you have not spoken one word."

"Forgive me, *Señor Gobernador,*" she managed.

"Why, there is nothing to forgive, my dear," he replied softly, as he smiled too directly at her. "But, tell me, what *does* go on behind those big gray eyes of yours?"

She was thankful to reach their tent. Fabia was waiting inside, her lined face impassive as she found makeshift seats for the visitors as they entered.

*"¡Jerez, bruja!"* Vicente ordered the old woman.

Oñate laughed and made the sign of the cross with his thumb and index finger as a protection against evil. "Captain Vicente," he said with a smile, "perhaps you should have a care what you call your servant woman—her powers with herbs are becoming well known throughout the camp. I understand she is a *curandera* of no little skill."

Vicente laughed loudly, but his eyes were hard as he glanced at the old woman who seemed to pay no heed to the conversation as she poured the amber sherry. "Eh, *bruja*," he laughed, saying to her as he picked up a deck of cards, "can you tell the future with these?"

*"Sí, señor,"* she answered quietly.

The Sergeant Major spoke up. "Let's hear what this *vieja* has to say."

Fabia shook her head. "*Señor*, it is sometimes best not to know what the future holds," she said quietly.

Vicente's face was stiff. "You will tell my friends their fortunes, *bruja*," he ordered coldly.

"As you wish, *señor*," she replied and took the cards. She pulled up a box and sat down on it next to a small table and began to shuffle the cards. Rapidly she laid them out in rows and then one by one she turned them up. "I see for the Sergeant Major a great victory in the near future. He will have descendants and live to an old age with honors bestowed upon him," she spoke tonelessly.

The Sergeant Major gave a snort of approval. "I knew it," he laughed. "I am destined to great things!"

"Tell mine, *vieja*," Oñate said with a laugh. "Surely the Sergeant Major isn't the only one with a bright future!"

Again Fabia dealt the cards and turned them up. She paused a few moments. "You will suffer a great disappointment and disgrace, but you will be exonerated and will live to an old age. You will die in the motherland."

Oñate was not smiling. "I will die in Mexico?" he asked.

"No," Fabia answered, "in *España*."

"How can that be?" Oñate asked with displeasure.

"I do not know, *señor*," Fabia answered quietly, "the cards say nothing more."

"What about *my* future?" Vicente asked impatiently.

Fabia reshuffled and laid out the cards again. "You will discover a mine of great richness," she spoke, but Vicente interrupted with a loud whoop before she could continue.

"I knew it!" he shouted with laughter, and to María Angélica's chagrin, he picked her up and swung her around. "I knew it!" he laughed gleefully. "Go on, go on," he urged Fabia as he let go of María Angélica abruptly. Quickly she backed away from him, and when she saw the Maese's eyes on her, she dropped her own in embarrassment.

"You will discover a mine of great richness," she repeated, "but no one will believe you. You will lose your mind and die a pauper."

Vicente's face flushed a dark red. "Lying old bitch!" he shouted at her. "*¡El diablo te engendró en el culo de una puerca!*" He repeated his words with even more venom. "The devil begat you in the butt hole of a pig!" He drew back his hand to strike the old woman who looked at him unafraid, but the Maese de Campo stepped forward and grabbed his arm as he laughed good-naturedly.

*"Amigo,"* he said, "she is just a harmless old woman. Don't take her so seriously. How can she know the future any more than one of us? Here," he said with a laugh, as he released Vicente's arm, "it's my turn. Let's see what she has to say about me!"

Vicente relaxed, but his face was full of hatred. "Tell the Maese's fortune, *bruja,*" he commanded imperiously.

*"Sí, señor,"* she responded colorlessly as she began to shuffle. She turned the cards up one by one but suddenly stopped.

"Don't quit, *bruja!*" Vicente shouted.

*"Señor,"* Fabia said deprecatingly, "you are right, the cards lie—I am just a foolish old woman—I know nothing."

She started to gather up the cards, but Vicente slammed his hand down on hers. "Keep going, you old hag."

Slowly Fabia turned the remaining cards over and sat there for an agonizing moment before she opened her mouth and spoke. Oñate, the Sergeant Major, and Isidro Inojosa riveted their eyes on her while rage filled Vicente's. The Maese de Campo tried to smile, but his face was taut, and the stillness in the tent was so heavy it prevented them from breathing. At last the old woman spoke. Her voice was like dry, fallen leaves crushed under a boot heel. "You will die before this year is up."

The Maese de Campo turned ashen for a moment, and María Angélica gasped. The Maese's brother lashed out and backhanded the old woman across the mouth, knocking her from the wooden box onto the floor of the tent.

"No!" the Maese shouted in fury at his younger brother who stepped forward to strike the old woman again. "Stop!" he shouted, his voice filled with absolute authority. "Don't you dare touch this woman again." He turned quickly and knelt beside the wrinkled old lady who lay unmoving on the floor, blood trickling from her mouth.

"Oh, Fabia," María Angélica cried as she dropped to her knees beside her servant.

The Maese slid his arm under the old woman's head and pulled out a handkerchief. He dabbed at the blood that ran from the corner of her mouth, and slowly she opened her eyes.

"Forgive my brother, Fabia," the Maese said gently. The old woman started to speak, but brought her hand to her mouth instead. Into her palm she spat two bloody teeth.

Isidro Inojosa's penetrating eyes gleamed with an unusual light and the corner of his mouth twitched in what might have been a smile. His and María Angélica's were the only fortunes not told that night.

# Chapter 8

Well before dawn the camp was bustling, preparing for the day's journey. Straps of leather creaked, and wooden carts groaned noisily as they were loaded. The dresses of silks and satins had been returned to their trunks the night before, to be worn again no one knew when. The tents of frieze came down, and red-embered fires glowed here and there, dotting the sandy river area with spots of flickering light in the gray pre-dawn. Cooking tripods perched over the fires, heating water for the hot chocolate that all would drink for breakfast.

Chocolate had been introduced to the world and was drunk by royalty in the capitals of Europe, but to the Spaniards who had come to the New World and had adopted the drink of the Aztecs, the dark, hot, foamy beverage had become a necessity of life. There were many who thought they could not face the day without at least one cup of *chocolatl*, and many were troubled as they saw their supply dwindling. Grapes might grow in *Nuevo México*, but not cacao, which grew only in the hot, wet lowlands of the Mexico they were leaving.

María Angélica drew her woolen shawl more tightly about her. How could it be so cold at night and yet so hot during the day? She leaned back against the large wooden wheel of the high-sided *carreta* as she sipped her hot chocolate, knowing this was the last moment of rest she would be able to snatch for many hours. Shortly after dawn, with loud protesting creaks and squeals, the carts would once again roll forward as mules and oxen strained to put the heavy, lumbering two-wheeled vehicles in motion.

It would be a long day. She had not slept at all the previous night. The horror of it kept coming back to haunt her, robbing her of sleep. She had heard Fabia say many times before that the cards do not lie, but surely what the old woman saw in them last night could not be true. Oñate in disgrace; Vicente, her husband, insane; the Maese de Campo, dead within the year! No! She would not believe it. Only God in heaven knew the fate of men's lives. What had possessed the old woman to say those things? María Angélica felt that she should reproach Fabia for having read the cards, but how *could* she, when Vicente had ordered the old woman to do it?

The one deserving of reproach was Vicente, but even if she could censure her husband for his actions, it would have been impossible now. He had risen several hours previously to ride out on the detail with the Sergeant Major and several others with orders to find natives of the region who could lead them to the good ford of the river. She was glad he was gone.

The hot chocolate warmed her, but she could not shake the chill of the pre-dawn nor that of the previous evening, and as she finished the hot, bitter beverage, she reluctantly pushed herself away from the heavy wheel and went to help with the preparations for the march.

She had not known what work meant before this journey. In the beginning she sat and waited for everything to be done by the servants as it always had. Nothing had ever been expected of her save learning prayers and embroidery. It had been her loneliness on her father's isolated *hacienda* and her own desire to read that had taken her past the rudimentaries her mother had taught her. She had never *worked*. Guilt, she was ashamed to admit, had motivated her to help in the labors of the journey. In her father's house it had never occurred to her that her help might be needed. Had she considered it, she would never have been allowed to do the work of servants, but on the journey it was sorely apparent that all help was needed, and as she sat genteelly watching others sweat and toil, she saw that her help was needed to ease the burden on the others, and although she had blisters on her hands and in the evening after a particularly gruelling day fell exhausted into bed, she felt better. She had no choice in this journey, but since the decision had been made, she was determined that she would endure the difficulties. She would make a home in the new land. What else could she do?

She rinsed her chocolate cup, wiped it with a linen towel, and carefully stored it away. Silently she helped Fabia gather up the remaining items and wedge them into the back of the cart. A Tlascalan Indian whom Vicente had hired as muleteer for the wagons brought the pairs of oxen with their heavy yokes and began to hitch them to the cart.

The gray of the pre-dawn quickly gave way as the sun rose in a cloudless sky. The remainder of their carts began to arrive, each pulled by oxen or mules in the charge of a Tlascalan Indian. At first she could not understand why Vicente had taken her inheritance to purchase so many carts and the services of Indians to drive them, but as other colonists' supplies began to run dangerously low, she and Vicente still had ample provisions.

He had also invested her money in livestock: beef cattle, oxen, horses, mules, sheep, goats, pigs, and fowl. They had by far the most provisions of anyone on the journey, due partly to the fact that they were latecomers to the group. Those who had spent three years waiting for the royal sanction to proceed had seen their once liberal supplies dwindle to barely sufficient for the sustenance of their families.

With her husband gone so frequently on scouting patrols, she had taken to overseeing their possessions. After some things had been stolen from their carts, she had put a trustworthy Tlascalan in charge, and he reported to her. Likewise, the most able *vaquero* who looked after the stock kept a head tally, which she entered into a ledger, noting as well how many lambs, kids, calves, or other stock were consumed for food. Occasionally she rode her mare back to take a look at the stock, but as the animals frequently trailed the carts by a league or more, she usually stayed with the rumbling, groaning carts as they rolled slowly and joltingly over the terrain. Walking, which almost all did, was preferable to riding in the pounding, jostling carts.

*"Todo está listo,"* Fabia said as she came round the cart. "All is ready for the journey."

María Angélica gasped when she saw the old woman's face in the light. In the dark shadows of the pre-dawn, the evidence of the blow she had received the previous night had been only slightly discernible as a swelling of the lip and in a slight slurring of the speech, but now that she saw the old woman's face in the full light, she was horrified. A dark, purplish bruise puffed out along the length of the weathered cheek and the old woman's upper lip was completely disfigured, swollen to over half again its size, and there was a black, blood-clotted split where her teeth had cut it.

"Oh, Fabia," she whispered, "I did not realize how badly you had been hurt. Let me make a pallet in one of the carts for you."

Fabia tried to smile but could not. "No, *querida*," she spoke with a slur, "only my lip is hurt. Do you want to break these old bones, too, by making me ride in the wretched *carreta?*"

"Of course not," María Angélica answered, "but isn't there anything I can do for you?"

*"Gracias, niña,* but no," Fabia spoke as she patted the hand that rested on her arm.

The order to move out was given up ahead and echoed down the line. Slowly the carts began to move. She and Fabia walked alongside. Up ahead she saw the Maese, erect and tall on his horse, supervising the orderly start.

That day they traveled two leagues along the river before camping for the night; the next day only a league and a half. The Sergeant Major and his detail had not yet returned as darkness fell. María Angélica sat on a woolen blanket staring into the embers of the campfire. The night was cool and a small breeze stirred the leaves of the cottonwoods that grew along the river. She knew she should go to bed soon for they had another hard day ahead of them tomorrow, but in spite of the fatigue that made her limbs heavy, she sat there. She pulled her *rebozo* more closely about her and hugged herself against the chill and the hollowness she felt inside.

"With your permission," a voice spoke.

She looked up to see the Maese standing there, and she smiled, unable to hide her feelings. "Certainly," she answered, "please join me."

She had not talked to him since the night of the fortune-telling, and she had prayed fervently every evening that Fabia's words would not be fulfilled. Juan de Zaldívar sat down at a respectful distance and smiled too, making her blush.

"I'm so sorry," she spoke in a rush. "I don't know how to ask your forgiveness for the other evening. I can't imagine what possessed Fabia to say those terrible things. I know that she must be wrong. Certainly within the year . . ." Her words trailed off into an embarrassed silence.

"Even if she is right," the Maese answered, "it is God's will, and I accept it completely."

She looked at the Maese's gentle face etched in the firelight and could not believe that it was God's will that that good man should die so young. The Maese was twenty-eight, the same age as her husband, ten years older than she.

The Maese smiled. "I hope I am not the cause of that distraught look on your lovely face," he said lightly.

She tried to smile. "I cannot help but worry," she said, unable to erase the concern from her voice.

"God is gracious," the Maese answered, "we must trust in His will."

Fabia approached and sat down a short distance from them. "Your *dueña* always watches out for you, doesn't she?" the Maese asked with a quiet laugh.

María Angélica glanced over her shoulder. "Yes," she said, "Fabia is like my shadow. I'm sure she would protect me from anything—no matter what form it might take."

"You are fortunate to have someone so devoted to look after you," the Maese said, "as fortunate would be the person whose job it was."

Her eyes dropped from his, and her blush was hidden by the firelight. "When do you expect we will reach the river's ford?" she asked.

"I don't know," the Maese answered smoothly, "certainly within a few days."

The Maese was right. On the following day, the Sergeant Major and his detail returned to camp bringing with them some Indians of the river area.

Later that day, eight more Indians appeared in camp on their own. The Indians called themselves "peaceful ones" although by their looks, one would not have thought so. Their skin was sunburnt copper and leathery, and their long, coarse, greasy black hair was held down by strips of woven fibers. Their faces, arms, and chests were painted with ocher and blood, and the stench of their bodies could be smelled at ten paces. They carried bows like the Turks used and arrows tipped with flint. The Spaniards quickly nicknamed them "muleteers" because they spoke with a heavy trilling of their tongues as they said their word for "yes." It made the Spaniards laugh when they said it because it sounded as if they kept saying "giddy-up." But they were friendly and supplied the weary Spaniards with good news—the river's ford was less than one day's journey farther. The Spaniards gave the Indians presents of iron-bladed hatchets, blankets, beads, and hawk bells. There was rejoicing that night.

Once again Vicente invited Oñate, the Zaldívar brothers, and Isidro Inojosa to partake of some of the *jerez* that was such a luxury. There was no fortune-telling that night and all became quite contented as they drank the amber liquid and began to talk of gold.

Early the next morning the carts rumbled out, and before noon the first ones were sloshing through the muddy water crossing into the land they had come to conquer. The teams of oxen were doubled in order to pull the heavy *carretas* across the sandy-bottomed river.

It was the Maese who rode back to guide the horse on which María Angélica had decided to ford the *Río del Norte*. She had no idea where her husband was nor did she care. The Maese rode alongside, the bridle rein of her mare secured in his hand. As the horses plunged ahead, the river water splashed up, soaking the hem of her dress, sending a spray of droplets that wet her face. She laughed with the exhilaration and urged her mare faster. The Maese laughed, too, and kneed his horse forward to keep up with her. They reached the other side dripping.

"Thank you, Maese, for seeing me safely across the river," she laughed, out of breath.

"It was a dampening experience," he said jokingly as he smiled at her. He was unable to hide in his eyes what he felt at that moment. He gave a slight bow. "If you will excuse me, *señora,* I must see to the rest of the caravan."

"Of course," she murmured, the smile leaving her face.

Close to forty more *manso* Indians came to the ford as the carts were crossing. They, too, were friendly and gave assistance in transporting the sheep across the river—a difficult task because the animals' wool quickly became water-soaked the moment they entered the swift stream.

By nightfall all had crossed, and camp was made not far from the banks of the *Río del Norte*. Stark mountains, bare of vegetation, rose on that side of the river, and the *manso* Indians offered to show them a pass through the foothills. With signs, the Indians told them that there were villages of natives along the river eight days ahead. Those would be the pueblos that Coronado had reported more than fifty years before when he and his group of men had passed through the land looking for the cities of Cíbola and the Great Quivira.

The fifth of May dawned clear, and the slow-moving caravan, oxen straining heavily, inched its way through the rough, rocky pass. Camp was made, and there they remained for a day to allow the oxen to rest. On the seventh, only half a league was made over an even worse trail that took its toll on the lumbering carts. Axles broke and the march could not continue until they had been repaired.

When they finally came out of the pass, the carts and animals found the going easier, and the caravan was able to make three leagues on a good day. The sun was hot, the land dry and barren. It scarcely seemed like spring although low-growing flowers made pretty dots of yellow and lavender here and there. Stickery spikes of ocotillo added their red blossoms to the sparse desert spring as did the prickly pear and cholla with flowers of gold and magenta. Fortunately the river was near, for there seemed to be no other water in the arid, mesquite, and cactus-studded land.

Dorotea and María Angélica trudged together beside the creaking cart, their shoes and the bottoms of their dresses gray with dirt. Draped around their heads and shoulders they wore thin rebozos that gave them some protection from the sun and kept a certain amount of the fine, gritty dust out of their hair.

"Did Vicente go with Captain Aguilar, too?" Dorotea asked as she wiped a thin film of perspiration from her upper lip.

"Yes, thankfully," María Angélica replied with distaste. "He volunteers for all the reconnaissance patrols, and I'm glad to have him gone. Thank God for Pedro, who is in charge of the carts. I try to help, but he is the one who sees to the other drivers and the oxen, and Cipriano and Domingo have charge of the stock. They were foremen on my father's ranch and are the best *vaquero* and *caballerizo* there are." She paused and put her hand above her eyes as she peered into the distance. "Have you seen the water that is always up ahead of us, but that we never reach?"

*"Sí,"* answered Dorotea, "how can it disappear so quickly?"

"It must be a mirage, but it looks so real," María Angélica said, her face unsmiling. She returned to the previous topic of conversation. "They have orders not to enter any settlements. The governor said they are not to enter under pain of death."

"That seems awfully harsh," Dorotea responded, "but then our governor has become more like a tyrant than a leader. He has people whipped for the slightest reason. Why, they couldn't even prove Joaquín Guerra stole that sheep, and yet Oñate had him publicly humiliated."

"I know," María Angélica answered. "I wish the governor did not have to use such drastic measures, but he has a difficult job and an enormous responsibility. He must maintain control."

"True," Dorotea said, coughing as the wind swirled a puff of dust around them, "but there are ways of maintaining control without cruelty."

"Of course that's right, but Don Juan says it is imperative that the Indians not be frightened. He is insistent on that point. It's not out of interest in the Indians, however, that Vicente volunteers. I think he does so in order that he may get a first look at the land, be the first to spot the gold. And then," she continued, "he wants to get in the good graces of the governor for whatever favors he may bestow."

Dorotea laughed. "Either he is already in the governor's good graces or you are!"

"Why do you say that?" María Angélica asked, looking at her.

Dorotea laughed again and put her hand on María Angélica's arm. "How many other captain's quarters does the governor frequent?"

"He comes for the *jerez,*" María Angélica responded.

"Don't be naive," Dorotea answered, her voice losing its mirth, "have a care. The governor's wife is back in Zacatecas. This is a long, lonely journey, and Don Juan, for all his gray hair, is still vigorous and very much a man, I would suppose."

Shock registered on María Angélica's face at Dorotea's words. "You mustn't speak like that, Dorotea. The governor is a religious man. Don't you see how he reveres the friars and how intensely he prays?"

Dorotea looked penetratingly at her. "Anyone can make a great show of piety. Don't be deceived." She paused a moment.

"I hadn't meant to be so blunt, but I am going to tell you what Isidro said last night when he came home from your tent." She paused again and took a breath. "He laughed in that cruel way he has and told me, 'That good friend of yours, that tasty gray-eyed *paloma,* is going to be given by its master to the old gray fox!' "

María Angélica's face turned pale, and for a moment she didn't speak. "It isn't true," she whispered. "How could you believe a man like Isidro?"

Dorotea laughed bitterly. "Better than anyone, I know what kind of man Isidro is. That's why I think there may be truth in what he says." She paused and added softly, "*Querida,* I just want to warn you. Keep old Fabia near." María Angélica nodded mutely, and in silence the two women continued over the harsh terrain.

As the caravan prepared to camp for the night, María Angélica spoke to Dorotea. "Do you want to have supper with us tonight? There's plenty."

*"Gracias,"* Dorotea replied. "I hope we find a place to settle soon, for our supplies are almost gone. I don't see how we can go many more days."

María Angélica saw the concern on her face. "You are that low on food?"

Dorotea nodded. "Everyone is beginning to get worried. Francisca Osorio's baby is sick. She doesn't have enough milk for the poor little thing because she hasn't had enough to eat herself."

"Let me give you some of our food," María Angélica replied. "We still have sufficient, and I must take some to Francisca tonight."

"Francisca," María Angélica said as she stepped into the tent, but she could say no more as her eyes fell on the child the woman held. Its head seemed too large for its scrawny, bird-like body, and its chest heaved with exertion each time it breathed.

Fabia stepped around María Angélica. She put a bowl of *frijoles* and a cloth-wrapped stack of tortillas on a chest near the woman. She spoke and her voice was light and pleasant. "I made too much food tonight—I forgot the captain would not be here. The *señora* thought perhaps you could use it so that it would not go to waste." Fabia reached for the baby and took it from the woman. "Eh, *hijito*," she cooed as she rocked it in her old arms, "this is quite a journey we're on, eh?"

Francisca took a tortilla and stuffed it into her mouth as she reached for the bowl. She took another tortilla and began to scoop the beans noisily as she ate.

María Angélica could not bear to watch the ravenous way the woman consumed the food and slipped out of the tent and ran back to her own. When Fabia returned, María Angélica was kneeling at her cot, praying. Fabia knelt beside her and took her hand.

"Let's go to bed, Angelita," she said presently. "We have a long hard day ahead of us tomorrow. I will look in on Francisca and the baby first thing in the morning before we leave."

At dawn the next day when Fabia stepped back into their tent, María Angélica saw the look on the old woman's face and her hand went to her mouth. Fabia nodded.

"The *niño* is dead."

María Angélica sat down on the edge of her cot and sobbed. Fabia sat down next to her and took her in her arms. "Angelita," she said softly, "we must pack up our things. The caravan pulls out right after the funeral."

Few spoke that morning when they heard the news. The crowd was stony-faced, and the mother wept with grief as the Father Commissary intoned the sentences of the Burial Office and the tiny handmade coffin was lowered into the barren alkali soil of the new land. When the carts groaned heavily as the caravan pulled away from the tiny mound with only a crude cross to mark it, silence fell over the group of colonists.

María Angélica could scarcely control her sobs as she turned to Fabia. The old woman embraced her.

"Why hadn't I noticed others did not have enough to eat, Fabia?" she asked with anguish. "How could I have been so blind? Had I shared our food with Francisca, perhaps that tiny child would have lived."

"Angelita, the caravan is not your responsibility," Fabia said gently. But the old woman knew guilt lay heavily on her mistress's shoulders as the carts continued the long journey.

"Will we never reach a place to found a settlement?" María Angélica asked again and again as they trudged slowly over the rough terrain.

That night when they camped, María Angélica stopped Pedro as he was preparing to unyoke the teams of oxen from their carts. "Pedro," she said, and there was a tremble in her voice, "please open the *carretas* that contain food supplies and help me distribute them to the needy."

*"Señora,"* the Tlascalan said with alarm, "you cannot do that. The journey is not nearly over. You will have need of your provisions."

"People do not have enough to eat, Pedro. Please open the *carretas*."

*"Señora,"* he repeated, but she interrupted.

"I insist you open the *carretas*." Her voice was scarcely more than a whisper, but her tone and the look on her face made him obey, and he began to untie and pull back the tarpaulins that covered the contents of the carts.

"Angelita," Fabia spoke as she walked up, "these are not the *carretas* that hold our tent and daily necessities."

"I know," she said.

"Then why are you having Pedro open them?" the old woman asked.

"I'm going to distribute the food to the people who are hungry."

Fabia grasped her by the shoulders. "Angelita, what has come over you? You know you cannot do that."

"Yes, I can," she whispered, "and I must. That baby didn't have to die. If I had given some of our food it might still be alive."

"You don't know that, Angelita," Fabia replied with emphasis. "That baby wasn't strong when it was born—I could tell that the moment it came into this world. It didn't even have the strength to cry. It sounded like a tiny mewling cat."

"It does not matter," María Angélica said, her eyes vacant. "People are hungry."

Fabia tried to make María Angélica look at her, but her eyes would focus on nothing. Fabia let her hands drop, shook her head "no" to Pedro, and scurried off.

When she returned, the Maese was with her. *"Señora,"* he spoke to María Angélica. "Do not open your carts. There is enough food in the caravan, I swear to you. It is not necessary that you do this." But before he had even finished speaking, a small boy came running up followed by a growing crowd.

"Come," the boy shouted back to them, "the *Señora* de Vizcarra is giving out food."

María Angélica stepped forward. "Thank you, Paquito," she said to the boy and pressed a small sack of raisins into his hand. She turned to the crowd of people who had gathered. She raised her voice and it cracked, but she forced it out. "Please take of our food to relieve your hunger and that of your families."

The people pushed forward and María Angélica started dragging out sacks from the *carreta* and pushed them into the grasping hands. Fabia and the Maese stood by helplessly and watched as the carts were emptied of their supplies.

When she had given out the food, and everyone had left, María Angélica sat down on the back of the *carreta* and wept. She was alone, for Fabia and the Maese had both gone to see to the setting up of camp, knowing they could have no effect on what was happening. There had not been enough food to go around—their supplies would not nearly ease the hunger of the people. As María Angélica sat on the back of the cart and wept, she felt a hand on her shoulder.

*"Hija,"* the gentle voice said, "do not cry."

"Oh, *Padre,*" she said, looking up at Fray Alonso. She pushed herself off the back of the *carreta* and went to her knees. She kissed the hand of the priest. "There wasn't enough to go around! So many are hungry still."

"I know, my child," the Father Commissary replied, lifting her to her feet, "but *Dios* sees your generosity and He in His Goodness will reward it. Just as He succored Moses and the children of Israel in the desert, so He shall succor us if we have faith."

*"Sí, señora,"* Oñate said as he approached. He took her hands. "Your God and your governor see your generosity, and it will not go unrewarded, I can assure you."

"I want no rewards," she whispered.

Captain Aguilar and the scouting detail had been gone for over a week in search of the first villages. The morale of the people began to sag as hunger increased and the caravan made its slow painful way north, covering sometimes only half a league in a day's journey.

On the twentieth of the month the captain and his detail returned. The first carts saw the dust rise in the distance and the word passed down the caravan. "They're back!" Eyes strained into the sun trying to glimpse the returning men, each person wanting to assure himself it was not another deceiving mirage.

The governor ordered the caravan to halt, and everyone rushed forward, eager to hear what the men had seen. There was a loud shout. The group had reached the first pueblo. Voices rose in rejoicing until Don Juan bellowed with rage at Pablo de Aguilar.

"You entered a village, you say?!"

Oñate's face was suffused with crimson and a blood vessel in his temple throbbed. "How dare you defy my orders!" he thundered at the captain.

"I simply thought, Governor," Pablo de Aguilar replied woodenly, "that since we had come this far, it wouldn't matter if we entered the village and took a look around."

"Wouldn't matter! What do you think an order is? The penalty for disobeying my order was death! Death! You knew that! And yet you entered the pueblo after I had told you that it was absolutely *vital* that we not alarm the natives! We *cannot* frighten them because then they will hide their food supplies from us. We must have food—and *soon*. How many times have I said this? My orders are supreme. I shall not be disobeyed! Sergeant Major! Arrest this man!"

The governor's voice calmed to a cold, impersonal tone. "Prepare a gallows tree."

There was a hushed silence as Pablo de Aguilar stared at Oñate, a hard look on his face. The Sergeant Major shouted, "Bring manacles and a rope. I want three men to find a large cottonwood at the river—on the double." Within moments the iron manacles appeared and Aguilar was put in chains. He threw a defiant look at the governor, no trace of contrition on his face.

"Confess this man, *Padre*," Oñate ordered the Father Commissary.

"Please, *Señor Gobernador*," the priest said with a conciliatory tone, taking him aside, "the captain has committed a serious wrong by disobeying your strict order. But do not take his life. Be merciful, like our Lord *Jesús Cristo*. The man is a mere mortal. We are all desirous of reaching the natives—forgive his foolhardiness. Had I been along, I myself might have entered the village out of sheer enthusiasm. It would have been wrong, but I wouldn't have done it out of blatant disregard for your wise order."

The Maese de Campo approached the two men. "Listen to him, Uncle," he spoke earnestly. "Show that you are a magnanimous leader. Do not let Aguilar's death be a blot on our glorious expedition."

"Bring Captain Vicente," Oñate said, "I want to talk with him." Shortly the Maese returned, Vicente accompanying him.

*"Sí, Señor Gobernador."* he said. "You wished to speak with me?"

"Yes, Captain," Oñate responded, "you were with Aguilar. Tell me with what attitude did he determine to enter the pueblo against my orders?"

"Sir," Vicente answered, "Captain Aguilar said your order was foolish, that there was nothing wrong with entering the village—that we should see what it was like."

Oñate's face purpled. "I will not have my authority ridiculed," he shouted. "Aguilar must serve as an example!"

"Uncle," the Maese interjected, "many of the soldiers are becoming discouraged, food is running low, people are hungry. You must keep morale high, you must keep them on your side."

"And you must keep God on your side, too," the Father Commissary added. "This expedition is for the greater glory of our Lord to spread his Gospel of mercy to the heathen. Show that you too, Governor, know how to be merciful."

"Captain," Oñate said as he turned toward Vicente, "do you have anything to add?"

Vicente's pale eyes were cold and his voice emotionless. "If you don't kill Aguilar now, you will have to do it later."

"Sergeant Major," the governor shouted to his nephew who stood some distance away with the manacled prisoner, "prepare to carry out my orders within the hour."

"Yes, sir," the Sergeant Major answered.

Oñate walked toward the people who stood silently, waiting. "I will be in my tent. Those who wish an audience may seek it. Father," he reiterated to the priest, "confess this prisoner."

A constant stream of colonists filed through Oñate's tent in the long hour that followed.

When María Angélica entered, she knelt in front of him. "Please, Governor," she said, anguish in her voice, "spare his life. I know he defied your express orders, but we have just buried Francisca Osorio's baby. Let us not have to bury another of our own."

His face was hard, but then he took her hand and held it between his own. "What has Aguilar done to deserve your heartfelt pleas for his life?" he asked.

"He is a human being, Governor. He is one of God's creatures," she said quietly.

"Your name suits you," Oñate remarked. "First you open your wagons and give away your provisions, and now you plead for Aguilar's life. It does seem that you are the angel of the caravan." He brought her hand to his lips and kissed it. She shivered involuntarily and remembered Dorotea's words. She could not bring herself to look at him.

"I beg your mercy," she said in scarcely more than a whisper as she rose.

When the governor emerged from his tent at the end of the hour, he spoke briefly to his page. The royal notary was summoned and joined Oñate in his tent.

After some time, the page stepped outside and shouted so that everyone might hear, "The governor orders that all, save the infirm, gather at the gallows to witness the execution of his orders."

There was silence for a moment before the people began walking toward the river's edge where a henniquen rope dangled ominously from the branch of an enormous old cottonwood. One of the soldiers detailed to prepare the gallows stood below the noose, the reins of a bay horse secured in his hands. The horse snorted and danced nervously in the sand as if it felt the tension of the crowd that gathered.

The iron of the chains clanked as the Sergeant Major led the prisoner toward his fate. The Father Commissary followed them, stole around his neck, crucifix in his hand. When they reached the champing horse, the Sergeant Major removed the manacles and bound Aguilar's hands behind him and dropped the noose over the condemned man's head. The Father Commissary held up the crucifix and Aguilar kissed it. Neither the face of the Sergeant Major nor that of Aguilar showed any emotion as the prisoner was mounted on the horse.

A hush spread over the crowd as Oñate approached, the royal notary walking behind him, a parchment in his hand. The governor's page placed a chair to the right front of the silent group, and Oñate sat down as the Father Commissary made the sign of the Cross over the condemned man.

In a loud voice the royal notary began to read. "On the twelfth day of this month of May in the year of our Lord fifteen hundred and ninety-eight, our governor upon whom Don Felipe the Second, our king and monarch, has bestowed all authority and jurisdiction in this province of *Nuevo México*, sent Captain Pablo de Aguilar, along with six others, to find and reconnoiter the first settlement of natives along this *Río del Norte*. The said Captain Aguilar was forbidden on pain of death to enter any villages and admitted that he understood the reasons for his orders, which were based upon the safety and success of this expedition. So that the natives might not be frightened nor have time to prepare traps for this expedition, undertaken in the name of our temporal King and Lord Don Felipe II and in the name of our Lord Jesus Christ, Don Juan de Oñate did impress the necessity of this order upon the said Captain Aguilar. But, upon reaching a settlement of natives, said Captain, with complete disregard for his solemn orders, entered the village. Based upon his legal jurisdiction and supreme authority, the Governor Don Juan de Oñate has condemned the said Captain Aguilar to death by hanging."

The only sound to be heard was a soft rustling in the leaves of the cottonwood and the quiet murmur of the *Río del Norte* as it flowed past the stone-faced crowd. The royal notary continued. "Beseeched by the soldiers, friars and colonists alike, the Governor, Don Juan de Oñate, has shown that he is a kind and merciful leader by revoking the penalty of death that was just and rightly imposed upon this transgressor." It was as if the entire group had been holding its breath and then, as one, exhaled in relief. "Therefore," the notary continued, raising his voice in order to be heard, "let the condemned man admit his mistake in front of this expedition and ask their pardon and that of his temporal master, the Governor, Don Juan de Oñate."

There was a moment of tense silence. The notary repeated the command.

"I admit my mistake," Aguilar said tonelessly, "and ask the pardon of this expedition."

The Sergeant Major removed the noose from the prisoner's neck and dismounted him from the horse. The crowd stood silently as the Sergeant Major took him by the arm and pushed him toward where Oñate sat, grim-faced.

"Kneel," the Sergeant Major growled, as he pushed the prisoner to his knees, his arms still bound behind his back, "ask your governor's pardon and express your gratitude for his mercy."

Aguilar looked directly at Oñate, and there might have been defiance in his eyes as he said in a tone that had no contrition in it, "I ask your pardon, Governor." He paused. "I am grateful for your mercy."

"Get him out of my sight," Oñate whispered.

As the Sergeant Major lifted Aguilar to his feet and led him away, the people broke into a cheer. "*Viva* Don Juan de Oñate! Long live our governor! *¡Viva! ¡Viva!*"

Oñate stood and a smile broke the harsh lines of his face as he acknowledged the people's approval of his decision.

# Chapter 9

"I want thirty good men," Oñate spoke harshly as he sat in his tent. "And I want you three to go with me, also," he said as he nodded at the Maese de Campo, the Sergeant Major, and Captain Vizcarra. "Captain," he said addressing Vicente, "you were along with Aguilar. You will be our guide."

*"Sí, Gobernador,"* Vicente answered, his pale eyes bright and hard.

"Maese," Oñate spoke to Juan de Zaldívar, "bring the Royal Ensign here. Bring Peñalosa. I am going to leave him in charge of the expedition while we go on ahead. It's imperative that we reach the settlements as soon as possible because we *must* have provisions. We cannot give the natives time to hide their stores of corn, otherwise we will all perish from starvation."

"It is that serious?" asked the Maese.

"Yes," his uncle responded, running his hand through his graying hair, "I have tried to keep it quiet so no one would panic, hoping we would soon reach the settlements where they have large stores of food." He paused and drove his fist into his hand. "But if the natives have hidden their food, we will perish, and by the holy name of our Lord, if they have, I will kill Aguilar with my own hands!

"Now," he continued, "pick thirty good men. See that they are well armed and ready to march within the hour, and send Peñalosa to me immediately!"

"Get my armor ready, Mateo, and bring it to me quickly! *¡Ándale!"* Vicente shouted to his slender, dark-eyed page as he threw back the tent flap and entered.

María Angélica's eyes widened as he rushed in, and he laughed harshly. "Come give your husband a kiss."

He had to repeat the command before she reluctantly approached him and grazed the whiskers of the side of his face with closed lips. He smelled revoltingly of horses, and even his red beard stank after a week of hard travel on the reconnaissance mission. As she stepped back he yanked her into his arms, bruising her mouth as he kissed her roughly. He let her go, pulled off his gloves and threw them on a low table.

"We leave in an hour," he said sharply. "Oñate's taking thirty men on ahead." She stood there stiffly, saying nothing. Vicente looked up at her, his ice-blue eyes riveted on her for a moment. "Yes," he said as if making a decision right then, "there's time. Get on the bed."

She backed away, but he grabbed her arm, yanking her to the bed. "Don't fight me," he growled in her face, "I'm not in the mood. We wouldn't want that little *coño* of yours to rust, would we? Everything needs a little oil now and then to keep it working smoothly." Vicente pushed her down on the bed and roughly pulled up her skirts.

His animal sounds had scarcely died away when there was a clanking sound of metal within the tent. Vicente's head jerked up and as her eyes flew open, she caught a glimpse of the embarrassed young page who stood dumbly holding the captain's polished armor.

Vicente let out a guffaw as the dark-eyed young man mumbled something incomprehensible and backed hurriedly out of the tent. "Stay," the captain said without the slightest embarrassment as he pulled himself off her and readjusted his clothing as he rose. He yanked her skirts down and stepped away from the bed, pulling the drape shut behind him. The boy stood trembling, eyes downcast, horrified at his blunder.

"Your sense of timing is somewhat lacking. Perhaps you should announce yourself before entering." The boy mumbled a scarcely audible apology.

*"Dios,"* Vicente swore as he saw the quilted cotton protective doublet that he wore beneath his armor. "Is my *farseto* wet?" he demanded furiously.

*"Sí, señor Capitán,"* the young man whispered, stammering an apology. "I, I, I . . . did not know you would be riding out again so soon. I thought perhaps you might want it washed. It smelled and . . ."

"Washed? Whoever in hell washes a *farseto?* You *pinche* mestizo! Even yet, the goddamned Indian comes out in you—always washing! You might as well be a woman!"

*"Perdón, señor,"* the boy whispered, "I only try to please you."

"Get out of my sight," Vicente said with disgust.

"Please, *señor,*" the boy begged as he dropped to his knees, his slender hands pressed together, supplicating.

Vicente kicked him viciously, and the boy fell to the side but did not whimper. "Get my leather doublet. I can't wear that sopping thing! I hope to hell you haven't washed my wheellock pistols. Don Juan wants us well armed and I would hate to have to tell him my pistols were in the laundry."

The boy flushed. "No, *señor,* they are in fine condition. I oiled them just now."

The well-armored and well-armed contingent set out at a gallop. A few supply wagons carrying munitions and provisions for the men pulled away from the rest of the cart train to follow the governor's advance detail. Not only did they leave a cloud of dust over the camp but also one of apprehension. The expedition's leader as well as the men next in charge, the Maese and the Sergeant Major, and the bravest officers and soldiers were in the group. What if something should befall them? Would Peñalosa be able to keep order?

Oñate had ruled with an iron hand in order to keep violent tempers, petty disputes, and factionalism from undermining the expedition. The long hard months of waiting at Santa Bárbara before final permission to march was granted had caused discontent among the colonists, and it had not dissipated on the journey north. Rivalries and hard feelings still stewed below the bright surface of optimism and expectation. But hunger had a way of gnawing at optimism and hope, and almost everyone was beginning to feel its pangs. What would become of them if they were forced to eat their seed wheat and the animals that were to breed their herds in the new land?

It soon became evident that they could no longer follow the river. The rocky crags came down to the edge of the *Río del Norte,* scarcely allowing passage of a horse much less a team of oxen with its lumbering cart. To the right of the mountains stretched a wide, flat plain. They would have to leave the river and follow that route, praying there would be water in the barren expanse.

Oñate and his men spent that night without water. Some of the men were sent to take the horses to the river over a league away.

During the day the sun beat down upon them through a spotlessly brilliant blue sky that offered not a puff of cloud to mitigate its strength, and their armor became so hot they could have boiled a cup of soup in their morion helmets. But at night, as soon as the sun had dropped behind the mountains in the west, the heat vanished, radiated into the night sky, and in its place was a chill that by morning made them stiff with cold.

That night as Oñate and some of his men sat around the winking campfire, their armor having been removed, they drew their cloaks around them to ward off the chilled fingers of the night air.

"Ah, Vicente," Oñate laughed as the red-bearded captain approached the group with a wineskin in hand, "you travel prepared!"

"But of course, my Governor," Vicente replied, "one may survive a day or two without water but not without wine!"

"My sentiments exactly," added the Sergeant Major, laughing. The wineskin passed from hand to hand, each man tipping his head back and drinking a long draught.

"That warms the insides," said Captain Gaspar de Villagrá, as he rubbed the wine off his beard with the back of his hand. "What a luxury on a cold night to have something more than a thin blanket with which to warm oneself."

The governor laughed. "Not only does Captain Vicente have wine to warm him at night," he said with a broad smile, "but with the caravan he has something even better—a warm, soft woman! Would that we all were so blessed!" The rest of the men concurred with loud expressions of agreement. Neither the two Zaldívar brothers nor the Captain Villagrá were married.

"Not only is she beautiful," the Maese spoke up, "but she is kind and generous also. What an example of Christian charity when she opened your wagons, Captain Vicente, and shared your stores of food with the less fortunate."

Vicente's smile was taut. Had it not been for the priests who had commended her actions and set her up as an example to the rest of the caravan, he would have beaten her for that stupid act. Even if it was her money that had bought the supplies, they were *his* now, not hers to dispose of as she so desired.

The Sergeant Major laughed. "It's not her charity," he said irreverently, "that I should admire if she were my wife!"

Oñate laughed also. "Although I admire Doña María Angélica's Christian virtues, I must agree with my nephew. She is 'angelic' in another more important way!"

Vicente grinned and laughed good-naturedly. It did not seem to bother him in the least that the woman whose charms they were discussing was his wife. It pleased him that the governor found her desirable. He would need Oñate's favor for prospecting. She had already served admirably. He knew Oñate liked *jerez,* but the fact that he frequented their quarters to the extent he did indicated that there was a magnet of another kind that drew the expedition's busy leader there. Yes, he mused, his wife was an asset in spite of her stupid religious convictions, and he fully intended to make her more worldly.

Conversation subsided as the wineskin passed around the group of men. Vicente looked toward Oñate before he decided to speak. The governor had had several long draughts of wine, but it was impossible to tell if it had eased his mood. The affair with Aguilar had infuriated him, and the intensity of his anger burst forth from time to time. It was obvious that one must not disobey his orders. If that were true in the case of making contact with the Indians, then it would be doubly true in the case of gold.

It was expressly forbidden, likewise under pain of death, to search for gold on one's own. Official expeditions sanctioned by the governor and made for the purpose of searching for minerals were the sole avenue for exploration. None were allowed on a personal basis. And Vicente was convinced that no intercession by any priest nor any colonist nor any woman would persuade Oñate to be lenient in the matter of gold.

The governor might propound the idea that the search for souls for Holy Mother Church was the paramount purpose of the expedition, but there were few men who would spend personal fortunes for such a noble end without expectation of some reward other than a heavenly one. The search for lands that would yield rewards of gold and silver was the motivation that sent the sons of Adam into unknown, desolate, and hostile countries—countries that exacted a great sacrifice from those who dared to enter.

Vicente knew he must go slowly and carefully with the governor if he were to succeed. Some of the barren, craggy mountains they passed reminded him of the harsh mountains of Zacatecas that had yielded so much wealth in precious metals, and he avidly wanted to explore them, but he knew he must wait. He must cultivate the governor until the right moment. Surprisingly, the cultivation was proceeding more quickly than he had hoped.

He was wise to have talked to a close friend of the governor's and to have learned of Don Juan's predilection for *jerez,* which he then went to great pains to acquire. And of course, arriving late on the scene, the governor had no grudges against him. In fact, Oñate was glad to have someone new on his side. Although he could not be blamed for the disastrous and demoralizing delays, the soldiers and colonists were becoming disenchanted with his leadership. That Vicente de Vizcarra brought to the caravan many well-supplied wagons, great amounts of livestock, as well as many men to oversee his goods and animals, did not lessen the governor's reception of him.

Soldiers and colonists had already deserted in significant numbers; to have someone so well supplied join the expedition would not only help Oñate meet his contractual agreements but would raise the morale of the others who were beginning to feel that the caravan was a sinking ship.

When they had joined the group, Vicente was given the rank of captain, and it had been easy to insinuate himself into the governor's confidence. It was then that he recognized his young wife's potential to aid his cause. She might not know it, but he was preparing her; she would serve him well when the time came.

Vicente looked at the men sitting around the fire. The governor's thoughts were obviously on the Indians and their food the expedition so badly needed. Vicente decided he would interject another thought into Don Juan's head. He didn't want the situation with the natives to completely dominate the governor's thoughts; there needed to be a constant germ of gold fever lurking there.

Vicente took a long drink from the wineskin. "There is one thing," he said, as he wiped his beard with his sleeve, "that is more important than wine or women." He paused for effect. "Gold!"

All vigorously assented and echoed his sentiment, and the captain continued. "I think this is going to be a profitable expedition. The mountains are barren, but that may be a good sign. Who knows? Maybe they are solid gold underneath!" Everyone laughed hopefully with him.

*"Ojalá que sea así,"* Oñate murmured. Vicente said no more as he passed the wineskin to the governor.

The land was cruel and deceptively barren. A gray-green expanse stretched out between two mountain ranges. On the west, impeding travel, were the mountains that edged the *Río del Norte*. To the east rose another chain of rough peaks that were black in the dawn, silhouetted by the sun that would soon rise behind them.

The plains that stretched out before them appeared gentle and even benign as if covered with short grass, not yet fully green. But the land was deceiving—rather like quicksand that consumed and dealt death to those who dared to tread upon it. In fact the land was a harsh desert masked by short dry bunch grass, wicked-thorned mesquite and bayonet-leafed yucca, some of it alive, much of it dead. The trunks of dead yucca lay brown and twisted like the rotting legs of a corpse.

The color of the ground was misleading, too. The treacherous expanse was covered by a dark, red-brown sand that appeared solid earth from its color, but reach down and grab a handful of it, and it sifted dryly and finely through the fingers. The slightest breeze would take a bite of it and swirl it chokingly into the air, and the heavy wheel of an ox cart or the hooves of a horse would have the same effect. A strong wind or a herd of animals was an even more dire prospect.

Here and there the desert was broken by small knolls, on closer inspection small sand dunes—more evidence that the wind was no stranger to that flat, mountain-hemmed expanse. Perhaps a dead yucca fallen to the ground, or a thistle caught in a small clump of close-growing mesquite, or the bones of some animal picked clean by a wolf or a vulture had caught the sand and made it drift.

The advance detail of the governor and his men rose shortly before dawn, their throats already dry. They would proceed by forced marches in order to reach the settlements, covering as much distance that day as possible. They prayed they would find water. No one wanted to consider the possibility that they would not.

As the group began its march, the fine dark sand raised by the horses' hooves and by their supply carts made them cough and further dried their throats. They pushed on through the day and the sun beat down upon their armor, forcing them to remove it. They could not afford to become more dehydrated. Nasal passages were parched and lips cracked from the lack of water. By afternoon the group had slowed to a crawl. The sun was merciless and blinding, and the men had spots before their eyes. The dizziness that many felt scarcely allowed them to keep to their feet. All walked now, their horses in as desperate condition as they.

The sun fell behind the mountains to the west. God alone knew how many leagues they were from the *Río del Norte*. Camp was not made. The men merely stopped in their tracks. Provisions were low, but everyone was too thirsty to eat. Vicente checked his wineskin. He did not realize they had drunk so much. He took a long quick drink, hoping no one saw him. Then he carried it to the governor. Oñate took the wineskin eagerly and drank.

"As governor, I must keep myself able to lead," Don Juan spoke as he lowered the wineskin. It sounded like an apology.

The next day they continued north, still finding no water. On the twenty-fifth of May they came to an arroyo they named *Los Muertos*, for they feared they were dead even though the arroyo had a small amount of water. They tried to wet their throats with it, but its brackishness made it undrinkable.

The Father Commissary, who had accompanied them, fell ill with gout. He lay in one of the carts moaning with the excruciating pain as the solid-wheeled *carreta* jostled and jolted over the terrain. The pain was so intense that he could not even pray. They could go no farther without water. Leaving the carts behind, the larger portion of the group struck out toward the west for the *Río del Norte*, and barely more than walking dead as they came through the rugged mountains, they reached the cool waters of the swiftly flowing river.

Wild with thirst, two horses died when their stomachs burst from the great quantity of river water they consumed. A detail took a barrel of water back to the carts that then continued north over the killing plains while the rest of the men on horseback pushed on ahead following the river. Everyone prayed the supply carts would also soon be able to travel near the *Río*.

The next day the men on horseback covered seven leagues, and there was great rejoicing as they came to a huge marshy area by the river's edge. A large distinctive mesa rose up a few leagues farther on. Vicente informed them they were within a day of the first settlement That night they feasted on duck and other water fowl that abounded in the marsh.

All drank their fill as they sat around the campfires and devoured the crispy, succulent meat. Because the Father Commissary was sick and with the carts, Father Cristóbal de Salazar, the governor's cousin, said a prayer of thanks for their deliverance.

The next morning at dawn, with the sky as the cupola, he said Mass, and all took communion so that their entry into the first settlement might be propitious. As they rode on that day, the men were tense and nervous with the anticipation of encountering natives.

Like reflecting mirrors, their armor flashed in the sun carrying the message of their arrival. By late afternoon they reached the village. They saw it nestled at the base of the black mesa, its three-storied houses a welcome, civilized sight. Well-tended, cultivated fields surrounded the communal dwellings, revealing their new green shoots of corn. Vines that would produce some kind of melon by summer's end grew close by. The men wanted to shout their joy at the sight of the village but Oñate had ordered silence. Under no circumstance did he want the natives frightened. He ordered the group to halt as he picked a few men to go with him to the village. Perhaps the Indians would see their peaceful purpose if only a small delegation approached. As they came near the houses, the silence was ominous. Slowly they rode forward, wondering if the dark doorways of the upper stories hid figures in their shadows. And if they did, were the figures holding bows and arrows, waiting until the riders were at close range?

Vicente's gauntleted hand opened and closed on the reins, prepared to wheel his horse instantly if required. Still they rode on, and the silence of the village screamed in their ears. At the base of the windowless first-story walls, Oñate reined in his horse and the others followed suit. The royal notary called out a greeting from the King of Spain and the admonition to come out of their homes, as the emissaries of the King of Spain came in peace. There was no response. Again the notary called out the message, not that any native would understand what he had said. Silence prevailed.

Oñate nodded to the Sergeant Major, who dismounted and walked slowly to one of the ladders that leaned against the wall. The Maese and Captain Vicente, as well as the others, prepared their arquebuses in case they would need to protect the Sergeant Major. The metal of his armor clanked loudly in the silence as he ascended the ladder. Briefly he paused before stepping onto the roof. Still there was no sign of life anywhere in the quiet village. Crossing the roof, the Sergeant Major ducked into a dark doorway. Long moments passed and he did not come out of the dwelling. Hands nervously held their weapons, and sweat trickled down inside polished armor.

Suddenly the Sergeant Major reappeared, a wide smile on his face as he stuffed something into his mouth and began to eat. "It appears they've abandoned the place," he shouted down. "Their food's still here, though," he added with a smile.

"*¡Alabado sea Dios!*" Oñate replied. "Praised be God!" he reiterated as he crossed himself. He turned to the Maese, Captain Vicente, and Captain Villagrá. "Help the Sergeant Major search the place. I want to know if there are any natives hiding anywhere, and I especially want to know how much food they have. But," he added in warning, "do not take or disturb anything. We must make a good impression upon the natives and show them we mean them no harm."

The three men dismounted and climbed the ladder. The governor sent a man back to report to the others that the village was deserted. That night they made camp by the river as Oñate ordered. Some urged that they occupy the abandoned village so that they might have the luxury of sleeping with a roof over their heads after the long gruelling journey they had endured, but Oñate forbade it.

Darkness fell and a gentle breeze made the cottonwoods along the river rustle softly. The governor posted sentries and ordered everyone to gather near the large fire that had been built. Stars winked in the dark sky that would have no moon that night to help the sentries in their duties. The gray-bearded leader's face was unsmiling.

"As I feared," he said harshly, "the Indians have fled. They have not hidden their stores of corn as it appears, but we *must not* avail ourselves of it. In this land we cannot afford the hostility of the natives. I cannot impress this fact upon you enough. You can see the land yourselves—it is obvious we cannot sustain ourselves off it—we must have food from the inhabitants of this province, but we must not take it by force. Certainly," he continued, "we could go back to this village and take all their supplies and go to bed with a full stomach. But is there enough food to last the winter? And where would we put it? Let's say we take this grain. What are we going to find in the next pueblo? An abandoned village to be sure, but in it there will be no corn. Having heard what happened in this village, the natives will hide their grain.

"Use your minds," the governor pleaded. "I would like to have a full belly as much as anyone, but I would rather be patient and live meagerly until we can plant our own crops next year, than to satisfy my hunger now and die of starvation this winter." He paused for the effect his words might have before he continued.

"I have tried to keep the caravan, especially the women and children, from panicking at the knowledge of how few food supplies we have left, but I am telling you men now in all honesty that our situation is desperate. If we do not find supplies soon, we will perish, but if we take the food of the natives now, we are only delaying the inevitable. We must purchase the food with knives, bells, and trinkets or receive it free from them as an example of their obedience to our monarch Don Felipe who will rule over them with peace. When they know the good news of the Gospel of our Lord *Jesús Cristo,* which we bring them, they will give us their corn in gratitude for so great a gift."

Oñate paused again. He stood with his back to the fire and watched the faces of the men in its yellowish flickering light, their bearded faces hard to decipher in the deceptive shadows. He had no way of knowing what were their thoughts save the occasional nod of a head that indicated some were in agreement with him. Don Juan silently cursed the Viceroy, knowing that the delays in the expedition setting out were the main cause of their dire situation. At times he regretted ever having applied for the honor of pacifying this godforsaken land. However, if he had to do it over again, he would probably choose the same path.

His inheritance had dwindled alarmingly and he was not as rich a Zacatecan miner as all thought him to be. His father had founded Nueva Galicia; his ancestors were covered with glory and would be remembered by history. No one would forget the name of his grandfather-in-law—Hernán Cortez. If he, Don Juan de Oñate Zaldívar de Salazar, conquered, pacified, and discovered gold in the far reaches of the north, in the vast expanses of *Nuevo México,* he would be remembered by history. His name would be inscribed in the pantheon of conquerors of the New World; his children, grandchildren, and great-grandchildren would carry the mark of honor he had won for them. Yes, he would do it again, and he would see to it that no one now would destroy his plans.

Oñate's voice carried the sound of a command. "Let's go to bed and pray that God grants us his graciousness on the morrow and that he brings the cart train safely across the deadly *jornada.*"

# Chapter 10

The wind whipped up the alkali soil and whirled it wantonly through the cart train, stinging eyes, burning throats, and choking the weary travelers who trudged head down, leaning into the wind, trying to lessen its force.

María Angélica and Dorotea walked side by side, their *rebozos* wrapped around their faces in a vain attempt to ward off the dust. They walked slowly, their steps heavy with a rhythm common to marchers whose purpose is lost.

"God in Heaven," María Angélica whispered beseechingly as she fell to her knees on the hard ground, unable to continue. "Please stop the wind. Have pity on the poor children."

Dorotea reached down and grasped her by the shoulders. "Stand up," she said firmly. "God can hear your prayers while you walk. Don't get behind. We have a privileged position near the front of the caravan. If you think the dust is bad here, what do you think it's like at the back of this cart train?"

"But what about the poor ones who *do* have to travel at the back?" María Angélica asked.

"Pray for them. We all have an obligation to live. You are creeping close to despair; you're losing the will to live, only you won't see it. You want to sacrifice yourself for others—for the children. That is a noble sentiment, but self-sacrifice is often a mask to hide from the fact that one has lost the will to live. It is really slow suicide."

"Dorotea!" she said with horror, "that isn't true. The Church teaches that sacrifice is good."

"I know, but I'm telling you there are different kinds of sacrifice. I love children, and it tears my heart to see them suffer, but tell me, how long could the young survive in this land without us? The adults must live to care for the children. Fabia has told me how you are not eating and are giving your food to the young ones. *Everyone* must eat. I know the food is meager—we are all hungry—but there is enough for everyone to have a little. The adults must survive to build a home for the children."

"But I have no children, and these little ones need the food."

"We all need to keep our strength on this difficult journey," Dorotea said with emphasis, but there was also a note of resignation in her voice, for she knew her words had fallen on deaf ears.

The wind died at sunset, and everyone said a silent prayer of thanksgiving. "Please, don't let it begin again tomorrow, Lord," María Angélica whispered, "have pity on the children."

"Angelita, have a little broth," Fabia urged. "The wind has stopped. Things are going to be better."

"Thank you, Fabia. I'm not hungry. Why don't you take it to Juana's little boy—he's not doing very well."

"I made an extra large pot of soup," Fabia said grimly. "I have already taken some to Juana as well as to others. Angelita, you *must* eat—there is enough. You must keep your strength for the journey. Tomorrow we leave the river and start across the plain. Who knows what *that* will bring?"

The oxen labored with difficulty, straining to pull the heavy carts through the red-brown sand that stretched in front of them. They could not make more than a league a day as cart after cart sank into the sand and had to be pulled out by a double team, and the mule teams suffered more than the stoic oxen.

The sun beat down mercilessly on the marchers, and although there was no wind, clouds of choking sand were raised by the straining hooves and the heavy wooden wheels. The scrubby, wicked-thorned mesquite bushes tore at skirts and pants and left mean scratches on arms and legs. The barrels of water, filled days before at the *Río del Norte,* were almost all empty, and parched throats cried out for water. The caravan had slowed to a snail's pace. Ensign Peñalosa, whom the governor had left in charge, called together the *padres* and the few officers who had remained with the cart train.

"We cannot go farther without water. A decision must be made tonight. Do we turn back—return to the river, make camp there, and send someone to tell the governor we cannot make it, or do we continue on, praying we will find water?"

Pablo de Aguilar spoke up. "How do we know the governor and the others are not dead, killed by the natives or dead from thirst? How long has it been since they rode out—three weeks, more? Why has the governor not sent word to us? This whole expedition was doomed from the start. Most of us have nothing left. Let's turn back while we still have our lives."

Fray Francisco rose.

*"Sí, padre,"* Peñalosa spoke to him, "we would welcome your views."

"I agree that we have had many trials and tribulations placed in our path," the priest spoke with feeling, "but how do we know that the Lord is not testing us? Did He not test Moses? We have been given the sacred duty of converting the heathen tribes that Coronado found in this land. It is a responsibility not to be taken lightly. We must place our trust in the Lord and continue, and if we perish, so be it. We will have died in the service of the Lord attempting to spread His Gospel."

The other friars concurred vigorously with Fray Francisco, and the officers who may have been sympathetic to Aguilar's words did not speak up.

"Then we continue," Peñalosa said, "and God help us."

"But we *must* have water," Aguilar spoke with vehemence.

"The caravan will stay camped here tomorrow," Peñalosa said. "I will send a detail west to the river to bring back casks of water so that we may continue on, but the horses will not be able to carry a very heavy load. *Padres*, pray hard that we find water along the way."

But no water was found, and what the detail brought back quickly disappeared, and the cart train's suffering increased as they battled against the heat and sand. María Angélica trudged beside the cart, the beads of her rosary twined in her fingers. Her lips moved in ceaseless prayer, but no sound came forth as she said *Ave* after *Ave* and then began again. Fabia and Dorotea trudged along beside her, but they said no prayers, their eyes fixed on the ground in front of them.

Each day the animals that died were butchered on the spot. Their blood was drunk by the thirsty travelers, and the meat was divided among the colonists, giving each person a few mouthfuls of mule or tough oxen. Many wolfed it down voraciously, but no cajoling on Fabia's part nor any reasoning on Dorotea's would convince María Angélica to eat. They had succeeded once or twice, but each time she ate something of substance she would complain of sharp pains in her stomach and could not keep the food down.

Tears slid down her face. "When are we ever going to get out of this horrible desert? Are we all going to die?" Her voice rose. "Where is the advance detail that went with the governor? Why have they not come back? Are they all lying dead somewhere? Where is the Maese? He is a good man, he would not let us starve."

Fabia led María Angélica into the tent and put her to bed. She took a jar from a trunk and stirred together a large spoonful of Campeche honey along with a few herbs and a bit of Vicente's *jerez* from a wineskin he had left behind. "Here, Angelita," she said as she lifted the young woman's head, "here is some medicine to make the stomach pains stop." Obediently María Angélica swallowed the sweet concoction. "Now, sleep," Fabia urged. The old woman came out of the tent and sat down next to Dorotea.

"She is starving herself," Fabia said softly. "She is so weak from hunger, her mind is not working properly. She thinks if *she* eats, the children are going to starve."

"What can we do?" Dorotea asked with concern.

"I just gave her some honey mixed with herbs to make her sleep. Hopefully it will make her so drowsy tomorrow that she cannot walk, and I can make her ride in the *carreta*. I am going to try to tell her she is sick, and maybe I can get some food into her in the guise of medicine, like she took the honey just now, but I don't know. She has not been the same since Francisca Osorio's baby died. She has blamed herself for that baby's death."

Vicente volunteered for the last sentry duty before dawn, knowing that if an attack were to be made, that was the time it would occur. He volunteered for any duty that might offer him the chance to render service to the governor. When the time came, he expected to be well rewarded for his efforts.

The night passed without incident although few slept soundly. The camp had just begun to stir when there was a sudden commotion. Vicente came leading a young Indian, hands bound, into camp. The native looked terrified as he glanced furtively at the bearded pale-skinned faces who approached him.

Oñate, hearing the commotion, stepped outside.

"Governor," Vicente said as he untied the native's hands, "this young heathen was snooping around in the trees. I thought you might wish to show him some Spanish hospitality so he could tell his people how friendly we are."

Don Juan smiled broadly. "Well done, Captain," he said and then turned to the terrified young boy. Oñate raised his hand, crossing his fingers in the gesture learned from the natives they had encountered at the ford of the *Río del Norte*. He had no idea if this sign of peace was universal, but he tried it anyway.

If only, the governor wished fervently, they had a translator like Cortez had found in Malinche, the woman renamed Doña Marina by the Spanish soldiers. The conquest of the Aztecs was due in no little part to the woman who had become Cortez's mistress. Since they, however, had no one who knew the language of the pueblos of the *Río del Norte,* they would have to rely on signs.

Upon witnessing the governor's gestures and seeing his smiling, unmenacing demeanor, the young Indian seemed to relax. Through signs Oñate tried to ask if he was from the nearby village they had visited. The boy responded affirmatively, and Don Juan attempted to find out where the others had gone, but very little information could be deciphered from the motions the young native made. Then using the language understood by men everywhere, the governor gifted the boy generously with hawk bells, blue and red glass beads, and a sharp metal hunting knife. Beaming with pleasure, the boy spoke words Oñate did not comprehend but assumed were words of thanks. Finally, he indicated to the boy that he was free to go back to his people.

By mid-morning the Indians began to come in. A few natives approached the camp and more could be seen reentering the village. The few supply carts the soldiers had left behind as they had ridden on ahead to the first village finally arrived, and because the Father Commissary's gout was much worse, the governor decided to stay there camped by the river. Perhaps if they waited at this spot for a week or two, the main body of the caravan would arrive, and they could continue together. He worried about the cart train he had left in the care of Peñalosa. How were they faring? What would it be like for them crossing that terrible land? Could the women and children survive? Captain Vicente had said that any man crossing the infernal land was a dead man. The waterless expanse was like the road to hell—a dead man's journey. And so the name had stuck: *Jornada del Muerto.*

The governor tried not to think about the caravan. He knew he was responsible for it, but he had left Peñalosa in charge. The man was mature and levelheaded; Oñate prayed he would see it through. What he must occupy himself with was the problem of the pacification of all the villages: their acceptance of the sovereignty of Don Felipe II and their acceptance of the true Word.

If only they had someone who could translate.

Two weeks passed quickly but still no word from the caravan. The governor began to feel uneasy. It was the middle of June. He must push on. They were in desperate straits for food. Diego de Zubia, the Purveyor General, had managed to round up some corn from the Indians at the pueblo of Qualacú, the name by which they now knew the nearby village at the foot of the black mesa, but Oñate feared they had already asked for more than the Indians had willingly wanted to give them. They would have to continue northward.

On the fourteenth of June they resumed the march.

They pushed on until they reached another pueblo, this one on the western bank of the *Río del Norte*, where they halted. The Indians here had not abandoned their village, and to the governor's profound relief and joy, the natives came out in great numbers to greet them, bringing corn in large pottery jars. The village was immediately christened "Socorro" because of the succor the village brought them.

Their chief, a man who called himself Letoc, communicated well with signs and supplied them with many details of other pueblos farther on. The generosity and friendliness of the people of Socorro did much to raise Oñate's spirits, as well as that of his men.

They were now truly in the land of the pueblos of which Coronado had spoken. As they continued north following the river, each day's journey brought them to another village, most of which were quickly abandoned upon their approach. On June 24, the feast day of St. John the Baptist, they arrived at a newly built pueblo that had only recently been abandoned, and in honor of the Saint's day, Oñate ordered a feast and general holiday. Great fires were built. The *Río del Norte* abounded in fish, and within an hour after having begun, great piles of catfish, trout, silvery chubs, and garpikes lay on the sandy river bank ready to be roasted. The governor ordered that much corn be prepared in spite of the fact that their stores were not excessively large even with the generosity of the natives at Socorro.

The highlight of every holiday was staged. Not only did the men enjoy the sham battle between Moors and Christians because it gave a chance for them to display their skills of horsemanship and weaponry, but it also recalled the glorious and noble past, and they could once again be caught up in the mystique of the age of chivalry.

Much to the governor's pleasure, Indians began to trickle into camp, their faces covered with a mixture of wonderment, curiosity, and sometimes fear. He greeted them with hospitality and gave them generously of the food prepared for the feast, and before long, increasing numbers of natives came. Having sufficient food for the newcomers created no problem because soon the Indian women came bringing native food to add to that of the Spaniards'. Gray-blue paper bread filled baskets that were set next to bowls of stew in which swam chunks of deer meat and squash. Merriment was general although hosts and guests could not understand a word the other spoke.

Many of the men who had not experienced the touch of a woman for many long months looked with hungry eyes at the girls and women who entered their camp. The governor found himself staring at a head of long, sleek black hair, or a slender copper arm, or a satin-smooth dusky cheek. Natives, both women and men, approached the pale, metal-plated newcomers to touch the hair that sprouted on their faces. To the natives, some of the strangers looked more animal than human with their heavy eyebrows and the filthy hair under their noses and around their mouths. Some of the Spaniards had hair the color of the red fox, and their pale eyes inspired fear, causing the natives to wonder if perhaps the strangers' mothers might not have been a coyote bitch or a vixen. Perhaps they were half animal, half man. Their smell was nauseating. Did they have paws for feet? Did they hide a bushy tail under the hard, shiny turtle-like shell they wore on their bodies? Curiosity gradually got the better of fear as more and more natives ventured to touch the pale skin, or the metal that they wore, or the strange giant-dogs that they rode.

The governor forced himself to quit staring at the fresh-looking native girls and turned his attention to his men. He had seen one or two touch the face or arm of a young girl who might be inspecting them thus. He must allow nothing to happen that would cause ill feelings; they were already outnumbered many times over. If something should happen to anger the natives, was the Spaniards' body armor and superiority in arms enough to save them in the midst of raging heathen? He would alert some of the officers to keep an eye on the soldiers as well as the natives. Slowly Don Juan made his way through the people, stopping to talk briefly here and there with the Maese, the Sergeant Major, Captain Vicente, Captain Villagrá, and others. They too began to mingle, calling the attention of the soldiers to the disproportionate number of Spaniards and natives.

Oñate called for the sham battle to begin. The two "armies," one headed by the Maese and the other by his brother the Sergeant Major, took their positions as the villagers watched, entranced. The loud trumpet blast that signalled the start of the battle sent fear through the natives and many fled, later to return when they saw nothing had befallen their comrades.

The fighting was fierce, and the Indians stood in awe as the strangers fought and "killed" each other. They could not comprehend what was happening. Suddenly the battle was over just as quickly as it had begun and all the members of one band lay dead on the ground. Shouts of *"¡Rey y Santiago!"* rang out thunderingly. And then to the great surprise of the natives, the "dead" arose, laughing and slapping each other on the back. The Indians began to smile and laugh and point as they realized what had happened.

There was more feasting after the battle, and the governor was in extraordinarily good spirits. The natives were friendly and becoming more generous as they brought presents of food—corn, beans, dried melons, jerked meat, live turkeys, beautifully embroidered cotton blankets, and soft, supple skins, tanned as expertly as was done in Flanders. Oñate was admiring the presents when suddenly a native dressed only in a breechclout approached. Two others, similarly dressed, followed.

*"Miércoles, jueves, sábado, y domingo,"* the *indio* said in a loud voice.

Don Juan's mouth dropped in astonishment. The Indian had spoken the words Wednesday, Thursday, Saturday, and Sunday in Castilian.

"Where did you learn to say that?" the governor demanded, but the poor native only quaked at his forceful tone. "Detain these men," he shouted and the Sergeant Major and two others seized the three Indians.

"We absolutely cannot let them get away," the governor said. "We must find out how they learned these words in *castellano!* They may hold the key to our conquest like Malinche did for Cortez."

*"Tomás, Cristóbal!"* the Indian spoke in terror at being restrained. He pointed north, repeating again and again, *"Tomás, Cristóbal. Tomás, Cristóbal."*

"Tomás? Cristóbal?" Oñate asked. "Could it be that there are men in this land that speak our language?"

"What about the other expeditions?" the Sergeant Major said. "Coronado. Alvarado. Espejo. Could some *mestizos* have stayed behind?"

"*Ojalá*. Would that God could be so kind!"

The governor tried to ask the Indians more questions, but it became apparent that they knew nothing more in the Castilian tongue. By signs, however, he thought he understood that two people who had taught the natives those words lived two days' journey to the north. Who were these men, this Tomás and Cristóbal, who knew the Castilian language?

"Bring some presents for these men, quickly!" the governor shouted. "We don't want them to fear us." He smiled at the natives and patted them on the shoulder. "*No se preocupen*. We're not going to harm you." He turned to Juan de Zaldívar.

"Maese! Prepare to march at dawn. And God save the cart train, we cannot wait for them."

# Chapter 11

With the fleeting quickness of a ground squirrel skipping over barren rock, the runner's moccasin-shod feet chinked into the toeholds of the sheer escarpment of the White Rock as he ascended. Without pausing at the top to catch his breath, he raced down the row of houses directly to Mauharots. He scrambled up the ladder to the roof of the *kiva* and then slowed as he descended another into the chamber. West of the fireplace he passed along a wall painted with white half-circle *shiwana* cloud faces. Symbolic lightning zigzagged down the wall, and drops of lifegiving rain decorated the mud plaster while a plumed water snake wound itself along the opposite wall. He carefully seated himself in the cool darkness of the room. No one spoke. He was brought a gourd dipper of water.

"With your permission," he said respectfully to the men who had gathered in the ceremonial chamber. A head nodded and he spoke. "They are here again. The men of the pale eyes who wear the clothes-that-shine have returned. The story we heard is true. They are here. They have been camped near the Big River near the village by the black mountain; they go always to the north. There are as many men as six hands." He made the motion for thirty.

One of the chiefs spoke. "Is their purpose known? For what reason do they return?"

The young man shook his head. "No one knows. There seems to be no reason that can be discovered. They are of much friendliness to the people and give many gifts." The young man withdrew several glass beads from the pouch that hung at his waist. He handed them to the chief to inspect who then handed them to the others. The men nodded and looked carefully at the rounded pieces of color through which light could pass. Except for the color, they were similar to the stone the crystal gazer used to see sickness.

"They did something very unusual," the young man went on. "A short distance from their camp, half of the men went to one side and the other half to the other. When a man put his lips to a strange, shiny thing and made a loud, terrible noise, the two groups began to fight fiercely. At last all of the members of one side lay on the ground as if dead. When the game was over, they rose and all laughed. It made me think of the K'atsina fight at Kacikatcutya that we reenact. Could it be that they know White House?"

The old chief shook his head. "Who is to know? But what we need to discover is their purpose. It was fifty-eight growing cycles ago that the first group of these strange pale intruders came into our land. I had twenty summers when the small detachment came here to Áco. It is something I can never forget. We thought these must be the sons of Nautsiti, Iyatiku's sister who left her and went to the East to create her own descendants. Iyatiku told our grandfathers that one day the children of Nautsiti would return and they would be pale-skinned like Nautsiti.

"When they first came, the big pale chief did not come to Áco; he stayed at the village of Pauray through the snow time. He massacred many of the people. They said he was looking for seven cities made of something hard and bright and yellow. Why he looked for these cities no one knew. Forty growing cycles passed and no more of these strangers came. But one day they appeared again. They, too, asked about the bright yellow substance, and the strangers who wore the long robes talked about a man who had died on crossed sticks. They carry small crossed sticks that they put their lips to, and they wanted us to put our lips to the crossed sticks also. Three of the long robes stayed in the villages near the Big River. They wanted the people to obey the crossed sticks, but the people killed them, and since then two more small groups have come and left." The old man paused. "What is the reason these new strangers come into the land?"

There was silence in the chamber. At length the old chief spoke again. "We will send more runners to keep us informed of what the pale strangers do. Perhaps then we learn their purpose."

"My husband," Rohona's young wife said as she ran to him when he stepped onto the roof of their dwelling. "Is it true what we have heard?"

"Yes," he answered unsmiling, "the pale ones have returned."

"What does it mean?" she asked, her eyes searching his face.

Rohona looked at her and his features softened as he reached out and stroked her shiny hair. "Do not be afraid, Kakuna," he said gently, "they will undoubtedly leave just as all the others have. We are safe here on our high rock home." He touched her cheek and then her slightly rounded stomach. "Let me see you smile again," he continued. "You have been so happy recently that I have become accustomed to see your face smiling, and now it bothers me to see the look of happiness gone from it."

She tried a valiant smile. "But I can't help be frightened of such creatures as are these pale ones," she said, a tremor in her voice.

"I remember when I had only five summers," Rohona spoke, "I caught a glimpse of a few that came up here on the rock. I was terrified. I thought they were terrible gods or animals, but," he added with a reassuring smile, "my grandfather told me they were just men—men with a different color of skin and hair and eyes—but they bled and died just like any human. When the very first ones came into the country almost fifty growing seasons ago, the people thought they were gods—they thought they were a part of the tall animals on which they sat, but they soon learned that they could be killed like any man." Rohona paused. "I am not afraid of them as men, but it is wise to know what they do here in our land."

Kakuna looked apprehensive again. "Will you be sent to gather information?"

Rohona smiled. "It is probable. But think, if I am one of the ones chosen to go, then you will have a firsthand report when I return—you will not have to hear the news from the other women."

Kakuna was not happy. "I do not like it."

"Nor do I like waiting for my supper," Rohona replied with slight chastisement.

The young woman's eyes widened. "Oh, husband, forgive me," she whispered and motioned toward one side of the roof where a fire had been made in the outdoor fireplace. "Our meal is ready." Now that summer was here, they ate and slept outside on the roof where it was fresh and cool.

Rohona knelt and Kakuna placed a pottery bowl in front of him. The aroma of venison, squash, and corn wafted upward from the dish and he smiled, pleased he had married a talented girl. She placed a stack of gray-blue *guayave* near his bowl of stew. The flat, highly polished baking stone sat in the fire. Kakuna knelt beside it and deftly smeared a bit of deer grease over the flat surface. She swirled the contents of an ochre-colored pottery bowl and quickly poured some of the thin blue-gray cornmeal batter onto the sizzling stone griddle, spreading the thin gruel with a corn cob over the smooth, hot stone. The edges of the batter curled up like paper, and when the sheetlike bread was done, she removed it from the griddle and added it to the stack near Rohona's bowl.

"Will you go down to the fields tomorrow?" she asked him as they began to eat.

"Yes, I shall have to be there for a few days. I will need food to take with me. The corn has sprouted and looks good. But the weeds also look good, so I shall have to take care of them."

The sun sank below West Mountain, and the pale intruders were forgotten as Rohona and Kakuna unrolled their hide and fur bed-bundles and lay down together on the terrace rooftop. Rohona pulled her toward him, caressed her cheek, and beneath the minute flickering lights that were scattered across the black, moonless night, he made her content that she was a woman.

When Rohona returned from tending the fields, another messenger arrived with more news of the pale strangers who were in their land. They were still travelling north, and they had reached Castixe, but still their purpose was not known. The runner, however, carried other, more disturbing news. The men they had seen who numbered thirty more or less were not alone. Many more of the pale strangers had entered the villages to the south. They had with them rolling baskets made of wood and many animals, some very strange indeed.

The men were gathered again in Mauharots. "Rohona is clever," one man spoke up, "like his namesake the jaguar-of-the-south. He can see what other men cannot. Let him go amongst the pale strangers and see if he can discover their purpose." There was general approval of the choice. Rohona *was* like his namesake—swift, untiring, canny, and fearless in the pursuit of his prey. He would see the pale men's purposes in their faces if he could not discover it by other methods.

Kakuna sat stiffly when she heard the news. Rohona reassured her as she packed food for him in a leather pouch. She stuffed parched corn, piñon nuts, jerked venison, and paper-bread into the pouch as if she were angry at it. She thrust the pouch at him. Rohona reached out and instead of taking the pouch of food, put his hand to her cheek and caressed it. Tears sprang to her eyes and slid down her cheeks. He wiped them away and pulled her to him.

"Forgive me," she whispered, "I do not like the thought of your journey."

"I will return soon."

But it was many days before he returned to his village perched on the flat mesa top. He had trotted for two days and arrived at Castixe at dark. He went immediately to the home of his mother's sister, who always made him welcome in that village. In Castixe they spoke Queres as they did with some modifications in Áco, but they could understand each other. It was not like the Tegua spoken at Caypa or the Tigua spoken at Tsugwevaga. The languages of those pueblos the Ácoma could not understand, and they had to use signs in order to talk or they had to find a person who could speak in both tongues. Rohona's aunt was delighted to see him and immediately brought him food as was the polite custom. When he had eaten and exchanged information about all the relatives, the subject went immediately to that which had brought him to the village.

"They were here two days ago," the aunt's husband said, making the sign for two with his fingers.

"Do you know for what reason they have come into our land?" Rohona asked.

"It's strange," the aunt's husband answered, "we do not fully understand." He paused and although Rohona was impatient to hear everything, he was polite enough to allow his uncle-in-law to take his time. The uncle continued. "The pale strangers found two men at Quigui who speak their language. These two came into the land with the last group of pale ones, but they stayed at Quigui and took Quigui women as wives. They are called Tomás and Cristóbal. They are big men now. They talk and tell us what the pale ones say, but what they say is very odd. They talk about giving us a man who died on a big stick, or 'Good Things to Hear.' They tell us about some pale chief who lives many, many moons to the east across a great expanse of water. This chief is to be our chief. They say this thing but it does not make sense."

"Where are they now?" Rohona asked, his dark eyes intense. "Where do they go?"

"They are still at Quigui," the uncle answered. "They always go to the north, but to where, no one knows."

"What does this mean?" Rohona asked. "That their chief will be our chief—when he lives so many moons away? I do not like these pale men coming into our land, bringing rolling baskets and many strange animals. What can they want?"

"They will undoubtedly leave like the others," the uncle said.

"Perhaps." Rohona was unconvinced. "But I have a feeling about these men. I fear their coming may bring harm to our land. They bring women and children. Is it not possible that they plan to stay?"

Before dawn the next day Rohona left the village that nestled at the base of the rocky mesa on the west side of the Big River. He swam the chilly, swiftly flowing stream and continued his journey on the opposite bank. Within an hour he came in sight of the village of Quigui that lay on the east bank of the river at the base of barren, strangely rounded hills that contrasted sharply with the tall, pine-robed mountains that jutted upwards behind them in the north. He kept to the river's edge among the cottonwoods, using the early morning shadows to conceal his presence.

The strangers had erected their odd cloth houses to the south of the village near the river's edge. Unusual cooking smells reached Rohona as did the strong odors of the tall animals they rode. He could see some of the pale strangers walking around the camp, but he was surprised at seeing dark faces among the light ones. Their features were heavier than the people of Rohona's land, and he surmised they must be natives from the south whom the pale ones had brought with them.

At that moment one of the pale strangers began walking directly toward him. With the silence of a jaguar's stalking step, Rohona pulled an arrow from his quiver and readied it in his bow. Had he been seen? The stranger kept walking straight ahead, directly toward where he crouched behind a cottonwood and willow brush. What did the man want? He carried no weapon in his hand and he walked without any concealment.

Rohona saw the man's eyes and thought he must be a witch, and he wished he had rubbed ashes on himself that morning. The eyes were odd and terrifying, so pale blue they appeared as if they blended into the white. The man must surely have died at some time before and have now come back to walk the earth. The white eyes were cruel and cold and seemed to be staring through everything they looked at. The man glanced in Rohona's direction, but it was obvious that he did not see him concealed there.

Red bristly hair sprouted on the man's face and covered his head. He was so close Rohona could see the red hairs on the backs of the man's hands. Suddenly the man stopped, not more than three arm's lengths away. Rohona's bow was poised, the string pulled taut. *I should kill you,* he thought. It would be a simple matter. An arrow through the neck severing the big vein. The man would drop dead in his tracks, no sound made other than the crumpling of the body as it sank to the ground. But Rohona did not release the arrow; instead, he saw the man free himself from his clothing and relieve his full bladder there in the brush. When he had done, he turned and started back toward the camp.

*I want to see them gone,* Rohona said to himself. *They will bring nothing but misery to this land.* Silently he continued upstream and entered the village of Quigui, determined to find the reason the strangers had come.

Four days later Rohona was still at Quigui. Something was in the air. People were pouring in from all the surrounding villages. Food was being prepared in great quantities. Rohona had been unable to talk to the two men, Tomás and Cristóbal, who spoke the strangers' language, for they were always with them, but the two men had told the people to prepare for a ceremony, which was necessary that their chiefs attend. Rohona would be there, too, although the strangers would not know a man of Áco was in their midst.

On the hard-packed earthen floor toward the back of the crowd that had gathered in the *kiva* of Quigui, Rohona sat inconspicuously. A tall, gray-haired man descended the ladder, his back to the rungs. Rohona was shocked. Only the Koshari or Tsitsunits were allowed to enter that way. It was bad luck for anyone else to enter the *kiva* thus, but the tall gray-haired man had presence, and it was easy to ascertain that he was the leader.

Among the pale, metal-plated strangers who entered the *kiva*, Rohona recognized the man with the red hair that sprouted on his face, the one whom he could have killed so easily. He did not like the man with the pale eyes; he knew deep within himself that he and the pale-eyed man were enemies.

Vicente looked at the expressionless faces of the heathen who sat in the stuffy *kiva*. He hated them. He hated their dark eyes that revealed nothing of their thoughts. He hated their ability to appear disinterested and unafraid. His pale eyes moved around the room trying to discern any emotion whatever on the dark faces. There was none. And they all looked the same—how would one ever tell the difference between one savage and another?

The governor began to speak. His words were slow, and he paused carefully, allowing the interpreters time to render his words into the native tongue. With elegant motions, he addressed the assembled group, among whom were seven chiefs from surrounding villages.

"The most powerful ruler in the world, the King of Spain, has sent me to you that your souls might be saved and that you might be this ruler's subjects in order that he might protect you and bring justice and a better way of life to you." The governor sought a sign of comprehension on the natives' faces as the translator spoke but saw none. He continued. "All this the great King is doing for you at tremendous expense and enormous effort, and it behooves you that of your own free will you accept this King and render obedience and submission to me his emissary, Don Juan de Oñate, who acts in his name."

Again the faces of the natives showed nothing. The governor's voice rose. "By giving yourselves in vassalage to the greatest ruler on earth, you will live a peaceful, contented life, protected from your enemies, and your food will be abundant with new kinds of crops and new animals to raise. You must know also," he said authoritatively, "the main purpose that persuaded the mighty ruler Don Felipe to send me as his emissary to this land: the salvation of your souls! Know ye that your bodies have souls that do not die even though the body may. If you receive the water of Holy Baptism your soul will live eternally in great bliss with God Almighty in heaven, but if you do not accept the holy water of baptism and do not become good Christians, you will go into the bowels of the earth to live for eternity in Hell, suffering the most cruel and everlasting torment."

He paused, then continued. "This religion will be taught to you by the most reverend Father Commissary, the vicar of his Holiness the Pope, who is God's ruler here on earth, and by the reverend fathers who have come with him from the Seraphic Order of St. Francis. You must obey and revere the holy fathers and take them to your villages so that they may teach you the ways of righteousness in order that you may escape the pain of Hell. You must treat them well, support them, and obey them in all things."

Oñate paused and instructed the translators to allow a moment for the chiefs and people gathered to discuss what he had said. His eyes scanned the dimly lit ceremonial chamber trying to judge the reception of his words, but there was nothing in the faces nor in the tone of the words they spoke that gave any indication as to how his words had been received.

Rohona sat motionless, his face a mask of stone betraying nothing of the anger that consumed him. How could the chiefs even consider submitting to this stranger who had so suddenly appeared in their land? Why were they afraid of this place called Hell that the gray-hair spoke of? Iyatiku had come up from below the ground to live on earth. She had never told them of this Hell underground where people suffered cruel and everlasting torment. Iyatiku was their mother; she cared for them. She would not let this happen. How could the chiefs do this? He wanted to shout "No!" but his was not the place to voice his opinions in the *kiva* of Quigui.

The chief of Quigui rose and spoke to Tomás and Cristóbal. In turn the interpreters relayed the message to Oñate: the chiefs agreed to accept this king who lived so far away. They could see no harm in it.

The governor smiled. He could scarcely believe their answer. This had been far easier than he had ever imagined. For a moment he felt gratitude toward the natives who submitted so docilely to him and made his job so easy, but scarcely had that emotion surfaced in his chest when another rose to take its place. He fought to keep the contempt he felt from showing on his face. What kind of men would allow a small handful of others to come into their land and subjugate them without so much as lifting a finger? Perhaps they did not realize just what they were agreeing to. He would make it abundantly clear to them. He spoke again, his voice reverberating in the chamber.

"You must realize exactly to what you have agreed. Let there be no misunderstanding. By rendering obedience and vassalage to Don Felipe II, the King our lord, you will be subject to his will, orders, and laws that I as his emissary shall declare and enforce. Let it be known that if you do not comply with and observe them, you will be severely punished as transgressors of the commands of your King and master. Therefore," Oñate paused, looking intently at the chiefs seated in front of him, "reflect carefully upon your decision and know what it requires: absolute acceptance of and submission to Spanish authority."

The translators finished rendering the governor's words into the native tongues, and the reply was likewise transmitted to Oñate. The natives understood everything and would submit to his majesty and become his vassals.

Don Juan smiled. There was a touch of condescension at the corners of his lips. "Now, as a sign of your submission, fall to your knees and render obedience and vassalage in the name of his majesty."

The chiefs arose and knelt in front of the governor as the translators ordered. When all had assumed the submissive position, Oñate continued, his tone imperious. "As proof of your vassalage and submission, kiss the hand of the Father Commissary in the name of God, and that of myself, the Governor of *Nuevo México*, Don Juan de Oñate, in the name of his majesty the King of Spain."

There was complete silence in the chamber. The seven chiefs in turn kissed the hand of the Father Commissary and that of the governor.

All eyes were on the act of submission of the chiefs, and none noticed the dark eyes toward the back of the chamber as they flashed with hatred and fury.

Rohona knew now why the strangers had come into their land.

# Chapter 12

He pulled aside the tent flap and stepped inside.

"Oh, Maese!" she cried as she looked up from where she lay on the bed. She pushed herself up and ran to him, throwing her arms around his neck and clinging to him so she would not fall. Tears made grimy rivulets down her dust-covered cheeks, and she sobbed as she buried her face against his leather-covered chest.

The Maese de Campo was caught by surprise at her action, and for a moment his hands remained at his sides, but then his arms went around her, and he held her as her shoulders shook. He trembled imperceptibly as he felt her body pressed against him, clinging to him, and he wished for the leather doublet he wore to be gone so that he might feel more distinctly the softness that sent agony through his nerves. It had been so long since he had held a woman in his arms.

One of the Maese's hands went to her tousled hair and smoothed it gently. She seemed scarcely able to stand. He bent his head slightly so that his cheek rested against her hair, and he closed his eyes to better savor the moment. Her sobs eased, but still she leaned against him. Then she brought both hands to her cheeks to wipe away the tears, smudging her face even more in the process.

"I'm sorry," she whispered, her eyes downcast, her body swaying.

The Maese's hands dropped to his sides, and he smiled at her as he looked at her tear- and dust-stained face. He lifted her chin gently. When her large gray eyes, fringed with wet black lashes, rested on his, he felt his composure weaken. How could one woman be so beautiful?

*"Señora,"* he said properly but gently, "there is nothing to be sorry for. I have heard the terrible trials the cart train underwent crossing the *Jor-*

*nada del Muerto*. I have heard that you would scarcely eat or drink. You have no reason to be sorry for a few tears."

He took her hand, looked at the long slender fingers and realized how thin she had become. Veins made a faint network on the backs of her hands, and he looked up at her, unable to keep the concern from showing in his features. He had been so taken by seeing her again that until now he had not noticed the shadows under her eyes nor the hollows in her cheeks that made the fine bone structure of her face more prominent.

"Fabia sent me," he said quietly. "She told me . . ." his words trailed off. María Angélica swayed as if she might fall, and the Maese reached out and took hold of her. He led her to a chair and pulled one near for himself. "Sit," he said gently and she complied. He spoke again as he held her hand. His voice was filled with concern.

"You must eat, María Angélica." He had dropped the *"señora"* with which he had been addressing her. "There is food now. I have brought many provisions for the cart train. The natives have been generous, and there is plenty now. You must preserve your strength."

As if she had been waiting, Fabia stepped into the tent, a bowl in her hands. She pulled up a stool and sat down beside her. "Come, *querida*, eat a little soup," the old woman cajoled.

"No, please," María Angélica said, but the Maese nodded for her to take it and she complied.

Fabia held a spoonful of the soup up, and María Angélica swallowed the liquid. The old woman continued to feed her as if she might have been a child, and she did not protest although spots of color tinged her cheeks. Suddenly the young woman put her hand to her mouth and ran behind the curtain.

They heard the sound of retching, and the Maese came quickly to his feet, concern etched on his face. Fabia put a hand on his arm. *"Por favor,* wait," she whispered and ducked behind the curtain where the young woman knelt, bent over a chamber pot, as her stomach rejected the soup she had just eaten.

Fabia wet a cloth and wiped María Angélica's face and helped her lie down, placing another damp cloth on her forehead. Fabia ducked around the curtain and approached the Maese. Her voice was scarcely more than a whisper. "The *señora* is starving herself to death."

"My God in heaven," he answered, stunned. "Surely it cannot be."

"Yes," the old woman whispered, "I don't know how many days it has been since she has kept anything down. If something is not done soon she is going to die."

His face was a stark white. "Can't you do something, Fabia?"

"I have tried, but nothing has worked. She will not eat for me. At times I think she has lost the will to live." Fabia's dark old eyes looked at him intently. "I think she will make the attempt if you are here, Maese, just as she did today. You must help me. But," the old woman added, "we have to go more slowly."

"I will do whatever you tell me, Fabia. She cannot die. God will not permit it."

*"Ojalá,"* the old woman whispered.

For the rest of the day, the Maese de Campo was in and out of María Angélica's tent. He ordered the caravan to rest and remain camped for several more days although there were those who wished to proceed and catch up with the governor and the advance group of soldiers.

Between checking the caravan and seeing to his duties, he stopped at the Vizcarra tent. When he entered, Fabia was close behind him with a bowl of broth.

María Angélica protested when the old woman sat down on the edge of the bed where she lay. "Please, Fabia, no. I am not hungry."

The Maese pulled a chair close and sat by her bed. He picked up her hand and held it between his own. "Please," he urged, "eat a bite for me." She saw the concern on his face, and then he laughed. "Please," he said again, "you know your *dueña*. She won't let me rest unless you eat."

After María Angélica had eaten a few spoonfuls, he began to chat lightly about the villages of natives they had seen.

He left the tent but every so often would reappear, and Fabia would be behind him with a bowl of broth.

In the evening he came and stayed longer. "I brought a *folleto* of popular plays that Captain Farfán had. Would you like for me to read one to you?"

"Oh, yes," she said, "that sounds wonderful." She felt a little stronger, and his presence gave her strength, too. She found herself watching his long tapered hands as they held the *folleto*. How much better a book looked in them than a sword, she thought. She watched his expressive, chestnut-bearded face as he read. Occasionally he would look up at her, and his clear brown eyes would smile at her. She smiled in return, and he quickly resumed his reading.

At last he rose. "I must not interfere with your rest and recovery," he said quietly.

She felt suddenly abandoned, and not wanting to lose the security his presence gave her, she reached out. He took her hand and brought it to his lips, placing a light kiss on it, and he bid her good night. *"Buenas noches."* But her fingers clutched his and their eyes held for a brief moment, and he brought her hand to his lips again, and that kiss was not as light as the first had been. *"Duérmete bien,"* he spoke softly.

She lay back on her pillow, a slight flush on her cheeks. He had used the familiar form of address with her. At that moment Fabia stepped up to the bed.

"Where have *you* been all evening?" María Angélica asked.

"Just inside the tent door, mending some poor stockings that scarcely have anything left to mend," Fabia answered. So she had been there the whole time. She must have heard his words. Fabia must have heard him use the familiar form to address her.

The following day she felt stronger, and when Juan de Zaldívar came, he did not have to urge her to eat. She ate a small cup of barley broth, and when she looked up, he was smiling at her. Fabia had gone to one side of the tent and was going through a trunk as if occupied.

María Angélica smiled at him. "See what a good girl I am?"

"Yes, I see," he answered with a light laugh.

Then her face sobered. "Thank you, Maese," she said, "I think perhaps you have saved my life."

"I thank *Dios* that he granted me the privilege of being here with you," he murmured.

The following day she asked the Maese not to delay the departure of the cart train any longer because of her. She said she would walk, but Fabia protested, and he insisted she ride in the *carreta*. Several times during the day he rode back to her cart and inquired about her strength, but he could tell from her gray eyes whose luster was beginning to return that she was faring better, and he felt thankful.

As their journey continued northward along the river, in the evenings when they camped, the Maese and sometimes Dorotea came to her tent, and they would talk until it was bedtime. On the evenings when Dorotea was not there, old Fabia acted as chaperone, and from her reputation, no one in the cart train would have entertained the slightest thought that there was anything improper in Juan de Zaldívar's visits. Fabia commanded the respect of all the colonists from the lowest Tlascalan Indian to the governor himself. But María Angélica had noticed a difference in Fabia's manner. Always before she had been like an old mother hen, hovering near should any danger—particularly of the male kind—come near her baby chick. Always before she felt Fabia had breathed down her neck if any man were present, but now on the evenings that the Maese came to visit, the old woman seemed to make herself inconspicuous in some corner. She appeared to fall asleep.

He also noticed the change, for he commented on it one evening. "I do believe old Fabia trusts me now," he said with a smile.

The day's travel no longer seemed as tiresome because she had the pleasure of the Maese's company in the evenings. He related all the details of the journey—how they found Tomás and Cristóbal, how the natives at the place they named Socorro gave them a great quantity of much needed corn, how the governor was preparing for the first ceremony of submission of the villages when he sent him to bring the cart train to meet them.

She told the Maese what their crossing the deadly plain of the *Jornada del Muerto* had been like, and when she could not restrain the tears that the memory brought, he wiped them away, and she closed her eyes as he gently dried her cheeks. When she recounted one of the few comic occurrences of the journey, she laughed and placed her hand on his arm. He covered her hand with his, and they sat there for long silent moments, each as if not wishing to destroy the contact with the other. It was the Maese who removed his hand first, and it had seemed with regret.

At first when he bid her good night, he would take her hand, bring it to his lips, and place a light kiss on it. But now his lips lingered.

Late one afternoon as camp was made, huge clouds piled up in the sky and turned indigo as the sun began to sink behind the western mountains. It was already raining on the slopes. Dark bands of blue reached the ground in numerous places along the horizon, and as darkness descended, lightning lit the sky, increasing in frequency as the storm approached. María Angélica stood outside the tent and looked at the ominous clouds.

"Oh, Fabia," she said to the old woman as she came around the corner of the tent, "do you think the frieze can withstand a heavy rain?"

Fabia patted her hand in reassurance. "I have doubled the anchors, *querida*, I think it should be all right." Then she laughed. "I'm certainly glad to see it rains in this *desierto*."

María Angélica smiled as she turned to enter the tent. "Yes, I suppose we should be thankful for moisture."

Just as the first fat drops began to fall, the Maese stepped into the tent. He had scarcely commented, "It looks like we are going to get a soaking!" before the rain began in earnest. It came in sheets driven by the wind, and the sound in the tent was deafening.

"I am going to check the cart," Fabia shouted and started for the door.

"No," he said, "you stay here. Let me do it."

Fabia blocked the tent door. "No," she said with emphasis, "you stay here with the *señora*. I will check it." The old woman took a breath and said pointedly, "I won't be back until the rain is over." She ducked out the door, and the Maese grabbed the tent flap and secured it against the pounding rain.

He turned and looked at María Angélica. Her gray eyes were wide with some emotion. Fear? Astonishment? He could not tell. The rain that had been deafening suddenly slackened and they both seemed to relax. She smiled nervously at him, but just as quickly as it had eased, a new onslaught of wind-driven rain battered the tent and she trembled visibly as the frieze swayed. A flash of brilliant lightning illuminated the sky and for an instant made it appear daylight in the tent. The bolt of lightning was so near that almost instantaneously, a thundering crack rent the air, and she fell to her knees as she crossed herself and began to pray. The Maese knelt beside her and put his arm protectively around her shoulders as he watched her in the flickering light of the tallow candle.

Sheets of rain pounded the tent and continuous barrages of cracking thunder drowned out the prayers that came from her lips. Water began to seep under the edges of the tent and the candle flickered out. She trembled with fear and prayed more fervently to the Mother of God. The Maese took her by the shoulders and lifted her to a standing position.

"Come," he shouted so that he would be heard above the thunder. "Come. Sit on the bed. The water will soon cover the floor."

They groped their way to the bed and she sat down, pulling her skirts up around her feet and tucking them under her. He sat down beside her, and when he pulled her close to him and put his arm protectively around her shoulders, it seemed the most natural action in the world. And when she leaned, trembling, against him and her head came to rest against his chest, that, too, seemed natural. No longer did she feel afraid. The darkness was a protective shroud and the only thought or feeling she had was one of security. It was a warm, rich sensation, and she felt a contentment that she had not experienced since so very long ago. She felt no surprise when the Maese turned his face and buried it in her hair. When his lips touched her temple and his hand went to her cheek in a gentle caress, she was not startled.

In a movement with the smoothness of rich, dark honey falling from the edge of a spoon, they lay backwards on the bed. He caressed her cheek and placed his lips on her temple. She felt him raise his head and then she felt his lips on hers in a light kiss that brushed her lips quickly and then was gone. She felt his beard against her face and his hand buried in her hair, and she felt her own hand resting on his side. They no longer noticed the deafening noise of the wind and rain and thunder, for the sense of hearing had been subordinated to those of taste and touch and smell. Everything the Maese did was born of gentleness, and she had no fear. When the Maese held her face in his hands and kissed her eyelids, when his fingers traced the outline of her ears, when his lips nestled in the curve of her neck and caressed her there, or when his hand moved softly over her breast and down the curve of her body, she felt like silken ribbons fluttering gently in the breeze. Her fear of the journey flowed from her and exhaustion consumed her. She felt safe, secure. Time had no more reality than death as they lay there, and when sleep overtook her, it was not recognized, for all had seemed like dreaming.

* * *

She awoke to a gentle shaking and to old Fabia's papery voice. "Angelita, Angelita, it is time to arise."

Her eyes fluttered open, reality still a stranger to her mind. She saw Fabia's age- and sun-wrinkled face smiling at her, and she returned the smile feeling as if she were a girl again and Fabia had handed her her morning cup of frothy hot chocolate.

Only when the old woman said, "You have slept a long time, child," did the vague memory of the previous night seep back into her mind. Quickly she glanced around expecting to see the Maese there, but the bed was empty and she still wore the dress she had worn the previous evening, though a light cotton blanket was now spread over her. She glanced with embarrassment at Fabia, a look of incomprehension in her eyes.

The old woman smiled. "The Maese assured me that there was no impropriety last night when you were alone together. He said you fell asleep, Angelita, in the midst of the rain and thunder. I marveled that you could go to sleep so soundly while the heavens were rent asunder." The old woman grinned. "I think the Maese marveled at it, too! But, I'm glad you had a good night's sleep, *querida*. You have been in much need of rest and security. The Maese is a good man. Perhaps too good." María Angélica's face was red with embarrassment.

"Because of the rain," the old woman continued, "the carts are unable to travel until the ground has dried sufficiently. The Maese said he will let us know at noon if we travel any distance today, and since the sun is almost at its peak now, I thought you should awaken if we are indeed to continue our journey this afternoon."

"You mean it is almost noon?" María Angélica asked as she threw back the cotton blanket and swung her feet onto the ground.

"*Sí*, as I said, the *señora* was much in need of rest, and I thank the Maese that he made you feel so safe that sleep came easily to you."

María Angélica glanced up at Fabia, but the old face told her nothing. Fabia reached out and smoothed María Angélica's tousled hair.

At noon the order came that they would remain camped until the following morning. The ground was still muddy enough to make it difficult for the carts and the oxen that must bear the burden of pulling them.

María Angélica did not see Juan de Zaldívar that day and by evening she was tense and nervous. She scarcely touched her dinner, and when Fabia asked pointedly, "Am I going to have to get the Maese again?" she started as if she had touched her finger to a hot iron.

"No," she said. "I will eat." She had scarcely finished her food when he appeared. She was caught by surprise, and stood quickly, her face lighting up. A smile spread across his face as well, but before her features could register embarrassment, he had crossed the short space between them and took her in his arms. Fabia's presence there did not seem to bother him.

María Angélica's face was buried against the Maese's chest, and she felt his lips brush her temple. She felt him lift his head, and he spoke to the old woman.

"Well, Fabia," he said lightly as he smoothed María Angélica's hair, "how has our sleepyhead been today?"

The old woman chuckled. "Fine, Maese, just fine." She added, "Can I get the *señor* some food or drink?"

"Thank you, but no. I've already eaten."

"Then please won't you be seated?"

He released María Angélica and smiled at her. "You are loved deeply," he said, touching her cheek. "Fabia knows that I would give my life before I would harm you or see harm come to you. She and I want only your happiness. I would die a happy man if only I were allowed to gaze on you from time to time or if you would favor me with a smile. That is all I ask of you—ever." María Angélica raised her eyes to his.

"How beautiful you are," he said as he cupped her face in his hands, "and how my heart is filled with love for you. Tell me only what you wish of me."

Her voice trembled as she spoke in a scarcely audible whisper. "But, Maese, I wish nothing." A look of deep regret and sadness spread across his face, and she added quickly, "I, too, wish only for your happiness."

"You, beautiful lady," he said sadly, "are the only thing that can give me happiness. That you wish nothing of me is the source of my greatest unhappiness."

"I wish your presence, Maese," she whispered.

# Chapter 13

On August 18, 1598, toward evening, the cart train reached the pueblo of Ohké, rechristened San Juan de los Caballeros, chosen by Don Juan de Oñate as the first capital of his new kingdom of *Nuevo México*. Of the eighty-three carts that had set forth from the valley of Santa Bárbara many months and many leagues ago, only sixty-one arrived in the new capital. The guns boomed deafeningly and shouts of joy filled the air. The Maese had brought the cart train north; the colonists and remainder of the soldiers were finally to be reunited with the advance guard.

María Angélica pushed a wisp of hair from her face and smoothed her hands over the dusty skirt of her dress as she looked at her new home in the distance. Dwellings rising three and four stories caught the lengthening rays of the sun and appeared golden against the green of scattered cottonwoods and the purple of the hills behind. A hard knot formed in her stomach. The sight she had so longed for those many months did not fill her with the joy that she had imagined it would. She felt instead an enormous sense of dread.

More than the village, it was other thoughts that disturbed her. The thought of her husband revolted her as did the thought of the Maese's brother, the cruel-faced Sergeant Major. The thought of the governor's suggestive flattery, the malevolent look on the scarred face of Isidro Inojosa, all made her shudder.

She had grown accustomed to the Maese's presence, sharing her evenings with him while Fabia sat quietly in a corner as if asleep. She had no idea whether the old woman slept or not, but she did not care. She and the Maese would read to each other or talk. He would hold her hand against his cheek or against his heart, and his eyes would caress her face.

But the caresses of that night of rain and thunder had not been repeated on the long evenings as the cart train made its way north.

On the previous night, however, the night before they were to reach San Juan, he had come to her tent as he had done each night of the journey. He seemed quieter than usual and there was sadness in his eyes. His manner filled her with a pain she could scarcely endure, and tightness constricted her chest. There were long, heavy pauses in their conversation and upon more than one occasion, her eyes clouded with tears, and Fabia left the tent.

It became late and still they sat there, only intermittent conversation breaking the silence. The Maese had not held her hand nor touched her cheek. At length he spoke. "I promised myself I would ask nothing of you, but I no longer care anything for my honor this evening." His eyes searched her face, and she felt her body tremble.

"May I hold you once more before we reach the village?" he asked, his voice soft and anguished.

"Oh, please," she whispered, "hold me and put your lips on mine." The look on Juan de Zaldívar's face filled her with such emotion that she felt as if she were being torn apart. She saw his hands tremble slightly as he reached to take her in his arms, and she felt his lips tremble as he covered her mouth with his. Her body molded against him and her arms went round his neck, and her tears made his cheeks as wet as hers.

There was urgency and necessity in his kiss. And then he lifted her into his arms and carried her unprotesting to the bed. Gently he laid her down and sat on the edge of the bed beside her. He cupped her face in his hands and covered it with kisses. He unlaced her bodice, baring her breasts, and there was no movement in her body as if she were no longer breathing. Tentatively his hands reached out and touched her, and she trembled visibly; his lips descended to her breasts.

As if pulled away from her by invisible hands, the Maese sat back, a deep groan wrenched from his throat. "God forgive me," he whispered. "I made a vow to *Dios* that I would not make you an adulteress. I love you too much to cause you to break God's commandment. Take my life, *Dios,* before I make this woman, whom I love more than my life itself, commit a sin."

She sat up and touched his face. "I love you," she whispered, "I love you, Maese."

He took her in his arms, and rocked back and forth, cradling her. She had no idea how long they sat embraced. Gently he fastened her bodice as she sat there numbly. When he finished, he took her into his arms again and stroked her hair as her head lay against his chest.

"I love you, Maese," she whispered pitifully. She wanted to say more, but no other words came forth.

"God, how I love you, too," he said softly. Then he pushed himself up abruptly and left the tent.

She crumpled to the bed sobbing, suffering pain she thought not possible. She felt a hand on her shoulder and heard Fabia speak. "Angelita, do not cry. Come, let's get dressed for bed."

María Angélica sat up and fell into the old woman's arms. "I love the Maese, Fabia," she whispered with anguish, "I love him. What on earth am I going to do?"

"I know you do, *querida*," the old woman spoke, but she left María Angélica's question unanswered.

The next day as they trudged the last few leagues toward San Juan, she caught sight of the Maese only a few times, but that evening as she stood looking at the village in the distance, he rode up and dismounted.

"Well," he said softly as he nodded in the direction of the village, "there it is—our new home."

"Yes," she murmured, "it is not the joyous sight I had expected it to be."

"Nor is it to me," he replied. The sadness she could not bear filled his eyes. "You are the only joyous sight for me."

She whispered softly, "You once said, Maese, that I could have your presence whenever I should wish it."

"Yes, that is true," he answered, his voice low and husky.

She raised her eyes to his. "Things will not be the same. There will be a great deal of work now that we are at the village, but, please, do not deny me your presence."

"I would not deny you my life."

He left her and rode to the front of the column to lead the weary caravan into the village. The Indians of the pueblo watched them approach, some from ground level, many perched on rooftops. She saw the gray-haired leader standing in front of the men who had accompanied him. She could not make out any others. A deafening volley was fired by the arquebusiers, and loud shouts filled the valley air. The natives watched in silence as the two groups were joyously reunited.

She stood unmoving by her cart. She did not hear Vicente approach. A small gasp escaped her throat as he grabbed her and swung her around. Roughly he covered her mouth with his in a harsh kiss, and then he let go of her and pulled something from a pouch, not noticing her hand as it wiped the repugnant kiss from her mouth.

"Look," he said loudly, his pale eyes strangely intense, "look at the ore we have found! We will be rich." He shoved his hand toward her, but all she saw was a handful of nondescript rock.

She tried to smile. "I'm very happy for you."

He shoved the rocks back into the pouch and swung her around again. She pushed helplessly against his chest. "Please, let me go. You are embarrassing me."

He laughed harshly and continued to swing her until she was quite dizzy. When he set her on the ground, she could scarcely keep her balance and fell against him.

"That's better! I knew my little wife had missed me!"

She had just recovered from her encounter with her husband when another voice startled her. She turned to see the governor smiling and making a deep bow toward her.

"Ah, the angel of the caravan," he said, stepping forward, taking her hand, and bringing it to his lips. "What a delight to the senses to see you once more. How I have missed the loveliness of your face these past three months. It scarcely seems possible that it was the twenty-second of May that I last saw you—and now it is August."

"God has been merciful to us, Governor," she murmured.

"Indeed He has," Oñate said, "and tomorrow being the feast of the blessed San Luís Obispo, we shall offer him great thanks for the safe arrival of the cart train." He paused. "And I shall add a special thanks that he has brought you safely here."

"That is very kind of you, Governor," she said, trying to keep her tone polite.

"Come," Oñate said, taking her arm and placing it in his. "Come," he repeated, "you must see your new quarters. I saw to it that you and Captain Vicente received one of the best dwellings." He glanced toward Vicente who stood nearby showing the ore to a group of soldiers who had gathered about. Don Juan smiled at her. "Your husband is adamant we will find gold."

"I know, but as we are told, it is better to store up riches in heaven than here on earth."

"Yes," the governor allowed, "but many good works for the greater glory of God have been accomplished with riches stored up on this earth." She did not respond and remained silent as he led her to the earth-colored dwellings.

"This," he announced proudly, "is your new home. A doorway has been made here on the ground floor for your convenience." He pointed toward the other buildings nearby where Indians stood on the roof. "See," he said, "the heathen do not have doorways on the first floor, so it is necessary to climb a ladder onto the roof and then descend by another ladder into the ground-floor room."

"How odd," she said as she glanced about.

"But it's not so odd as you might think. It's for defense. If the village is attacked, they merely raise the ladders and the village is like a simple fort. Now that we are here, fortifications are no longer necessary. Our arms are far superior to native weapons."

She shuddered at the prospect of bloodshed. Oñate patted her hand and smiled benignly at her. "Dear *señora*," he breathed, "I would never let any harm come to you. But we have been very fortunate to have received the vassalage of many villages without the slightest reluctance of any native. Indeed, they have accepted our dominion joyously. The heathen in this land are all as docile as children."

She heard the condescension in his voice as he continued. "They will be good workers for us. With their labor we shall build a worthy kingdom in these lands."

"I thank God that our reception by the natives has been so peaceful," she said. "Perhaps He has made them docile toward us so that they may quickly receive the salvation that the holy fathers bring them. *Dios* must desire greatly to have the natives of this land as *His* children."

"Indeed He must," Oñate added smoothly. "Now," he continued, "won't you step inside and survey your new home?"

She entered the cool dark room, straining to see in the dim interior. A musty smell enveloped her, and the only spot of light in the room came from a square opening in the ceiling through which the pale evening sky was visible.

"There are several rooms on the ground floor, one behind the other," he said, taking her arm again. Both she and the governor were startled by the voice that came from behind them at the entrance of the dwelling.

"Ah, there you are, Angelita," Fabia spoke.

Oñate laughed when he realized who it was, but the laugh was taut. "I see your *dueña* is still as watchful as ever."

"Yes," María Angélica said, "nothing escapes her, not even when she is sleeping."

"Well," he said smoothly, "since you are here, old watchful one, perhaps you, too, would like to see where your mistress will be living so that you may plan how best to keep her safe."

Fabia gave a noncommittal grunt and followed the governor and María Angélica into the back rooms as they inspected the house. When they returned to the entrance, Don Juan excused himself.

"Unfortunately, angelic lady, my duties call, but I am looking forward to seeing your lovely face later at the banquet that has been prepared for your arrival." The kiss he placed on her hand lingered too long, and María Angélica withdrew her hand.

With the governor's departure, she felt a tiny spark of excitement begin to flicker within her. After the long, grueling journey, she actually had a roof over her head, a home to call her own. It did not occur to her that only a few weeks previously it had been someone else's. Had it, she might have wondered whether the owners were pleased to give it up to strangers.

"Fabia," she said quickly, "get some candles so we can better see what it is like in here."

The following day their possessions were brought into their new home, and she worked alongside Fabia and the other servants cleaning, moving furniture, and unpacking until she was exhausted. When a carved rosewood bedstead was unloaded, María Angélica ran her hands over the smooth wood. What a luxury that bed would seem after the one that had sufficed during the journey.

"I want one of the upper rooms for a bedroom," she told the young *mestizo* who was Fabia's helper. "It's much too dark and stuffy in the ground-floor rooms. It will be much easier to catch a breeze up higher."

*"Sí, señora,"* he answered. He put the heavy carved headboard on his back and attempted to climb the ladder to the upper stories, but the combination of weight and unwieldiness made the task impossible. After several unsuccessful attempts, the young man begged her forgiveness for being unable to negotiate it up the ladder. Another servant came to help him make a new attempt, but that too proved unsuccessful.

"I'm afraid, Angelita," Fabia spoke, "that you must resign yourself to having your bedroom on the ground floor."

"No!" she replied adamantly. "Get some ropes and wrap blankets around the headboard. We will pull it up."

So by attaching ropes and resting the padded headboard against the ladder that served as a track, the young servant men were able to pull the rosewood bedstead up to the second floor, and so in the room off the terrace roof, María Angélica placed her ornately carved bed. She looked longingly at it and thought how wonderful sleep would be. But she shuddered when she thought about her husband.

Now that they had a home, they would have their separate bedrooms, as was the custom. She hoped that since she had chosen a room off the terrace and Vicente's room was down below that he would seek her bed less often. Still, she knew there was no way to avoid him.

The night before, the bed she had used during the journey was set up in the downstairs room, and she had fallen into it exhausted. She ached with fatigue, but sleep evaded her as she lay in fear, expecting Vicente to come in at any moment. She did not know when sleep had overtaken her, but in the morning when she awoke, she realized she had been spared. She was thankful for the reprieve.

She had not seen the Maese since the cart train reached their new capital. That evening when he arrived after supper, Fabia came up to her and whispered, "*Cuidado,* Angelita. Be careful that your face does not betray the love you feel."

Others, too, came to the house. The governor was there, drinking Vicente's *jerez,* which had arrived in the carts of the caravan. The Maese's brother came, his cold eyes so different from those of his older brother. Isidro Inojosa and the forty-year-old Captain Villagrá, whose dog, Blanco, had found water holes on the *Jornada,* also came.

She sat unobtrusively and listened to the men talk. They did not appear to notice her, so happy were they to be reunited with the others. She should have excused herself and left the men to their wine and words, but she could not bring herself to leave. It was the first time she had seen the Maese since they arrived. He sat across the room from her, and while she had no opportunity to speak with him, to merely look at him filled her with warmth. She knew he was aware of her presence also.

At first the men laughed and joked telling amusing incidents, but gradually the talk changed, and in spite of the Maese's presence, she began to feel an increasing apprehension.

Provisions were not as ample as she had been led to believe. She assumed they had been given sufficient food for the winter by the Indians at the pueblo the governor had named Socorro. From the talk of the men, however, she learned there was not even enough to get them through the fall. Would they starve as they almost had on the journey? She did not care then; now she did. She looked at the Maese's face in the candlelight of the room. She did not want to die now.

She heard the harshness of the Sergeant Major's voice. "There is already reluctance among the villages when Zubia goes to collect food supplies for us. To date there has been no outright refusal, but it is bound to come. It must be dealt with."

"And it will be," Oñate remarked coldly.

Vicente interrupted. "There is another matter that is going to require your attention, Governor, and that is your own soldiers. Although you pardoned Aguilar for disobeying your order not to enter any village, I would wager gold he is one of the main ones still fomenting discontent."

Oñate sat brooding, staring at the floor, as Vicente continued. "The journey was damnably long and hard. I know there are whispers of turning back, of returning to Mexico. *You* know it. It's easy to see that the land in this country is no more than a desert. It will never produce food in great quantities, and ground cover is so sparse it will never support great herds of cattle. Anyone can tell that. We have all seen the natives—they are poor and miserable.

"At the moment, it appears they raise only enough food for their own needs, and, save a few hides and coarse cotton for *mantas,* what products do they produce that we can buy cheaply and resell at lucrative prices in

Mexico? All in all you must admit the picture of a life of ease for this new kingdom of ours is bleak on all sides."

He paused but continued in spite of the frown on Don Juan's face. "The only hope we have is that we discover gold or the South Sea, which they say abounds in pearls. Ore has been taken from a few places but until it can be assayed, who can say if it holds any mineral worth? There must be no returning to Mexico until we find gold!"

Everyone nodded vigorously, the governor included. The wineskin was passed around again, and Villagrá spoke up. "Perhaps now that the carts are here, the soldiers' discontent will diminish."

"It is no better now that the carts are here," Isidro Inojosa interjected, his dark eyes as harsh as his voice. "As you wanted, Governor, my *mozo* has been keeping his ears open around the suspected malcontents. They only feel reinforced now that the others are here. Those that had to travel with the cart train are the ones who curse most vehemently the day they ever joined this expedition."

The Sergeant Major scowled. "Their curse should be for the mother who copulated with a he-goat to beget them. They are traitors to this expedition." Heads nodded in agreement.

Oñate sat staring at the hard, mud-packed floor before he looked up and spoke. "This expedition *will* succeed. Harsher methods must be used. I will not let a group of lazy, weak-livered troublemakers destroy the glory of my conquest. I will chain and publicly humiliate *anyone* who even breathes discontent!" His face had reddened, and he pounded his fist into his palm.

The others in the room, warmed by the liberal amount of sherry they had imbibed, assented loudly, but the Maese de Campo's words rose above the others for attention. "Our conquest *will* be glorious. God will assure it, but, Uncle, I urge you, be understanding and lenient for the moment. It has been a difficult journey for everyone. Give the discontented a chance to adjust to this new land."

María Angélica nodded in response to the Maese's words and felt the uneasiness that had been growing in her dissipate. Later that night, however, as she said her prayers, it returned. "What is in store for us, dear Lord?" she whispered with anxiety.

The governor was not given a chance to allow the malcontents time to adjust. They did not want time, for on the very next day a conspiracy to desert, led by Aguilar, was discovered by Isidro Inojosa's servant. Those involved were put in chains, and the governor said they would be hanged. Once again the Maese, the friars, the women, and some soldiers prevailed upon Don Juan to show leniency. Oñate reluctantly pardoned the conspirators and their lives were spared.

The people began to settle into their new homes and construction of a church was started. Working day and night with the help of uncounted natives, the walls went up and by the eighth day of September of that year of 1598, the church was ready for dedication. Dressed in their finest clothes, which had not been worn since the Act of Possession on the banks of the *Río del Norte* leagues to the south, the people gathered in the newly constructed edifice as the Father Commissary blessed it and consecrated the altar and chalices.

María Angélica took communion, having gone to confession the evening before. She prayed that she was in a state of grace. Her embarrassment had been acute and her voice trembled when she said, "Father, forgive me for I have sinned." She found that the words to describe the Maese's visits to her tent would not come from her lips, and she asked to be forgiven for unpure thoughts. She hoped that covered her situation. Thankfully there were many people to confess so that they might take communion at the dedication on the morrow, and the priest did not question her about her transgressions.

She saw the Maese take communion at the dedication service, and she had occasion to wonder what he had confessed. She found it difficult to believe that loving a man like him could be a sin, but she was troubled nonetheless. She did not like to consider the future. *That* unknown terrified her.

Elaborate festivities in honor of the dedication were held, and the natives looked on in awe at the sham battle between Moors and Christians. Her eyes never left the Maese de Campo as he showed his superb mastery of the art of horsemanship. Under his leather doublet, near his heart, she knew he carried a small piece of mulberry-colored silk ribbon.

"Please," he had whispered to her that morning after the dedication, "could this *caballero* beg a small token to carry with him into battle?"

She nodded and smiled and returned unnoticed to the dwelling that was now her home. She found a pair of scissors and snipped off a small piece of ribbon from the many that adorned her dress. Later that afternoon she held it in her palm when the Maese kissed her hand.

It touched him deeply that she had given him a token from the gown she wore, and he silently dedicated the battle to her.

At the banquet that night she had an opportunity to talk with him for a short while alone, the first in days. Nothing was said other than polite conversation, which would not have raised an eyebrow.

"I thoroughly enjoyed the battle, Maese," she said. Her words sounded stilted to her.

"Thank you, *señora,*" he replied formally.

"And the horsemanship was superb," she added.

"You are too kind."

"Oh, Maese," she started but could not continue, nor did he.

They sat there unspeaking and she found it difficult to keep from looking at him. He seemed tense, and occasionally he would look at her in a way that would make her blush and lower her eyes.

The succeeding days brought no more opportunities to talk with him, for everyone was occupied with the job of settling into their new capital. When she was outside her dwelling or at church, her eyes searched for him, but infrequently did they find that which they sought. When they did, he would nod or give a small bow, but out of propriety he did not smile at her.

Once houses were set in order, the women had the occasional luxury to pay visits to each other. Although they had lived in close proximity on the long journey, the requirements of the march precluded social intercourse of any refined nature, but now visits could be made. Although their *salas* had only mud floors, the dwellings were made into homes, and each woman made her living space as comfortable and attractive as her ingenuity and belongings would allow.

Dorotea and María Angélica visited each other as often as possible, and Doña Eufemia, the wife of the Ensign Peñalosa, started a weekly sewing session so that the women could chat and exchange gossip.

"You are looking much stronger," Doña Eufemia said to her at one of the first of the sewing sessions. Health was a constant topic of conversation; no one wanted to think about the graves that marked their long journey north.

"Thank you," María Angélica replied, "*gracias a Dios* my health has returned. I owe it to Fabia's skill." She could not mention the name of the other person who had given her the will to live. The women nodded.

"Yes," Diego de Zubia's wife concurred, "your *vieja* is truly gifted." She patted her large abdomen. "I hope when my time comes that she will be able to assist me."

"Of course," María Angélica assured her.

That fall the natives harvested their crops and food was abundant for the moment, but María Angélica knew there was concern that it would not be sufficient to last the winter. She had heard the men talk although the women appeared ignorant of the status of the colony's food. She did not know whether they were simply fooling themselves or whether their husbands kept them uninformed. Surely they knew the status of their own storerooms.

One morning shouts and bugle calls brought everyone from their quarters.

"Someone has stolen horses!" shouted one of the *caballerizos*.

The Maese ordered an immediate review. The soldiers poured forth from their dwellings and formed in lines. When all were at attention, the

Sergeant Major shouted the names, reading from the muster roll clamped in his hands.

"Abeyta, José," he shouted.

*"Presente."*

"Acevedo, Manuel!"

*"Presente."*

The list was completed. There had been no response to four names. Juan González, Manuel Portugués, Juan Rodrígues and his younger brother were unaccounted for. They were nowhere to be found.

The goveror was livid with rage, cursing viciously in spite of the presence of women. He managed to bring himself under control. "Leniency is no longer possible," he shouted so there would be no mistaking his words. "From this time forward the justice I mete out for desertion, conspiracy, or disobeyal of orders will be swift and harsh. My ears will hear no pleas for mercy. None!"

He detailed a group to go after the deserters. "Villagrá, you and Captain Márquez will lead the detail." In a booming voice, he gave the deserters' sentence. "On my order you will behead them the moment they are apprehended, and you will bring back the right hand of each traitor so that all may know that they received their just punishment."

A hush fell over the group of colonists and soldiers, and the only voices heard were those of Captain Villagrá and Márquez who acknowledged the governor's order.

The village was subdued for a day or two following the desertion. People spoke in scarcely more than whispers. One morning the governor ordered all the colonists and soldiers to gather in the open area near their quarters. He mounted a *carreta* so that all might hear his words. The people gathered slowly, their steps heavy.

"What is it this time?" Dorotea asked María Angélica wearily.

"I don't know," she answered, "I haven't heard a thing."

The governor held up his arms and his voice boomed. "I order the Sergeant Major to take fifty soldiers and make an expedition into the land of the *cíbola!*"

There was a moment of silence followed by an outburst of voices shouting with wild enthusiasm. The people's mood had changed instantly. Oñate raised his arms for quiet.

"Coronado saw the animals, so did Leyva and Humaña who came later." He gestured broadly. "Many leagues to the east on the great sweeping, treeless plains, they live—the large, dark woolly beasts that travel in herds so vast the eye cannot see their limit. Nomad Indians hunt them for food and robes. They are the native cattle Coronado wrote of, they are the buffalo. Let us see them also!"

The governor paused and let the people raise their voices again in approval before he continued. "The Sergeant Major is to go to the land of the buffalo, to bring back meat and hides, and to see if some of the strange cattle might be domesticated. If we could raise herds of the native animals such as travel the plains, that would be a source of food that would last us for years, and from what is left over, we could realize substantial wealth. You all know how buffalo hides and dried meat would sell in the mining outposts of northern Mexico. What revenue we could reap while we await our discoveries of gold!"

The clamor of the colonists and soldiers rose deafeningly, and the Indians of the village of Ohké looked on with incomprehension.

"Maese," Oñate shouted, and Juan de Zaldívar pushed his way through the crowd and mounted the *carreta* alongside the governor. "Maese, detail fifty men to accompany the Sergeant Major." The noise was deafening as the soldiers shoved to the front, wanting to be chosen for this first foray outside their new capital.

Juan de Zaldívar raised his hands. "Men," he shouted, "present yourselves at my quarters within the hour if you wish to volunteer for this expedition." The soldiers who had shoved to the front pushed quickly out of the crowd and rushed *en masse* to the Maese's quarters, hoping that being near the front would assure their being chosen. None of the soldiers had joined the conquest of *Nuevo México* to sit in a mud village. Adventure and gold were what they sought.

Everyone watched the soldiers rush toward the dwellings where the Maese had his quarters—all except one person. María Angélica stood looking at Juan de Zaldívar. He turned and saw her and placed his hand over his heart as if to say *You are here*. She looked down but not before she smiled at him.

That evening Vicente informed her he was going with the Sergeant Major and she found it difficult to hide her pleasure at the announcement. She knew that he cared nothing for the prospects of domesticating shaggy beasts, but the opportunity to look for mineral prospects was another matter. She could scarcely bring herself to look at her husband, so strong had grown her feeling of revulsion toward him.

That first night the cart train had arrived in their new capital he had not come to her bed, but her horror had been realized on the following. What he did to her seemed like the most vile act possible. How could that act not be a sin, when the gentle caresses of the Maese were? With her husband it was so horrible, such a terrible violation, and yet when Juan de Zaldívar had held her in his arms and caressed her . . .

When she heard that the Maese would not accompany the expedition, her spirits soared, and she had to be careful not to show her happiness. She thought of the evenings they had shared on the journey, and she could not wait until they could once more spend their evenings alone together.

The visits of the women grew stifling to her, and she grew impatient with their gossip. She could think of one thing and only one.

When Vicente rode out with the expedition, she was overcome by a deep sense of relief, but she soon realized that she would not have as many occasions to be alone with the Maese as she had expected.

The evening before Vicente departed with the expedition, the governor came to their quarters ostensibly to bid her husband good-bye. "I wanted to wish you a safe journey, Captain," Oñate spoke as he entered the *sala*. Vicente did not miss the glance the governor gave his wife who stood silently to one side.

"It is an honor for you to come personally, Governor," Vicente said. "If I may be so bold, I have a favor to ask of you."

He walked over to María Angélica and put his arm around her waist possessively. She stood stiffly, her face unsmiling. "I worry about my wife here alone while I am gone. Would it be presumptuous to ask you if you would look after her while I am on the buffalo plains?"

The governor seemed caught by surprise at the request, but then he smiled broadly. "Of course it would not be presumptuous to ask, Captain. I would consider it an honor."

María Angélica's eyes widened as she glanced from her husband to Oñate. Vicente looked at her, and there was a steely quality in his eyes. When he spoke, his words were a command. "You will make Don Juan welcome in our home at whatever hour, and you will see to it he has as much *jerez* as he wants."

She nodded weakly even as she saw the hungry, waiting look in the governor's eyes.

# Chapter 14

"My dear *señora*," Oñate said as he stepped into the room, taking her hand in his, "how lovely you look in the candlelight." He brought her hand to his lips, keeping his eyes on her face as his lips lingered.

She felt her body tense. Every evening since the buffalo expedition departed, the governor had come to keep her company, but there was something in his manner that evening that made her nervous. On most of the evenings the Maese accompanied him, and she was thankful for his presence, but not once had they had an opportunity to be alone. When the Maese was not there, however, at least Fabia was, her hooded eyes in watchful scrutiny, and Oñate himself seemed ill at ease under the old woman's dark gaze.

There was great respect among the people for *curanderas* not only for their healing abilities but also for their powers, which many believed went beyond medicine, and it was obvious the governor respected old Fabia and would be reluctant to cross her. But at this moment Fabia was absent. At María Angélica's request, she had gone to take a bowl of goat's milk pudding thickened with corn flour and flavored with cinnamon to one of the servant's children who had not fared well on the journey and still looked pitifully undernourished. She prayed Fabia would return quickly for she knew the Maese would not be there. He had gone to the pueblo of Caypa that day and had told her that it would be late when he returned.

She withdrew her hand from Oñate's and was about to ask him if he wouldn't be seated, thinking that surely Fabia would be returning soon, but before she could speak, the governor did.

"I saw your *criada*," he said. His tone was casual, but a smile played at his lips. "The wife of my secretary's servant is quite ill, so knowing old Fabia's abilities, I asked her if she would look after the woman during the night."

María Angélica turned pale. Don Juan said matter-of-factly, "I am glad that I can keep the *señora* company tonight. It must be very lonely having one's husband away."

"Please," she murmured, putting her fingers to her forehead, "I fear I must ask your pardon this evening, Governor, but I have a frightful headache, and think I shall retire early."

He smiled at her and took her hand. "Dear *señora*," he said smoothly, "I could not possibly leave you alone if you are ill."

"No, please," she stammered as she retrieved her hand, "I will be fine—it is merely a headache."

"Nonetheless," the governor said with emphasis, "I would be remiss if I should leave the *señora* by herself when she was ailing."

"No, please," she replied weakly.

He reached for her hand again as she stepped backward in retreat. "Perhaps you would like to lie down?" he asked solicitously, but his eyes carried not the same message as his words.

"Oh, no," she responded quickly, retreating to a straight-backed chair. "Please be seated," she said hastily, motioning to a chair opposite. How on earth was she going to get rid of him?

She desperately began to talk. Words poured from her lips, and she was aware of the amusement in the governor's eyes as he watched her. While she talked, Don Juan interjected words of flattery, but she acted as if she did not hear and kept the stream of words from her mouth constant. She had little idea whether what she was saying made any sense, but it did not matter, for she was quite certain he was paying no attention. His eyes devoured her, and he smiled sensually at her.

"How long will the men be gone on the buffalo plains?" she asked with urgency, not because she cared but because she had to have something to say.

"Long enough," Oñate replied with an insinuating smile.

She immediately chose another conversational gambit. "How is the friars' holy work progressing? Have they brought many natives into the fold yet?"

"They are working as assiduously toward their goal as I am working toward mine," he said.

"And what specifically is your goal now that the natives have accepted the King's rule, Governor?" she asked and instantly regretted her question when she saw him raise his eyes to heaven and laugh. She was mortified by her stupidity.

"Why, dearest lady," he said softly, his voice filled with mirth as he looked back at her, "my goal is to wrap within the fold of my arms and to show my most penetrating love to one of God's most exquisite creatures." Her face burned, and she sought madly for something to say. He took the opportunity to continue with his flattery. "Your beauty is such that did I not believe in God, I would have believed in Him the instant I laid eyes on you, for such a creature as you could only have been created by a god."

"Please," she whispered, "do not say such things. All of God's creations are beautiful."

"But He outdid himself on you," he continued unfazed. "Gazing upon you is like a benediction, a blessing from the Almighty. My soul quivers when I look upon you, and I know that God could not have created such beauty for the joy of one man alone. God wants happiness for His children; He would not have created something so exquisite had He not intended that it give joy to many, for such a face, such a body were meant to show the love of God. It would be contrary to God's purposes, if such beauty were wasted."

"Please," she said, "what you are saying sounds close to blasphemy."

"Far from it, my dear. I am merely attesting to the infinite love and power of Our Lord."

Her cheeks felt as if they were on fire. "Governor," she said quietly, "it's getting late. I think it is best that you go."

Oñate gave no indication that he was preparing to leave. "Angelic one," he said with an insinuating smile, "your husband is not here to partake of your beauty. He has offered me the hospitality of his house, surely you would wish to make your governor welcome."

"Please go," she said as she sat with downcast eyes, her hands clutched tightly in her lap, praying furiously that she be delivered from her distress.

At that instant, the door reverberated with a loud bang, and she found herself on her feet, running toward the sound. She threw the door open and saw Juan de Zaldívar standing there.

"Maese," she said with breathlessness, "how nice to see you." She fought to bring her voice under control. "Won't you come in?"

Bewilderment covered the Maese's face as he stepped into the room. He, too, sought to control his expression when he saw the governor. "Uncle," he said, unable to mask a note of concern in his voice, "Fabia sent me an urgent message that you wanted to see me immediately."

Oñate laughed unpleasantly. "Why that crafty old hag!"

María Angélica could tell by the governor's eyes that he was far from amused. "The *dueña* has sought to protect her charge even if she could not be present. Old Fabia had to sit by a sickbed tonight and it seems she did not trust me with her mistress!"

Juan de Zaldívar found it difficult, but he forced himself to laugh lightly. "Yes," he said, "I would hate to be the one to try to outwit old Fabia."

Oñate turned to María Angélica, a tight smile on his face. "Yes, *señora,*" he said smoothly, "you are fortunate to be so well looked after." He turned back to the Maese and spoke. "The *señora,* unfortunately, has a headache. Perhaps we should retire to my quarters."

"Of course, Governor," the Maese replied. "Good night, *señora,*" he said to María Angélica, bringing her hand to his lips in proper form, "I hope that you are feeling better on the morrow."

"Thank you," she said quietly.

As the two men left the house, she slid the wooden bar down, bolting the door behind them. The feigned headache was no longer feigned—it was quite real and painful.

Following that one evening, she was never alone with the governor much to her grateful relief, for Fabia would not leave her side in spite of Oñate's several attempts to send her on some errand. The old woman's eyes pierced the governor when he made a request, and he seemed unwilling to make his request a command.

Fall was truly on its way. Patches of yellow and gold were beginning to appear on the high slopes of the mountains as the trees were touched by the cold of the nights. María Angélica shivered in the mornings when she arose, but she loved the changing season. She marveled at the brilliant blue of the sky that seemed more intense now in the chilled air than it had in the warmth of summer. The scent of burning piñon wood wafted fragrantly from the houses in the early morning.

When the riders were first spotted, everyone assumed it was an advance group from the buffalo plains, and voices rose with excitement, anxious to hear the adventures of the first expedition in their new land.

María Angélica grasped Fabia's arm. "Oh, no, not yet, please," she whispered. Fabia patted her arm and squinted dourly into the distance.

"No!" someone yelled. "That's Captain Villagrá. That is his big white horse."

"You're right. And that's Captain Márquez alongside."

"Praised be God," Fabia muttered, and María Angélica sighed with relief.

The horsemen rode into the plaza where the governor and colonists awaited them. Captain Villagrá dismounted and handed Oñate a leather bag.

"My Governor," Villagrá said in a loud voice. "Your orders have been carried out and to the letter!"

Oñate grasped the bag, opened the drawstring, looked at the contents, and smiled with grim satisfaction.

"Bear witness!" he shouted as he raised the sack and dumped its contents onto the ground. "Bear witness to the fate of traitors!"

Salt spilled from the sack and four blood-blackened severed hands fell to the ground.

María Angélica was not the only woman who nearly gagged at the sight. The men, however, pushed forward, wanting to hear the details of the capture and the subsequent execution of the governor's orders.

"Well, that's certainly a lesson for deserters," Fabia said matter-of-factly as they hurriedly returned to their dwelling, "but if I were the governor I wouldn't be too complacent."

"Why would anyone desert after seeing that?" María Angélica asked with a shudder.

"Much worse than that will be committed before this conquest is completed," Fabia said darkly.

The governor seemed to grow impatient with his visits to María Angélica's house now that Fabia was always in attendance, her eyes burning into him, and he began to speak of how he was anxious to bring all the native villages under his dominion before winter came.

"When is the Sergeant Major returning from the buffalo country?" he asked with impatience one evening as he and the Maese sat in María Angélica's *sala* eating the *pastelitos* that Fabia had made.

"*¿Quién sabe?*" the Maese answered. "Surely it can't be much longer."

"There are villages to the west," the governor spoke, "villages that do not lie along this *Río del Norte*. It is the vassalage of these that I especially want in order to consolidate my dominion in this land." Oñate made a sweeping gesture with his hand. "But there is one pueblo in particular that has captured my imagination. They say the village is perched high on a flat rock mesa, impregnable and inaccessible except to individual ascent by means of ladders and toeholds chipped out of the rock face of the mesa wall. It is reputed that the natives there are unfriendly and acutely suspicious of any stranger. I must subjugate this village!"

Don Juan licked the remnants of a *pastelito* off his fingers. "I wonder if they will accept our domination as readily as the other villages have? If I can control this pueblo, I will have all of *Nuevo México* in my power."

The governor sat brooding for a few moments. "Why should I sit here waiting for the buffalo expedition? I could go south and inspect those salines that they say lie to the east of the *Río del Norte*. Salt might be a good export for us." The Maese nodded, and Oñate continued, his voice animated, "From there I could head west, toward the villages lying in that direction." The governor sat back with satisfaction at the thought.

"I'll do it. I'll go ahead and set out with a group of soldiers. It's almost November—I don't want to waste any more time before winter is upon us. However, I want you to remain in charge here at San Juan, Maese, and await the return of your brother."

Juan de Zaldívar dared not look at María Angélica. His heart soared to think that he would have a few days, if not a few weeks, alone with her again. Her smile, her voice, her movement came back to rest in his mind. His desire for her consumed him. How could he love her so much when that very love could be the instrument of her damnation? He could not count the number of times each day he prayed to conquer his desire, but to little avail.

Why could not his love for her be pure—as in past ages when a knight could love a lady whom he could never hope to have? The futility of the situation was abhorrent to him. His choices were two: send her immortal soul to eternal damnation or deny his very life, which she had become. She sustained him. When he did not see her, he felt like a starving man, but one glimpse of her was enough to renew him and prolong his life until the next time he might gaze at her.

He still did not understand old Fabia. Why had she become his ally? When he was around, she dropped the vigilance with which she always protected her mistress—even the night on the journey when he almost lost control, she had done nothing. Was it because she felt he had saved her mistress's life when the young woman was near starvation? But that was not a sufficient answer. He had the strange feeling that Fabia would not object if he expressed his love to her mistress in the most intimate way possible. In fact, after the night of rain and thunder, Fabia's words to him might have been interpreted thus.

He had blurted out that María Angélica had fallen asleep in his arms and that there was no need for Fabia to worry about her mistress while absent from the tent. The old woman seemed unconcerned.

"The *señora* needs love. She needs the love of a man—a good man," she said. "I want only for the happiness and well-being of my mistress."

"That, too, is my only wish," he had replied.

"I do not care what the *padres* say," she continued pointedly, "they do not know the needs of a woman."

From that time on, she had furthered his cause, allowing him to be alone with her mistress, and had even enlisted his aid in protecting her from the governor. Yes, the old woman was clever and was his ally, but he would have preferred it otherwise. If she were not, then his situation would have been much easier. The burden was now his, and his conscience wrestled with his passion, and he prayed for strength.

It would have been far better had he stayed away from María Angélica's house, not allowing himself to visit, but she had asked him not to deny her his presence—and he had given his word. But he knew that made no difference. Even if he had not given his word, he knew he could not have stayed away.

"As you command, Governor," the Maese said, shoving his thoughts from his mind when he saw that Oñate was awaiting a response from him.

"I shall await the return of my brother and the expedition from the buffalo plains."

María Angélica kept her eyes riveted on the floor and prayed neither the governor nor Juan de Zaldívar would look at her, for she feared she could not restrain her emotions from showing with all their intensity.

As it was to be, the Maese had exactly a month and two days with her.

In high spirits he saw the governor and his group of men off. The hours of the day dragged unmercifully, and evening seemed as if it would never come. Juan de Zaldívar paced in his room, unable to think of anything else save being alone with her.

María Angélica feigned a headache to avoid the sewing group that afternoon. She tried to busy herself in the *sala*, but when she knocked a pottery cup onto the floor and it shattered into small pieces, she swept up the fragments and gave up her efforts to keep busy. She went to her bedroom and tried to read, but it was useless. Although she turned the pages, she had no idea what the words had said.

In the evening when the knock finally came at the *sala* door, she fumbled opening it and felt ridiculous when she heard her voice, a pitch too high, say inanely, "Why it's you, Maese. How nice to see you."

Juan de Zaldívar seemed no more at ease than she. "*Buenas tardes, señora*. I hope I am not intruding?"

"*Claro que no*, do come in."

They sat stiffly for a few moments, making small talk, each growing more nervous as they sat there facing the other.

Fabia entered, bringing Vicente's *jerez*, and poured them goblets of the wine. She filled the glasses to the rim when she heard the stilted conversation and turned to the Maese, affecting a simpering tone. "*Buenas tardes le dé Dios, Señor* Maese." She gave an elaborate curtsy.

Juan de Zaldívar burst out laughing. "*Buenas tardes* to you, too, Fabia." María Angélica laughed, and the tension was broken in the room.

"Oh, how I have missed you, Angélica," the Maese said, turning to her and taking her hand and placing a kiss on it.

"And I you."

Fabia turned and left the room, a broad smile on her face.

They sat and talked, their faces animated. He only held her hand, but the love in their eyes would have been evident to anyone who had stepped into the room. The steel of Juan de Zaldívar's considerable will was tempered well.

Much later when he rose to go, he brought her hand to his lips. The kiss he placed on it conveyed clearly all the emotion he kept within him, and she was left as breathless as if the kiss had been on her lips instead.

*"Buenas noches, corazón,"* he said softly.

*"Buenas noches,* Juan," she managed to whisper.

Captain Gaspar de López Tábora, who had gone with Oñate, came riding into San Juan two weeks after the governor had set out. He went directly to the Maese's quarters.

"The governor has decided that since he is going to the western villages, he will continue on to the discovery of the South Sea. They say it isn't too distant from there. The governor believes that if we can make important discoveries, perhaps the soldiers and colonists will be pacified, and, even more important, the King may be inclined to grant more royal favor."

"There is truth in that," the Maese replied.

"God knows we need something to sustain our conquest in this desolate land. Those were the governor's very words," the captain spoke as he handed the Maese a folded paper. "These are the orders he sent you."

The Maese broke the seal and unfolded the paper. His eyes scanned it rapidly. "To the *Maese de Campo de la Provincia de Nuevo México*: When the buffalo expedition returns from the eastern plains, you, along with thirty men, are to start with all haste toward joining me for an expedition to the South Sea. The pueblo of the high mesa that they call Ácoma has, thankfully and without bloodshed, rendered vassalage unto the King. You may reprovision yourselves there before you meet me at the pueblo of Zuñi where I will await you. By seeking your reprovisions at the pueblo of Ácoma, we can test their willingness to obey our dominion, but nevertheless, *take great care* while you are there as I do not believe they are subjugated at all in spirit. I eagerly await your arrival. Don Juan de Oñate, Governor and Captain General."

The Maese refolded the orders slowly. He prayed the buffalo expedition would delay.

For two more weeks he managed to keep from taking her in his arms. Their only touch was when he took her hand and kissed it in greeting and departing, but it was a lingering kiss, and on more than one occasion, he felt her hand tremble faintly, and he wished he could feel her body next to his.

Although they did not touch, their time together was warm and intimate. They talked or read or laughed softly, savoring just the presence of the other. Her eyes sparkled and smiled at him while his caressed her. They existed in a world of their own, and once Fabia brought them refreshment, she kept herself discreetly busy in another room.

The Maese knew that his brother could not delay many more days on the buffalo plains, and the tension began to grow in him as he thought that each day might be his last alone with the woman who consumed his waking thoughts as well as all his nighttime dreams.

The days had grown quite chilly, and all the cottonwoods in the valley along the river brilliantly attested to the fact that winter was coming to that north country. Burning golds and flaming yellows lined the river and might have looked like long, fluttering silk ribbons to the cranes and geese that flew overhead, their honking audible below as they made their way southward. The women wore heavier wool *rebozos* about their shoulders to keep out the chilly drafts. Everyone smelled of the piñon smoke that wafted fragrantly through the houses from the fires that had been built against the chill.

María Angélica's quarters had begun to look like a home. The interior walls had been finely plastered by the native women, so deft and quick with their hands as they applied the thin, gruel-like mixture, bringing an incredible smoothness to the surfaces. The interior was whitewashed, helping to brighten the dim windowless rooms. Sconces with hammered tin reflectors were mounted on the walls and their tallow candles gave off a flickering light that danced and played along the walls and in the shadowy corners. Coarsely woven Mexican rugs could not hide the fact that the floor was handpacked dirt, however.

As María Angélica sat on a cushioned *banco* and the Maese in a chair opposite her, they could hear the wind outside, swirling dust and leaves. The fastened-down hide that covered the hole in the roof through which, by means of the ladder, one reached the upper stories, quivered and snapped noisily as the wind tugged at it. A low, sibilant howl would occasionally emit from the battened-down cover.

Had it been her apparent uneasiness, the chill of the room, the look of disquietude in her eyes that brought him to her side? Without conscious thought he moved across the small space that separated them and found himself sitting next to her on the *banco*, her hand grasped in his. He knew it *had* been the look in her eyes that made him take her in his arms.

When he came to sit by her, she looked up at him, her eyes smiling at him with a look that made his heart pound.

He gathered her into his arms and cradled her head against his chest as he fought the desire that stabbed through him like a sword thrust. *Dios*, how he wanted her.

*God, why do you do this to me?* he asked himself with agony. *What do you want of me? Why do you rip my guts out with love for this woman when I am not supposed to have her? Why? I have always sought to honor your commandments, but why are you putting me to this test, this torture I can hardly bear?*

He smoothed her hair. Surely the love he felt for her could not be born of evil. *If there is a purpose for my loving her, just show it to me so I may understand.*

The sound of the wind whipping at their sanctuary was the only answer he received.

His hand caressed her cheek and then lifted her chin; his mouth covered hers. The kiss he placed on her lips was gentle and demanded nothing of her, but he felt in her response that she would not resist any demand he might have made. He caressed her face with kisses and pulled the pins from her hair, letting it fall around her shoulders. The piñon smoke that permeated the dwelling had lightly scented her hair, and as he buried his hands in the luxuriant darkness, the dusky smell of the aromatic wood penetrated his senses, and he thought that every time he smelled that fragrance, it would remind him of her.

And so the evenings into November passed: the Maese expressing his love with gentle caresses and tender kisses but nothing more. When he returned to his quarters each night, however, he would kneel and pray.

"*Dios*, if this is a sin, forgive me and give me some sign, please, that this love is wrong for it is of a beauty so deep that it seems impossible that it was not created by your Almighty power."

Then he would ask of God a bargain, as mortal man has done since the beginning of time. "*Dios*, if you will grant me this love to continue as it is, I will not ask more. I will be content. I will not seek the ultimate fulfillment."

# Chapter 15

The evening the messenger arrived, riding ahead of the buffalo expedition to inform the inhabitants of San Juan that the Sergeant Major was nearing home, filled the Maese with aching regret. His evenings with her had become as indispensable to him as eating or breathing, and he could not bear for them to stop.

When Fabia opened the door, he entered the *sala* without a word and crossed the room in long, quick strides and pulled María Angélica into his arms. He crushed her to him and his mouth devoured hers, uncaring that Fabia watched. There was pain in his eyes as he spoke. "The messenger just arrived. The expedition to the buffalo plains is within one day of San Juan." The color left María Angélica's face and tears welled in her eyes.

Fabia approached them, her dark eyes inscrutable, her face unsmiling. She put her hand gently on María Angélica's arm. "Go to your room, Angelita," she said as if she were speaking to a child. The young woman looked at her with surprise and incomprehension. Fabia only repeated her words, "Go to your room."

Fabia took her by the arm and led her to the ladder. María Angélica hesitated and looked back at him. Juan de Zaldívar nodded, and she ascended the ladder and disappeared onto the roof.

Fabia turned back to the Maese. Her eyes were penetrating as she looked at him, but her words were quiet. "I once told you that the *señora* needed the love of a good man." He nodded, and she continued. "The *señora* is like a flower. Just as a flower will wither and fade on the vine if it does not have water, so will the *señora* wither and fade if she does not have love. The only thing in this world I truly care about is the happiness of my Angelita. These old hands delivered Angelita's mother, and these old breasts nourished her mother when my own baby died. I raised her mother to womanhood, and these same hands delivered Angelita, and these old arms rocked her and raised her to womanhood—only to see her married to a cruel man whom she could never love. I will not see my Angelita wither and fade in this barren land, Maese."

He swallowed and spoke quietly. "I love your mistress more than life itself. Her happiness is the only thing *I* truly care about."

"Then go to her," Fabia said softly.

He stood on the terrace roof feeling the cold November air biting at his face and hands, but within, a fire consumed him. He no longer remembered his bargain with God. He opened the door and then quietly closed it behind him. He stood for a moment leaning back against the heavy planking. A tallow candle sat on the bedside table, its flickering light illuminating the woman who sat on the edge of the bed, unmoving.

He crossed the room and sat down beside her. "I would not hurt you for the world," he whispered.

She looked at him, her eyes luminous in the candlelight. "Your love could never hurt me."

He took her in his arms gently and cradled her against his chest. Slowly, unable to control the trembling in his hands, he began to undress her. He undid the bodice of her dress and cupped her breasts in his hands, caressing her. She pressed her body against his in a gesture of wanting. Desire stabbed through him as he pulled her clothes from her. When she lay naked on the bed, he stopped, his chest heaving.

"My God in heaven," he breathed, "but you are beautiful."

His hands touched her lightly here and there as if he could scarcely believe she was real and not some figment of his thoughts gone wild. He leaned forward, and his mouth began to caress her breasts. His hands moved down her sides and over her belly, bringing sounds of desire from her throat as her hips arched toward his fondling. His lips descended along the path of his hands, and what she had thought was an abomination seemed now like exquisite torture as his mouth caressed her in ways she had never dreamed possible. Suddenly she gasped for breath and could not stop the sounds that came from her throat as something inside her shattered and she felt the unbearable pleasure of it. Juan de Zaldívar ripped his own clothes away, and he was thrusting into her, quenching the passion that felt as if it would destroy him. The feel of her breasts pressed against his chest, the feel of her desire for him, the feel of her silkiness wrapped around him drove him wild.

* * *

When he finally lay still, he held her tightly against his chest as if he were afraid she might vanish. "Only God in Heaven knows how much I love you," he whispered hoarsely.

She turned her face to his and spoke against his mouth. "Juan, I, too, know."

He kissed her passionately on the lips and ran his hands down her back, cupping her buttocks and pressing her against him. "God, how I want you still."

Exhausted, they slept, and later somewhere near dawn they both awoke. With infinite slowness, he made love to her again, savoring each kiss, each caress, each thrust. She cried out and clung to him, and her desire intensified his own.

It took every ounce of will he possessed to leave her. When tears began to trickle down her cheeks as she watched him dress, he thought his heart could not endure. He took her face in his hands and kissed away the salty tears. "Do not cry, dearest heart of my heart," he whispered, "I cannot bear to see it."

"I love thee, Juan," she murmured with passion.

"And how very much I love thee, *ángel de mi alma,*" he said softly.

"What are we to do?" she asked.

"God will give us the answer."

Save for two people, there was great rejoicing in the small, shabby capital that afternoon as the Sergeant Major and his fifty soldiers came riding into San Juan.

The men returned tired, yet in good spirits. They had brought much meat, tallow, and many hides that would help keep them warm that winter. No one really knew what to expect during the cold months in that north country. The natives spoke of snow and freezing rivers, but the Spaniards could not, until they had seen it themselves, know what winter there would truly bring.

The meat of the shaggy creatures was perhaps more welcome than the hides. Food was meager and no one ever seemed to have his fill. On the order of Diego de Zubia, numerous forays were made to acquire grain from the natives of the pueblos scattered throughout that country.

Above all else, the colonists needed to preserve their livestock. Unless they had sheep, cattle, and horses to breed, they could scarcely hope to survive, much less prosper in that harsh land that had required such sacrifice to reach. So it was with general thanksgiving that the people received the meat the Sergeant Major brought back to the village. His hopes, however, of bringing back some of the humpbacked wild cattle to start domestic herds had been sadly deflated after several attempts to corral the spooky, lumbering giants failed.

Vicente returned impatient. The flat plains of the east showed no prospects of mineral wealth whatever, and although the dark, woolly beasts were entertaining to chase and kill, they held little other interest for him.

When he heard that the governor had proceeded toward the west and was destined for the South Sea, he was at first furious that he had been left behind and then insistent that he would join the Maese's small group that would shortly depart to join forces with the governor. Vicente cared little that for weeks he had been on the march. Success depended on his seeing as much country as possible; *he* would be the one to discover gold.

Upon return he paid scarce attention to his wife whom he had not seen for weeks. He came to her bed, however, that first night. He did not even bother to bathe and remove the smell of the long journey. As he thrust into her again and again, she thought she would go insane from the revulsion and violation she felt. When he was finished with her, he began to snore, deep in sleep.

She pushed herself out of bed and was sick as she leaned over the chamber pot and retched again and again. She pulled off her nightgown that smelled of his body and groped in the dark for another that she pulled on. She wrapped herself in her *rebozo* and trembled with cold as she stepped out onto the roof terrace. She made her way down the ladder and through the *sala* to Fabia's room.

"Fabia," she whispered, trying to control her voice as she shook the old woman's shoulder.

"*Niña*, what is it?" Fabia asked with concern as she came awake.

"Please, may I sleep down here?" she asked in a quavering voice.

"Of course, *querida*," the old woman said as she moved over on her cot to make room for her. "There, there," Fabia crooned as she patted her gently.

It was decided the next day that the Maese's party would leave the following morning. Both Fabia and María Angélica had to work furiously that day preparing foodstuffs for the march since Vicente was insistent that he would go.

That afternoon María Angélica sat exhausted, unable to stop the tears that ran down her cheeks. She had not seen the Maese since he left her bed at dawn the day before.

"Do not cry, Angelita," Fabia said gently when she came into the *sala* and saw her. The old woman touched her shoulder. "You must learn to be strong, Angelita. Life requires it."

María Angélica put her hand over the old one that rested on her shoulder. "Yes, Fabia," she replied softly, "that is what I know I must learn."

That night Vicente joined the Sergeant Major and some of the soldiers in a game of cards. It seemed he scarcely remembered he had a wife at home. The Maese, however, excused himself from the game. He was tense and nervous. The darkness of the cold November night hid him from view, and the gusty wind muffled his steps as he made his way to the dwelling where during the past weeks he had spent so many evenings. All of them, save one, were blotted from his mind, but that one night lived in his memory, consuming him.

Fabia opened the door and let him quickly in. María Angélica flew into his arms. "Oh, how I have missed you!" she breathed as she threw her arms around his neck and kissed him.

"Oh, *mi ángel,*" he whispered, "I had to say good-bye."

"I'm glad you came," she whispered tremulously, touching his cheek.

Silently Fabia dropped the wooden bar down so no one could enter precipitously, and just as silently she crossed to the ladder and ascended it to the roof, whispering down, "I will watch the street."

María Angélica embraced him again. She held onto him in desperation.

He felt the need in her body and whispered hoarsely, "You can never know how much I cherish the love you gave to me." She had on a simple dress and as he ran his hand down her back, he could feel the curve of her buttocks through the material. He brought her hips against him tightly, and pressed himself to her intimately, wanting to possess her and make her his once more. Her breasts tantalized his chest, and her mouth opened under his. He pulled open the bodice of her dress and kissed her breasts hungrily as her hands pressed his head closer.

"Oh, Juan," she whispered with necessity, "love me again before you go, please."

"Oh, *ángel,* how I need you," he groaned. Urgently he freed himself from his clothes, and lifting her skirts, he entered her with a force that caused her breath to be expelled in a small gasp. She clung to him and cried out when he did.

He covered her face with kisses, which she returned voraciously. "My God, how I love you," he said, his arms cradling her.

A raspy whisper returned them abruptly to reality. They could not see her face, but they heard Fabia's voice and felt the sudden draft of cold as a corner of the buffalo-hide roof cover was lifted.

Fumbling, she readjusted her skirts and he his clothing. She pulled the bodice of her dress closed as she sat quickly down on the *banco* and sought to calm herself, smoothing her clothes as old Fabia descended the ladder with a rapidity unexpected for her age. They scarcely breathed as they heard the sound of jangling metal approach and then pass by their door.

"I must go," the Maese said hoarsely, his voice filled with emotion. Turning to Fabia he said quietly, "God willing, I will see you both after this expedition to the South Sea." He grasped Fabia's hand and kissed it.

"I shall always be indebted to you for your kindnesses toward me. Guard over our Angélica while I am gone, for you know that I love your mistress as you do."

He turned to María Angélica, whose eyes were wide and filled with pain. It mattered not to him that Fabia stood watching them. He lifted María Angélica to her feet, took her in his arms, and kissed her passionately, crushing her to him, and then he kissed her tenderly on the mouth and eyes and forehead.

He spoke quietly and touched her cheek. "You are my life. I will miss you, *corazón de mi vida*. God willing, we shall quickly find the South Sea, and I will return to you and be able to show you once again how much I love you."

"And I you," she answered, her voice choked with emotion. She went to the sideboard and from a small silver box took a coral rosary, the beads carved into tiny pink roses. "Take this," she said softly, "as a remembrance of my love." The Maese took the rosary and brought it to his lips.

"God be with thee, Juan. Come back to me soon. I cannot bear to be without you." She stood on tiptoe and placed a kiss on his lips.

Juan de Zaldívar tried to consider his situation as he rode across the great expanse of rugged, barren land that was now their domain, but he could not bring coherent thoughts to his mind. He knew only that he loved a woman and that there was nothing he could do to stop himself. It mattered not that she had a husband nor that he had made a promise to God that he would not make a sinner of her. *Dios, she is my life. I cannot leave her.*

The land was barren, but the subtle shadings of color gave beauty to its immensity. Earthtones ranged from deep ochre to brassy gold, from the most delicate shades of pink and lavender to the dark black-purple of volcanic rock. Slopes of talus encircled century-worn mesas, and solitary volcanic cones rose in the distance. Deep, dry, sand-bottomed arroyos gave evidence of the waters that, as a result of summer mountain showers, rushed headlong from the elevations ultimately reaching the *Río del Norte*. All of these made up the immense landscape that engulfed the small contingent of men who crossed it on horseback, their armor glinting in the cold late November sun.

On the first of December, Juan de Zaldívar awoke to a dusting of snow that lightly covered the ground. His breath made small white puffs as he blew to warm his hands. He calculated they were within a day's journey of the mesa of Ácoma—there they would get provisions. The village of the mesa citadel had sworn allegiance to the King of Spain and was now under his dominion. As the governor had said, it would be an excellent place to stop and reprovision before continuing on to the pueblo of Zuñi farther to the west where Oñate awaited them. Their supplies were running low, and it would be advantageous to be amply outfitted for the expedition to the South Sea. The Maese hoped fervently that the governor had misjudged the spirit of the village citadel and that the natives there would receive them with hospitality.

Later, Juan de Zaldívar reined in his horse on that bright December day and sat with awe as he viewed the solitary mesa that rose up from the floor of the valley that was rimmed on all sides by encircling mountain mesas. The huge rock in the distance was magnificent and starkly beautiful. In the sun, the sides of the towering citadel appeared ivory and pale pink like a majestic carving that a god had placed in a bowl. It was difficult to believe that a village of some fifteen hundred natives was perched on its summit, reached only by scaling the sheer, craggy walls with ladders and toeholds. But as the small contingent approached, the several-storied dwellings became visible on the north end of the massive rock. What a sublime feeling it must be, the Maese thought, to live there and look out for miles around over the valley below.

They did not hurry, for they wanted their expedition to attest to the peaceful intent of their mission. As they came within a league or so of the base of the mesa, natives came out to meet them. It was perhaps four in the afternoon when they reached the base of the *peñol*, and the winter sun was well on its way toward its early repose behind the western mesas. Its angle turned the rock citadel a pale reddish color and shadows began to lengthen.

Tomás, the Maese's translator, explained to the gathered natives that their small expedition was in need of food supplies and would be grateful if they could furnish them.

The Maese glanced around. In order to make camp they must have water for drinking and wood over which they might cook their food. There was nothing to be had there at the base of the mighty rock the natives called home. He motioned to his servant Jusepe to bring some trade items forward. Night was not far distant. The Maese gave a native Tomás said was the spokesman some iron hatchets and a few other trade items.

"Water and firewood," the Maese said, and Tomás translated.

The native nodded in understanding and pointed to the top of the high cliff, indicating that such things were available in the village.

"Captain Márquez," the Maese shouted, "take six men up on the *peñol*. The natives said they would furnish us wood and water."

"*Inmediatemente*, Maese," the captain replied as he turned to detail the men to scale the impressive cliff.

When the detail was ready, some of the natives started with them to the base of the cliff, but the majority chose to remain with the other Spaniards. The Maese hoped, now that the group was divided, that it was their curiosity that kept them down below and not some other reason. The natives touched the horses, marvelling at the huge animals that carried the strangers on their backs, and the more inquisitive touched the cold metal the strangers wore. The weapons—wheellock pistols, arquebuses, pikes, and swords—held their eyes in fascination.

The Maese watched the small detail led by Captain Márquez climb the rocky, sloping base of the mesa to a cleft in the gigantic rock. They made their way gradually up the cleft, and then by means of tall ladders that reached from one rock ledge to another, facilitating the ascent, they made their way to the top. When they were out of sight, he turned his attention to setting up the camp, calling out orders here and there as he saw fit, and keeping an eye on both his soldiers and the natives.

It was not long before Captain Márquez and his men descended from the high perched village, bringing with them only a small amount of water and a little wood. In their tow, also, were two men of the pueblo.

"Maese," Captain Márquez addressed Zaldívar, "the natives were not generous with wood and water as you can see." He paused and glanced at the two chiefs they had brought with them and then turned back to the Maese as he continued. "It is my opinion that they gave what little they did unwillingly. We got no food as you can also see. I brought along these chiefs thinking that perhaps if we detained them here, we could make certain that the natives would furnish us the provisions we need."

"No," the Maese said with emphasis, "we must in no way use force to coerce the people. We must see to it that they are not harmed or abused in any way. They must see that we wish only to be their friends. If we can gain their confidence, then they will be more willing to furnish us with the provisions we need—and must have."

He approached the chiefs and thanked them for the wood and water they had given, and Tomás told them that the Spaniards needed food supplies also and that they were willing to buy them. He called for more hatchets and iron goods brought forth, which he gave to the chiefs as payment for the food they might give. The chiefs accepted the items and indicated that on the morrow they would have corn for them.

The following morning natives descended the mesa, the baskets they carried on their backs secured by forehead straps. They brought tortillas and three or four *fanegas* of corn. The Maese was disappointed with the quantity of corn. What they needed most of all, however, was ground corn, for they had not the time nor the manpower to spend grinding it on the march.

"Explain this to the natives, Tomás," he said, and the translator did as ordered.

"They say that there is not sufficient ground meal available in the village for our needs."

The Ácoma spokesman stepped forward and spoke again in Queres to Tomás who relayed his words.

"If you wish to retire to the stream you crossed about two leagues away, you will find there water and firewood. The women will start grinding corn and tomorrow you may come and get it."

The Maese was not pleased with the delay because he knew the governor was anxious to start for the South Sea, but it was better to wait and allow the Indians time to grind the corn than to proceed without proper provisions.

"Prepare to move camp," he shouted.

That evening on the orders of Juan de Zaldívar, the Spaniards gathered around the large fire that was built with the scrub juniper found near the arroyo. The warmth the fire emitted was more than welcome in that icy December air. The Maese stood with his back to the fire facing the soldiers. His tone was not harsh, but it was resolute as he began to speak.

"The natives are giving us *their* food—provisions that were to be for their own sustenance. The food they are going to give us tomorrow is food that they raised with the sweat of their brow—food intended for their children and families. We must treat them kindly," he said with emphasis.

On the faces faintly illuminated by the glow of the fire and the moonlight, he thought he discerned a look that prompted him to add, "There will be no looting or taking of any indiscriminate possession of any native under pain of *death*. We will take only those foodstuffs that they freely offer." He paused. "Am I understood?" he asked sharply.

*"Sí, señor,"* they answered, but he made a note to repeat the order in the morning.

Later that night, the Maese strode away from the light of the campfire. He went some distance along the arroyo and then knelt on the cold, hard ground. The moon illuminated the landscape, creating a strangely two-dimensional black and silver world. He crossed himself and kissed the small crucifix of the rosary. The *Pater Noster* rolled off his lips followed by the *Ave Marias*. Never before had that devotion had as much meaning for him as when he touched the tiny carved coral roses that belonged to the woman he loved.

Later when the decades of *Aves* had been said, he again kissed the crucifix and, stiff with cold, rose from the ground. Pain shot through his knees, but he welcomed it as a sign of penance.

*"Dios,"* he prayed aloud as he stood there on that crystal cold December night, "I am a miserable sinner, unworthy to ask anything of you, but without your help I am lost. I love a woman I should not. Show me, I beg you, what I must do. Whatever is your will I accept completely." He looked up at the uneven globe of the waning moon as if there might have been some answer there. Then he looked in the direction of the mesa citadel. "Lord," he whispered softly, "I pray that on the morrow the natives may be kindly disposed toward us and give us the food we need. Amen."

* * *

Juan de Zaldívar awoke early the next morning stiff with cold. He made a point to speak personally to some of the men he felt might be inclined to take more than the natives were willing to give. He knew he must be tactful.

"Captain," he said as he approached Vicente de Vizcarra and clapped him amicably on the back. "I would appreciate it if you would help me see to it that the men respect the natives' possessions. If we take more now than we should, we certainly cannot expect much generosity from them in the future, and indeed, our lives depend upon the kindly disposition of the inhabitants of this country."

He had never liked Vizcarra. He recognized the captain's fearlessness and courage, but as a man he had no respect for him, and when it came to native people, he knew how the captain treated them. The Maese didn't like what he was going to have to say, but he would say it, hoping it might keep the captain from causing problems in the village.

He found it painful to have to be pleasant, for he could scarcely endure the thought of that man as her husband. It was abhorrent to him that the captain had the right to her love but he did not. How could any father have allowed such a man to marry his daughter? She had never spoken about what she felt toward her husband, but the Maese had seen on a few occasions what looked like loathing in her eyes. He gloried in the memory of what he had seen in her eyes when she looked at *him*. He knew with all certainty that she loved him, but he was filled with jealousy at the thought of the captain possessing her.

"What we must keep in mind," he continued, hating his own hypocrisy, "is that it would be to our advantage to keep the natives happy until gold has been discovered—which, we well know, takes time. We will need much Indian labor for the mines. If we could firmly establish and consolidate our dominion over the native villages, then conscripting labor would be a much easier task. As the proverb goes, 'You catch more flies with honey than with vinegar.' " He laughed and the captain laughed with him.

"You're right," Vicente answered, "the most important thing is the gold. We must find the gold. We'll let the good fathers make docile children out of the heathen, and they will be ready to work the mines for us." His pale eyes were bright and hard as he looked toward the massive towering rock.

"*Jesús*, what a fortress," he said between his teeth, not seeing the look of deprecation in the Maese's eyes. "I'll bet they're an arrogant bunch of bastards—perched up there on their rock."

# Chapter 16

Rohona was not even breathing hard as he scaled the sheer sandstone wall and entered the village at a trot. The air was cold and brittle, but he wore only a breechclout and high-topped moccasins lined with rabbit fur. He did not feel the temperature. The exhilaration of the early morning air and his run across the valley floor filled his chest. He did not let the thought of the strangers intrude upon the peacefulness of the transparent dawn. That would come later—when he reached the *kiva*.

Thin twisting ribbons of fragrant juniper smoke rose from the houses into the frigid early morning air. The sky was a bright, hard blue and water in the small stone hollows used for plastering or washing was covered with a sheet of ice. It was the moon of the shortest days. As the weather grew colder and North Mountain sent the clouds that would bring snow, Rohona knew that the men would be spending more and more time in the warmth of the *kiva,* making moccasins and ceremonial objects and weaving the cotton they had gathered that fall from their fields near the edges of the stream on the valley floor.

But that early morning the men were not gathered there to weave. Pale strangers were in their land. Some days previously a group of them had come to Áco mesa, and now more of them had appeared.

The translator with the first group, called Cristóbal by the newcomers, explained to them why the bearded ones had come. What he said made little sense. What was this thing called a soul about which they talked and for which they wanted food and clothing? The longrobes would save their souls, but they must give the strangers much corn and many blankets for the privilege.

Rohona spoke in the *kiva* that day a moon ago. "I would rather keep the food I have raised and the blankets I have woven, for *those* I know will keep me warm. But a soul? Of what good is this thing called a soul or this man who was once nailed to crossed sticks? Can this man keep us warm and put food in our bellies and in our children's bellies?"

His thoughts had been echoed by many in the *kiva* that day the first group arrived. Rohona understood the real reason the strangers were there and told his people when he returned from the ceremony in the *kiva* at Quigui, but many of the village said it was not possible.

There were too few of the strangers to rule over the whole land, they argued, and most did not accept this explanation for the purpose of the pale ones. How could so few rule over all the people of the land and make them do their bidding, the people asked again and again. Nevertheless all were apprehensive and suspicious.

When the first group came to Áco, it was decided after much discussion that the chiefs would kneel in front of the metal-plated leader as the chiefs of the other villages had done. The reasoning was simple. If they knelt, the strangers would leave more quickly and once they were gone, Áco would continue as it always had. Why shed the blood of the Ácoma if simply by kneeling, they could get the intruders to leave? Had not the intruders left Quigui and gone on north?

Perhaps the Ácoma would not have knelt so readily had they known that the leader would demand such large quantities of cornmeal to take with him, but they gave it, desiring only that the strangers depart. The younger men, filled with anger, urged killing the newcomers, but the counsel of the old prevailed.

Rohona knew, however, that at some point there would be a clash between his people and the strangers. It was as inevitable as the wind that swept brutally over their mesa home in wintertime.

And now another group of the metal-clad strangers had appeared. Although fewer than the first, they, too, wanted corn. They were willing to trade knives and other objects for food but the Ácoma knew that their corn was essential for their own survival.

The men met in Mauharots to discuss the arrival of this new group of pale ones who had come to Áco mesa. One old man rose in the ceremonial chamber and spoke in a rustling, ancient voice. "The Apaches have come to our village to trade the things of the buffalo that they have hunted in the East, to trade them for our corn. We trade only what we want. But other times the Apaches have come and attacked our village to take by force what they want. We well know their treachery, and the rocks and stones we keep on our rooftops are always ready to answer it. How do we know that the new pale ones will not do the same? They come with hatchets of cold brightness to trade for corn. But they want much, much corn. How do we know that they may come to take and not to trade?" With the unsteady legs of old age, the man seated himself and many voices seconded his query, indicating that there were few who had not had the same thoughts.

Many spoke with angry words, and tempers flared as the men in the stuffy *kiva* voiced their fears and concerns for the well-being of their village and the preservation of their ceremonies.

"Will the K'atsina send the clouds that bring the rain if we bow down to this man on the crossed sticks to whom the pale strangers have begun to make the people at Ohké and Quigui and Castixe, and all the villages to which they go, bow down?" That had been one of the questions asked.

"They say we must give up our old way," another had spoken. "Does this mean we can no longer send our prayer sticks to Wenimats?"

The same ancient man who had spoken earlier gave his advice, and it was accepted by all. "Let us make no quick move against these strangers, but let us be ever alert and prepared in case the bearded, shining ones show treachery in their actions. Let no one be coerced into giving corn or blankets or anything that they might have and with which they do not wish to part. If one wants to barter with the strangers for some of their wonder tools or their many colored beads, that is his business to strike a bargain to his liking. But if one does not want to give his corn in exchange for something the pale ones have, that is his right. Let us wait and see what is to come with these men of the pale skin."

All agreed to the advice, but many spoke with determination, saying they would not barter with these new strangers.

Rohona rose and reasoned thus: "If the pale ones who have no food of their own cannot secure corn and foodstuffs from the inhabitants of the land, then they will be forced to return from whence they came. Is that not so?" Many nodded in approval.

The people of the White Rock were a wary, distrustful people as their choice of a home perched high on a solitary rock evidenced, and the sight of bearded, armor-clad, beast-riding strangers did nothing to change that. From the resolution on the faces of the men in the *kiva*, it was clear that the newcomers would not be able to expect much generosity from the inhabitants of that particular village.

Rohona was not afraid. His prayer-arrow long ago had carried his fear into that inaccessible crevice where it still lay, but fear is not the only thing that causes an uneasy feeling in the pit of the stomach. As he walked back to his home after leaving the *kiva*, he gazed toward the north to the ravine by which the strangers were encamped. It was as if he could see them in his mind, for he knew his eyes could not. An occasional glitter of reflected light flashed or a telltale ribbon of smoke rose into the sky, and although he could not see the bearded ones, they were etched vividly in his mind. He had a feeling of deep distrust and dislike when he went to the villages along the Great River to the east to see the strangers who had come into their land, but last night, the knot of uneasiness came to rest in his stomach.

He had gone down to the valley floor and across to the ravine to reconnoiter. He watched the pale ones' leader walk away from the camp into the darkness, unarmed and alone. He saw the bearded man kneel and saw him pray as he fingered something he held in his hands.

The man's action was not unusual. Many had been the times that Rohona himself had gone out alone to pray and make offerings to the K'atsina at Wenimats, but when he heard the man speaking in his strange-sounding manner, exhorting the god to whom he addressed his passionate words, it was as if a stone had suddenly been dropped into Rohona's stomach.

He knew not a word of what the man was speaking. Nevertheless, he understood with perfect clarity the vehemence with which the man was addressing his god. What could the man possibly be requesting in such a manner? Rohona could not begin to guess. He felt, however, the power of the man's words, and the stranger's intensity made him understand the absolute conviction the man had in his god—just as his people had absolute conviction in the K'atsina at Wenimats.

When the stranger looked into the star-flecked black of the sky, Rohona's eyes, too, lifted to the immense vault, wondering if the stranger saw something there that he did not. At that moment he had begun to feel the disquietude. Who was this stranger's god whom the man addressed so forcefully? For what had the pale one been asking? Did this man's god answer his prayers as the K'atsina answered the prayers of the Ácoma? Rohona was gripped by an intense need to see these strangers gone from his land.

When he reached the roof of his house, he knew that he would give nothing to the strangers that day when they came again to barter for the food they wanted. Kakuna was kneeling at the grinding bins, at work with the hand stone, quickly and efficiently turning the kernels of corn into meal.

"Grind no more, wife," he said tersely as he took his lynx-skin quiver from its peg on the wall.

Kakuna looked up, startled at the harsh sound of his voice. "Do the strangers not come today for cornmeal?" she asked.

"Yes, they come," he responded, his angular, high-cheekboned face hard. "But we will give them none. We do not need their things. Our child that is coming soon will not need their things either."

Kakuna did not question why. She rose from the grinding stones and wiped the smudge of cornmeal from her face that she had placed there as a prayer before she began to grind. She did ask one question. "What if the strangers do not get as much food as they want?"

Rohona shrugged, but it was not a casual motion. "I do not know." He said nothing further as he checked the arrows in his quiver and checked the tension of his bowstring.

Friday, December 4, 1598, was a crystal cold day. The sky was intensely blue, marred by nothing save a red-tailed hawk that flew up from a cluster of scrub cedar. Juan de Zaldívar squinted into the distance at the pale ivory-pink sandstone citadel. Not even the rock at Gibraltar seemed as imposing.

It was mid-afternoon when they reached the base of the steep cliffs, edged here and there by high-drifted pale pink sand dunes ground from the mesa rock by centuries of wind and rain. The Maese dismounted and turned to Bernabé de las Casas.

"Remain here," he ordered and motioned to three soldiers, "you, also, remain and watch the horses." He spoke to the others. "Once more I exhort you—do not molest any native, and, furthermore, I order that no one leave the group at any time when you reach the top of the mesa. In addition," he commanded, "under pain of strict disciplinary action, *all* must remain within my sight, for I will have no native bothered in any way!" After he spoke, fourteen men accompanied him from the camp where the others of the party remained. The group climbed to the top of the mesa, followed by the delegation of Ácoma who had come down to meet them.

The Maese was asked in sign language to wait in one of the open squares among the house rows while a village crier went through the streets asking all who had cornmeal or other goods to barter to come out, for the strangers had arrived. While the crier went about his job, the Spaniards waited, taking advantage of the chance to survey the village they had heard so much about.

They marveled at the tiered, well-constructed houses built in long rows. The Maese noted the long, thick beams of pine that supported the roofs. No vegetation grew on the mesa top and there was nothing more than scrub trees on the valley floor, and he realized with awe that the beams had to have been carried by hand from the distant mountains and up the sheer cliffs to the summit. Only the tall mountains to the north or west could have provided those pine beams. The Maese felt a growing respect for these high-mesa dwellers.

He had lost track of time as he surveyed the dwellings, but suddenly he realized that they had been standing there a considerable length of time. The soldiers were becoming restless. Captain Gaspar Tábora leaned over and whispered to him.

"What's taking the devils so long to come up with the provisions? They've had two days to be grinding. I think we'd better demand the cornmeal or we'll be here all day."

A look of displeasure crossed the Maese's face. "We are not here to demand. We are here to buy food with hatchets and iron knives."

At the end of another long span of time, he was forced to act. Tempers were becoming short having to wait for what seemed to the soldiers an interminable length of time. Many derogatory remarks were being uttered at the natives and hissing murmurs of "Let's take the goddamned corn and go!" reached the Maese's ears.

In a loud, angry voice, he ordered all the soldiers to stand at attention. The natives who were in the square could not mistake the attitude of the Spaniards even though they understood not a word the strangers said. The Maese was furious at the soldiers. "You shall stand this way until sundown if the remarks continue," he spoke angrily. "We are visitors to this village, not overlords."

Leaving them there, he along with Tomás turned and approached the native with whom he had spoken earlier. The translator asked about the cornmeal.

The Indian made a gesture with his hands. "I do not know why the villagers have not come forward."

"Tell him," the Maese suggested, "that perhaps he should make his rounds again."

And so it was done. Not more than half a dozen Indians came bringing cornmeal, and what they brought was pitifully small.

The Maese tried not to let his disappointment show. He spoke again to the native, imploring, "We need *much* cornmeal for we are going on a *long, long* journey to the west. We will pay you well for your food."

Tomás translated.

"Perhaps if you were to go from house to house asking, you might receive more," the Indian suggested to the translator.

The Maese did not like the idea, but the long rays of the sun told him that the short winter day was quickly escaping. He nodded his agreement and walked back to the soldiers who still stood at attention. He told them what had been decided, and their pleasure was obvious.

"Once more," he commanded, "you have my express orders not to molest the natives. This half of you," he shouted, motioning with his hand, "will go with Captain Núñez de Chaves and Captain Vicente to the eastern part of the village. The remainder will come with me this way."

The two groups could not have been apart for more than fifteen minutes when the sound of unmistakable altercation reached the Maese's ears. Whirling, he started at a run toward the sound, but many Indians had gathered in his path. Anger covered their faces and they began to hurl stones at him and the men with him. In response, the soldiers with the Maese quickly aimed their arquebuses at the crowd that approached them.

"No!" he shouted. "There must not be bloodshed if at all possible. We must show them we have not come to fight. When they see that, they will cease." But they did not cease. The stones were joined by arrows, and the Maese was forced to retreat out of the streets of the house rows and into an open area where an outcropping of rocks rose up behind them.

"Fire into the air!" Juan de Zaldívar shouted. "Scare them, but do not harm them!"

"Maese!" Captain Gaspar Tábora yelled above the din of threatening natives. "They intend to kill us! Let us fire at them!"

"No!" he ordered, but at that moment Hernando de Segura fell dead at his feet, an arrow piercing his neck. "Fire at will," the Maese shouted, countermanding his order of only seconds before, and he fired his wheel-lock pistol into the oncoming rabble as did those with arquebuses. As natives fell dead from the blast, screams of fury and terror rent the air, and momentarily the surging Ácoma stopped. It gave Captain Núñez de Chaves and two soldiers who had fallen back trying to reach the Maese enough time to achieve their goal.

"What in God's name happened back there?" Juan de Zaldívar shouted to the captain as he reloaded his wheellock.

"Martín de Biberos wanted a turkey a woman had," the captain shouted. "They got into a scuffling match over the damned bird, and Biberos hit her across the side of the head with his arquebus. Must have killed the poor woman."

"Good God, no!"

They retreated toward the rocks in a hail of stones and arrows. Núñez continued."The side of her head was smashed, and she fell lifeless to the ground." The report of the Maese's pistol drowned out the next words, but he heard the captain finish as they reached the rocks, saying, "When Biberos was dead, they turned on the rest of us."

"Maese! What is it?" the captain yelled just then as he saw Juan de Zaldívar go down on one knee.

A grimace of pain crossed the Maese's face as he grabbed the arrow that had pierced his thigh just below the armor of the cuisse. He broke the shaft off and yelled, "Come on!" as he turned and began to climb the rocky rise, his wounded leg dragging. As he scrambled higher up, he saw Núñez fall backward, wounded by what, he could not tell, but it was with horror that he saw the natives leap forward and grab the officer, dragging him backward, pounding his head with stones. Blood flew everywhere and shortly all that remained of Captain Núñez was a mangled corpse. The Maese felt sick to his stomach at the sight and glanced around him. There were only three soldiers left with him. Where were the others? Had they all been killed?

Suddenly, in the midst of deafening clamor, he experienced a moment of utter quiet and stark revelation. God had granted his request. He had given him the answer he had sought. Last night he had begged God to show him His will, and *now* was that moment.

A wrenching pain gripped his heart, but it was not caused by any manmade weapon. A fleeting picture of a graceful dark-haired, gray-eyed woman passed in front of his eyes. "I truly loved thee," he whispered, "more than life itself."

He scarcely felt the rock as it smashed against the morion helmet at his temple. His knees buckled and he was in a kneeling position. His body crumpled forward, and he felt sand and blood in his mouth as he began the ritual, "Forgive me, Father, for I have sinned . . ."

# Part Three

# EL ESCLAVO

## Slave, February 1599

# Chapter 17

"Angelita, Angelita, wake up," Fabia said, gently shaking the young woman's shoulder as she lay with her head slumped against her feverish patient. "Wake up, *querida*. We must give the *indio más agua*. He must drink."

María Angélica pushed herself away from the edge of the cot. "I didn't realize I had fallen asleep."

"Come, let us try to get more water into him."

María Angélica lifted the Indian's head and shoulders as best she could while Fabia tried to pour cool water down his throat. "He must have liquids," the old woman said.

He frequently choked on it, but every half hour they gave him water although he was unaware of anything that was going on around him. María Angélica looked tired and haggard, but in spite of Fabia's protests, she would not leave his side.

Vicente stepped into the room once in the early evening while his wife was ministering to the Indian. He looked with contempt at the savage and said scornfully to her, "I'm gratified you're going to so much trouble to keep the filthy heathen alive—it'd be a shame to lose twenty years' worth of servitude. He's young enough and looks like a strong bastard, I ought to get a lot of work out of him. I asked the governor for him, and I sure as hell hope he doesn't die on me."

María Angélica's eyes were narrow with anger as she stood. "Perhaps it would be more merciful to let him die," she said with biting disgust. She had never spoken to her husband in that manner before and was surprised to hear herself.

"You're probably right," he said before he turned on his heel and left the room.

She reached down and put her hand on the feverish man's arm as if in reassurance that what her husband had said was not true, but the Indian was aware of nothing. Or so she thought. But when she put her hand on his arm, he moved as if in response. She took his hand and held it. Some moments later in a scarcely audible rasp, he whispered, "Kakuna." María Angélica whispered, "Kakuna"—his wife as she had learned from his sister who now belonged to Dorotea's household.

It suddenly occurred to her that he must have loved the woman who was his wife. It was the first time that she had ever imagined that the heathen were capable of love or any other sentiment, for that matter. They were pagan; she had only envisioned savage acts and abominable rituals. "Dear Lord," she whispered, feeling shame, "they are your children, too, aren't they? Forgive my blindness."

She slipped to her knees beside the cot as she held the hand of the savage. *"Dios,"* she said quietly, "I have hated this land. I still hate it. I'm sorry, I cannot lie. This land took the Maese from me, but have you brought me here for some purpose? I know I am weak and shallow. I must have help—I cannot endure my life as it is now. If you want something of me, you've got to help me."

The man moved again and it seemed to her that in his weakness he might be trying to pull her closer. She leaned down toward him and spoke his name softly.

"Rohona."

She saw his other arm lift slightly off the cot. And then somehow she was lying with her cheek resting on his chest, her hands clasping his. Her head flew up.

"Fabia! Fabia!" she shouted. "Come quickly! The fever has broken!" She wanted to laugh and cry at the same time. "Thank you, *Dios,* for the life of this native," she murmured. "I swear I will teach this man about you."

That following morning the Indian opened his eyes for the first time since he had been brought to San Juan. María Angélica smiled at him and spoke his name, but he made no response. He looked at her, but there was a vacant look in his eyes as if he saw but knew nothing. She was alarmed and went to get Fabia. When they returned, his eyes were closed.

"He has been sick for many days," Fabia said. "The fever sometimes weakens the mind. God willing, he will return to himself. What we must do now is get some food into him. Look how gaunt he is."

In all her care of him, it had made no impression on María Angélica that he must have been a powerful man. The hollows in his cheeks made his high cheekbones more prominent, and in spite of the obvious weight loss from the sickness, it was readily apparent he had been strong and agile. For the first time she realized he was taller than the average native and was lean with long, sinewy muscles. How fast he must have been able to run; with what strength he must have been able to pull a bow string.

For the first time, she saw him as a man and for some reason blushed. Before, she had seen him only as one of God's creatures and a heathen at that.

Fabia made a rich broth with marrow bones and María Angélica sat behind the Indian to hold his head and shoulders so that the old woman might feed him. Fabia had washed his long, matted hair with yucca suds, and it gleamed blue-black, the long, coarse strands falling across María Angélica's lap as she sat propping him up.

In the beginning it had revolted her to touch him, but that had gradually changed. Now there had been another change. She still ministered to him, rubbing salve on his wrists where the manacles had abraded the skin. He would always carry the scars of his ordeal, but it no longer bothered her to look at the stump that had also begun to heal, and she could even change the bandage by herself.

He seemed to like her touch, for if he were tormented by a dream, she could calm him by placing her hand on his arm or by holding his hand. She bathed him gently, but she could never overcome her embarrassment, and much to her relief Fabia took care of the most intimate matters.

She did not dislike ministering to him. She felt useful in caring for a human life. It gave her something to do, something to occupy her and keep the horrible memories from flooding back and consuming her. She devoted all her energies to trying to restore his health as if by saving a life she might atone for a death that weighed heavily on her. As she cared for the Indian she marveled at the smoothness of his skin and its deep bronze color. She was surprised at his lack of body and facial hair, although she knew that in Mexico the natives were beardless. When she bathed him, she ran her hands over his muscles in what was very similar to a caress, although she would never have admitted it.

The Indian gradually began to regain some weight from the nutritious food Fabia fed him. Although it seemed he had back the physical strength to eat, he did not. Fabia tried showing him the food and handing him a spoon, but he just looked at it blankly and did not eat. They had Dorotea bring Siya to see if he would talk to her, but he looked blankly at his sister also. He did not even say the name "Kakuna."

Siya had learned a few words in Castilian, and it was obvious that Dorotea and she were becoming friends. They had one thing in common—hatred for the man who was the source of their misery. One day when the two women were preparing to leave after visiting María Angélica's patient, Siya approached her and knelt, taking her hand.

*"Gracias,"* she said softly.

María Angélica lifted the girl to her feet and embraced her. "It was not I, but *Dios* who saved his life," she said gently. Siya looked at her and shook her head, indicating sadly that she did not understand. María Angélica pointed to the Indian and then to herself and shook her head "no." She pointed to him again and then looked and pointed upward to indicate *Dios*.

Siya looked up, also, but saw only the roof. She looked back at María Angélica, not comprehending. The young Spanish woman hugged her and smiled. "One of these days you will know what I mean," she said, and patted the girl's hand reassuringly. Siya smiled and María Angélica realized how beautiful she was with her even white teeth, long, shiny black hair, and high-cheekboned face with its large dark eyes. Theirs must have been a fine-looking family, she thought, if brother and sister were both so handsome.

Gradually the blank look left the Indian's face, supplanted by a look of perplexity. When she came to feed him or change his bandages, his dark eyes never left her face. His look was not unpleasant, but it made her uncomfortable. Sometimes when she sat by his bedside feeding him, for now he could sit up, propped against pillows, he would reach out and touch her hand or arm as if to see if she were real. One day he stroked his fingers across her cheeks and touched her eyes and hair.

She became nervous and uneasy when he touched her but made an effort to smile and be calm, hoping that by reassurance he might regain his understanding. He even looked at his mutilated foot with complete incomprehension. She asked Fabia if he would ever return to normal; the old woman shrugged and said, "Only the Almighty knows."

The Indian improved steadily, but he seemed plagued at times by excruciating headaches, for all of a sudden a grimace of pain would contort his features, he would cover his face and hold his head with his hands, and when the pain had gone, he would go into a deep sleep for several hours.

Gradually María Angélica was becoming used to his inquiring touches, and it seemed as if a kind of greeting had evolved, for when she came into his room and neared his bed, he would put out his hand and she would come close so that he could rub his fingers on her cheek. She smiled at him, but he never smiled at her. For some reason she would have liked very much for him to.

She sat and talked to him, and she had even begun to bring a book, which she read to him. She knew he understood nothing, but likewise he did not seem to understand his native tongue, for when Siya talked to him, his reaction was the same as when María Angélica spoke to him in Castilian. Nor did he speak. Once or twice it seemed to her that he might have tried to say something, but no sound came forth.

"We need to start getting him up to begin to learn to walk with his crippled foot," Fabia said one day. "He is going to be weak, having been in bed for so long, and it will undoubtedly take him a while to learn to balance without the front part of his foot."

Fabia slipped cotton trousers on him, and together she and María Angélica tried to help him stand. As they supported him, he wavered for a moment before his knees buckled, and with a thud, he half fell, half sat down on the cot. Again the two women got him to stand for several seconds. They did that several times, and then let him rest, for just that effort seemed to tire him.

The next day they again helped him to stand and let go of him to see if he might be able to remain upright on his own. He lost his balance, however, and pitched backwards onto the cot. María Angélica grabbed for him but was unable to break his fall. Fearful that he might have hurt himself, she knelt down quickly on the cot and started to lift his head, her eyes wide with concern, but the Indian sat up on his own, and seeing the look on her face touched her cheeks with his fingers. She blushed without being able to help it. The Indian attempted to stand on his own and did so for a very few seconds before his knees buckled.

The following day he took a few wobbly steps as they supported him on either side. He was heavy for the two of them, and although she was taller than Fabia, she found it difficult to support him. It would not have occurred to either woman, however, to have asked Vicente's help. Fabia would never have asked the captain anything; María Angélica would not have asked him for fear he would have done something cruel to the Indian. As it was, Vicente paid scarce attention to the new member of the household who had as his quarters one of the small, dark rooms to the back. Only on infrequent occasions did the captain even bother to look into the room, and then it was to inquire how much longer it would be before they could get any work out of him.

"I want him ready by planting time," Vicente said.

One morning as María Angélica was taking food to the Indian, she heard a terrible crash. She dropped the bowl of food and ran headlong into the room. She gasped as she saw him lying sprawled on the floor, motionless. Yelling for Fabia, she ran to him and fell to her knees beside him, placing her hand on his chest to see if he were alive. Undoubtedly he had decided to get up and try walking by himself.

Fabia came running into the room and rushed to the Indian's side. Still he did not move. Fabia, too, felt his chest to assure herself that his heart was beating, for he lay so still he looked lifeless. Fabia surmised what had happened, and very carefully she ran her hands over his head and found the already rising lump on the back of his head. When she withdrew her hand, there was blood on it.

"It is not bleeding badly," the old woman said as she pressed a piece of folded muslin to the back of his head, "but he is unconscious. He must have hit something *muy duro*." They both glanced at the corner of the rough cot.

It took three days for him to regain consciousness. María Angélica had become so distraught with worry, she had asked Father Cristóbal to come. She wondered if perhaps the Indian should have last rites.

On the third day after he had fallen, she was alone in the room with him, sitting beside the cot reading, when out of the corner of her eye she glimpsed a movement. Her head jerked up, and it was true—the fingers of his hand were twitching. She slid off her chair and took his hand in hers, speaking his name, "Rohona."

His eyelids fluttered and then opened, staring for a moment at the ceiling. "Fabia," she shouted, "he is waking up!" At the sound of her voice, the Indian turned his eyes toward her, and she gasped.

Never before had she seen such a look on a person's face. The color drained from her own, and she tried to say something but no words would come from her throat. He pulled his hand from hers, sat up abruptly but then grabbed his head in pain and fell back on the cot. She scrambled to her feet. She wanted to reach out and touch him when she saw his pain but was afraid after having seen the look in his eyes. When the pain had passed, he glanced around the room and back at her, questioning fury and hatred etched on his face.

"What is it?" asked Fabia, stepping into the room. Instantly, the hate-filled eyes fell on her, and she whispered, "He has regained his memory, *querida*, how different things will be now."

"Go get Siya," María Angélica said in scarcely more than a whisper. "She can tell him there is nothing to fear."

The Indian tried sitting up again, this time more slowly, and María Angélica took a step toward him intending to help him, but he looked up at her, the fierceness in his eyes making her stop in midmovement. He started to swing his legs off the bed and that was when he saw his stump. A look of horror washed across his face.

He fell back on the bed and lay there staring at the ceiling. He remained that way even after Siya entered the room and ran to his side. She spoke to him, but he did not answer. Again she spoke. He turned to face her, and it appeared as if she, too, recoiled at the look in his eyes. He spoke viciously to her. María Angélica could not understand the words, but there was no mistaking the fury in them. Siya replied to him, and it seemed as if she were trying to placate him, but it did no good. Eventually she rose and left the room and the other women followed her.

Once outside, she turned to María Angélica. "Rohona . . . angry," she said haltingly in Castilian. "I sorry." She wanted to say more but knew no words and shook her head sadly.

María Angélica patted her arm. "I am sorry, too," she said quietly.

She spent the rest of the morning pondering what she was going to do. Finally she knelt in front of the statue of Our Lady and asked for guidance and for patience. She had given *Dios* her promise that she would teach this man about Him. She did not bargain on so much hatred, but if one cheek were smote, she would turn the other. The Lord had faced the hatred of the mob, she could face the hatred of this man. She would not turn away; he must see that not all Spaniards were vicious monsters.

With that resolve, she took lunch to him that day. Her hands trembled as she entered the room, and she tried to steel herself to the look she knew would be in his eyes. She walked in, a smile pasted on her face, and spoke to him. Of course he would not understand, but eventually he would learn.

"I have brought you food," she said, trying to sound cheerful. He turned to look at her, and in spite of all her resolve, she recoiled at the sight of the hatred but continued walking toward him and set the bowl on the small wooden carton that served as a bedside table.

"Do you want me to feed you?" she asked, making the motions. He stared at her with narrow eyes but made no response to the signs. She picked up the spoon, dipped it in the broth, and reached to feed him. He knocked the spoon from her hand, splattering broth over himself, and when she took the linen napkin and tried to wipe it off, he pushed her hand away. She picked the spoon up off the floor, wiped it on the napkin, and held it out to him. He would not take it.

"Well," she said rising, "here is your food. If you wish to eat, please do so." She took a small silver bell from the pocket of her dress and rang it. "If you need anything, just ring this," she said and pointed to herself, "and I will come." She had scarcely stepped out of the room when she heard the bell tinkle. She stepped back inside but the Indian's look told her he did not want her there. Again she left, heard the bell, and stepped back into the room. The Indian looked at her and then at the bell and tossed it on the floor as if it were trash. She swallowed at what she knew was an insult, but she walked forward, retrieved the bell, and placed it on the carton near his bed.

When she came back later, the broth was gone. At least it appeared that he was not going to try to starve himself. She pulled the chair nearer the bed and sat down. She had resolved that she would begin teaching him Castilian at once, whether he liked it or not. She would not let his hate drive her away. The Indian lay on the bed and stared at the ceiling as if she were not there.

"You, Rohona," she said. Without thinking he turned and looked at her as he heard his name rather oddly pronounced. Just as quickly, he looked back at the ceiling, his face scornful.

"I am María Angélica," she said and pointed to herself. "You, Rohona. I, María Angélica." She kept repeating the phrases again and again, although the Indian might have been deaf for the apparent attention he was paying. Eventually, he even closed his eyes, but she was sure he was not asleep, and so she continued with the lesson.

"Bed," she said, tapping on the cot, "chair," she added, tapping on the chair. She pointed to her hands, feet, mouth, eyes, and to other objects in the room, repeating the names again and again. For half an hour she talked to the man who lay ignoring her. Then she rose and left with a cheerful, "I'll be back later."

She and Fabia came to the room to help him with his walking, but he pushed them away. Not long after, she realized that when they were out of the room, he was attempting to stand on his own and trying to take a step or two. He was obviously not making much progress. She went to one of the men, a carpenter, and asked him to make a cane. When it was ready, she took it to the Indian's room and demonstrated how it was to be used. He did not even look at it. However, later she thought she heard him trying to use it.

She was persistent with the Spanish lessons, spending a half hour each morning and afternoon at the language. That the Indian appeared to pay no attention whatever did not bother her. She would be like the tiny drop of water that with persistence eventually cracks the granite boulder. Each night, however, she did pray for patience, but only once had she wept from frustration, and that was in her room, unseen by anyone save her statuette of Our Lady of Guadalupe. Perhaps the Virgin would aid her in her quest to bring *Dios* to the Indian as Our Lady had aided in converting the natives of the valley of Mexico by appearing to the Indian Juan Diego in 1531. Surely the patron saint of the New World would help her.

One day she walked into his room and caught him on his feet attempting to walk. Without hesitating, she walked directly toward him and stopped in front of him. "Very good!" she said, smiling, but it was obvious he was angry that she had come in.

Abruptly he stepped backwards to move away from her but lost his balance in the process. She grabbed frantically for him but was unable to stop his fall, and lost her own balance, tumbling with him in a heap onto the low bed.

She fell on top of him and frantically struggled to get up. He tried to push her off but the edge of her shawl and the hem of her skirt had caught under him. For a few seconds they struggled to get free then ceased at almost the same moment. Putting his hands on her waist, the Indian rolled over on top of her, freeing the edges of her clothing from beneath him. He was on top, pinning her to the cot, and for a fraction of a second, they looked at each other. Her gray eyes were wide, and she was acutely aware of his body pressed against her own.

The hate in his eyes returned with all its original fierceness, and he pushed himself off her as if repelled. She got quickly to her feet, and it took all her willpower to keep from running from the room. She did not return to his room that day.

# Chapter 18

Spring came late that year. It was the first week of May when the last frost tipped the new leaves with white. What the Spaniards did not realize was that spring always came late in that high north country. It had been cold, bleak, and windy throughout March and April, and only a few courageous little blooms sprouted on low sprangly plants. It was a pitiful display of reawakening nature that did nothing to revive the spirits of the colonizers.

Winter seemed to drag on forever. Their houses were drafty, cold, and lice infested. Their eyes burned constantly from the smoky interiors with their poorly vented fires. Hands and lips were chapped from the dry, bitter cold. Food was scarce and often rancid, and everyone had a gaunt, pallid look. Hunger and discontent stalked the newcomers. Small groups of soldiers gathered at Pablo de Aguilar's dwelling and there were whispers that they spoke of desertion. Diego de Zubia, whose job it was to requisition corn from the neighboring pueblos, reported to Oñate that the natives were becoming defiant, refusing to give but meager amounts of their stored grain.

"If you ask me, Governor," he had said on more than one occasion, "sooner or later we are going to have to use force to get the corn."

"That must be avoided," the governor reiterated. But the situation became so dire that in March he sent a desperate plea to the Viceroy for food, supplies, and reinforcements. They had to have food or they would surely perish.

The *Río Bravo* ran cold and swollen from the melting snows and the Spaniards found it exceedingly difficult and unpleasant to ford the river in order to reach the flat land on its west bank where they were going to plant their first crops in their new land. Fields had to be cleared, plowed, and harrowed, and the irrigation ditch they had begun in the fall must be completed before planting could be done, but the Spaniards were not counting on their labor alone to supply their needs.

Shortly after they had settled into their new capital the previous fall, the governor called a general meeting with the hope of quieting some of the discontent. "Men," he began, "so that our conquest may proceed more quickly, I am going to grant Indian pueblos in *encomienda*. By this method we can acquire the food and labor we need if we are to be successful in this new country. I have decided to grant entire villages to my officers and soldiers. This grant entitles the grantee to collect a specified amount of tribute from the Indians who live within their allotment. The tribute will be in the form of *fanegas* of corn, woven cotton blankets, and free labor. In return for this tribute, you, as *encomendero*, are to insure the natives' well-being, not only in temporal matters but also in the spiritual realm. That is to say, you are to protect the natives under your jurisdiction from hostile tribes that might attack them, and in addition, you are to see that the heathen are instructed in the Catholic faith and all that attains thereto."

The soldiers were enormously pleased, considering what they might reap from the Indians they would be allotted. What the governor was instituting was a kind of feudalism transplanted to the soil of *Nuevo México*.

Many of the Spaniards had brought servants with them from Mexico. A few were blacks from Africa, but the majority were Mexican Indians or *mestizos*, half white, half Indian. The infantry brought to New Mexico by Oñate was, in fact, almost entirely made up of Tlascalan Indians from New Spain. Among the servants brought were household menials, but many were stockherders and horsemen whose duty it was to care for the stock and help produce the large herds that the colonizers hoped to raise for profit in the new country. The Spaniards, however, had not counted on such arid land, land that in many places could support no more than one or two cows per *caballería*. The climate was harsh, and the vast herds the colonizers had hoped would make them wealthy were not going to materialize overnight. Most of their expectations rested on what they might acquire from the inhabitants of the land.

Priests were sent out to the nearest pueblos to begin sowing the seeds of Christianity as the colonizers sowed their European grains of wheat and barley. Just as the grain was foreign to the new soil, so the Catholic faith with its god who had been nailed to a cross was foreign to the people of the new land.

There was little difference in the natives' minds between the long-robes and the metal-clothes. Both demanded labor and foodstuffs. The long-robes wanted a very large house built for their god on the cross as well as a house for themselves. They wanted people to cook and clean for them, and to plant many acres of grain for them, and to take care of the livestock that belonged to them. They said the food was for the long-robes to keep, so that if there were ever a famine, they could distribute it to the people. But the people always had at least two years' worth of food stored in the bottom rooms of their houses. Why was it necessary for the long-robe to make them plant for him?

Not only did the Spaniards bring new kinds of grain and animals into the land, they also brought tomatoes, chiles, melons, cabbage, onions, potatoes, herbs, and other comestibles that they hoped would carry them through the long, harsh winters ahead.

The spring had been cold and miserable, but once summer came that year, the weather became beautiful. The newcomers continued to marvel at the intensity of the blue of the sky. The cottonwoods and willows along the *Río del Norte* burst into fluttering, shimmering greenery, and the new soil was accepting the foreign seeds with a rapidity that was in stark contrast to the seeds of the Faith the friars had sown.

Although the days were hot, the nights were pleasantly cool, and the air was clear and clean—a welcome difference from their stuffy, smoke-filled homes of wintertime. Spirits rose as the men felt the exhilaration of being able to ride again. Horsemen all their lives, the soldiers as well as the officers grew restless cooped up in their small, mud-plastered quarters. There was much talk of gold, of the South Sea, of a place called Quivira in the east that was said to hold many riches.

"Governor," Vicente spoke as he approached Oñate who had just ridden up from an inspection trip to Santa Clara pueblo. "Fabia has made some of those *pastelitos* you appreciate, and I have a new pipe of *jerez* that needs christening. Would you care to join us this evening?"

*"Por supuesto,"* Don Juan replied with a laugh, "I was afraid that *jerez* of yours was all gone. It has been a while since I have had any."

"Forgive me, Governor," Vicente said, "but with the roundup and *herradero*, as well as the planting, it seems there has been little time for the more pleasant things of life."

That evening Vicente was more liberal with the *jerez* he had begun to hoard than he had been for some months. The governor seemed in fine spirits as the captain poured another round.

"The men are eager—impatient—I would say, for an expedition," Vicente said as he broached the subject he had been waiting for. "Leave the servants and the Indians to tend the crops. Let them take care of the harvest. The soldiers are not farmers, nor are the officers. We are *conquistadores!* We came to found a kingdom and to find gold!"

The smile on the governor's face disappeared. "I am well aware of the fact that the success or failure of this conquest depends upon the gold or silver I am able to discover, but the colony must have food or we shall perish. I do not have to tell you how desperate the situation was in March, when I sent the plea to the Viceroy for supplies, and I pray to God they arrive before this winter. Before the snow had gone, you felt your stomach gnaw painfully from hunger as did we all." His voice rose. "It is quite conceivable that we may all die of starvation! It is warm now, and some of the cows that have had calves are giving milk. The harvest of the crops we have planted along this *Río del Norte* must be successful or when the snows come again, our conquest will die with us."

They did not notice María Angélica who had just stepped into the room. The color left her face and she stood unmoving, the tray of *pastelitos* clenched in her hands. Unaware of her presence, the governor continued. "We can press the natives only so far. They are all complaining. The first thing I was met with this afternoon at Santa Clara was a group of the tribe's elders with grievances against the Purveyor General and the *padre*. And my own men are complaining. Does Pablo de Aguilar think I do not know what he is about? He knows how I deal with deserters. He saw the severed hands of those bastards that Villagrá and Márquez brought back preserved in salt, but there can be no conquest if we have no food to eat!"

"But, Governor," Vicente said, "any offenses that may be committed against the natives or the growing number of malcontents among the soldiers will be forgiven or overlooked in proportion to the wealth you send out of New Mexico for the King's coffers. Is that not true?"

Oñate was silent for long moments, and Vicente shifted nervously. "You're right, Captain," the governor said at last. "You are right. I have let the lack of food cloud my thoughts. We must begin the search for gold—we cannot wait for the harvest because then winter will shortly be upon us. We will requisition the necessary grain for an expedition from the pueblos, despite their complaints. But I shall not lead the men. I will stay to insure the harvest does not suffer neglect."

Toward the first of July the expedition Oñate had authorized set out. Led by the hero of the battle of Ácoma, the Sergeant Major and thirty men dressed in armor, their curved morion helmets hanging from the armor-hook for travelling, rode out of the tiny capital of their kingdom amid loud shouts of encouragement. They were bound for the South Sea with its riches of pearls. Each man, envisioning his own wealth, communicated his excitement to the horse he rode. All the animals champed at the bit and stamped nervously, scarcely held in check by their riders. With the group rode Captain Vicente, his eyes bright and hard, the prospect of discovering gold along the way foremost in his mind.

As she stood watching the dust swirl in a cloud as the men rode out, María Angélica's heart rose to see her husband depart. As winter dragged on, he had grown more and more discontented and foul-humored. He talked of nothing but the necessity of finding gold. Usually it was to the other officers and soldiers, but if he were at home, the snow heavy on the ground, she was forced to listen to the interminable ranting about the imperative need to find the precious yellow metal. Sometimes his eyes would take on a strange luster, and she avoided looking at him.

She turned away from the cloud of dust and started back toward the dwellings. She knew that one of the most important reasons she was happy to see him leave was that for several months, at least, she would be relieved of having to fulfill her wifely duty to him. She shuddered at the thought of how she had to make her mind a blank when he came to her bed, and she had to endure the animal grunts and thrusting by silently praying. She felt filthy when he had finished with her. The next morning she always said a prayer for the soul of the Maese. The pain she felt had finally lessened some. The wound was beginning to heal, but it left her completely hollow inside. To her relief, Vicente did not come to her bed often, for he spent late hours drinking and playing cards with other soldiers, and, she suspected, there were many poor young Indian girls who were forced to endure his attentions. She had seen Indian girls of only twelve or thirteen already showing large bellies, distended with the bastard seeds the Spanish soldiers had planted there.

"Thank God, they're gone," Dorotea spoke as she walked up to María Angélica. It seemed their thoughts had been on the same thing. "Thank God Isidro's gone," she continued. "Poor Siya can now have a respite from his constant demands."

María Angélica turned to Dorotea and put a hand on her arm in sympathy. Dorotea looked away and spoke bitterly. "He uses her vilely. He is so rough with her that some mornings it appears painful for her to walk. It's almost more than I can stand. I have begged her forgiveness for being unable to alleviate her suffering, and many times I have even offered myself to Isidro to ease the burden on her, but he just laughs at me."

She wiped roughly at the tears that had sprung to her eyes. "It is so humiliating to offer myself to a man I despise and then have him laugh at me. I don't know how the girl bears it so stoically, but she never complains. She did show me, though, an herb she uses to avoid getting with child. Thank God Isidro doesn't know," Dorotea said, crossing herself, "because he would certainly beat her and might even kill her if he was enraged enough. God knows why, but he wants a son more than anything else. He calls me the barren old hag and says if he cannot get sons out of my belly, he'll get them out of some Indian girl's."

María Angélica shuddered. "God forgive me, but I cannot believe He made all men in His own image." There was anger in her voice. "This morning I was in the main *sala* putting some of my books in a pine bookcase the carpenter, Jacobo, had made for me, and Vicente came into the room. He spoke harshly. 'Come here, wife, and give your husband a good-bye kiss.' He startled me and I turned around, despising the cold smile on his lips. Although it took every shred of willpower I possess, I went over to him, and placed a quick peck on his cheek. 'What kind of good-bye is that?' he said, and yanked me into his arms and brought his mouth roughly down on mine. He bruised my lips with his teeth, and as if that weren't enough, he yanked down my blouse, and," she paused with embarrassment, "he bit at my breasts and it really hurt, and as I tried to push him away, over his shoulder I saw the Indian standing there watching with his hate-filled eyes. Oh God, Dorotea, I can't tell you how mortified I was, and at that moment I despised my husband with an intensity that made me understand why some people might be tempted to kill. I know it is sinful, but . . ."

Dorotea interrupted, ice in her voice. "It may be sinful, but I have felt the same thing."

"I was horrified that the *indio* had to witness such a thing," María Angélica said, "but I was thankful Vicente didn't see him, for I have no idea what he might have done—to me, or to the Indian, or, for that matter, whether he would have even cared.

"I am so relieved to have him gone, for I fear constantly that he will vent his cruelty on the *indio* who, *gracias a Dios*, has finally recuperated physically from his long ordeal." Her voice had defeat in it. "But, Dorotea, his hate is such a vivid, palpable thing that at times I wonder if he will ever lose it. I am persevering in trying to teach him Castilian, though with no apparent success whatever, I must admit."

She stared off into the distance. "At times I have used his own stubbornness to keep me from giving up my attempts in frustration. I am not about to let that heathen wear me down when I have made a promise to God. Surely Our Lady will stand by my side if I continue to ask for her help." She crossed herself, and Dorotea patted her on the arm.

"You have more perseverance than I do," Dorotea said with a laugh. "That native has the most fearsome look on his face that I have ever seen. Don't you ever worry?"

María Angélica laughed. "It has never occurred to me. God has given me a big chore, and I can tell you I am only trying hard not to fail."

"Well, you must have succeeded to some degree," Dorotea answered, "because by the time planting season came, he was navigating under his own power and was as good a worker as anyone. I can tell you he surprised all the soldiers and Mexican overseers with his industry. Everyone sees the anger and the obvious hatred he does nothing to hide. I think they would have understood if he had refused to do anything, but the unrelenting way he works has baffled everyone and, oddly enough, he has instilled fear in no few number of them. I have even heard Isidro talk about him with a degree of respect in his voice, if that is possible. He said the Indian talks to no one, but whenever he is working, those around him work harder, glancing over their shoulder occasionally at him as if he were compelling them somehow. He said your crops are the most abundant and hardiest of all the colonists, and it looks as if you will have a good harvest."

"I know," María Angélica said. "Vicente would not have noticed, had others not mentioned it to him, and he, too, was surprised at how the *indio* works. At first he was amused and complacent, feeling proud that he had done so well in choosing his slave, thinking that the heathen warrior had learned his lesson in defying the mighty Spaniards. But there is nothing groveling or subservient in the Indian's eyes, and I have seen Vicente's amusement disappear. He keeps his wheellock pistol oiled and primed, and besides the sword that usually hangs at his side, he keeps a knife in his boot top, and he has fallen into the habit of glancing over his shoulder. He even told me that at times he almost wished the slave would try to attack him because he would enjoy running his sword through him and seeing his guts spill on the ground."

María Angélica trembled as she spoke. "But in my husband's words, 'the heathen bastard has never made the slightest move.' In spite of that, Vicente now stops for a moment before he enters a room, and he has made a practice of never entering a dark room without first lighting a tallow candle to disperse the shadows. In truth, I find it amusing," she said as her mouth curved in a smile, "but I would find anything amusing that gave Vicente pause. I just pray to God, though, that nothing happens."

The two women walked on without speaking. When they neared the horse corral, María Angélica nodded in that direction. "It appears the Indian might have made one friend, for he has taken to going to the corral, touching and looking at the animals. He sometimes makes signs to the *caballerizo*, but if you ask Domingo if he has become the Ácoma's friend, he shakes his head and says, '*¡Santa María!* That *indio* does not want a friend!'

"Perhaps Domingo is right," she continued, "if he is talking of the human kind, but the man has become friends, it seems, with the horses. Domingo himself—who you know loves the four-legged creatures more than he likes most men—said he respects the Indian's way with the animals. Perhaps out of that respect there will grow a kind of unspoken friendship." She paused and added softly, "I truly hope so."

She loved horses, too, and she had had her own for as long as she could remember. Her father bred stock on their *hacienda*, and the sorrel mare she had brought to New Mexico had been a present on her sixteenth birthday. Domingo was the one who had pronounced the filly, moments after it was born, one of the finest he had ever seen.

Domingo had been her father's *caballerizo*, just as many servants whom Vicente had brought along had worked for her father. She was deeply grateful for the people she knew she could trust and count on in a place and circumstance that seemed as precarious as their new colony.

She had noticed the *indio*'s interest in the horses and wished there were no order forbidding natives to ride them, for perhaps that might have been an avenue by which his hate could have been broken down.

# Chapter 19

The rider came galloping into San Juan from the south. His horse was lathered with sweat, and foam was flying from the corners of its mouth as the rider yanked it to a stop in the plaza.

"Tell the governor there has been an uprising among the Jumanos," the man gasped as he slid off his horse. "We tried to get our supplies for the journey to the South Sea from them, but they refused."

Fear rippled through the colonists who heard the messenger's words. Dorotea grabbed her skirts and ran to María Angélica's house with the news.

"*¡No lo quiera Dios!*" María Angélica gasped, crossing herself. "Are we in danger?" Her face went white. "What if the natives of the whole province rise up in revolt against us?" she whispered. "All we have heard recently is of their growing discontent."

"If they rise up," Dorotea answered matter-of-factly, "we would surely die for we are so few in number." María Angélica crossed herself again, and the two women rushed to the plaza for more details.

Oñate was already there, his voice thundering. "Have the natives of this land not learned from the destruction of Ácoma what the mighty Spaniards can do?" The governor shook with rage when he heard the story the messenger told. "How dare the Jumanos bring baskets of stones to the Sergeant Major instead of the corn he requested!"

With fifty men gathered quickly, Oñate galloped south to the Jumanos pueblo that lay east of the *Río del Norte* near the salines. He would no longer counsel against violence toward the natives who failed to bring forth food. They *would not* defy his authority. As governor his prime responsibility was to the King and the new province. The settlers and soldiers must eat. He could not allow the Indians to become recalcitrant in sharing their quantities of corn.

As soon as they reached the village, he shouted to the soldiers, "Put it to the torch! We'll burn this stinking pueblo to the ground, and then we'll see if they bring us stones instead of corn!"

The warriors of the village were prepared for the attack and sent a rain of arrows at the metal-clad men, but they were not prepared for the killing musket blast that Oñate ordered. The Jumanos had not seen the carnage at Ácoma and did not know the real killing power of the Spaniards' weapons, but they had heard of the aftermath and knew what had happened to the warriors there. When they saw the mangled bodies of their kinsmen, they laid down their weapons. The uprising was extinguished before it had really begun, but the governor called for the ringleaders and they were brought forth.

"I sentence you to hang for your insolence!" he shouted, and before the horrified eyes of the entire village, in moments their bodies dangled grotesquely from the ropes that held them.

"I repeat my order," the governor shouted. "After you have taken the corn for the Sergeant Major's expedition, fire the houses. We will teach these heathen that they dare not defy Spaniards."

He clasped the hand of the Sergeant Major. "God's speed and good luck."

The expedition continued on its journey, and the governor returned to San Juan, hoping desperately that the men he had sent in March for reinforcements would arrive that fall. Little did he expect that over a year and a half would elapse before the awaited recruits, ammunition, and foodstuffs finally rolled into the shabby little capital of San Juan.

The rain was sufficient that summer and the harvest was adequate for the moment, but not nearly enough grain had been sown. It was obvious that it could not last the winter; it would again be necessary to obtain food from the natives. The governor knew the complaints would be many and bitter, but there was nothing to be done. The colonists must eat.

September brought a crispness to the air, and it was a relatively pleasant life that they would have until the cold weather arrived and the food began to give out. At the moment, their stomachs were full, and there were no more rumors of Indian uprising. Tables had iron pots of meat in thick, red chile sauce; stacks of off-white wheat flour tortillas stood next to those of corn; *ollas* of white beans with chunks of cabbage, carrots, and a few turnips added fragrance to the cool fall evenings. Melons for dessert tasted sweet as honey.

María Angélica had been eager to go horseback riding, to ride along the river and among the cottonwoods, but Fabia had forbidden it, and there was scarcely anything Fabia forbid with which she did not comply, for the old woman usually had good reasons for what she did.

But she needed to get away by herself. She had grown up on a large, isolated *hacienda,* and she had become accustomed to and desired long periods of time alone. The Spaniards' quarters, there in the pueblo of San Juan, were cramped and close together, privacy and solitude a scarcity.

"I can't bear it any longer. I just can't," she told Fabia. "I was allowed to ride by myself on my father's *hacienda;* you remember that."

Fabia scowled, but after several days of constant importuning, the old woman agreed. "On one condition, Angelita," she said sternly, "and that is that the *indio* go along, riding on a burro and taking with him the bow and arrows I have seen him make. This wild country is not the same place as your *papá's hacienda*."

There had been only one Spaniard with whom Fabia would have allowed her mistress to go riding alone, and that man was dead, but the old woman refused to allow her to ride by herself. "There are wild animals as well as snakes and gopher holes that can throw a rider, and who knows when a band of Apaches might appear?" Fabia said sharply. "It is too dangerous to go alone, but if you insist, you may go riding as long as the *indio* goes along. I am sure Domingo will supply him with a burro, not a rapid source of travel but the best available under the circumstances. I would rather see him on a horse, too, but that is out of the question."

María Angélica's face flushed. "I refuse to be escorted by an Indian! How can you suggest that? I can take care of myself. You know how well I ride." Fabia's look was hard and resolute, and María Angélica lowered her eyes in the face of it.

After some moments the young woman sighed with resignation. "All right, I will agree. I cannot fight you when you get that look on your face, but it's only because my desire to escape is so great that I will go ahead and do as you say."

Fabia patted her hand. "You know it's best, *niña*."

María Angélica looked up at her. "Perhaps it might be an opportunity to chip away at the *indio*'s hatred. Maybe if he were away from the Spaniards and this colony and in relative freedom, he might begin to see that life is not really so bad."

"Perhaps," Fabia said noncommittally.

It took the translator, Tomás, to explain to the Indian what was expected of him. He took the announcement without any show of emotion even when Domingo gave him a couple of lessons on riding a burro.

She and the Indian began to ride three or four times a week, and she would have done it more frequently had she not felt she should attend to her chores.

She loved the freedom and peace away from the village. She would ride for a long distance and then dismount to sit under a cottonwood or to dangle her feet in the cold *Río del Norte*, and she had even on a few occasions brought a book to read. She spoke to the Indian sometimes, but he seemed to pay no attention. She thought perhaps the hate was muted in his eyes when they had their rides of "freedom," but she could not be sure. He had, much to her joy, begun to understand a few words in Castilian, but he would make no attempt to speak the language.

On their long rides, he had taken to killing game that he would bring back to Fabia for the supper pot. Sometimes it was squirrels, sometimes rabbits, or fowl of different kinds. The skill he had with his bow was astonishing and his eyesight even more so. Frequently he would shoot when she saw nothing in the distance, invariably bringing down some animal or bird.

Fall, she decided, was the most beautiful season of the year in the new land. Winter was cold and harsh, spring bleak and pitiful. Summer was hot but not unpleasant. Fall, however, was glorious. Long *ristras* of bright red chiles hung from pegs outside the houses to dry. Stacks of melons and pumpkins lay waiting to be cut up and dried. Shocks of cornstalks for horse fodder stood in the fields. The cloudless sky was brilliant. The fall air early in the mornings had a sparkling crispness to it, and the smell of piñon and juniper smoke perfumed it. The days were warm and golden and made one want to lie in the sun and take an afternoon catnap.

It was on days like that, when she could ride far from the village, that she was happiest. At other times she did not allow herself to consider whether happiness was ever to be her lot. She had accepted her life, both the hollowness and the hard work, knowing there was nothing else, but she did feel that perhaps *Dios* had brought her there for some purpose. She could not fathom what it might be and no longer cared. She prayed constantly for strength, but never found happiness. It was much better to refrain from such thoughts because they brought nothing but pain.

The only thing to spoil the delight of fall was the return in late September of the Sergeant Major and his expedition. They had wandered for over three months searching for the South Sea, but hostile Indians and lack of food had made them return to San Juan before they could accomplish their goal. Spirits sank in the capital when it was learned that no gold or other mineral wealth had been discovered either.

Vicente's hair and beard were matted with dirt. He had the look and smell of a Visigoth barbarian, and his demeanor was the same—hostile, quarrelsome, and abusive. She did not realize how peaceful their existence had been for the previous three months. Even the Indian's silent hatred was easier to endure than her husband's contentiousness.

Her cheeks burned with revulsion when Vicente walked into the room and saw her. She knew the look on his face and shuddered, but Fabia, Domingo, and the Indian were there, and she was thankful for their presence and the reprieve it offered for the moment.

"God, what a miserable journey," Vicente said as he walked over to her. "Day after day of desolate country, pounding our asses in the saddle." He took her roughly by the arm. "Am I ever in the mood for something soft," he said. She gasped in horror as he yanked her along and spoke over his shoulder to the others, "You'll excuse us, but I need a little welcome home."

She wished she could have died at that very moment. She felt as if she had been ground into the dirt by a boot heel and spat upon.

Later when Vicente finished with her and lay snoring to the side, she slipped out of bed. She saw his knife lying near the bed where he had dropped it with his clothes. She picked it up and fingered the cold steel. A surge of desire to stab it into him again and again rushed through her, but she dropped the knife on the pile of clothes as if it had burned her hand.

"God help me," she whispered with horror, "what am I coming to?"

She ran and pulled on riding clothes, grabbed her shawl, and slipped quietly out of the house and to the corral. Out of the makeshift lean-to that served as tack room, she took a bridle and put it on her mare.

The cold nights had made a yellow blaze of the cottonwoods along the river and the leaves had begun to fall, fluttering to the ground with any slight breeze. They made a yellow carpet beneath the trees, and on the *Río del Norte* floated an occasional leaf like a tiny yellow boat.

She rode out without looking back, the wind whipping her hair into her face. She urged her horse across the hills but then turned and rode down to the river and along its bank, stopped where the river made a bend and tied the mare to a willow branch near a clump of cottonwoods. She walked down the gravelly bank of the river and sat looking at the water flowing past, not allowing any thoughts to enter her mind, trying to make everything blank, trying to blot out the hate that gnawed inside her.

Suddenly she jumped up and began stripping off her clothes. Perhaps the icy water would make her feel clean again. She dropped her clothes on the rocks and hesitantly put one foot into the swift river water. It was like ice, but she put the other foot in also. The rocks were sharp and her feet ached from the cold, but she waded farther out. The icy water stung as she splashed it up onto her legs and body, and she gasped for breath from the shock of it. She was covered with goose bumps and shivered, but still she stood in the water and scooped it up, trying to remove the stench of the man who had used her.

"I hate him, I hate him!" she shrieked into the silence and pounded the water, sending a cold spray of droplets into her face. Her arms dropped limply to her sides as she wept bitterly. When she could stand no more, she stepped out of the water and threw her shawl around her. She rubbed herself dry, her teeth chattering as she pulled on her clothes and climbed the gravelly bank to where she had tethered her horse. There beside it was the burro the Indian rode.

She gasped and jerked her head around, but she did not see him anywhere. She rested her forehead against her mare's neck but could not stop trembling. Had he seen her? At length she reached to take the mare's reins and her eyes fell on him. He was leaning against a tree about fifty paces away, looking at her.

In his peculiar hobbling gait, he walked toward the burro. She saw the hate in his eyes and recoiled. When he reached the burro, he said, "Domingo made come."

Those were the first words in Castilian she had ever heard him speak. She smiled, forgetting her embarrassment, and walked round her mare to where he stood.

"You spoke," she said, smiling, putting her hand on his arm. "You spoke *castellano*. Thank you."

He knocked her hand away, his eyes angry. "No—thank you—don't want!"

The smile evaporated from her face. "Why do you hate me? I have been good to you. I have never done anything to hurt you. Why are you so angry at me?"

"Angry," he said scornfully, and she was surprised he had understood what she had said. "I am slave," he continued bitterly in halting, heavily accented Spanish.

"But I did not make you a slave. Why do you hate *me?*" she asked.

"You woman of pale eyes," he said with loathing on his face.

Large tears sprang to her eyes. "I am a slave, too," she whispered. "I have no choice, either." She had placed her hand on his arm again without thinking.

He looked down at the hand resting on his arm, and then it happened. He grasped her by the shoulders and roughly put his mouth on hers as he had seen the red beard do. He did it in anger, but he did not know she would taste so sweet, and that he would like the touch of his mouth on hers. And then he was pushing her down onto the golden leaves, and she was fighting, and he had a need that burned white hot in him, and he was entering her with need and hate.

She cried out and then her struggles ceased and she moaned softly, and the hate was gone in him. He wanted her as a man wants a woman, and strangely he felt her wanting him, and he knew freedom for the first time since the terrible killing on Áco mesa.

She felt his hate turn to passion, but she did not know that she arched against him, accepting him deeply. They lay in the golden leaves, in the golden fall, and when the last spasm died away, he put his mouth once more on hers, softly, to taste her again in that pleasant way. He felt her lips tremble under his and part, and he felt himself momentarily come to life again inside her.

Her hands clutched his back but then fell away from him. He lifted his mouth off hers and looked at her. Her dark lashes lay feathery on her pale skin, and on her cheeks were bright spots of color. Her eyelids came open and her large, wet, gray eyes looked at him apprehensively.

"No hate," he said softly, and she saw in his eyes that he spoke the truth.

Tears rolled from the corners of her eyes. Gently he lifted himself off her, covering himself, and awkwardly she pulled her skirts down. He sat beside her, his chin on his knees, staring into the distance, saying nothing.

She sat up and spoke softly and slowly without looking at him. "Take the horse. Go. You are free. No longer slave." Rohona turned and looked at her, but she would not look at him. She repeated in a whisper, "Go. You are free."

Rohona rose and went to the mare. He rubbed its nose and it nuzzled him. He untied the reins and hobbled around to the side. With effort, he threw himself onto the horse's back. She made no protest at the new rider. Rohona looked down at the gray-eyed woman, but her head was bowed and she did not look up. He touched his heels to the horse's side, and they were soon gone from sight.

She rose and went to kneel on the gravelly river's edge, welcoming the sharp pain as the small stones cut into her knees. "Father, forgive me for I have sinned," she whispered as she began the Act of Contrition. When that was finished, she prayed softly. "Father, forgive me for breaking your trust. I know I promised to teach this man about you, but I have failed. Do not punish him for my failure but give him the freedom that he so desires.

"*Dios*, I do not understand your ways," she continued. "I feel unclean when my husband touches me, but when this man touched me, I did not. Please give me understanding, I beg you. Am I so sinful that I cannot do anything you wish?" Her head dropped forward, the sounds of her crying mingling with those of the *Río del Norte* flowing southward on its journey to the Gulf.

# Chapter 20

She waited many minutes before she mounted the burro and started back toward San Juan, hoping to give the Indian as much time as possible to escape. She worked on her story: a rabbit had jumped up out of the brush scaring her horse, and it bolted, throwing her; the Indian gave her the burro to ride back to San Juan to get help, and he went after the horse, hobbling as best he could. She last saw him cross the river, heading west, but she would say the horse raced off to the east. She prayed they would believe her.

It was dusk when she came riding into San Juan. Domingo was the first to hear the story. He took her home where Fabia was beside herself with worry. Vicente had been at the governor's since he awoke that afternoon, but the old woman sent no word to him when it became late and María Angélica had not yet returned.

"I will go get the captain," Domingo said in a rush. "There is still a little light left. If he started now, perhaps he could find the horse and the poor *indio*. That is a good man, that *indio*." Domingo had believed the story.

Fabia took one look at María Angélica's face and was not fooled. "No, no," the old woman said. "It is much too late to send the captain out. It will be dark within moments. In the morning he can go out with several men; if he goes now he will only wander around in the dark and perhaps his horse will step in a hole and throw him."

"*Sí*. Of course you're right," Domingo said, thinking of the danger to the horse and not the rider.

Vicente did not hear until late that night what had happened. Fabia put María Angélica to bed, and Domingo waited in the *sala* until the captain returned. Vicente was furious.

"*¡Jodidos!* I'll never see that horse or that *pinche* Indian again! *¡Maldito* *de la vida!*" He whirled around and faced Domingo again. "Have my horse ready at first light of dawn—I'm going to ride out and see if I can find the mare at least. That *zopo* better not be on her! I'll kill him. A horse is worth more than a slave—or even a wife, for that matter!"

But Vicente did not have to go after the mare the next morning. At dawn Domingo came running to the captain's quarters and pounded loudly on the door. Fabia let him in, and Vicente, who had risen just a short time previously, came rushing to see about the racket.

*"Capitán,"* Domingo said, out of breath, "the *indio* has brought back the mare!"

"I'll be damned," Vicente said under his breath. He returned to his room, pulled on his leather doublet, and buckling on his sword, followed Domingo to the corral.

The Indian and the mare were there. "You're a cunning bastard," Vicente said to the stony-faced man. "Why the hell did you not run away?" He did not expect an answer, nor did he get one, but he turned away before he saw the look on the Indian's face. Rohona realized he was not going to be put in chains.

María Angélica had heard the commotion. "What's going on, Fabia?" she asked with worry, pulling her *rebozo* around her shoulders as she descended the ladder into the *sala*.

"The *indio* has come back with the mare," the old woman said. She was still agile enough to reach her mistress's side and break her fall before the young woman crumpled from the last steps of the ladder.

María Angélica remained in bed all that day—because of the fall from her horse, according to what Fabia told people. The young woman did not even want to see Dorotea, who came to inquire about her well-being.

"She'll be fine," Fabia told her friend. "She bumped her head when she fell. She just needs some sleep for it to wear off."

Late that night when everyone else was asleep, María Angélica rose and walked out onto the roof from her bedroom. She pulled her woolen shawl more tightly about her to shut out the cool fall air. Sleep would not come.

Why had he returned? Why did he come back to a life of slavery when he could have been free?

*"Dios mío,* what am I to do?" she whispered, looking up at the black dome with its millions of flecks of light. "Are you up there somewhere? You seem so far away. Forgive me, please, but I feel as if you have deserted me."

She glanced at the stairstep wall that formed a division between the next quarters and which also served as a way to the third-floor roof. She gathered up her nightgown and climbed the steps. Maybe *Dios* would hear her better nearer heaven. When she reached the upper roof, she breathed the chilled night air and looked down on the dark village, feeling as if she were a tiny speck suspended in the blackness of the sky. She knelt and crossed herself.

"*Dios*, what do you want of me? What? Forgive me my failures and grant me some understanding, I beg you. I cannot go on. *Virgen María*, have mercy on me."

It was then she felt she was not alone on the roof, and she rose in panic and whirled around. She stepped backwards, losing her balance, and he came out of the shadows to keep her from falling. She leaned against him weakly, and his arms held her. She did not know how long they stood there. He took her hand and led her to the pallet on which he had been sleeping. He sat down and pulled her unresisting with him. The only thought that came to her was that surely *Dios* or the Virgin had led her to the rooftop.

Gently Rohona laid her down and touched her face and then put his mouth on hers. Her lips and body quivered, and his hand moved down her side, feeling the curving length of her as he pressed her against him. He pulled up her gown and ran his hand over her belly, then was on top of her, holding himself above her, looking at her white body gleaming in the pale starlight. He entered her, her breath expelled in a small gasp, and there on the roof in the chill night air, a canopy of stars decorating the heavens above them, they knew each other again as man and woman. Later, in spite of his limp, he helped her down the stairstep wall and tasted her mouth once more, and she clung to him.

When he mounted the horse the day before, he had no intention of ever seeing a Spaniard again, but as he rode, with an exhilarating taste of freedom on his lips like honey, he realized they would come after him. It was not necessary to understand the language of a people to learn what was important to them, and it was clear that horses were vital to the strangers. He did not know whether the woman would tell them what had happened or not. He did not think so, but he did not know.

He fully expected to be thrown in chains for having the horse, especially if he were found riding it, for he knew it was forbidden to any native. He also fully expected to be hanged, for the gray-haired leader had hanged other offenders for less. He no longer cared. He had wished to die many times. Let it now be on the strangers' consciences—let their god punish them, for he had heard that for them to kill a man was sinful and their god would mete out punishment to those who sinned.

And so he returned, but nothing happened to him, save the one thing he wanted more than the death he sought: the gray-eyed woman. He wanted this woman with hair the color of wet pine bark; he wanted this woman with large gray eyes the color of the soft feathers of the dove. He wanted this woman more than anything he had ever wanted. When he had her, he felt as if he were free; he felt as if he were whole again. He was no longer a slave, no longer a cripple.

María Angélica knelt at the *reclinatorio* in her room, her head resting on her hands. "Sweet Mother of God, can you help me? I am as desolate as this desolate land. Has your Son destined this to happen? I truly loved the Maese, and he showed me the joy of being a woman. Is it wrong to know joy? Am I sinning now? I swear upon Your Sorrows that I no longer know."

The following day she arose and went to Mass. She prayed for guidance but none came. She saw the Indian later and could not look at him, but in the afternoon she told Domingo that she wanted to go riding.

"But, *señora*, you took a bad fall."

"I'm fine. Thank you for your concern, Domingo, but when I was little, didn't you always put me back on my pony after I fell?"

Domingo nodded and smiled. *"Sí, señora."*

He saddled her horse and a burro and summoned the *indio*.

She did not look at him but tapped her horse with her heels and rode away from the corral.

They forded the *Río del Norte* and followed the Tzama and then she turned her horse north along a tiny dry streambed. She dismounted and tethered her mare to a low-growing shrub. She leaned back against a lone cottonwood that stood by the streambed.

He hobbled over to her and, putting a hand on the tree on either side of her, looked down at her. "I need," he said haltingly, touching himself over the heart. "I need you," he repeated, touching her, *"no me siento esclavo, aquí."* He tapped his chest.

"I need. You make *me* feel free," she whispered.

He turned away from her, and she leaned back weakly against the tree. She watched him as he limped to the mare, took the saddle blanket off, and placed it on the sandy streambed. He removed his shirt and laid it at the end of the saddle blanket, and then he came back for her and led her to the pallet.

"I want to see," he said simply. She stood perfectly still as he began to undress her. He was intrigued with the undergarments she wore. She saw him smile for the first time as he looked at her underdrawers and tried to figure out how to remove the lace-edged tubes that fit over her legs but left the crotch open. For so long she had wanted to see him smile, and when he did, it was because of her undergarments. She could not even be embarrassed and smiled, too, touching his lips. She reached down, untied the ribbon at her waist, and the underdrawers fell to the ground, and she was completely naked. He took her hand and seated her on the pallet and sat down opposite her.

"I want to see," he repeated, and sat looking at her for long moments. "Much beauty," he said, making a motion with his hand that indicated her entire body.

She gloried in the desire she saw in his eyes; she wanted him to look at her, and she wanted to look at him. Shyly she pointed to the loose trousers he wore. He rose and took them off. She loved the hard, sinewy body that she had bathed when he was sick. He wore a breechclout under the trousers and that, too, he removed and stood naked in front of her.

He sat down opposite her again and began to touch her in different places. He ran his fingers over her face and down along her collarbone. He touched her nipples with both hands. "Pink," he said, "women from Áco, dark." Then he looked at her breasts, remembering being surprised when he saw the red-beard put his mouth on them. "Taste good?" he asked, leaning forward and taking the tip of one into his mouth. He flicked his tongue across it. "Mmm. Taste good," he murmured.

"Yes, and feel good."

"Like?" Rohona asked, straightening up and looking at her.

"Yes, like."

Rohona lowered his head to her breasts again. His hands slid along her legs and reached her most private part, and he caressed her there as she closed her eyes. Gently she felt him lowering her to the pallet. His mouth came down on her breasts, and she felt his hand slide down her belly again and between her legs, nudging them apart. There was a tension winding tighter and tighter in her belly, and she felt her hips tense and rise and suddenly it happened, exploding and sending waves through her. She gasped and moaned and when she opened her eyes, he was smiling at her.

Later, when they lay sated, he turned on his side toward her, propping himself up on his elbow. "I cannot say name," he said as he pointed to her.

"María Angélica," she said slowly.

He made several attempts at pronunciation, none of which were successful. "Big name," he said and tried once more. He seemed unable to say much more than two syllables that sounded like "mía."

"I call 'Mía,' " he said.

She smiled. "Do you know what 'mía' means?" Rohona shook his head. " 'Mía,' " she said, hugging herself, "means 'mine.' "

Rohona smiled. "You're mine. You're 'Mía.' "

"*Sí. Seré Mía y tuya*. Mía and yours both."

They were approaching San Juan when Rohona stopped the burro. He looked seriously at her and spoke. "Mía, you should not look at me. Be like an Indian—do not show emotion." He touched her face.

"I will try," she said solemnly.

But Fabia knew they were lovers the moment she saw her mistress when she returned alone on the burro. The old woman feared for the girl she had raised, but she was filled with happiness. The *indio* was a real man, and her darling needed a man like him so she would not wither and die as she had once told the Maese.

María Angélica went riding as often as she felt they could, but it was not as frequent as she would have liked, and every night that it was possible, she would slip up to the roof and they would make love. With his arms around her she felt strong and invulnerable. Afterwards in her room she would kneel. "*¿Qué quieres de mí, Dios mío?* I will do Your will; simply tell me, and it is done."

When she learned Fabia had known from the start, María Angélica's embarrassment was acute. "Please don't think terribly of me, dearest Fabia," she said, and she put into words for the first time what she had come to know. "I love him, Fabia."

The old woman took her into her withered arms and cradled her as María Angélica continued. "I was so miserable, and he has given me happiness."

"I know," Fabia said gently, smoothing her hair. "I know you love him, and I am happy. He is a good man, that *indio*. You have this old woman's blessing, *niña*."

"Oh, Fabia," she said, looking up at her, "thank you. You don't know how precious that is to me. I have prayed to *Dios* and the Virgin every night to tell me what to do."

*"Querida,"* the old woman said, "we must think about practical things." She thought a moment. "I know that it is not possible to wipe the look of love off your face, for that comes from within, but you do not want to see your husband hurt."

"Vicente?" María Angélica asked incredulously.

"Bah," Fabia said with disgust, "there is only a piece of paper that says that beast is your husband. I am talking about your *real* husband—the man who owns your heart and your body—the man *Dios* knows is your husband."

"Do you truly think so?" she asked.

"I know so," Fabia said with finality. "Now, you do not want to see the *indio* hurt, and I do not want to see you hurt, *querida*. Therefore, you must be very careful. The *indio* has a face of stone. He has already instilled a strange kind of fear into the people. They do not know why he works like a demon when the hate he has for Spaniards is blazing. That they fear him is good, for it will not occur to them that you could love that man. But you, *querida*," she said, patting her cheek, "you do not have the face of stone. Your face is full of love, for everyone to see. The *Señora* Dorotea has even mentioned the new beauty of your already beautiful face. I have said it is that we have plenty to eat now that the harvest is over, but once the gaunt months of winter come, that answer will not serve."

"What am I to do?"

"I cannot tell you everything, for I do not know," the old woman sighed. "It must come from within you. But perhaps there are a few things I can say that may be of use to you." The old woman paused and took María Angélica's hands in her wrinkled ones.

"First of all, you must not feel guilty or think that you are doing something wrong—*that* people see instantly. Guilt shows on the face. You must never think that what you do is wrong. Perhaps now you do not think so because the love is just new, but the *padres* have taught you well. There will come a time when you will remember what they say, and you will be filled with guilt. You must talk to *Dios* and *Nuestra Señora* and tell them this is your real husband, although they have probably known it for a long time."

María Angélica nodded solemnly and Fabia continued.

"Perhaps it was He or Our Lady who made these things come to pass. Who knows? But you must trust in *Dios* and in the Virgin and not in the *padres*. Do you understand?" the old woman asked urgently.

"Yes, yes, I do."

"When you ask your forgiveness, ask it from Our Lord—not from the *padres* in the confessional!" Fabia added.

The old woman talked on, giving instructions and suggestions, and María Angélica listened closely, knowing that her fate and the fate of the man she loved were in her own hands. She knew she would need the help of *Dios*, too, and was not afraid to ask, for it must have been the Virgin or he who led her to the roof that night.

In the following days, she made many decisions about her life. One decision had been repugnant, but she knew she must make it. She steeled herself and sought to forge strength from her new happiness. She needed help and prayed fervently for it; she must not hate the man the Church said was her husband. She loathed Vicente and felt disgust just at the thought of him. She must learn to feel nothing for him—neither hate nor loathing nor disgust, simply nothing. As she prayed for patience, it occurred to her that perhaps he was part of God's plan, too. It was because of him that she had been brought to this land. When she thought of him in those terms, the hate diminished a little. She saw his cruelty and his inhumanity, but she tried to look upon him with compassion for the misery in which he must live, so separated from *Nuestro Señor*.

An unusual thing happened when she stopped hating him. He began to look at her differently, as if he did not quite understand something, almost as if he did not know her. Before, he had been insolent, overbearing, contentious, obscene. He still was at times, but there was occasionally a haunted look in his eyes, in the pale eyes that had always before been cold and hard.

When she no longer hated him, she realized she no longer feared him. Perhaps he had somehow become aware of this, and it had done something to him. He had no power over her if she were not afraid. Perhaps he sensed this. It almost seemed that now he somehow felt a strange fear of *her*, or at least uneasiness in her presence.

Whatever the case, the most dramatic difference she was to note came in the wifely duty she had to perform. Before, he had always taken her forcefully whenever he had wanted without even so much as a consent, verbal or otherwise, on her part. When he knocked at her door one night, asking to come in, she was stunned and mumbled *"entre,"* wondering what on earth had happened.

He came to the bed and slipped in beside her. "You are my wife," he said, almost apologetically.

"Yes," she answered simply. Then he touched her and held her in his arms before he rolled on top of her. Never before had he made any attempt at gentleness.

She did not feel the same revulsion and humiliation that she always did. In fact, she felt nothing. The act was of no more significance to her than darning one of his stockings or doing some other menial task for him. She even experimented with not answering his knock when he came to her bedroom, and he went away without a word. But she did not do that often although she would have liked to. She knew that making her body available to him was a requirement of her marriage. If she was allowed her love of the Indian, she would begrudge nothing that would allow it to continue. As to the change in Vicente, she attributed it to the graciousness of *Dios* as well as His approval.

Vicente spent many evenings at the governor's quarters, and likewise the governor and other officers would pass certain evenings in their *sala*, never failing to comment on her beauty or grace. All seemed to notice a change in her because they remarked on it. She tried to be gracious.

"This new country must agree with you, *señora*," the governor said to her upon one occasion.

"With certainty," she said. "It is a beautiful land."

"I would that all the colonists held the same view as you, beautiful lady," he said earnestly.

* * *

Vicente's passion was gold, and it had steadily been intensifying as the days passed and none was discovered. He raved about the need to find the coveted metal, and a fleeting worry would prick María Angélica if she glanced at him while he spoke. An unusual light burned in his ice-blue eyes. She would notice his hands jerk oddly when he gestured, and his voice cracked when he berated Oñate for not allowing individuals to search on their own.

"It takes too many provisions and too much manpower to make organized expeditions!" he ranted as he paced back and forth. "How much more simple if a man could go alone. But our illustrious governor is adamant—he has made the penalty for personal prospecting death!" Vicente clasped his hands on top of his head. "Somehow I've *got* to convince him to let me go out by myself. In a couple of months, winter's going to be upon us and that will make it next to impossible to search the mountains where we'll most likely discover good ore. *¡Qué culo de gobernador!*" He flopped down onto a chair and stared into the distance.

María Angélica winced at the obscenity and glanced at Vicente from the corner of her eye. It seemed his mind dwelt on only one thing, but if Dorotea had been correct that day long ago when she told her that Vicente was going to give her to the governor, then something had changed. He no longer pushed her toward their gray-haired leader.

The trees along the *Río del Norte* had lost their glorious yellow, and water left outside had a sheet of ice on it in the morning, but the days were still warm as fall progressed.

It was near the first of December that María Angélica knew for sure. She suspected it, as had Fabia, it turned out, but it wasn't until then that the signs became obvious. *Las reglas* had not come for two months now. Her breasts felt tender and the sickness at food was an unpleasant, frequent occurrence. She was beside herself with joy—until she realized that the baby she wanted so badly would undoubtedly show the dark stamp of its paternity. She knew within her heart that she carried Rohona's child.

# Chapter 21

"God will provide."

That had been Fabia's statement and that was what María Angélica pinned all her hopes upon.

Rohona was filled with joy as he saw her belly begin to round. When they lay together after making love, he would run his hand over the enlarging curve of her stomach and feel pride deep within himself. He did not tell her about his other unborn child. He only thought now about this woman and the child that she would give him. He, too, worried, knowing that the child could not hide the identity of its father, but she told him her god would provide, and because she believed it, he believed it.

That winter Rohona's speech improved rapidly, astonishing everyone but María Angélica. Domingo remarked that the *indio* could speak the castellano *"muy bueno."* The *caballerizo* was also surprised at the Indian's ability with horses and asked the captain if he could keep him at the stable to work. Vicente grudgingly admitted that the heathen had a way with the animals, but he would not give permission for the Indian to work solely for Domingo. He would be needed to oversee the planting. It had become obvious as the winter wore on and food became painfully scarce that Vicente's household's relative abundance of food was due mainly to the efforts of the Ácoma slave. Just as the game they had that winter was due to his skill with bow and arrow. Vicente even allowed him to take a horse—not to ride but to transport back the deer he might shoot.

Rohona made a loom and María Angélica had cotton bought from some of the more southerly pueblos where the native fiber grew. To the surprise of the Spaniards, the men of the pueblos were the weavers. During the long, cold months of winter, they would gather in the warm *kivas* and weave the cotton *mantas* that the Spanish had come to desire, as their own blankets and clothing began to wear thin.

Rohona remained a member of the household, never having been moved to the quarters of the other servants after his recovery. Save Fabia, he was the only other servant who lived in the household, and as he sat weaving during the winter months, María Angélica and Fabia sat sewing and embroidering tiny garments. Vicente sat either staring into space, thinking thoughts of gold, or spent the long days in card games with the other soldiers. It seemed he tried to avoid the presence of the stony-faced Indian. There had never been a question raised about the savage remaining in the household. When the two men met in the dwelling, the Indian's dark gaze never fell from that of the pale-eyed captain who always averted his eyes first from those of his slave, a slave who seemed more to control than to be controlled.

Knowing she would have to tell Vicente sooner or later that she was pregnant, María Angélica steeled herself for it, trying to show nothing on her face, but when she made the announcement, he evidenced a happiness that she had never expected nor thought him capable of. It caused her much more concern than had he met the news with complete indifference. One other result of telling him was that he had not come to her bed since. Many nights, however, she would slip quietly down to Rohona's room, and they would make love on his small cot.

In late winter the Spaniards began to suffer from extreme deprivation. As in the previous winter, food was scarce and the neighboring pueblos were complaining bitterly about the corn that they were forced to give the Spaniards, corn that had been grown for their own families. Clothes that had been brought from Mexico two years previously were wearing out, and many of the poorer colonists were in rags, many shoeless. Gums bled from lack of fresh or dried fruits, and many suffered from diarrhea caused by lack of fat in their diets. Skin lesions which cracked and oozed in the bitter cold of winter, affected many, while some of the older ones developed persistent, hacking coughs and the little ones' eyes grew bright with fever. There were those who survived, but many were carried out of their homes in crude wooden boxes to be buried in the frozen earth. Would reinforcements and supplies sent for over a year ago never arrive? Bitterness, despair, and anger grew daily. Many were of the opinion the conquest should be abandoned, and they should make their way back to Mexico before they all perished.

Oñate stopped the flagrant talk of desertion, but he could not stop the whispers. He knew Pablo de Aguilar, whom he had almost hanged at the ford of the *Río del Norte*, was the main proponent of desertion.

"I knew I should have hung the bastard then and not listened to the pleas of the Fathers and the women," the governor said one evening as he sat in María Angélica's *sala* along with his nephew the Sergeant Major, Captain Inojosa, and Vicente de Vizcarra who sat staring at his hands, apparently paying little attention to the conversation.

"That, Uncle, is one of the dangers of being magnanimous—the recipient of one's magnanimity is seldom grateful," Zaldívar said.

Oñate scowled and nodded as he took a bite of one of Fabia's *empanadas*. He always wondered where the old woman found the lard to make her delicacies when food was so low.

"But Aguilar's a good soldier," Captain Inojosa said as he, too, availed himself of an *empanada*. "He distinguished himself at Ácoma mesa. I will give him that."

"You're right. And that's the main reason I've tried to look the other way when I hear the whispers," the governor said. "We need good soldiers, but if Aguilar isn't careful, he may find out too late that he has become a liability to me."

"Just tell me when, Governor," Vicente mumbled.

The captain had listened to some of the conversation Oñate realized. If he could hold the colony together until the reinforcements arrived, he was confident the conquest could proceed, and it was only a matter of time until gold was discovered. The governor knew the value of men like Vicente de Vizcarra. He was a little unbalanced, but his single-mindedness was what was called for in these circumstances. One must have the absolute conviction that gold *would* be discovered, otherwise one would give up against the terrible condition in which they were forced to live. He would have to keep Vizcarra encouraged. He needed his optimism and drive for gold. He was glad, too, he had granted the captain's request for the Ácoma slave.

That was a strange case. He had never seen quite so much hate in one man's eyes, and yet the savage worked with curious, un-slavelike diligence. Some of the poorer, more superstitious colonists seemed to fear him, but Domingo, Vicente's *caballerizo*, had nothing but praise for the Indian. It was a strange situation, but it served Oñate perfectly. The Indian, it appeared, would keep the captain's household out of desperate straits, and he would not need to turn his attentions to his family. Especially now that his splendid wife was pregnant, there would have been more possibility that Vizcarra would have begun to worry about her welfare instead of the discovery of gold. Since the Indian seemed to be providing for the household, however, the captain would have no need to take his mind off the precious metal. Oñate decided he must find something to encourage him. Perhaps it might not be a bad idea to let him do a little looking on his own. Hadn't Fabia predicted the captain would find a mine of great richness?

* * *

Although he did not discover gold that winter, Vicente did discover something else of importance to the governor. One night at cards he heard two soldiers talking about plans for a desertion Pablo de Aguilar was masterminding. Knowing the importance of that information to the governor, Vicente made his way as quickly as possible to Oñate's dwelling.

"He must be killed," the governor said evenly upon hearing the news. "There is no longer any other way." Vicente nodded. "Tomorrow morning," Oñate continued, "find some pretext, but bring Aguilar to my quarters. While here, he will be killed and we will say he tried to kill *me*. I'm not about to let that bastard escape punishment again. I'll not give him the opportunity to rally his co-conspirators. Let them fear me—let them know I'll kill any traitorous *hijo de puta* with my own hands. Besides, I want the personal satisfaction of watching that son of a bitch die."

Early the next morning, Vicente de Vizcarra and Aguilar arrived at the governor's quarters.

"Come in, come in," Oñate greeted them with a broad smile. "Damn but it's cold out there." He closed the door behind them. "I've got some matters I want to discuss, but let's go into the next room—there's a nice fire going."

He opened the door and held it, but just as Aguilar was about to step into the room, Oñate gave him a push to knock him off balance. Behind the door two servants armed with knives were stationed. As Aguilar stumbled, the two men stepped out, shoved the captain to the floor and stabbed him.

As Aguilar fell wounded, Oñate drew his sword quickly from its scabbard. He kicked Aguilar to turn him over. Slowly the man pushed himself to his knees and looked up.

"For the love of God, Governor," he said, "get me a priest to hear my confession before you kill me."

"Why bother?" Oñate snapped. "You're going to Hell anyway, you sonofabitch." He stepped forward and thrust his sword through Aguilar's heart as the doomed man made a valiant attempt to draw a dagger from under his doublet.

"I should have done that a long time ago," the governor said as he withdrew his sword from the body.

"Get his dagger, Captain," Oñate said to Vicente, "and rip my sleeve to put a little reality in this charade."

Pablo de Aguilar's death, however, did not stop the discontent. In late March Captain Alonso de Sosa Albornoz, whose family was close to starvation, came to Oñate asking for permission to return with them to Mexico.

"For the love of God, Governor," he said with a desperate voice, "I have buried two of my children this winter. How can a man stand and watch his children starve to death? Please, let me return to Mexico. I am ruined financially, and I cannot bear to see any more of my children die before my very eyes."

Oñate put his hand on the man's shoulder as if in consolation. "I will grant your request within eight days, but not until we can finish the spring roundup of the horses. I need all the soldiers and captains for the job."

"Of course, Governor," Captain Sosa said gratefully.

Early the next morning, the Sergeant Major along with three other men mounted their horses and rode directly to a prearranged spot in an arroyo two leagues from the capital. Within half an hour, Captain de Vizcarra and Captain Sosa rode into the arroyo looking for horses that might have wandered there. When all the men had ridden out of the arroyo, only Captain Sosa remained, buried under four feet of sandy earth, his body punctured by stab wounds. When Captain Sosa had not returned after a week, the governor personally gave his condolences to the widow.

"*Señora*, I am so sorry," Oñate said as he grasped her hand. "Undoubtedly the captain must have met with an unfortunate accident because his horse has returned but he has not. I have had men looking for the past three days, but they have found nothing. We must hope he is safely in God's hands." Captain Sosa's wife burst into tears.

After the disappearance of Captain Sosa, the governor had no more requests for permission to return to Mexico.

In the spring, the Spaniards moved their capital from San Juan to San Gabriel across the *Río del Norte* just above the confluence of that river with the Tzama or Chama as the Spaniards were calling it. Improvements had been made in the existing houses of the pueblo and the colonists' living quarters were much more comfortable than the cramped ones at San Juan. In addition, they were much closer to the fields, and it was no longer necessary to ford the river to tend their crops. The move raised the spirits of the colonists as did the coming of warm weather, but discontent continued to seethe beneath the surface. When would the supplies and reinforcements arrive? Had the Viceroy completely forgotten them?

As summer approached, María Angélica became more and more apprehensive about the birth of her child. She was uncomfortable with the heavy weight of the baby and its constant kicking, and there was nothing to lighten her spirits. She continued to echo Fabia's words, "God will provide," but it began to sound more and more hollow as the time for the baby's birth grew closer. How on earth would God provide? He could certainly not change the baby's skin color. She found herself breaking into tears at unexpected times.

Rohona became increasingly worried. He considered the idea of fleeing with her and the child, but how far could a woman who had just given birth, a tiny baby, and a cripple get before they were hunted down? He began to pray that her god would provide, for he saw no other way out of a situation that predicted doom for all. When he thought that another child of his might die at the hands of the Spaniards, his hatred flamed anew and he could scarcely control it.

Fabia began to fear that María Angélica could not withstand the tension and that her nerves might drive her to some disastrous act.

"Perhaps the baby is the captain's," she said to María Angélica, thinking that the young woman might seize upon that as a possibility to ease her mind, but María Angélica would not accept that possibility.

As the time that Fabia calculated for the birth grew nearer, the old woman made the preparations for it. She appeared to have no plans to deal with the paternity of the child other than to delay the others' inevitable knowledge of it. To this end she instructed María Angélica that when the pains began, she was not to let anyone know and that even if the contractions became painful, she must not cry out so that others could hear. Then Fabia made the decision that they must bring two other people into their confidence. By that means they might also delay others' knowledge and perhaps find a solution to their dilemma.

Dorotea hugged María Angélica and passed no judgment on her when she heard the news. Siya, likewise, kissed her new sister-in-law, as she now considered her, and her dark eyes were filled with happiness, but both women were terrified when they considered what might happen.

"What can we do?" asked Dorotea solemnly.

"I don't know," Fabia said, "but I will call you when the birth begins. No one is to know when the labor starts except us."

Later that day, Fabia went to Dorotea's house to talk to the two women again. "I have something I wish to ask of you, but Angelita must never know," she said quietly. "I have thought about this a long time. I fear for their lives when this is known. All three may die." She pinned the two women with her unblinking gaze. "This is my request to save their lives: when the baby is born, I will give Angelita something to make her sleep. Will you, Siya, take the baby and slip away from here? Can you go among one of the isolated villages to live and raise the child of your brother?"

"I will do it gladly," Siya said softly. "I not want any to die. I will raise the child of my brother as my own."

"I will give you a skin of boiled goat's milk to nourish the child on your journey," Fabia said, "and God willing, you will find another mother who is willing to share her milk with your poor child."

"I think you are right, Fabia," Dorotea said, tears in her eyes. "María Angélica must think her baby is dead—in order for it to live. I will do all in my power to see that Siya gets safely away and that Isidro has no idea in which direction she has gone."

What Fabia did not know was that hidden in the makeshift tack room were a few small bundles containing foodstuffs and a quiver filled with arrows prepared for flight at a moment's notice. Little did she know that two horses were always tethered close in the corral, their bridles and saddles readied.

Two weeks before the baby was born, near the pueblo of San Marcos, gold was discovered. Vicente and six others had been given permission to take a look in the hills and mountains in that area. The news sent nearly all the soldiers riding at a gallop in that direction, Don Juan de Oñate at their head.

The pains began in the early afternoon. By nightfall they had grown much stronger, and María Angélica's face would blanch at the outset of one as she tried to keep from making any noise. Fabia went for Dorotea and Siya and had some fresh goat's milk brought to the house. The two women sat with María Angélica, sponging her face and holding her hands while Fabia saw to all the preparations. A cup with leaves brewing in it sat on the bedside table.

From the terrace rooftop as she had brought up a kettle of boiling water, Fabia saw the Indian slip furtively to the horse corral. She suddenly realized she had forgotten about the baby's father. What did he have in mind? She should have known he would have made his own plans, but she could not allow him to interfere with hers. The safety of her Angelita was paramount. He, too, must think his child had died.

Fabia left the bedroom and went downstairs to wait for him. María-Angélica would be fine for a while with Dorotea and Siya there with her. When Fabia heard the soft noise of the door being opened carefully, she sat down at the table and sipped from a cup as if the tea she was drinking came from the pot that sat in front of her.

"The baby is coming," she said quietly when Rohona entered the room.

He nodded, his face grim.

Fabia made her face impassive. "The first one always takes longer. Would you like some of the tea?" she asked, nodding toward the pot.

The Indian shook his head. "Not want tea tonight. Thank you."

He didn't see the flicker cross Fabia's face, but when she spoke there was no indication of any emotion in her voice. "It's going to be a long night. I can tell that baby's going to take its time coming. Me, I need this tea to keep me awake. These *hierbas* will help keep an old woman alert when the night grows long." She put the cup to her lips and drank.

"Oh?" he responded with interest. "Rohona take some tea then." She got a cup and poured him some of the tea from the pot. He drank it down quickly. "Baby take a long time?" he asked her.

"Yes," she answered, her eyes hooded as they awaited the response she sought in his pupils. When she saw it, she smiled and added, "but the mother is strong."

Rohona stifled a yawn. Fabia's voice was reassuring. "Go to your room and rest for a while. I will let you know the moment the baby comes." Rohona nodded and rose unsteadily. Fabia walked softly beside him to his room. He shook his head a couple of times as if trying to clear it while she led him to the cot. He sat down heavily, and she put her hand gently on his shoulder and eased him backwards.

"There," she crooned as she lifted his feet onto the cot and pulled a thin blanket over him. The old woman stood looking down at him. His eyes were closed and his chest rose slowly and evenly. "Sleep well," she whispered, "may God grant your child a long life."

Near midnight, María Angélica begged for a handkerchief to stuff in her mouth for she knew she could no longer keep from screaming. It was only half an hour later that Fabia saw the black hair and knew, as she had known, that the child was the *indio*'s. Quickly the baby came, a lusty, squalling, kicking boy.

"You have a healthy *hijo varón*," Dorotea said to María Angélica as she lifted her head and gave her a drink from the cup that had been sitting on the bedside table. After Dorotea laid María Angélica's head down gently onto the pillow, she went to join Siya who watched Fabia as she cleaned the child.

"He is beautiful," Dorotea whispered.

"Yes, beautiful," Siya answered, "and big. He will be a fine warrior."

"Take him," Fabia said as she handed the now-quiet bundle to Siya, "hold him while I see to the mother."

"Please," Dorotea said plaintively, as she held out her arms, "let me hold him for a few minutes. Let me see what it is like to hold a newborn child. Let me hold María Angélica's baby once." Siya handed the bundle to Dorotea and tears slid down the face of the Spanish woman. "I envy you, Siya," she said quietly.

"There," said Fabia as she turned to the other women, "she will sleep until morning." The old woman pulled up a chair and sank her weary bones onto it.

"When do I leave?" asked Siya.

"Not until close to dawn, I think," Fabia said. "That will give time to get away from the village, but you will not have to walk so long in the dark when you might take a misstep and fall."

"Yes," Siya answered.

The women had just relaxed to wait for dawn when a pounding came at the front door.

"*¡Madre de Dios!*" Dorotea whispered in terror as she handed the baby to Siya whose eyes were wide with fear. "Who on earth could that be?"

Fabia was instantly on her feet, running to the ladder and descending it with a speed that belied her age. "*¿Quién vive?*" she asked through the door of the *sala*.

*"Por favor,"* an Indian voice begged. "Woman dying."

Fabia opened the door a crack and saw a native man. "What is it?" she asked.

"Come, please," he said beseechingly, "woman dying. They say you good woman medicine. Please."

"Where?" asked Fabia.

"Ohké," the man said, "San Juan."

"Wait," Fabia said. She returned to the room where the two women huddled in a corner with the baby.

"There is a woman in San Juan who is dying," Fabia said in a whisper. "They want me to come."

"Are you going?" Dorotea asked.

"*Sí*, there is nothing I can do here." Fabia took the skin of goat's milk and handed it to Siya. "This is milk for the baby. One hour before dawn, leave." She handed her another pouch. "This is food for you."

Fabia took the baby from Siya's arms and lifted it, putting her weathered old lips to its cheek in a kiss. "God be with thee, *hijito*," she whispered. She handed the baby back to its aunt and turned to Dorotea. "Do not leave her," she said, nodding toward María Angélica, "until I return."

An hour before dawn Dorotea kissed the baby and hugged Siya. "Go with God," she whispered as the Indian girl slipped out the door.

Twenty minutes later Fabia came running up the ladder and into the room where Dorotea still sat at María Angélica's bedside, tears sliding down her cheeks. Fabia collapsed in a chair, so out of breath she was babbling incoherently. Dorotea was beside herself trying to understand what was of such vital importance that Fabia should have run, as it appeared, all the way from San Juan. Her clothes were dripping from having crossed the river. The old woman's chest was heaving, and she had her hand over her pounding heart as if she were trying to keep it from leaping out. Finally Dorotea caught a few words. "Siya. Must stop. God has provided."

"What has God provided?" Dorotea asked urgently.

"Must stop Siya," Fabia panted.

"Why?"

"The Indian girl just died, her baby died . . . We can say our baby is the girl's baby . . . We can say the captain's baby died." Fabia closed her eyes for a moment, sucking in air.

Suddenly Dorotea understood. "I will go after Siya. She is on her way north to Taos. You stay here. I will get her!" And with that Dorotea ran headlong from the room and down the ladder. She managed to get a bridle on a horse—she didn't even know whose it was. She must find Siya and get back before dawn. Clinging for dear life, she started up the river as fast as the horse would go. When she was out of earshot of the village, she began to shout Siya's name. Pale grey rimmed the east, and Dorotea kicked the animal as hard as she could.

Suddenly she saw a figure in the distance running toward her. "Thank God," she whispered.

She helped Siya mount by standing on a rock and handed her the baby. Then she mounted behind. They would have to go more slowly back to the village but she looked apprehensively at the lightening eastern sky. Again she prayed.

As they rode back to San Gabriel, Dorotea explained as best she knew what had happened. "Fabia went to deliver another baby," Dorotea said, "but the mother and child died. I think she intends to say the child lived and that this baby is it. Then she will say María Angélica's child died." Siya nodded, but Dorotea was not sure the girl really understood. Dorotea was not certain she herself understood either.

Fabia met them at the stable. Fingers of light were creeping into the eastern sky. "Quickly. Let me tell you the story," the old woman said. "A young girl, no more than twelve or thirteen, was in labor when I got to San Juan. I could tell she was dying. The baby was born but it was dead, choked on the cord. The girl died only minutes later. It was then I learned from her mother that a Spanish soldier had raped her. And I realized suddenly that God had provided. We will say María Angélica's—Vicente's—baby died, but the Indian girl's lived. So I took the poor motherless baby, a Spaniard's bastard, and brought it to my mistress who was distraught, insane with grief over the loss of her own child."

"Yes," Dorotea whispered, "I think it will work. God has truly provided."

"Now," Fabia continued, "we must plan what to do. I shall take the baby and go down by the river and wait until people are stirring so there will be men who see me bringing a baby across the river. Dorotea, you must go have the carpenter make a small casket at once. Weep and tell everyone you see that the captain's baby died. But get quickly back to María Angélica's bedside and let no one near her. Siya," the old woman said to the Indian girl, "dump the food out of the pouch I gave you and fill it with river sand. Let no one see you and hurry back to María Angélica's bedside."

She turned back to Dorotea. "When the coffin is done, take it by yourself into the bedroom and put the bag of sand into it and close it. Then have the carpenter nail it shut at once. We will say that the poor creature was deformed and that we baptized it the moment it was born, knowing it couldn't live. We will say it lived only a few minutes."

"Now," Fabia said, looking toward the east, "I must take the baby and go. I will be returning when the sun has risen."

* * *

Many people that morning saw old Fabia carry a newborn baby through the village to her mistress's house. When she got there, the *sala* was already filled with praying, weeping women. Fabia found it difficult to keep from showing her displeasure as she quickly climbed the ladder, the baby tucked securely in one arm.

Dorotea met her on the roof, apologizing as she nodded down toward the *sala*. "I could not keep them away."

"Perhaps it suits our purpose," Fabia said as she entered the bedroom and saw María Angélica, awake, sitting up, tears streaming down her face.

When she saw the bundle in Fabia's arms, she wailed plaintively, reaching out her arms. "My baby!"

*"Pobrecita,"* the women in the *sala* murmured, thinking the captain's wife was crying for her dead child.

# Part Four

# LOS HIJOS

## Children, August 1600

# Chapter 22

A telltale line of faint gray presaged the dawn. The lone figure climbed to the highest roof, its burden securely under its arm. When it had reached the top, the figure sat and disappeared into the shadows, indistinguishable on the high roof had anyone been about in the pueblo at that early hour. The burden rested on the crossed legs of the sitting man, and there was infinite patience in the way he waited there in the cool pre-dawn air. He wore only a breechclout. The sky became a violet arch above the expanding gray, and soon tentacles of pale yellow light crept above the horizon, and the stars of night faded in the wash of dawn. The figure rose. The sun, like one of the brilliant shields the strangers had brought to their land, rounded above the eastern mountain peaks, illuminating the figure and the burden it held outstretched. As the blinding, golden light struck the man, he spoke.

"Behold, Sun, the child whose name is Kakana."

Rohona gathered the tiny baby into his arms and taking a pinch of corn pollen from a small pouch at his waist, dabbed it on the child's forehead and cheeks, and turning toward the west, he offered cornmeal with a prayer that it go with wings to the K'atsina at Wenimats. He sprinkled cornmeal in the cardinal directions and prayed for a long life for his son.

Even at that sacred moment he could not but think of his hatred of the Spaniards, and his mind fomented plans of how the natives of the land could rid themselves of the detested strangers who took with force the food and clothing raised by the people's toil, leaving them to die of starvation and exposure.

The past winter he himself had seen the dead ones lying along the road and the pitiful starving ones who came to the Spaniards' camp with a small bundle of wood, a handmade clay pot, or their last worn blanket to try to trade for corn, but the strangers turned them away because what grain they had was for their own consumption though taken from the natives in the first place. There were other starving ones, lacking anything to trade, who came to the settlement offering to accept the strangers' god, to accept the water poured on their heads and the heads of their children if they would only be given food. The blue-robes poured the water on their heads, but there was usually little food forthcoming.

How he hated the strangers and burned to see them gone, and he knew that the only way to see this accomplished would be if the pueblos would unite. The Spaniards were few and the natives many, but the Tano distrusted the Tegua, and the Tegua distrusted the Tigua, and they all distrusted the Queres. Not until all joined together would there ever be a possibility of pushing the parasitic light-skins from their land.

Rohona hated the strangers, save one, but the thought of ridding the land of them left him with a hollow feeling. What if she were taken from his life? What joy and contentment would there be then?

The gray-eyed woman with hair the color of wet pine bark answered some need in him that he had not known. She gave him a sense of freedom and yet his greatest pleasure was to be near her, even if she only sat embroidering and he weaving with not a word passing between them. Her laugh made him smile and the mere sight of her made his passion smolder. Her naked body was the color of Áco mesa in the sunlight, the color of the cream that came to the top of the milk they took from their animals, and some parts were the color of the tiny, carved pink bead he carried with him. When she looked at him tenderly, or when she cried out with the pleasure he gave her, or when she took him deep within her—he knew no words to express the feeling.

When her stomach had begun to round with his child, his pride was deep. Her breasts showed tiny patterns of blue veins as if left there by Spider Grandmother, and he knew it was a good omen. As her belly grew larger, she would take his hand and press it against the roundness, and he would feel his baby move and know that it was strong.

As he looked down at his son cradled in his arms, he could scarcely endure the thought that he had almost lost this child, too. When Siya told him what the old woman had planned so that the Spaniards might not kill father, mother, or child, he felt something close to fear when he considered that he might never have known his son. The gray-eyed woman, however, prayed to her god and said he would provide a way, and he had done so. Perhaps her god did answer prayers as did the K'atsina at Wenimats. Perhaps it did not hurt to offer prayers to both.

The woman had given him a fine son. He was strong and healthy and would make a warrior of good stature. The woman was tall and the child would be tall. His limbs were straight and his features even and beautiful.

He had dark, thick hair, dark eyes, and his skin would be a tawny bronze color. Everything about him filled Rohona with immense pride.

He did not know how to make a prayer to the mother's god. He had already sent a prayer to the K'atsina by way of prayer sticks he made and cornmeal he offered, but the strangers did not do anything similar. He had seen the mother go down on her knees, touch her forehead, touch her breast in the center and then on each side. Would the god understand the language of Áco or did he only understand the language of the strangers? Rohona went down on his knees, and holding the baby in one arm, made a sign of the cross.

"Thank you for son," he whispered in Castilian.

He had not the words to say that he was grateful that he would be able to see his son grow to be a man and to teach him the ways of Áco, but he rose and spoke in Queres. "Thank you, Iyatiku. You are not forgotten nor will you ever be forgotten."

María Angélica was not awake when Rohona returned the baby to her room, but Fabia saw him enter, and although there was nothing to show on the old face, she felt contentment knowing the child had a father who would see to his child's well being.

Later that morning, after she had combed María Angélica's hair and put her good shawl about her shoulders, Fabia ushered Fray Francisco into the new mother's room. The priest had said the last rites over the tiny coffin that had left the house four days previously. The mother had not been able to attend the interment, so distraught was she over the death of her first born, or so Fabia and Dorotea told everyone.

Fray Francisco was upset that the coffin had been nailed shut so quickly, for he felt that he should have been called to baptize the infant, but Doña Dorotea assured him that she had done it properly and that she felt it was urgent to put the poor little dead thing in the coffin so that its mother could not demand to see it and discover how deformed the tiny creature was.

On the day of the burial, Fray Francisco had come to María Angélica's house to try to comfort the new mother on her loss, but she wept continuously while he was there. He had hoped that by now she was over the first grief and might listen to reason. On that first day he had seen the half-breed infant lying in the cradle that had been meant for her own child, and he was not sure the old woman had been wise to bring it to her mistress. Certainly it was the charitable thing to do, the poor little thing having lost its own mother, but there must be some Indian woman who could suckle the child. It seemed hardly proper that a woman of quality such as the captain's wife should feed a bastard half-breed infant.

Fray Francisco had come that morning to see if she wouldn't listen to reason. "I am gratified to see you looking so well, Doña María Angélica," he said, smiling. "The blessings of the Almighty be upon you this beautiful day."

"Thank you, Father," she replied, returning the smile. "Please, won't you sit down?"

The priest availed himself of the chair Fabia had placed next to the bed. There was a moment of silence before he spoke. "You are looking well," he repeated.

"I'm feeling quite well, thank you, Father," she said. "I think Fabia is being overprotective by making me stay in bed when I am feeling fine."

"I am gratified you are feeling recovered," Fray Francisco said, deciding that the time was appropriate to mention the infant. "And the child, how is it progressing? It is a boy, is it not?"

"Yes," she answered proudly, "he is doing very well, thank you."

"Doña María Angélica," Fray Francisco began, "you have done a charitable thing by taking in this poor orphan, but for a lady of quality such as the *señora,* it is not necessary that you be troubled any longer. I am certain we can find an Indian woman who would be willing to take the infant and nurse it along with her own."

"No!" she shouted, stricken with a terrible panic. She clawed the covers back and climbed wildly out of bed to reach her child. She grabbed the sleeping baby out of its cradle and clutched it to her breast. It awoke and started to cry.

"No!" she shouted again. "God has given this baby to me—and I *will* keep it. No one can take this baby from me!"

At her last words it was as if a bucket of ice-cold river water had been thrown in her face, and she instantly gained control of herself. Her voice took on a quiet, steely quality filled with absolute determination.

"God saw fit to take my own child," she said coldly, her eyes riveted on the priest's nervous face, "but He gave me this child to raise in its place so that it might learn to love Him. It is my holy and sacred duty to raise this child, and I shall not break the solemn promise I made to God that I would love and nourish this child as my own. Neither you, Father, nor *anyone* can take this baby from me."

There was something in her voice and in her eyes that made Fray Francisco regret he had spoken, and he recognized the conviction behind her words. "So you have made a solemn promise to *Dios* to raise this child as your own," he said smoothly. "I admit it is a gesture of true Christian piety toward the heathen, and Our Lord knows there have been precious few acts of generosity toward the natives since we have come into this land."

Her eyes pierced him and would not drop from his face. He clasped his hands in a nervous gesture and looked down at the floor. He cleared his throat and tried to sound comforting. "Certainly, *hija*, if you have made a solemn promise to God, then we must all abide by that promise. May your example of Christian love make this colony more aware of the true spirit of *Dios*, which we were sent to bring to this heathen people."

Unfortunately, Fray Francisco's words of that summer day did not come to fruition. Most of the colonists, men and women alike, were horrified to think that the beautiful, elegant wife of Captain de Vizcarra was suckling a bastard half-breed brat that she intended to raise in her own house as if it were her own child. A few made public expressions commending her Christian charity, reserving their real feelings for private comments, but the majority made no secret of their thoughts.

Dorotea made scathing remarks to some of the women who made a point of showing great public piety but who had disparaging things to say about María Angélica's actions. Many also wondered what Captain Vicente was going to think of his family situation when he returned to the capital from the newly discovered mines. The captain's antipathy for the natives had not gone unnoticed.

The comments people made angered Dorotea in the extreme, but she was grateful that it had not occurred to a soul that the controversial child was María Angélica's very own. The mother obviously cared little what anyone thought and seemed genuinely happy. No one doubted that the love she showed the infant she carried so fondly in her arms was anything but real. Even the people who whispered "wait until the captain returns" were disappointed. Precious metals were what consumed him.

Word had been sent to Vicente that his child had died at birth and that his distraught wife had taken in a half-breed infant. The news came as a disappointment to him because he had liked the thought of having a son to inherit the wealth he would discover. But there would be more children. The fact that his wife had taken in an Indian child only meant that there would be one more servant in his household—one he hadn't had to pay for. The news, in reality, scarcely affected him. In his mind dwelled one all-consuming thought: gold.

When he returned to the capital at San Gabriel, his enthusiasm almost made him pleasant. "The ore at San Marcos appears that it might assay with a heavy silver content!" he said with excitement. "We will be rich!"

He talked on to his wife about the good prospects of the mine, but it did not occur to him to console her over the loss of their child. He casually viewed the half-breed infant and remarked, "Well, at least it looks strong and healthy."

"Quite," she replied evenly and was surprised that she felt no flutter of nervousness.

Perhaps people were too afraid of the captain to comment to his face on the fact that his wife was suckling a half-breed bastard, but it appeared none had, and the fact that the situation at home seemed not to bother him took the last scraps of interest from the circumstance. The more pressing matters of hunger and discontent began to reoccupy the thoughts of the small colony.

María Angélica was not aware of the growing bitterness and dissatisfaction among the colonists. Her own contentment blinded her to the feelings of others. Her household was peaceful. Vicente was off at San Marcos again, determined to discover gold if he had to dig up an entire mountain. News filtered back that he was behind pick or shovel from before dawn until after nightfall, scarcely taking time to eat. The Sergeant Major was also there setting up an ore-crushing machine he had brought with him all the way from Zacatecas.

María Angélica named her son Alejandro after the great and handsome Macedonian who had conquered half the world by the time he was thirty. The culturally superior Greeks despised the Macedonians as barbarians, but Alexander, tutored by Aristotle, absorbed their culture and became their conqueror. She would see that her Alejandro, despised by the Spaniards as a barbarian, would absorb their own culture, and perhaps one day he also would rise to a high position.

She did not know that her son had another name in addition to the one that she had given him and that Fray Francisco had repeated on the day the child was baptized. She did not know that the baby also bore the name Kakana, Timber Wolf, a name chosen by the father because of the animal's traits. The timber wolf was a lonely animal but loyal to the small group with which it traveled. It was a fierce, fearless hunter and a survivor. Its soft coat of fur was also the color of a pair of eyes that reminded the father of one special person.

Rohona was in the fields from sunup to sundown, planting, weeding, harvesting. He labored with even more diligence than before. If he were not in the fields, he took the burro and another pack animal with him into the mountains to hunt. Some days he came back with a deer, some days with two dozen rabbits whose pelts, along with the others he had shot, would make a warm blanket for the cold winter nights.

He cut the rabbit skins into long, thin strips that he wound around a yucca cord so that the end of one strip bound the following strip of fur until a long fur rope was formed. He made a frame with a smooth pine pole at the top and one at the bottom. Over these poles he looped the long rabbit fur rope that formed the warp, and through the fur loops of warp he wove yucca string that made the weft. The result was a warm, soft blanket that made the beds cozy no matter how low a howling snowstorm might make the temperature drop.

The contents of the many loaded carts Vicente brought to the new land proved invaluable for keeping the household from suffering to the degree the other colonists were. Rohona had seen the bundles of trade goods stacked in the back storeroom, and at his request, María Angélica gave him beads, hawk bells, iron needles, awls, and other small items, which he took with him to the neighboring pueblos. There with the trade goods he purchased the labor that the three of them—he, Fabia, and María Angélica—were too few to be able to complete. He had their excess rabbit pelts and deer hides tanned, meat dried and jerked, *mantas* woven, and piñon nuts gathered. The purchased labor helped to provide stores of food and goods that would sustain the household through the coming winters.

Following the example of the pueblo natives who every summer carried corn and *mantas* to Taos to trade, Rohona, along with Domingo and Cipriano, took a small string of pack animals, loaded with trade goods, north to the village where the Querechos came with the *cíbola* they had hunted on the eastern plains. When the small pack train returned to San Gabriel, it carried buffalo hides, dried meat, and tallow.

Fabia, María Angélica, Dorotea, and Siya spent the days peeling squash and pumpkins, cutting them into rings to hang on racks to dry. Siya learned from them how to prepare the foreign foods they had brought to the land, and they in turn learned from her how to take advantage of native edibles. Corn was ground, candles and soap made, herbs dried, roots dug.

The blisters on María Angélica's hands had turned to calluses but she did not mind that her hands were no longer smooth. Her lot was cast. It had not been her decision to come to that land, and it had not been her intent to love a native, but both had happened and she accepted them as God's will.

In spite of the deprivations and constant toil the new land required, it would never have occurred to her to want to return to Mexico. That thought, however, had occurred to many. The deaths of Aguilar and Sosa caused the talk to merely await safe time and safe company for expression. Food was scarce; work was long and hard and seemed profitless. Although the accommodations in San Gabriel were better than those at San Juan, they were still lacking in many of the comforts the colonists desired, and as discontent, spoken or unspoken, grew, the governor became more and more tyrannical.

The natives had taken to hiding their grain, knowing that the soldiers would ransack their houses if they said they had none. The supply details sent out to the pueblos each month to collect food for the colony met with more and more bitter complaints from the Indians, and many villages' entire populations would flee to the mountains when word was received that a group of Spaniards was on its way. Upon several occasions, foraging details came back to San Gabriel empty-handed, having met with deserted villages everywhere they chanced to go. The colonists had to have food from the natives or they would surely perish, for they were unable to grow sufficient for their own needs.

Oñate found it necessary to torture a number of chiefs to find where they had concealed their food. One chief whose fingertips they crushed on a blacksmith's anvil at last revealed where he had hidden his grain. When they unearthed the small sealed pottery jar with its pitiful few handfuls of corn—the only corn the chief had managed to hide—those Spaniards who still had a conscience felt deeply ashamed, others were merely angry at the small quantity.

Their rapaciousness did nothing to endear the Spaniards to the natives, and the priests found the harvesting of souls a difficult task. Many of the friars suffered great frustration at their inability to bring the natives to the acceptance of *Jesús Cristo*. Ironically, their frustration was made more acute because the pueblos were among the most peaceful, well-organized, and virtuous of all the natives the conquerors had encountered in the New World.

There was no drunkenness among them as there was among those to the south who drank the powerful, fermented pulque of the agave plant. The Pueblos' only beverages were pure water and atole made by stirring toasted, ground corn into water. They did not steal nor lie; they were industrious and thrifty people. Had they not been so ill-treated by the soldiers, many of the friars felt they would have been willing and admirable converts. It was not surprising, however, that the natives were not inclined to emulate the newcomers nor accept the god they said was so loving.

As the summer of 1600, the new century, drew to a close, and it became obvious that the harvest would never last them through the winter, the governor began to suffer more qualms about the future of the glorious conquest he had envisioned. Daily his bitterness and depression grew.

"Why has the relief force not arrived?" he ranted. "It has been over seventeen months since I sent Captain Villagrá and Márquez along with the Father Commissary and my own cousin Fray Cristóbal to secure reinforcements for us and provisions for this precarious settlement. What has become of them? Am I going to have to see to the survival of destitute and starving colonists through another cold, harsh winter?"

Oñate felt attacked on all sides. The soldiers wanted food and clothing for their families, the priests wanted immediate salvation of souls.

"I know the men with families need food," he said, "but haven't I, too, felt the pangs of hunger along with the rest of them? Haven't I done my best to secure sustenance from the natives? But my very attempts to gather enough food so we will not starve have met with disapproval from the friars. They accuse me and my policies for the low number of converts.

Did I not spend over four hundred thousand ducats of my own fortune to finance this conquest?"

The hostility the governor faced on all sides did nothing to improve his imperious nature. There were a few people, however, who did improve his mood. Vicente de Vizcarra's single-mindedness and absolute conviction that they would discover gold was a welcome change to the soldiers who wished to find chunks of the precious metal lying strewn in their paths. And Oñate sought as frequently as possible the company of the captain's wife, made more beautiful it seemed by motherhood, although she had lost her own child.

Oñate saw her working right alongside her servants, doing work no lady of quality in New Spain would have considered, but she did it without complaining. He was quite certain she did not love her husband, which, if she had, might have been a reason to endure the hardships; but whatever quality it was that made her face the privations and the uncertain future with equanimity, he admired and appreciated.

He paid social calls on the Vizcarra household as frequently as his many duties would allow. Often he came ostensibly with news for her from her husband, but he well knew, in spite of her expressed appreciation for his kindness, that she was not interested in the mining operations at San Marcos.

The real reason he sought her company, however, was to enjoy her beauty and the obvious contentment with her life that was apparent in everything she did. He had once harbored hopes of having her as his. At one time he felt her husband was willing to use her to buy favors from him, but something had happened—some change had been wrought and he could not say what it was, but he felt it.

Maybe it was the baby, maybe it was old Fabia, maybe it was the woman herself, but in spite of the change, she somehow acted to calm him at his most angry, to buoy him at his most depressed, to sustain him at his most persecuted. He had even begun to unburden himself to her in the way in which a man will unburden himself to a woman but not to another man.

"I have done everything in my power to make this conquest a success," he said to her. "Why do they all act as if everything is my fault? Can I do anything about the lack of rainfall? Can I do anything about the fact that gold nuggets are not scattered on the ground?"

She always reassured him. "Of course you cannot do anything about those things, Governor, but I know the future will be brighter for us. We must not give up. God is merely testing us." She did take the opportunity, however, to urge kinder treatment of the natives. "You must admit we have placed a heavy burden on the inhabitants of the villages. We must treat them with more kindness, I think."

The governor spoke wearily. "I truly lament the situation, *señora*, but what can I do?"

They both knew that he would be compelled to continue as before in order to feed the colony; she knew there was little hope that the burden on the natives would be relieved.

One ray of hope did appear near the end of September of that year: a small advance group of the relief force arrived in San Gabriel. There were only seven soldiers accompanied by a new priest, but they had brought a few carts with provisions and news that the full relief force was truly en route. Spirits rose, and the approaching winter did not loom quite so ominous before them. To the isolated colonists the new soldiers and lone priest brought news from Mexico that was as ravenously consumed as were the foodstuffs they brought.

The governor, in a much better mood than previously, came to María Angélica's house. He handed her a small box.

"I hope you like it," he said, "it's a confection of sweetened apricot paste with ground almonds that the wife of Juan Guerra de Reza, my guarantor, sent me. She knows it is a favorite of mine."

"Oh, Governor, I can't accept such a precious delicacy when it was sent especially for you."

"Take it, dear *señora*. It is only a small way I can express my gratitude for your optimism that has done so much to raise my spirits and help me endure this so far thankless job."

In the end she accepted the sweetmeat, and later she shared the delicacy with Dorotea, Siya, Fabia, and Rohona. It had been a long time since she had had anything quite so delicious.

# Chapter 23

"They come! They come!" shouted the rider.

On the eve of the Savior's birthday in the year 1600, amid shouts of joy, the long-awaited relief force rolled into the small capital of San Gabriel. On that cold December night without regard to the fact that fuel was scarce, flickering lights of small pitchpine torches glowed from all the rooftops to light the way for the Christ Child and to give thanks for the arrival of the newcomers.

A total of seventy-three soldiers and seven new friars had made the long hard trek across the wastes of northern New Spain to the *Río del Norte* and thence northward across the infamous *Jornada del Muerto* that had claimed the life of Oñate's cousin, Fray Cristóbal, on the outward-bound journey of a year and a half previously. The mountain range to the west of the *Jornada* would forevermore bear the name of the friar-cousin of the conqueror of *Nuevo México*.

With the relief force came four lumbering, solid-wheeled carts pulled by thirty-two oxen. Besides guns and ammunition and new swords, the carts carried such luxuries as eighty small boxes of chocolate for making the hot drink the colonists had longed for; one hundred and forty-six boxes of quince and peach preserves; an assortment of anise, cinnamon, sesame, rosemary, saffron, and black pepper; barrels of olives; eight *arrobas* of sugar; two pipes of wine; bags of raisins and almonds; cakes of soap; colored silk and woolen stockings; Portuguese thread; Holland and Rouen linen; Campeche cloth; calfskin shoes; cordovan boots; silk doublets; green Chinese taffeta; five and one-half *varas* of lustrous blue satin of which María Angélica was the recipient.

The governor gave the material to Vicente de Vizcarra who had returned to the capital for the Christmas season. "This, Captain," Oñate said warmly, "is for your beautiful wife who has been such an example of Christian goodness for this colony. May this piece of cloth add a little joy to her Christmas."

When Vicente reached home he gave the material to María Angélica with the admonition, "Get busy and make a gown for yourself out of this. And make it low in front. I want the governor to see the good use to which his gift has been put." He fingered the blue satin and smiled. "This gift just goes to show how much in favor I am with our governor."

María Angélica sought to be pleasant. "The fabric is beautiful."

She was reluctant to make and wear a dress of such richness when so many had scarcely enough with which to cover themselves, but she said nothing, knowing that it would be useless to argue. The material would do little to keep anyone warm during the hard months of winter. It was an incredibly frivolous thing to have sent with the relief force.

Fabia and María Angélica both worked on the dress, and it was made quickly so that it might be worn to celebrate the new year of 1601. The governor hosted a ball, limited by lack of a proper ballroom, but not by the newly arrived wine. She expected she would have to endure Vicente's attentions that night, but he imbibed liberally before the evening was even old, and she saw him slumped in a chair and realized that sleep had superseded any amorous intentions he might have had.

More than she had ever expected, she enjoyed the beautiful new dress and the many compliments and appreciative looks she received. It felt good to be clothed in soft, silky folds of material, and she became animated at the ball. For a few short hours she forgot she lived in a mud village hundreds of leagues from civilization, forgot the precariousness from one day to the next of her life and that of her son as well as that of all the others, forgot the worry of whether they would even be alive one year hence.

Life for a few short hours seemed carefree and happy, and she returned home after the ball and found herself wanting the attentions of a special man. For that night she refused to let thoughts of the future have any access to her mind.

She slipped into Rohona's room carrying a tin candelabrum that filled the small room with soft yellow light. She saw the look in his eyes that she had wanted to see all evening. There had been desire in the eyes of many of the soldiers at the ball, but she cared only about the desire she saw in one man's eyes. She smiled at him and his eyes smouldered. He beckoned to her, and her dress rustled softly as she crossed the room to sit on the edge of his low cot.

He ran his hands over the smooth blue satin. "Much softness," he whispered.

She leaned forward and put her lips on his. "Much love," she whispered.

"Yes," he answered, kissing her tenderly, "much love."

After soft laughter and clumsy but successful attempts to remove the voluminous folds of material, he demonstrated to her just how much love he felt for her.

The joy and enthusiasm the relief force brought to the capital was short lived. They had not brought sufficient food supplies to relieve the hunger of the colony, and, in fact, they increased the burden. There had not even been enough in the carts to supply the new eighty-odd mouths much less add to the larders of the original settlers, so all suffered. Many of the new recruits felt outrageously deceived. The captains Villagrá, Márquez, and Bernabé de las Casas, whom Oñate had sent to enlist new soldiers and settlers, had given glowing reports of the north country and its prospects for mineral wealth. The true situation of the impoverished colony became immediately apparent to the recruits, and many were ready to turn around and go back to Mexico. When they heard what had happened to others who had deserted or asked permission to leave, they changed their minds. The grisly story of the deserters beheaded by Villagrá and Márquez, who brought back to the governor the right hands of the unfortunate men preserved in salt, was enough to deter even the foolhardy.

Just as the new soldiers and settlers were disgusted with the colony and the land, so were the friars. Even the new Father Commissary, Pedro de Escobar, seemed quickly to have become disillusioned. The Fathers considered their task impossible because of the mistreatment the Indians had received at the hands of the soldiers, and, in addition, some were reluctant to baptize even the willing ones, for they feared for the colony's permanence. How could they in good conscience baptize scores of natives only to abandon them later if the colony should collapse and all the Spaniards return to Mexico?

The colony, half starved and seething with discontent, managed to survive the cold, harsh winter they had come to realize was characteristic of that high north country.

Vicente returned to San Marcos after Christmas, and María Angélica spent a winter of contentment. She did not like the cold nor the smoky indoors that made her eyes water, but Rohona had made her and Fabia rabbit-fur moccasins that kept their feet warm and cozy on the cold dirt floors. Their food was simple and they never had quite as much as they would have liked, but they did not starve. María Angélica's contentment came from her child and from the man she considered her husband. The baby began crawling after Christmas and was not sick a day. He was robust, healthy, very inquisitive, and his mother's joy. He was a handsome child and would be a handsome man.

Fabia loved the baby fiercely, respected the father, and was deeply thankful to see the happiness and contentment of her *querida*, but as the winter wore on, a troubled look came frequently to her dark, old eyes. Her mistress, however, had not noticed it. Finally the old woman spoke when the worry had grown too great.

*"Querida,"* she said gently, patting María Angélica's hand, "the *niño* is getting big. It is no longer safe for you to visit the bed of the father so frequently."

"But Vicente is not here," María Angélica murmured. "No one knows."

"Ah," the old woman said, "that is not what I worry for. You are going to catch the seed of your *indio* again." María Angélica turned pale.

"You had not thought of that, had you, *querida?*" Fabia asked gently. "I will prepare you some herb teas to drink so that the seeds will not catch."

"No! I could not!"

"But, *querida*, it is too dangerous to take a chance. Your *indio* is *muy hombre*—he will plant another baby."

"God will provide."

"God has been good to you, *querida*, you cannot ask him for too many miracles."

"He provided once. If I believe in Him, He will provide again."

"Sweet *Madre* in Heaven," Fabia whispered, crossing herself as María Angélica swept out of the room, "guard my little girl."

There was a bitterly cold, dusty March wind blowing the day Vicente returned from San Marcos. His clothes were filthy and in rags, his boots, which were falling apart, were tied to his feet with strips of leather. His red hair was matted, his beard unkempt and stained. A frigid blast of gritty wind swirled into the *sala* when he entered.

María Angélica looked up from her sewing, shocked to see him and shocked at his appearance. His eyes had a strange quality to them, staring into the distance as if they focused on nothing. He crossed directly to the fireplace in the corner and stood warming his rough, red hands. She came to her feet and ran to close the door he had not bothered to shut against the cold wind.

"The mine's no good," he rasped, his voice hoarse from the cold.

"How do you know?"

"I want gold," he said, turning toward her, his pale eyes staring past her. "I've got to have *gold*. If there's anything in those hills it's silver. I won't have silver—I have to have gold!"

"But my father's riches came from silver," she said placatingly.

"Your father!" Vicente spat. "I'm going to be richer than your father ever dreamed! But I'm going to find *gold!* Gold is the only thing that matters!"

María Angélica took a step backward in the face of his sudden belligerence. She saw Fabia standing in a doorway to the side.

"Gold! I have to have gold! I won't stay here and rot while the governor sits on his ass doing nothing! I am going after gold!" He whirled around to stare into the fire.

Fabia moved to María Angélica's side.

"Go get the governor, Fabia," María Angélica whispered. "Maybe he can pacify Vicente before he does something foolish." Fabia slipped out the door and María Angélica closed it behind the old woman and pulled her shawl more tightly about her to ward off the chill of the cold, nasty wind. The captain stood, staring into the fire.

At length he turned to stare at her, and she recoiled at the sight of the wild look in his eyes, but at that moment Fabia and the governor entered.

"Captain," Oñate said jovially, "I'm glad you're back." He, too, saw the twisted look on Vicente's face, and he raised the wineskin he carried in his hand and laughed good-naturedly. "What do you say we warm our insides a little while we talk business—I have a proposition for you."

"Please, Don Juan," María Angélica said quickly, stepping forward, "won't you be seated? Let me get you some glasses for the wine."

"Thank you, but, no, *señora,*" Oñate said lightly, "we shall drink the way comrades drink!" He lifted the wineskin and tipped his head back.

The governor pushed the wineskin into Vicente's hands and sat down in the chair María Angélica had offered. "Have a drink, Captain, you deserve it!"

Vicente hesitated a moment and then threw his head back and let a long stream of the dark ruby-colored liquid arch into his mouth. He lowered the skin and wiped his mouth on his sleeve.

María Angélica slipped quietly from the room, leaving the governor and Vicente alone.

"So San Marcos doesn't have such good prospects after all," Oñate said.

"There may be a piss pot full of silver there, but that's all," Vicente said. "What I want is gold."

"And I, too," the governor said. "We must find gold—or at least thick, rich veins of silver for this conquest to be successful."

Oñate weighed what he intended to say. He hoped to throw a scare into Vizcarra.

"I have told this to no one, Captain," he said in a somber tone as he leaned forward, "but this conquest is about to collapse. If something isn't done soon, I will be forced to take this entire colony back to New Spain. I had hoped to bring the word of God to these heathen, settle new territory, discover new wealth for the king, but unfortunately it seems that it may not be possible, and I will have to admit defeat. I will lead the colonists back safely to civilization and then retire to my silver mines in Zacatecas."

The mixture of fear and shock on Vicente's face told the governor he had chosen his gambit wisely. He had not underestimated the captain's desperation for gold. If the governor pulled the entire colony out of the new land, the captain would be left almost penniless and with scarce hope of ever striking it rich.

The governor had no intention of admitting defeat so easily, but the captain need not know that. He needed men like Vicente de Vizcarra, whose driving passion would support his own position. Oñate went on.

"Captain, I must keep the soldiers busy. They must think the conquest is being carried forward. They must not for a moment think that it has come to a standstill. With the reinforcements, I now have enough men to make a real expedition to some of the places of which we have heard rumors. It could be another attempt to reach the South Sea to look for the fabled pearls or it could be to the eastern plains, to the land they call Quivira with its many inhabitants who are said to wear much golden jewelry.

"Captain, I need your help, and in return I will see that you are properly rewarded."

The governor paused for effect. "Help me raise the enthusiasm in the soldiers for a much grander expedition than we have made before. Help me execute it, and when we get back, if we have not discovered gold, I will give you written permission as well as my own blessings to search for gold on your own."

Oñate could afford to be generous with that offer. He had nothing to lose. If they discovered no wealth in jewels or precious metals on the expedition, he would not be able to mount another within the near future. One man alone, however, could go out on his own, and if Vicente discovered a rich deposit of gold—so much the better. The man who had led the conquest would receive the lion's share no matter who discovered it.

Vicente's horror at the thought of the *entrada* being abandoned changed to barely controlled glee when he heard the governor's offer. He finally had what he wanted. His pale blue eyes burned with intensity.

"You'll have my help, Governor," he said in a strangely quiet voice.

Oñate smiled broadly and nodded at the skin Vicente still held in his hands. "Now, let's do justice to that wine."

She tried to twist away, but even in his drunkenness he gripped her painfully and she could not escape. She smelled his filth and wine-sour breath as he tried to kiss her, but she yanked her head away so that his mouth did not come down on hers. Half stumbling, half dragging her, he pulled her to his bedroom and threw her on the bed. He yanked and ripped at her clothes and fumbled with his own until he had freed himself.

He wrenched her legs apart and stabbed into her, butting against her, grunting, heaving in spasms, his body jerking. And then he passed out, his body suddenly limp and heavy like a dead weight on her.

She bit her lip to keep from crying or being sick. Suddenly she was aware of movement.

"No! Don't!" she whispered with horror as she saw the knife poised above Vicente. "For the love of God, don't!" she said in near hysteria.

Rohona did not lower the knife but held it still poised so that one swift movement would have severed the red-bearded man's jugular vein.

"Please," she begged in a whisper, as she saw the murder in Rohona's eyes, "if you love me, if you love your son, don't kill him."

For agonizing moments Rohona stood there, knife poised, until slowly his arm dropped to his side. With his other hand he pushed the drunken, sleeping man to the side and reached to help her up.

"No," she sobbed, turning away and covering her face with her hands, "don't touch me. Go away. Go away." She did not see the look of pain and incomprehension on his face as he turned and left the room.

When Vicente recovered from his hangover, he was no longer in a vile mood nor did he have the strange light in his eyes. Occasionally a faraway look came there, but María Angélica was not forced to be in his company often. Most of his time he spent in the other soldiers' quarters, playing cards, laughing, drinking, and talking incessantly about the riches to be had on the upcoming expedition.

For three days following the episode with Vicente, she avoided Rohona. When she had overcome her feelings of shame, she slipped into his room on several occasions, but it appeared that he was not sleeping there. She became frantic with worry because she had not seen him. Fabia shook her head and said she did not know.

Finally she went to Domingo early one morning and told him she wanted to go riding and to send for the *indio* to accompany her.

Her plan worked, but there was an expressionless, unreadable look on Rohona's face as he rode behind her on a burro.

She rode west and then turned north along a small stream. It must have been noon or later when she saw the small pool and the round stones made emerald green by the moss that covered them.

The sun was warm and it finally seemed that winter had gone, although she knew that the weather was fickle, giving them a taste of summer one day and then a killing frost the next. Dismounting, she walked to the pool and knelt to scoop up a handful of the water for a drink. It had a faint mineral smell, and to her surprise, the water she expected to be ice cold was quite warm. She had heard that there were *ojos calientes* in the area, but she had been under the impression that the hot springs were near a group of pueblos called Jemez to the west and south. Here was one in the north.

She was delighted with her discovery, and the warm pool with its emerald rocks she found enticing. Her decision was instantaneous as she remembered a previous time.

Slowly she disrobed and stepped into the shallow pool and sat down on the slippery rocks. She knew he was watching her but could not bring herself to look at him. Then he was there in the pool with her, naked beside her, and he had her in his arms and was kissing her. She felt the warm water lapping at her, and then they were sitting facing each other, her legs entwined about his body, and he had entered her and she was moaning softly, her head thrown back, the sun warm on her face.

*"Mucho amor,"* Rohona said afterward, touching her body with his fingers, lightly. "Much hate for red-beard," he added.

*"Te quiero,"* María Angélica said, touching her fingers to his chest, "and, yes, much hate for red-beard."

# Chapter 24

Armor gleamed brilliantly in the June sun. Horses that had run free for the winter champed at the bit and pawed the sandy earth, nervous and high-strung at being restrained by bridles, *estradiota* saddles, and richly embroidered caparisons. The wagons carrying barrels of black powder, sacks of cornmeal, farriers' tools, miscellaneous pieces of leather, glass beads, and other trade items creaked and groaned as the barrel-chested, oak-yoked oxen lurched forward under the prodding of their Tlascalan teamsters. The royal red and gold standard fluttered gently at the top of its staff. The entire village—colonists, the soldiers who stayed, servants, and Indians—gathered to see the expedition off. They were going east to the land of Quivira, onto the vast plains where the *cíbola* roamed in huge herds like rumbling, rolling seas of brown fur, hoping this time to find more than wild beasts.

Francisco de Sosa Peñalosa, named by Oñate as lieutenant governor in his absence from San Gabriel, rode out to where the governor sat his handsome bay gelding. Oñate clasped Peñalosa's hand and gave him a final admonition before he gave the signal for marching.

"Try to keep spirits high, and deal immediately with malcontents. You have my full authority. Any hint or talk of desertion must be met with the severest of penalties. And remember, there is no prospecting except by my order. The men who remain must stay in San Gabriel to tend the crops. We must have a good harvest!"

"*Sí, gobernador,* I do not take my responsibility lightly," Peñalosa answered. "May God grant you a safe and profitable expedition."

Dorotea, Siya, María Angélica, and Fabia stood watching the large entourage set forth. Dorotea held Alejandro so that he might see better. His eyes were wide, filled with childish amazement at the shiny, metal-clad men and the large animals they rode. He made excited, babbling noises and jumped up and down in Dorotea's arms. She laughed and squeezed him tightly and kissed his cheek.

"You want to learn to ride a horse, eh, *hijito?*" she said, nuzzling him playfully. "Now that you are getting to be such a big boy, I am sure Domingo will soon have you astride a fine pony!" María Angélica glanced at her son and smiled as Dorotea set him on the ground.

He had been walking for only a month, but he toddled off as if he were bent on going somewhere important. María Angélica hurried after him. Both Siya and Dorotea's eyes followed the dark-haired baby. There was longing in Dorotea's eyes, and she turned to Siya and put her hand on the girl's arm.

"Oh, Siya," Dorotea said, "why don't you stop taking the herbs to keep from getting pregnant? I know you hate Isidro, and he uses you vilely, but think how wonderful it would be to have a baby around the house. I would love your baby as if it were my own."

Siya looked at her sadly. "I don't take herbs for a long time. I, too, think a baby would be nice to have. I'm afraid a baby will not come now—too many herbs, maybe."

Dorotea's eyes were brimmed with tears. "I am so sorry," she whispered.

"I, too," Siya said sadly. "We just have to give love to Alejandro and now the new one that comes."

Dorotea's eyes widened in shock. She glanced quickly around. No one was near. María Angélica had gone after the baby and Fabia had followed. Other women were some distance off in small groups.

"No!" Dorotea whispered. "You mean . . ."

"*Sí*, Rohona told me," Siya murmured, her eyes wide with fear. "What happens this time? How will God provide again?"

"I don't know," Dorotea sighed with worry. "I envy María Angélica her babies, but I am terrified."

"Perhaps the husband and soldiers will not come back until after baby is born," Siya said hopefully.

"But what difference does that make in the long run?" Dorotea asked. "How can this baby die, too, and be replaced by another?"

The small capital had the feel of a long-deserted village. Nearly one hundred of the men along with their pages, grooms, and other members of the entourage were bound for Quivira. The men who stayed behind were discontented, burdened with overseeing the crops they had no desire to tend. To a soul, save the friars, they had come for riches and not to raise a few miserable *fanegas* of corn and wheat in a land that received such scarce rainfall.

The days passed and in spite of Oñate's order to his lieutenant governor, Peñalosa was making no apparent effort to stop the men from going off in small groups to reconnoiter the surrounding mountains. Perhaps he felt it kept them occupied and kept them from forming a larger group that would pool its discontent.

María Angélica tried to keep from acknowledging her apprehension over the birth of the baby that was growing within her. She was pleased and happy to be with child again and would not think about the future, other than to say to herself as she had before, "God will provide."

Although María Angélica had not wanted to, Fabia insisted that she tell Vicente she was pregnant before the expedition left. The captain greeted the news distractedly, and she knew his thoughts were on gold, which was just as well as far as she was concerned. She was grateful for his upcoming absence, for her life would be much freer. She would not have to slip to Rohona's room clandestinely.

She was sometimes amazed at the fact that Vicente had no idea she had a lover living under his very roof, but all he thought about was precious metal. It would be pleasant and comforting to be able to live for a few months like man and wife with the man she considered her husband. She would not allow herself to think that her whole world might be ripped asunder when the child that grew under her heart was born.

Three months passed, summer ended, the harvest was gathered, and the expedition had not yet returned. María Angélica knew people were discontented because she heard the talk no one bothered to keep quiet now that the governor was gone. But she was not prepared for what happened at the end of September of that year.

"The colony is being abandoned!" Dorotea said breathlessly as she rushed into María Angélica's house.

"No!" María Angélica gasped. "That isn't possible!"

"But it is. I just overheard Diego de Zubia talking to Padre San Miguel. There is going to be a Mass this morning and after Mass, they are going to draw up plans for leaving."

"Peñalosa won't allow it. As lieutenant governor he will put a stop to it."

"No, you don't understand. He is in sympathy with them, and besides, his daughter is Zubia's wife."

"It can't be. What about the natives? The Fathers cannot desert them, not now after having baptized so many."

"Oh, but the priests are urging it just as loudly as the captains," Dorotea said. "Fray San Miguel said all the priests were with them, including the Father Commissary, Padre Escalona. The only exception is Fray de la Oliva, and he is in Santo Domingo. He's the only real priest in the bunch, anyway. He has converted more Indians there in one year than all the others have together."

"I just don't believe they will abandon the colony," María Angélica said, "not with the others gone."

She was wrong. Near the first of October, 1601, lumbering carts, filled with all the worldly goods the deserters possessed, began to roll southward. The lieutenant governor and the Father Commissary, although they were in complete agreement with the deserters and had urged them in their plans, remained in San Gabriel, as they oddly felt was their duty, to await the return of the governor.

They were both of the opinion that when Oñate returned to the capital, the desertion a *fait accompli,* that he would have no option but to follow and leave the barren land they had been foolish to try to conquer.

With the lieutenant governor and Father Commissary remained only twenty-five soldiers loyal to Oñate. Among them was Gerónimo Márquez, who was sent to Mexico with the loyal soldier's version of the desertion of the colony to contradict the many accusations the deserters planned to bring against the governor.

María Angélica and Dorotea wept in each other's arms as they watched the long row of carts rumbling south.

"What is going to happen to us?" María Angélica asked. "What is going to be the fate of this colony upon which we have staked everything?"

Her fear was of a much deeper nature than Dorotea's for she had far more to lose. Could she bear to lose the man she loved, the father of her son? And what would become of the unborn child that moved within her?

Rohona, unlike María Angélica, viewed the departure of the many strangers with satisfaction. He fervently hoped that their abandonment of the land meant that all the pale ones would go, leaving the land once more for the people. Hatred still smoldered in his breast, and he would have gladly plunged a knife into each one of the few strangers who remained.

He had even entertained thoughts of a conspiracy of the villages to rise up against their oppressors. It would take only a handful of men to fall upon the few soldiers in the unfortified capital. They could then lie in wait at Galisteo, and when the others returned from the plains they could pour down upon them and kill them. The land would once more be theirs.

Rohona had even gone so far as to talk to his uncle who had come up from San Felipe to find out what was happening. They had seen the cart train of the strangers and wondered why so many were on the move southward. Rohona mentioned his plan to his uncle who instantly seized upon it as the course of action they should follow. It was obvious his hatred was just as intense as that of his nephew.

"We must begin immediately and lay our plans carefully," the uncle said, "and we must have the support of all the villages together if we are to succeed in killing those with their clothes of metal and weapons of fire who will be returning from the east." Rohona concurred. His uncle's eyes glittered with hatred.

"And we will destroy all the strange animals they brought and all the plants that are not plants our mother Iyatiku brought up from under the earth for us. And we shall kill all their women—the women from whose wombs come the evil pale ones. And all the children that carry the blood of the vile strangers, that carry seeds of their paleness—we shall kill them all so that nothing remains to contaminate our land."

A coldness swept over Rohona. The people would kill his son? His son was vile in their eyes because he carried the blood of the hated strangers? His son, who would be tall and strong, his son who laughed and gave his father kisses as his mother had taught him. And his son's mother—she, too, would have to die? Her belly slit to kill the child she carried? The gray-eyed woman would have to die? The woman who made him feel the glory of being a man?

How could he hate the pale strangers with such venom and yet love a woman of them with such an intensity?

Rohona was filled with impotent fury. He wanted two things, but to have them both was impossible. He did not even hear what his uncle was saying. He knew only that he could not see his son killed—nor the gray-eyed woman. The thought was intolerable.

At length he became aware of his uncle who was still talking, formulating plans of how they should proceed. He listened and when his uncle finished, spoke, but the words were not what his uncle expected.

"I think we should let the strangers go of their own accord," Rohona said emotionlessly. "When those who have gone to the east return and see the others have gone, they, too, will leave this land. If we attack them, perhaps the others who have gone south will return to make war on us as they did at Áco when we killed only a few of their men." Perhaps the others would leave and the woman would stay, Rohona thought.

His uncle shrugged noncommittally, and they parted strangers.

That night when Rohona came to the bed he shared with María Angélica, now that Vicente was gone, there was an intensity to their lovemaking like that of new lovers, despite the fact that her stomach was swollen by the child that would be born in just a few short months. Afterwards she clung to him and he held her clasped against his body.

The beauty of fall went unnoticed that year. There had never been laughter and mirth in the dingy capital, but that autumn a pall of apprehension and gloom lay heavily like a rancid, mangy old *cíbola* hide over the mostly deserted mud-brick village.

Alejandro brought the only joy to María Angélica's household that fall, and Dorotea and Siya seemed drawn there for the laughter of the child. He toddled and climbed everywhere, his curiosity unlimited, and he was not a little spoiled with five adults who showered him with love. His mother and father loved him unreservedly as did old Fabia, and the only other two persons who knew his real parentage overflowed with love for him.

If Peñalosa's wife, Doña Eufemia, or some other woman came to María Angélica's quarters, Alejandro might crawl up in their lap. He seemed not to notice their ill-ease and obvious distaste, but his mother did. When the person was gone, she would scoop her baby up in her arms and kiss him fiercely as if she could protect him that way from all the cruelty he was sure to meet as he grew up.

She had to endure other unthinking cruelties also. Doña Eufemia, in trying to make conversation, had suggested to her, "I know you will be so much happier once you have your very *own* child—once you have the captain's baby."

María Angélica knew her face had paled at the remark, but she was unable to say anything and could only nod mutely, hoping Doña Eufemia could read nothing in her features.

Some days later she overheard the same woman talking to another after Mass. "When she has the captain's baby perhaps then she will return to normal and put that half-breed child in the servants' quarters where it belongs."

Not only did the comments stab into her heart like a dagger, but they began also to gnaw insidiously at her, leaving fear and worry in their stead. Until then she had managed to avoid thinking about the birth of her second child. She placated herself with the litany that God would provide, but as the time grew nearer for the baby to be born, the phrase became hollow and lost its ability to reassure.

She began to fear the return of the expedition from Quivira. They had been gone over four and a half months. Had something befallen them?

That same worry began to filter through the tiny capital. She, however, at times almost wished something had. If she could only have the baby before they returned.

It seemed that Rohona, too, had an interest in the return of the expedition, for he would go to the highest rooftop and look out over the land as if searching for a glint of sunlight that might mean something of metal was approaching. He went off on hunting expeditions, but he ranged south and east rather than north. Although he normally kept aloof from Spaniards as well as natives, he had made a point of talking to a few men from Yungue-Yungue, Ohké, and Caypa, but he had heard nothing of any plot to fall upon the returning expedition as he and his uncle had talked of. He kept alert, however, and kept horses ready, and in the makeshift tackroom hid several sacks filled with necessities should they have to flee suddenly. His main worry was the mother and the unborn child. How would she be able to ride in her condition? He, too, prayed for an early birth.

December was rapidly approaching, and Fabia calculated that the birth would occur within a week or two at most. María Angélica became nervous and tense, tears likely to come over the slightest thing.

"Can't you give me something to take?" she begged Fabia. "Something that will make the baby come early?"

"No, *querida*," Fabia said with utter seriousness, "one should not meddle with the coming of a child unless there is something very wrong."

María Angélica collapsed in tears, and Fabia held her, smoothing her hair, but worry creased the old woman's face. She prayed God would provide, but she was fearful that they might have already used up his provisions. She had no plan to follow with this birth. Perhaps it would be necessary for Siya to take this child away, but both mother and father now knew what the original plan had been, and the old woman did not know whether they would allow it or not. Fabia's shoulders slumped; she felt old and tired.

One evening when Dorotea and Siya came to visit and they were all gathered in the *sala*, Fabia broached the subject about which all thought but about which no one spoke.

"The baby will not delay much longer," the old woman said.

María Angélica paled, and Dorotea and Siya's eyes were wide with fear. Rohona's face remained immobile.

Fabia sighed. "I see no other way. This baby must 'die' also, but we cannot bring it back the way we did with Alejandro. It would arouse too much suspicion."

"No!" María Angélica gasped.

"Angelita," Fabia said, "then what do you suggest?"

"Go on," Rohona said quietly to Fabia.

"Although people will remark on both babies dying, I see no other way. Since the captain is not here, no one will know, and perhaps we can slip the baby away and get someone in Caypa or Jemez to care for it for a year or two and then bring it back here and beg the *señora*, knowing she took in another child to raise, to take this child so that it will have food to eat and a better life."

"I could go away with baby," Siya offered.

"I have thought about that," Fabia said wearily, "but I think if you disappear when the baby 'dies,' someone might put two and two together."

Siya nodded.

"I couldn't bear to send my baby away," María Angélica sobbed pitifully.

Rohona went to stand by her and placed his hand on her shoulder. "What else can we do, Mía?"

She shook her head, her face in her hands.

Rohona was the first one to spot the two riders. With amazing agility despite his lameness, he descended from the rooftop. Fabia was the first one he saw.

"Two metal riders come," he said.

Alarm was written on the old woman's face. Her plan hinged on the baby being born before the arrival of the soldiers. That was not to be.

Fabia scurried to find María Angélica. She was at Dorotea's, sitting and chatting while she embroidered a small garment that rested on the convenient shelf her large stomach provided.

"They come," Fabia said, "the *indio* just saw two armored riders approaching."

María Angélica came instantly to her feet. Her eyes went blank and she swayed momentarily before her knees buckled. Neither Dorotea nor Fabia reached her before she crumpled back onto the *banco* on which she had been sitting. Within seconds she recovered.

"*Madre de Dios*, have mercy on me," she cried, crossing herself.

Three days later, on November 24, five months and one day after they had departed, the entire force rode into the nearly deserted capital of San Gabriel. When the two riders reached the village three days before and told them the expedition was on its way, fresh men mounted horses and rode to inform the governor of the desertion of the colony by the soldiers and the friars.

Fury and disillusionment covered the faces of the returning men, most of whom bore injuries as a result of a fierce attack by hostile plains Indians while they had been in buffalo country. They discovered hundreds of savages inestimably more barbaric than the peaceful pueblos of the *Río del Norte* country, but they had not discovered a trace of gold or other precious metal nor anything of value save the thousands upon thousands of *cíbola* cattle.

By the time he reached San Gabriel, Oñate had recovered from his fit of apoplectic rage upon hearing the news of the desertion. His face was like chiseled granite when he rode into the capital, and the first thing he did was order a group of soldiers to leave immediately to try to overtake the deserters and arrest them.

Overcome by the tension, María Angélica was in bed when Vicente trudged wearily into the house. A livid red scar across his forehead was the only thing he had acquired on the long expedition. His page removed his armor for him, and Vicente sat slumped in a chair, staring at nothing. Fabia padded softly into the *sala* and stood in front him.

"Welcome home, *capitán*," she said. "Unfortunately the *señora* is not feeling well and has gone to bed."

Vicente did not respond and sat there as if he had not heard a word she said. She repeated her words but still he did not speak. She left the room and went about her business.

Some time later she glanced into the *sala*, and he was still sitting there staring at nothing, his hands twitching. Fabia went to María Angélica's room.

"The captain has returned very strange," she said softly. "He doesn't speak."

María Angélica pushed herself up. "I suppose I must say something to him," she said with a tremor in her voice, but she did not know what she should say.

"Welcome home," she said quietly, when she walked into the *sala* where Vicente sat. At first he made no indication that he heard her. When she repeated the greeting, he lifted his eyes, and it was obvious when his eyes fell on her large stomach that he had completely forgotten she was pregnant.

She was dismayed when a smile came slowly to his lips. "Well, I'll be damned," he said quietly. "I forgot I'd left something in the oven!"

He spoke almost kindly. "Don't worry, this one won't die. Although the governor has given me permission to look for gold on my own, I won't leave until this baby is born."

Terror etched María Angélica's face, but Vicente did not notice, for at the same moment she crumpled to the floor. He grabbed for her and broke her fall, yelling for Fabia.

# Chapter 25

That night she went into labor. She was in hysterics. Fabia sent for Dorotea and Siya, hoping their presence might have a calming effect on her, but it appeared to have none. María Angélica babbled incoherently, only occasional words understandable, most of which dealt with God coming to her aid. When a contraction came, she screamed at the pain, unlike during the birth of her first child when by sheer willpower she had kept from making noise.

The screams even affected Vicente. Many times he had heard the cries of agony from men dying or being tortured and they left him curiously unmoved, but for some reason, the screams of this woman trying to push out his baby filled him with a kind of awe—even fear. He drank too much of the wine the governor had sent him, and he became belligerent and yelled for Fabia. The old woman entered the *sala*, her eyes dark and angry, hiding the worry in them.

"What's going on?" he demanded.

Fabia snorted contemptuously. "The girl is having a baby, what more?"

"But why is she screaming?" he demanded drunkenly.

"Because it hurts, fool," the old woman said contemptuously.

Vicente drew back his hand to slap her but held back when he saw the look on her face that dared him to do it. "Do something, *bruja!*" he growled between his teeth. "Your life is worthless if you let this baby die. I want to see my son!"

The blood drained from Fabia's face as she turned abruptly and returned to the room where her mistress lay in agony.

Dorotea glanced at Fabia when she reentered the room. The old woman looked shriveled and ancient. Her eyes were sunken in her brown, wizened face. Her shoulders were stooped, and her hands looked like the claws of a bird. Dorotea was suddenly very afraid.

She had, until that moment, held out some hope that the old woman would contrive a way out of the present situation. The full impact of the danger in which María Angélica lay overcame Dorotea, and she fell to her knees, the Hail Mary rolling, in a tone of desperation, off her lips. Fabia and Siya, too, went to their knees and began to pray. Exhausted, María Angélica dozed for a moment only to awaken, contorted with the next pain.

No one saw the solitary figure on the highest roof of the house. He sprinkled cornmeal to the cardinal directions and then again to the west to Wenimats asking the K'atsina for their help. He knelt as he had seen her do and began to pray to her god. He tried again and again to think of some way to save her and the child.

The pain he felt was worse than losing his foot. He would lose a hundred feet rather than this, and he was reduced to desperation. Her god or the K'atsina were the only remaining hope. He prayed fervently in his meager Castilian, asking her god to help her and the child, but in the event that her god could not save her, he had to make a decision, and he had made it.

Rather than allow the strangers to deal with her or the child, he would kill the woman he loved and their baby quickly and painlessly so they would not suffer. And that meant he would have to kill little Timber Wolf also. He would have to kill Alejandro, for when the Spaniards saw the new child, they would know the parentage of the older one.

It was close to dawn. Rohona descended from the roof and went silently to find a knife. He took a sharp steel and slipped unnoticed into Alejandro's room. He would kill the boy first, and then before anyone could stop him, he would kill the woman and the new baby that would surely be born soon. He would follow them in death, and if she was right about her god they would be together after death.

A few low clouds painted the dawn with brilliant reds, pinks, and oranges, covering the entire land with color. It was a beautiful day to die, Rohona thought as he stood by the side of Alejandro's small bed and looked down at his beautiful son sleeping peacefully.

Fabia had been busy in María Angélica's room and had not noticed the approach of dawn. "The baby is coming," she whispered. Tears poured down Dorotea's cheeks as she held María Angélica's hand while the young woman pushed down, straining to bring her baby into the world. Dorotea's lips moved in prayer. Siya's eyes were wide with fear.

*"Rojos!"* Fabia said hoarsely. "They are *rojos!"*

Dorotea jerked her head around. "What is it?" she whispered, seeing the contorted look on the old woman's face. "My God, what is the matter, Fabia?"

*"Nada,"* the old woman said with a crooked smile. *"Nada.* There is nothing wrong. The baby's hair is red! A few more pushes and it will be here."

Fabia glanced up suddenly. "Siya, go quickly. I forgot the *indio*—go find him! Tell him everything is going to be all right. It is the child of the captain!"

Siya scurried out the door and slipped unnoticed to her brother's room then to the roof, but even on the highest level she did not see him. She looked in all directions as the dawn was beginning to pour its light over the east mountains. Quickly she descended, debating whether or not to go out to the stable to look for him. It occurred to her to check Alejandro's room. Just as she reached the door to the boy's room, she heard the squall of the newborn. She sighed with relief that the baby had made it safely, pausing before she pushed the door open to Alejandro's room. Rohona's head snapped around as she stepped inside.

"No!" she gasped as she saw the knife poised above the child. "No, Rohona, no!" She ran to him and grabbed his arm.

"No!" Siya said. "The baby has the red hair. No one knows about Alejandro—no one *will* know about him!"

He lowered his arm and looked at her in astonishment. "He did it," Rohona said. "Her god did it. He found a way to let them live."

"Yes," Siya responded, "it is the child of the captain."

"No," Rohona said. "It is not the child of the red-beard. It is mine."

Siya looked at him, not understanding.

In the other room, Fabia brought the tiny child for the exhausted mother to see. "It is a girl, *querida,"* the old woman said smiling, holding the baby down for María Angélica to inspect. "She is the captain's child. There is no need to worry. God has been gracious."

María Angélica took one look at the wrinkled, pale-skinned little creature and turned her face away. "No," she rasped hoarsely, "that is not my child. That thing is Vicente's!"

A look of shock crossed Fabia's face. *"Querida,"* the old woman said, "she is yours, too. She is a beautiful baby. She is a beautiful daughter to love."

María Angélica turned back to stare at Fabia. Her gray eyes were frigid. "Take her away!" she hissed. "She is not mine. I do not want her." She turned her face away again.

Dorotea came to María Angélica's side, her voice gentle as she spoke. "You will love her, you'll see. It has all been such a shock. Once you realize how lucky you are, you will love your little daughter as much as you love your son."

"Never!" María Angélica whispered and turned toward the wall.

* * *

When Fabia had cleaned the baby and wrapped it in a soft woolen blanket, she opened the door quietly and went out, carrying the infant.

Vicente sat slumped in the *sala*, the empty wineskin at his feet. His eyes were closed in either sleep or drunken stupor. Fabia shook him by the shoulder, and his eyes came open. At first they were bleary and angry, but then he saw the bundle in the old woman's arms and staggered to his feet.

"My son!" he slurred drunkenly.

"No, your daughter."

"Daughter?" He pushed back the edge of the blanket from the baby's face.

"Yes," Fabia said, "your daughter."

*"Mierda,"* he swore, "the goddamned woman was supposed to give me a son—I wanted a son!"

"Unfortunately, God allows us no choice in the matter," Fabia said in quiet scorn. "We must thank Him that He saw fit to grant us a healthy child, be it boy or girl."

"Bah!" Vicente replied, sinking down into the chair in which he had been sitting. As he reached for the wineskin, Fabia took the opportunity to escape the *sala*.

"Oh, *hijita*, it is not your fault who your father is. A baby cannot choose its parents," she whispered. "Old Fabia will love you even if no one else does."

María Angélica had gone to sleep by the time Fabia returned to the room. Dorotea was sitting by her bedside, exhausted, also, from the all-night vigil. She looked up at Fabia who had entered and saw the bone-deep fatigue that curved the old shoulders.

"Go to bed, Fabia," Dorotea said, rising and reaching out her arms to take the baby. "Get some rest. I'll stay here with them until you return. Everything will be all right."

The old woman did not protest, and shortly after Fabia had gone, Dorotea heard what sounded like quiet scratching at the door. Opening it, she saw Siya and Rohona standing there. Alejandro was in his aunt's arms, bouncing up and down, his eyes bright with excitement. Dorotea ushered them in quickly and shut the door behind them. She smiled at Alejandro and pulled the blanket back from the baby's face.

"This is your little sister, Alejandrito," she said. She had no more gotten the words out of her mouth when she realized what a careless and dangerous thing she had said.

"No!" Siya whispered. "Never say."

"Yes, of course," Dorotea said quickly, "how stupid of me. I shall never say nor think it again."

Rohona looked at the baby. "I have a daughter now," he said.

Dorotea glanced up. "It's the captain's child," she said gently.

"No," Rohona said solemnly, "it is my child. Your god made it look like red-beard so all is safe. It is my child."

Dorotea started to object but refrained. "Yes, God was truly gracious," she said instead. "We have much to thank Him for."

María Angélica slept for the remainder of the day, awakening only in the evening. She would neither look at nor touch the baby.

"But, *querida*," Fabia cajoled, "the baby needs to nurse or the milk won't come."

"I don't care," she said tiredly, her face turned toward the wall.

Dorotea, too, tried to convince her that she must give the child nourishment. "Otherwise the baby will die," Dorotea spoke, "and God will hold you responsible." But no argument was successful. They even tried to bring Rohona to see her.

"No!" she screamed. "I don't want to see him!" They did not attempt it again for fear someone might hear her.

Fabia brought her small cot into María Angélica's room that night. Somewhere near midnight the baby woke crying. Fabia lit the tallow candle in the *candelabro* and went to the small crib and carried the infant to its mother's bed and laid it next to María Angélica. But the woman did not stir in spite of the lusty howl the tiny kicking girl was making. Fabia shook María Angélica by the shoulder. Her eyelids fluttered and came open but her eyes were glazed and seemed to have no comprehension.

*"Querida,"* the old woman said, "the baby is hungry." María Angélica stared at her blankly and then her eyes fluttered shut. Fabia reached out to push back the young woman's tousled hair.

"Wake up, *querida*," she said softly. As her fingers touched María Angélica's forehead, she felt the fever. *"¡Dios!"* she whispered. "Not the *fiebre*."

By morning María Angélica was delirious. Fabia sent Siya to see if she could find a nursing mother in one of the nearby pueblos, for the baby would die without nourishment, and now it was not possible for the mother to feed her child.

Fabia made herb poultices and forced herb teas down María Angélica's throat. Everything she knew, she did, but her dark old eyes were sunken and worried. Dorotea, too, stayed by the bedside, sponging María Angélica's burning forehead, holding her hand as she thrashed in her delirium in the sweat-soaked bedding. Dorotea's lips moved constantly in prayer, her rosary entwined in the hand that held María Angélica's.

When she did not seem to improve throughout the entire next day, Dorotea asked Fabia, "Is there not something more you can do for her?"

For the second time, Dorotea saw a look of doom haunt the eyes of the old woman who crossed herself as if trying to ward off the possibility of it.

"There is nothing more I can do," Fabia said heavily, "it is up to God now. The girl does not want to live, it seems. And when a person no longer wants to live . . ." she made an expressive gesture with her hands, "then they do not fight for life, and it is up to God."

"But why is she like this?" Dorotea wondered, her voice edged with anguish.

*"¿Quién sabe?"* the old woman responded. "All I know is that sometimes the birth affects a woman—just like animals. What makes the mother deer or the mother rabbit reject her young?"

Dorotea felt suddenly very cold as Fabia continued. "I have a dark foreboding about this family," she said in a voice that sounded as if it came from the depths of a cavern. The old woman rubbed the back of her hand across her eyes to wipe away the tears that hovered there.

*"Mí pobre angelita,"* she whispered. "I brought her mother into the world, I brought my angel into the world, and now I have brought her little daughter into the world. I do not wish to see them carried out of it. It is too hard on this old heart. The old should not have to bury the young."

Vicente came to the room only once to look in on his wife. He seemed to view her illness with a mild irritation as if it were a weakness on her part. He did not even bother to look in the direction of the crib.

In Yungue-Yungue Siya found a young woman with a baby who for food was willing to move to their dwelling to nurse the little daughter of the Spaniards along with her own. Other than supplying nourishment, Siya had taken over care of the tiny red-haired baby as well as of Alejandro while Fabia and Dorotea remained occupied with the mother.

Rohona, too, would come occasionally to hold the infant and cuddle it. Once when he was holding the baby, Dorotea remarked quietly to Siya, "How strange to see a man care for a child."

"But among the Ácoma," Siya said, "it is not uncommon for a man to care for a child if the mother is occupied and he is not. Many are the grandfathers who, no longer able to work in the fields, care for their grandchildren while the mother and father tend the corn."

Many times, too, Rohona slipped noiselessly into the room to sit by María Angélica's bed. His face was a chiseled mask, but none of the women in the room thought for a moment that he was unaffected by the illness. What they did not see was the time he spent kneeling, praying to a god he could not even picture in his mind. He knew what the K'atsina looked like, and it was easy to pray to them. But her god? It was as if he were hiding behind a bush, always able to keep himself concealed.

* * *

It was the hour before dawn on the fourth day after the baby's birth that Rohona slipped into the bedroom where María Angélica lay gravely ill. Old Fabia slept in exhaustion on her small cot. Very carefully, very gently, Rohona lifted the tiny, sleeping baby from its crib and carried it out of the room. When he reached the uppermost roof, he sat down in front of the sand painting of a turtle he had made. He was not a medicine man and knew not all the proper preparations to make, but he did the best he could, just as he had done when his son was born. The early December air was sharp and cold, but he did not shiver although his only clothing was a breechclout. The baby, however, was wrapped snugly in a warm woolen blanket and lay, still sleeping, in the cradle of his crossed legs. Rohona made prayers to the K'atsina, singing softly.

Gradually the sun announced its coming, sending rays of pink light into the cold winter air. Rohona stood and faced the east with his small bundle. Just as the sun rose blindingly over the eastern mountains, he pulled the blanket back from the sleeping child and held it to the sun.

"Behold the child Ho-oka," he said to the source of brilliant light. Feeling the blast of cold air hit its skin, the baby girl let out an angry wail. Rohona laughed softly and quickly covered the child and pulled it close against his shoulder. "Hey, little Ho-oka," he said softly, "little gray doves do not make such an angry sound. You are supposed to coo softly. Have I misnamed you?"

The baby seemed soothed for a moment, but Rohona knew that now that it had been awakened it would feel its hunger and begin to cry. Quickly he descended from the roof and took the baby to Alejandro's room where the Yungue-Yungue woman slept with her own child. He gave the baby to the startled woman he had awakened and then went to see the mother of the baby girl he considered his daughter in spite of the bright red hair that curled against her head.

Old Fabia continued to sleep as he entered the room and crossed to María Angélica's bedside. He knelt as he did when he prayed to her god. The same prayer he had come to say so frequently poured from his lips asking for her god to save her. He rose after he had finished praying and reached out his hand to touch the woman's cheek. Abruptly he put both hands on her face and forehead, and his features were no longer stark and hard. A smile broke the harsh lines.

"Rohona thanks you, God of the strangers," he whispered quietly, "I thank you for the life of the woman."

Fabia awakened and saw Rohona's hands on María Angélica's face. Not completely awake, for an instant she thought he had been closing the young woman's eyes in death, and she cried out, "No!" and scrambled toward the bed.

Rohona turned and saw her agitation. "The fever, it has gone," he said smiling.

# Chapter 26

Gradually, María Angélica regained her strength.

"There will be no more babies," Fabia told her. "Because of the fever you will have no more children." The old woman added pointedly, "This is the last chance you will have to love a baby of your own. Do not give up that wonderful blessing."

María Angélica did not answer. Nor could she look at the father of her son, but she did watch him out of the corner of her eye when he came to see Vicente's tiny daughter. He picked up the child and talked to it softly.

He brought the baby to the bedside and she was unable to keep her eyes averted. It was as if some horrible force made her turn to look at the man she loved, holding the infant implanted in her by a man whose very touch revolted her. When Rohona smiled at her, her face burned with embarrassment and she could not bear his gaze.

"Thank you for daughter," he said to her. "Now I have a beautiful daughter and son. Your god is very powerful—he made my child look like red-beard so that we may live and be happy. I thank your god for my daughter, and I thank your god for making the sickness go away from you."

He reached out and touched his fingers to her cheek, but she could not look at him.

He pulled a chair close to the bed and sat down with the infant. "Why do you not want your daughter? Why do you hate your daughter?"

"I am ashamed," she whispered raggedly.

"What does ashamed mean?"

She made various attempts at explanation and then gave up, saying only, "I did not want *his* child."

Rohona looked at her and there was absolute conviction in every line of his features. "She is Rohona's daughter. Your god made her look like red-beard, but she is my daughter."

María Angélica could not believe that he truly thought that, yet there was total assurance in his voice and in his face. He stood and held out the baby to her.

"Hold your daughter," he said.

"No!" she gasped with a kind of horror.

Rohona looked at her intently, and she was not able to look away. "At first I hated you, Mía," he said slowly, "until I touched you. Then I knew that I had love for you, not hate. Hold our daughter."

The last was a command. He held the baby out to her, and the intensity of his dark eyes commanded her to do his bidding.

Gingerly she took the infant in her arms. Her hands trembled, and she felt agonizingly awkward. Tears rolled down her cheeks, and she whispered, "God help me."

Fabia came into the room at that moment and rushed to the bed when she saw María Angélica holding the baby. The old woman crossed herself and whispered an inaudible prayer.

The old woman fussed around her. "I will take her to the Yungue-Yungue woman for she is hungry, but we shall bring her here to you often so that your milk will return." María Angélica did not reply. Fabia took the baby and made comforting sounds to it.

María Angélica spoke quietly. "Does she have a name?"

"She has no name yet. I have called the poor little thing Alegría because of the happiness I felt at her birth."

"Then that shall be her name," her mother said.

When Dorotea came that afternoon, María Angélica grasped her hand and spoke. "What has happened? Fabia won't tell me a thing. I think she is afraid to worry me for fear I will have a relapse. I must know. What did the governor do when he found out about the desertion?"

Dorotea's face was somber. "You can imagine what he did. He turned purple with rage. He has thrown Peñalosa in jail and he has sent soldiers after the deserters to try to stop them. He wants them all tried for treason."

"I'm not surprised, but what about the colony? What about us? The deserters said we would all have to leave once the governor returned and saw the situation." Her face was pale.

"He has ordered everyone to the church this evening for an announcement," Dorotea said, "but of course you won't be expected to attend."

"I'm going to get out of this bed and go whether Fabia permits it or not. I cannot stand this torment of not knowing what will become of us."

* * *

Oñate entered the small church and walked slowly to the front. He knelt at the altar, crossed himself, rose and faced the assembled group.

"The situation of this colony is desperate." His voice boomed in the quiet nave. "I am ordering the Sergeant Major to Mexico to appeal to the Viceroy for help in light of the cowardly desertion of the spineless soldiers and priests. If he is unsuccessful at the court in Mexico City, he is to sail to Spain and seek an audience with the King and the Council of the Indies. It is our only hope. We cannot survive here without support. We will all die of starvation or be forced to return from whence we came, leaving our glorious conquest in ashes."

"What's going to happen to us?" María Angélica asked as she hugged Dorotea.

"I don't know." Dorotea answered starkly. "If it comes to it, we will all return to Mexico."

"But *I* can't."

"You may have to whether you want to or not. We'd all better prepare ourselves."

Oñate's voice reverberated in the small church. "I would suggest you all go to your knees and spend a great deal of time in that position throughout the next days beseeching God not to desert us as have the cowardly soldiers and the lily-livered priests."

He turned to the Father Commissary who stood by the altar shifting nervously from one foot to the other. Oñate's eyes were venomous, his words cold and hard.

"Lead us in prayer, *Padre*. Ask God to sustain this colony for His greater glory, to send us relief, and to punish the villainous cowards who would desert His holy work in this heathen land."

The Father Commissary knelt, and when he spoke his voice was hollow. "Let us say ten *Aves* for the preservation of this colony."

Oñate's face reddened at the insignificant number of prayers the *padre* intended to offer, but he said nothing.

As they left the church, few spoke. María Angélica walked with her arm linked in Dorotea's. Vicente appeared remote, absorbed in his own thoughts, scowling, unaware, it seemed, of his wife who had left her sick-bed to attend the meeting. But Oñate was aware of her presence and came walking quickly toward her.

"Dearest *señora*," he said, taking her hand and bringing it to his lips, "what a fright you gave us, but what a wonderful sight to see you up so soon. Surely you know you did not need to come out tonight. I would never forgive myself if you had a relapse."

"You're very kind to be concerned over me when you have so many other more serious matters to deal with, Governor," she replied, "but for my own part, I am much more concerned with the fate of this colony than I am with myself."

"I would to God all the colonists felt the same way as you, dearest lady," he said with vehemence. He turned toward Vicente who walked some paces away, oblivious to everyone.

"Oh, Captain, would you mind if I stopped by your dwelling for a few moments?"

"Not at all, Governor, not at all," Vicente said, coming out of his reverie.

Oñate turned to Dorotea. "Thank you, Doña Dorotea, but I can see the *señora* home safely."

"Certainly, Governor," Dorotea responded.

Fabia met them at the door. "Come, Angelita," she said, taking her arm without even acknowledging the governor's presence. "You must get back to bed."

"No, Don Juan has come to pay us a visit. I shall make him welcome. Please bring the governor some *jerez*. I shall have a cup of hot chocolate, and you may bring me a lap robe if you will."

Fabia looked at her intently for a moment but then nodded and left the room.

"Please," María Angélica said to Oñate, indicating a chair.

"Governor," Vicente broke in, "you cannot abandon this colony!"

"I know, I know," Oñate said bitterly, "but so far nothing has been accomplished that will make *any* impression upon those in positions of power in Mexico or on the Peninsula. *Nothing*. I have written glowing reports, but without any concrete evidence—that is to say gold, silver, or jewels—the reports will not for long convince anyone."

His hands were clenched, his knuckles white. "I made Peñalosa lieutenant governor in my absence and entrusted the well being of this colony to him, and he did nothing, absolutely nothing, to stop the desertion! In fact, he not only made no effort to stop the treason, he even aided the instigators, one of whom was his own damn son-in-law.

"And that treacherous Father Commissary, that liverless Escalona, aided and abetted the desertion, also, allowing all the priests to flee. They told me that from the pulpit itself he and the other priests urged desertion!" Oñate's jaw clamped shut with rage, but then he spoke again. "In the entire province of *Nuevo México*, there are only three *padres* left—the Father Commissary, Fray Francisco, and the lay brother, Fray Pedro—and both of the last two were with me on the plains when the desertion occurred. How do they expect to harvest souls for Holy Mother Church without priests?"

"Governor," Vicente interrupted impatiently, "do you remember our bargain?"

Oñate looked at him. "Yes?"

"You said that if we found nothing on the plains that I could prospect on my own. If I found gold, the colony would not be abandoned, would it?"

"No."

"Well?"

Oñate glanced at María Angélica who sat watching them closely, and then he turned back to Vicente.

"When the snows begin to melt in the spring and if we have heard nothing from Mexico by then, you may go."

The winter was hard and miserable that year in the depleted capital. The deserters had taken the lion's share of the grain that was meant to see the colony through the winter. The expedition that returned from the buffalo plains had brought some meat and hides with them, but it was not enough to supply the hungry colonists.

Daily as the long winter dragged on, Vicente had seemed to lose more touch with reality, ranting and raving about precious metal. The governor came often, a frown creasing his forehead as he watched Vicente whose eyes seldom focused on anything in particular. Frequently, the captain was scarcely aware of Oñate's presence as the governor sat talking to María Angélica of his own worries.

She did her best to ignore her husband's repetitive rantings, but she tried to pay attention to the governor's concerns. He was usually filled with anger, but occasionally sounds of doom would creep into his voice, and terror would clutch her. What would happen to the colony if Oñate admitted defeat? She knew the answer to the question, and it chilled her.

"Governor," she would say, "viceroys come and go, but this colony *must* remain. What if Cortez had given up? Or Pizarro? Those names carry glory in the history books, and so will yours. God would not have led Spain to the New World if He did not want its inhabitants to know the true Word, and He would not have allowed us to reach here if He did not want us to pacify this remote land."

"You are right, dearest *señora*," the governor answered, taking her hand, and she did not attempt to remove it from his. "This conquest must not be abandoned!"

So when the snows of winter began to melt, with the permission and best wishes of the governor, Vicente and his page set out.

"Return immediately if you discover any precious metal," Oñate commanded him urgently. "I will send a messenger with all haste to Mexico to counter what I know the deserters are saying."

A year and a half passed before the tiny colony saw anyone from the outside world. They raised their meager crops, barely managing to keep from starving; their clothes were more nearly rags than garments. María Angélica recovered gradually but remained thin, and although Dorotea claimed she was still beautiful, she knew that she was not. Her hands were rough and calloused, her skin tanned by the sun, and her cheekbones made too prominent by the hollows below them.

When six months passed and Vicente and his page had not returned, she wondered briefly if something had not befallen them. When a year came and went since he had ridden out, she assumed that starvation or hostile natives had taken their toll on the two men. She asked a priest to say a prayer at Mass for the repose of their souls. She added her own prayer that God have mercy on them, but she did not ask for their safe return. Just as she did, the rest of the colonists assumed she was now a widow.

Rohona was lean and hard from the constant work of providing food for his household. Without him they would all have faced starvation. If there were no planting or harvesting, he hunted, sometimes ranging far into the mountains to search for game. With him he would take back the skulls of the deer he had previously shot. When María Angélica first saw the skulls drying on the roof, she questioned him about them, thinking he was keeping them as trophies.

"No, after the skull is dry," Rohona said, "I must paint it so that it will look like a deer again. I must paint a black stripe down the middle of its face, and I must fill the eye sockets with cotton and paint black centers so the deer will have eyes again. After that I tie feathers to the antlers. When the head is ready, I take it back into the mountains. There it is necessary to pray that the deer will come alive once more. By doing this we assure that there will always be plentiful game."

Rohona's face showed his complete conviction in the belief, and she was well aware of his hunting success. She would scoff at nothing that might interfere with it.

Fabia was also aware of the conventions of the natives of the land and tried to heed them. Many were the times she crossed herself and thanked *Dios* for the Indian.

She still looked the same: ancient, wizened, and wrinkled, but she continued to work as she had when she was much younger, zealously caring for the children. Alejandro and his little sister Alegría, whose bright red curls were the delight and amazement of many, were the only ones who did not show the toil and lack of food in the miserable little capital.

As the days passed, and with Fabia and Rohona's constant urging, María Angélica had begun to care for her baby daughter. She saw to the child's needs, but even when the baby began to smile and gurgle happily, she could scarcely feel any tenderness for the little creature. She knew she would never love her daughter with the same intensity with which she loved her son. She tried very hard not to see Vicente in her daughter, but it was difficult.

Alejandro was delighted with the baby and experimented with new syllables around her, as if he wanted to learn to talk just so he could communicate with her, and the baby was fascinated with him.

As the months passed, the children became constant companions, always playing, always exploring as far as a three-year-old and a child of eighteen months could manage before an adult came looking for them.

There were comments at first about it not being quite proper for a full blood Spanish girl-child to be playing with a half-breed bastard, but soon the comments died for there were few children in the destitute colony. Everyone got a lift of spirits watching the agile, handsome little boy climbing or running, followed by the bobbing head of bright red curls of the little girl who followed him on legs that were still not yet expert at it.

Alejandro spoke both Castilian and the Queres of his father and aunt, and he had even picked up some of the Nahuatl curse words Fabia was frequent to employ. Alegría had begun to say a few words, most of which were unintelligible to all but Alejandro. She adored the Indian slave Rohona and the little toys he made her. She did not know her own father, for when she was barely four months old, he had gone off with his page to search for gold.

The colonists' only real concern was whether there would be enough to eat during the winter. That, too, was always Fabia's concern, but she praised the Lord for the recovery of her Angelita, delighted in both children and loved them fiercely and protectively. In spite of everything, however, occasionally there would come to her eyes that dark fleeting look that Dorotea had seen in the old woman's eyes the night of Alegría's birth.

# Chapter 27

Someone noticed a cloud of dust rising from the south. People rushed from their dwellings, straining their eyes to try to make out what approached.

Oñate yelled to a couple of soldiers. "Ride with haste! Find out what comes!"

Within moments the soldiers were mounted, the rowels of their spurs urging their horses forward with a leap.

"Mamá, Mamá," Alejandro said, pulling on her hand after the horses had galloped out of the village. "I want to see, too," he said with excitement.

María Angélica ruffled the dark hair of her three-year-old son. "The *soldados* will be back quickly, *hijito*, and we shall find out what it is."

Sometime later they saw in the distance one of the soldiers galloping back toward the village at a full run. It must not be natives or all the soldiers would have ridden back with haste. The soldier waved his arms and shouted.

"*¡Carretas! Carretas* from New Spain!"

*"Gracias a Dios,"* Oñate whispered, "the Viceroy has sent reinforcements!" Loud cheers rose from the people gathered there, and they hugged and kissed each other. "Thank God! Thank God. We have not been forgotten."

The wagons rolled into San Gabriel amid shouts of praise and joy, and tears filled all eyes. The Viceroy had sent out four friars and a small detail of soldiers to escort them. The colonists inundated the new arrivals, overwhelming them with questions about the outside world. Not only were they starved for food, they were starved for news. May of 1603 and they had seen no one from the outside world for over a year and a half.

Philip the Third was on the throne of Spain. The friars were pleased, for although the new King was known to be melancholic and retiring, he was also known to be deeply religious, and they expected the Church to benefit under his rule. The accursed Protestant English, under their doddering old-maid queen, were trying to wrest the rich sea trade from the hands of its rightful owner, the King of Spain. The Hollanders, Protestants also, were fighting the Spanish rule in the lowlands, and they, too, wanted a piece of the rich East India spice trade. In France, the Protestant Huguenots were fighting the Catholics, and hopefully Philip III could put a stop to the spread of the hated, devil-inspired Protestantism. Or so the friars prayed.

The joy of the colonists and of the governor, in particular, was of a very transient nature when they realized the implication of the size of the tiny group that had arrived.

Later that afternoon Dorotea came to María Angélica's dwelling. Her voice was hard. "It's obvious the Viceroy doesn't support this venture in the wilds of *Nuevo México,* nor our illustrious governor. If the Viceroy wished for its success, he would have made the deserters return or he would have at least sent a large number of reinforcements rather than this paltry group. Four friars and a handful of soldiers!" she laughed bitterly. "This is as much of an insult to Don Juan as a slap in the face would have been."

María Angélica nodded. "The governor must be furious. I know he was hoping for several hundred soldiers, at the minimum. He says that without more men there is no possibility of discovering anything—gold, silver, pearls—anything."

That evening Oñate took leave of the new arrivals and María Angélica found out how correctly she had assessed his response. He stood in her *sala* not availing himself of the chair she offered him. He cursed the Viceroy, damned the deserters, and execrated the barrenness of the land. He heaped vituperation upon everything and everybody whom he perceived to have hindered him in any way. At length he calmed and sank onto the chair.

"But," he said, his voice becoming more quiet, "I must be careful not to offend the new friars, for they may be of assistance to me." He spoke candidly to her.

"One, in particular, I judge it would be best not to anger. He might be a valuable ally, for he has the look of a fanatic. I am quite certain that if one got on the wrong side of him he would—in spite of his saintly profession—do absolutely anything to further his own ends."

María Angélica nodded. She could only agree with the governor, for she had seen the friar, too. Isidro Ordóñez was a hawk-faced man, his nose thin and aquiline. His small, riveting black eyes appeared to have no lashes, enhancing the eagle-like look. He was rather tall and bony, his hands and fingers long and narrow, and when he clutched his rosary, it seemed as if the beads were caught in the talons of a bird of prey.

"He has a hungry, ravenous look about him," Oñate said, "but I am sure it is not for food. I would guess it is for power. Of course that trait is admirable for the capturing of souls for Holy Mother Church, but what it portends for civil and ecclesiastical relations, I fear."

The friars had scarcely arrived, indeed it was on the following day that Fray Ordóñez had gone out from San Gabriel, without any rest after the arduous journey, to preach to the natives in nearby villages. Within weeks he had baptized many despite the fact that there was little in the Spaniards, nor in their way of life, that would have encouraged the Indians to emulate their culture.

A month later Fray Ordóñez returned to San Gabriel.

The governor came to María Angélica's house. "That friar wants *me* to give him more 'commitment' to the missionary effort," he said with exasperation. "How does he expect me to support him when the Viceroy sends me nothing except four friars and a measly handful of soldiers?"

Oñate's voice was bitter, but then it softened as he looked up at her and spoke. "I have no wife to act as hostess for me. Would you be so kind as to do me that small favor?"

She tried not to look surprised at his request. "What do you have in mind, Governor?"

"Priests are just like other men," he said speculatively. "In spite of their words or actions, they usually like their comforts like anyone else."

He saw a look cross her face, and he laughed. "Dear *señora,* it's not what you think. I want to keep this friar on my side. As zealous as he is, he could be an asset to this conquest, but as an adversary I shudder to think of the mischief he could cause me. Things are bad enough already.

"He has come asking for more commitment from me, but I have nothing to give him. However, the last thing I want him to think is that I will not or do not want to give him support." He smiled. "This is where you come in, dear lady."

She looked at him levelly. If Fray Ordóñez was in a position to support their colonization effort in *Nuevo México* then she wanted him on their side.

"What do you wish of me, Governor?" she asked.

"I knew I could count on you," he said with a smile, "but what I have to ask of you is really quite simple. I just want Father Ordóñez to feel at home. I don't want him to feel the desperation of this place that so many feel. I would like for us to be able to talk here at your dwelling."

He spread his hands to indicate the *sala*. "Your room is cozy and much more comfortable than most, what with all the things your husband brought in the cart train. You yourself have a serenity most of the women here don't have—as well as beauty. Even a priest could not be immune to the loveliness of your face."

"Just tell me what you want, Governor," she said matter-of-factly.

"I would simply like to bring the friar here and for you to offer us some refreshments so that we might chat in comfortable surroundings."

At that moment Alejandro came bounding into the room. "Mamá, Mamá," he said breathlessly as he held out his hand, *"¡mira!"* She scooped him up onto her lap to look at the treasure he held in his hand. She kissed him on both cheeks and looked at the shiny rock he grasped in his chubby little fingers.

"What a lovely *piedra, hijito,*" she said, smiling at him, "but the governor is here. You must greet him." She set Alejandro on the floor and he walked timidly to Oñate and went down on one knee.

Don Juan laughed and picked him up. "What a big boy you are getting to be," he said. "You are three now, eh?"

Alejandro nodded solemnly and held up three fingers. Oñate looked across at María Angélica. "This is also part of what I mean about your dwelling—it seems so much like a home. Have the children here when the friar comes. Bring that little red-haired baby in here, too."

María Angélica smiled. "She's hardly a baby anymore—she's a year and a half. But what if Fray Ordóñez doesn't like children, Governor, what then?"

"Then you will quietly remove them, and we will find what Fray Ordóñez does like." Oñate laughed as he set Alejandro on the floor.

"Just when would you like the good father to see this scene of domesticity?"

"Would tomorrow afternoon be acceptable?"

"That would be fine. I will have Fabia make some of her specialties."

"Wonderful. What would I do without you, dear lady?"

"You would manage, Governor."

The next afternoon Fray Ordóñez sat in the *sala* of María Angélica's house along with the governor. The priest sipped hot chocolate and ate the *pastelitos* and *empanadas* that Fabia had made.

"Ah," he said as he bit into one, "I have not had *huitlacoche* since I left Mexico City. Delicious."

Oñate smiled at María Angélica but turned to Fray Ordóñez. He had already praised the efforts of the zealous priest and flattered his ego, but he added more.

"If you, *padre*, had been with me from the beginning, I am quite certain this entire province would have already been converted for the glory of the Church and his majesty, Don Felipe."

The friar smiled his tight smile, and the governor realized he must be careful not to make the praise overlavish.

At that moment Fabia appeared in the doorway with Alejandro and Alegría, holding both their hands. It was obvious the children had been scrubbed within an inch of their lives, and they were dressed in their best clothes. Alejandro's dark hair was brushed back from his face and Alegría's bright red curls ran riot around hers. It was clear no brush would easily tame that hair. Fabia let go of the children's hands and they ran to their mother with excitement, not quite knowing what was the occasion for such hurried preparations.

Alejandro threw his arms around María Angélica's neck, and Alegría scrambled up into her mother's lap. María Angélica laughed and kissed them.

Oñate saw Fray Ordóñez's surprise as the children came running in and saw the smile that came to the *padre*'s eyes as he looked at them.

"The boy is a half-breed orphan the *señora* took in when her own child died," the governor said. "She has raised him as her own son. Her husband's surely dead, but she carries on with strength. There is no woman in this colony who has more Christian charity than *Señora* de Vizcarra."

When Fray Ordóñez spoke there was something in his eyes that Oñate could not decipher. "The boy's an orphan?" he asked quietly.

"Yes," Don Juan said, "but he has been treated like a real son by the *señora*."

"Children," María Angélica spoke, "the governor is here as well as *Padre* Ordóñez. You must greet them. Father Ordóñez has come all the way from Mexico to teach the natives about *Jesús Cristo*. He has a very important job to do."

She placed her hand gently on Alejandro's back and gave him a little nudge. He hesitated but then walked slowly over to Oñate and went down on one knee.

*"Buenas tardes, Señor Gobernador,"* he spoke in scarcely more than a whisper, and then he rose and knelt before Fray Ordóñez. *"Su bendición, Señor Padre,"* he whispered. Fray Ordóñez smiled and put out his hand for Alejandro to kiss. The little boy touched his lips to the bony fingers and then Fray Ordóñez made the sign of the cross on the boy's forehead with his thumb.

"*Dios te bendiga*, my son," he said. He cupped his hands around Alejandro's face and lifted it. His eyes glittered. "You are a beautiful boy," he said, and he placed his thin lips on the child's forehead and kissed him.

María Angélica set Alegría on the floor. "Greet the governor and the *padre, hija,*" she said, but Alegría turned and clutched her mother's skirt.

María Angélica tried to extricate herself from the little girl's hands, but Alegría began to wail and cling more tightly to her. María Angélica looked up with embarrassment at Fray Ordóñez.

"Never mind," the priest said, "the girl is just frightened of a stranger, but you are not frightened of me, are you, my son?" he asked Alejandro. The boy shook his head, but his wide eyes said otherwise.

Fray Ordóñez picked Alejandro up and set him on his lap. "There," he said, "you and I are going to be friends, aren't we?"

The priest reached and took a *pastelito* from the tray that sat near him and held it out to Alejandro, but the boy looked at it hesitantly and did not take it.

"Do not be afraid," Fray Ordóñez said quietly. There was something in the priest's eyes that made the little boy take the *pastelito* and eat it quickly, but then seeing his chance, he pushed himself off the priest's lap and ran back to his mother. Alegría let go of her mother's skirts and grabbed onto Alejandro as if he were her protector.

"You may go now, children," María Angélica said. "Say good-bye to our guests." The children bobbed their heads and mumbled a quick *buenas tardes* and were out of the room in seconds. "I'm afraid the children aren't used to strangers," she said apologetically.

"That's quite all right," Fray Ordóñez said with his taut smile that did not seem a smile.

Later that afternoon when the governor and Fray Ordóñez had left, Fabia was muttering to herself as she removed the trays and cups from the *sala*.

"What are you grumbling about, Fabia?" María Angélica asked.

"I don't like the looks of that friar. He is a scheming, clever man. I should not like to have him behind me, for I fear I might mistake him for Beelzebub."

"Perhaps you should not call a predicator of the Lord's Gospel Beelzebub," María Angélica said. "But I, too, have an uneasy feeling when I'm around that friar. He seems to like children, but it is as if with his lashless, eagle eyes he seeks the vulnerability in each person's soul."

A slight shudder passed through her before she continued. "But I pray he is good for this colony—anything to bring us some stability, some hope that all will not be abandoned. Each day I become more worried, for I fear the governor is losing hope."

The novelty of the new arrivals wore off quickly as the realities of life had to again be dealt with. It was planting season, which, next to harvest, was the busiest time of the year.

Harvest came and went. Winter bore down cruelly and the spring was bitterly cold.

# Chapter 28

María Angélica opened the door and smothered her shriek with her hand. The smell revolted her. She tried to speak but could not.

*"Señora,"* the soldier said, "it is a miracle. I spotted him some distance from the village on horseback wandering aimlessly. His page was following behind. When I went out to meet him, he just stared forward into the distance and didn't seem to see me or hear me when I spoke to him. I had to lead him here."

All had thought him dead. She, above all, had thought him dead. One month short of two years and he had returned. She was aghast at his appearance.

*"¿Señora?"* the soldier asked when she did not speak. "What shall I do with him?"

She swallowed and forced words out as she stepped back. "Bring him in. Set him in a chair, *por favor*."

The soldier led the filthy, stooped man to the chair she indicated, and eased him onto it. "What about Mateo?" he asked.

"Please," she whispered, "just leave him outside for the moment." He nodded and she walked him to the door. *"Gracias."*

"Do you think the captain *está loco, señora*?" he asked quietly.

"God willing, he will return to himself."

She closed the door behind the soldier and turned to look at Vicente. His beard had grown down to his chest and was matted and putrid. It had obviously not been trimmed during his entire absence of almost two years. He had odd rags and bits of leather tied to his body as clothing, and it appeared and smelled as if he had not bathed during the entire time he was gone. His stench overpowered the room, and his eyes had a morbid, vacant look.

She walked toward him and stopped. She started to speak but the words caught in her throat. "Can I get you something?" she managed to say.

He did not answer, and she tried again. "Are you hungry?" But he said nothing as he sat slumped in the chair.

After long moments, just as she was about to leave the room to try to find Fabia who had gone on an errand next door, he spoke, startling her.

"The silence was so loud!" He shouted the words, and she jumped. His voice cracked and he began to speak as if in a soliloquy.

"We rode north and then west and there were mountains and an enormous canyon such as I have never seen before and flat wasteland where we almost died of thirst, and at night red eyes watched us in the dark. The silence was so loud I had to cover my ears. *¡Dios!*"

He rambled on and on. She wanted to escape the *sala* but was reluctant to leave for fear it might anger him or cause him to come after her.

It seemed that he and his page had spent the winters in caves and used the animals as food, keeping them preserved in the snow, buried so that the wild animals could not dig them up. He talked about a great salty lake they had come upon and about the thirst that had nearly driven them insane.

Word reached the governor that Captain Vizcarra had returned, and Oñate rushed to their house.

He took one look at María Angélica's pale face when she opened the door and knew her husband had not found gold, but he could not stop his question. "Did he find *anything?*" She shook her head and stepped aside to allow him to enter.

He saw the filthy, rag-covered man slumped in a chair and stopped short. He was without words for a moment.

"I am dismayed at the condition of the captain, *señora,*" he finally spoke quietly to her.

At that moment Fabia came rushing in the front door and came to an abrupt stop much as the governor had. "God save us," the old woman whispered as she looked at the man in the chair who muttered to himself, making no indication that he was aware there was anyone else in the room.

Oñate spoke to Fabia. "Go get Alonso. Tell him to come immediately. One of my own servants shall attend to making the captain presentable."

When the governor left, María Angélica saw his shoulders sag. She turned back toward Vicente and shuddered.

Within a few weeks he began to seem a little more normal. He began also to talk again on the sole subject about which he seemed to have any interest. He talked about making preparations for a new foray. "I've got to go again quickly. It's out there. I know it's out there just waiting for me."

He had never made any indication that he recognized the little red-haired girl as his daughter. He did not seem to notice her; he asked neither her name nor anything about her. If she passed in his line of vision, it was as if he saw through her. He was that way with all people: his eyes appeared to focus on nothing, his only vision that which appeared behind his eyes. It was as if the children in the household did not exist, and they did everything in their power to avoid being caught anywhere near the stranger.

María Angélica was seized by a fearful dread that he might come to her bed. She knew that she would surely flee, screaming, if he attempted to touch her. No more could she submit to him.

Rohona sensed her worry. "Have no fear, Mía. He will not touch you," he said, his eyes intense as he looked at her. "If he should try, he will no longer walk among the living."

"No," she said with shock, taking his arm. "You must not kill him."

"Do not worry," he said quietly, "there are ways. None of the *españoles* would ever know what had happened."

"You *must* not kill him," she reiterated. "It would be a far greater sin than anything we have ever done. You *must* not."

Rohona looked away. "I will not kill him, Mía, for you, but accidents cannot be foreseen or prevented sometimes." Nevertheless he began to make a habit of returning frequently to their dwelling. His footsteps were silent and his eyes vigilant.

Although Vicente appeared to have regained a measure of normalcy at times, María Angélica wondered if he weren't mad. She feared, too, that his young page may have followed in his master's footsteps, for since returning, he appeared mute, only grunting occasionally in response to a question. Most of the time Vicente seemed unaware of much that happened around him.

He had ordered a cot for Mateo put in his room, and she thought that perhaps having spent the winters in caves with his page, he was no longer comfortable sleeping alone. Then one night an unusual sound awakened her.

Her first thought was that something was wrong with the children, but both were sleeping peacefully. She saw a flickering light coming from Vicente's partly open door, and the strange whimpering drew her to glance in.

For an instant she did not understand, but in the next, she knew all too clearly. Her hand flew to her mouth, and she fled to her room.

That such things existed was almost more than she could believe, but it did not keep her from realizing that by Vicente's perversion she was perhaps saved from the thing she feared and dreaded more than death itself.

Relief washed over her, and she crossed herself. "Forgive me for my hypocrisy," she said softly, and the next day she told Rohona, "I think there is no longer any need to worry about Vicente."

He looked at her questioningly for a moment, but when he saw the assurance in her face, he said nothing and only nodded.

It was a strange household indeed. Little did the rest of the colony have any idea just how strange it was, but everyone recognized that Vicente was unbalanced, and the Indian slave in the Vizcarra household was no more than one of the captain's possessions in their minds.

The governor seemed to recognize Vicente's condition for when he visited, he always directed his words to María Angélica because the captain seemed unable to follow a conversation. As the days passed Oñate grew agitated as if the man's unresponsive state was urging him to action.

One day when he came to visit, he paced in her *sala* unable, it seemed, to remain seated. "In spite of the destitute condition of this colony, I must do something!" he said.

She thought his voice sounded desperate, and she started to say something placating, but he interrupted.

"I must make a new attempt at discovery—I cannot simply sit in this dingy little capital and hope riches will fall into my lap!"

He looked at the captain for a moment before he walked over to him and took him by the shoulders. He shook him with as much enthusiasm as he could muster in the face of Vicente's blank stare.

The governor shouted, "Think no more of personal searches for gold in the near future, Captain, because I am planning another expedition! An expedition!

"As soon as harvest is over and we have sufficient provisions for the march, I will make another attempt to reach the South Sea. I think there is more chance of discovering pearls than gold, and if I could discover a good water route and ports for the Philippine trade, I might be able to recover some prestige for this conquest. I am certain what we had is being tarnished with each succeeding day as those goddamned deserters regale the officials with the conditions in *Nuevo México* and the supposed excesses of its governor."

Vicente's face began to register some understanding. He jumped up and Oñate stepped back. "An expedition?" the disheveled captain said. "An expedition? Good, oh, good, good." He sat back down and knotted his hands into fists. "Good. I'll be able to keep looking."

* * *

On October 7, 1604, the paltry expedition of thirty soldiers, two friars, and the governor set out for the western reaches seeking once more riches and glory. María Angélica crossed herself as the expedition rode away into the distance and prayed they would return quickly.

She remembered standing and watching another expedition leave, praying then that they would take forever to return. She looked at the curly red head of her daughter who was playing in the dirt with Alejandro. In another month Alegría would be three years old.

María Angélica knew she had a great deal for which to be thankful, but she could not keep from praying silently as she watched her daughter, "Please, *Dios*, let there be none of her father in her."

The warm fall days were quickly gone, and winter wrapped them in its cold, snowy blanket.

"I never thought I would see the day I wished for the return of an expedition," she spoke one evening to Rohona as the wind howled around the door of their dwelling, "but I pray this expedition returns quickly and that God grants them success. They *must* find something of value for I know the governor is losing hope."

Exactly six months and eighteen days after it had set out, the expedition returned, having made the discovery of an extensive body of water into which a large river flowed. No pearls were found but the soldiers returned triumphant and rejoicing. The governor was in the best of spirits, his enthusiasm unlimited.

"This is what I have hoped for," he shouted to the assembled colonists, "what I have prayed to God for! We have found a fine port. More than a thousand vessels can anchor in it without hindrance to one another. Soon we shall see cargoes of silks and satins from the Philippine trade landing on those shores. Great numbers of peaceful Indians fill the region—souls for Holy Mother Church to reap!"

María Angélica rejoiced with the other colonists and gave fervent thanks for the fortuitous discovery. "Governor, I am so happy," she said when he came to their dwelling that night.

He was elated and took both her hands, kissing them numerous times although Vicente stood nearby. "Captain," he said as he turned to Vicente and clapped him on the back, "I'm going to carry our wonderful news to Mexico myself. I'm going as far as San Bartolomé where I will await word from the Viceroy if he wants to see me personally about the discovery. Come with me. Share the triumph of our discovery!"

The staring quality had returned to Vicente's eyes. "I've got to find it!" he shouted. "We found nothing on the march—nothing."

"What about the four sample stones we brought back?" Oñate asked. "They may be of value."

"But they are not gold!" Vicente yelled. The governor glanced at María Angélica, but nothing showed on her face as her husband whirled around and shouted again, "I've got to find it! I'm going out again!"

"Go, then," Oñate said quietly. "If you discover gold, so much the better. Perhaps the *vieja*'s prophesy will come true."

At dawn the next day, Vicente and his page set out. He said no word of good-bye to María Angélica, and she did not acknowledge his leaving other than to stand at the door and watch him ride away.

Later that morning, the governor came to her dwelling.

"I am off, dearest lady," he said with a smile as he kissed her hand, "when I return I intend to satisfy a long-held desire of mine—one I should have taken advantage of long before now."

She started to withdraw her hand, but he held it securely. "You know as well as I that your husband is no longer quite right in the mind. He may not return this time."

"God looks after children and madmen, Governor," she said quietly.

"Perhaps not this time," Don Juan de Oñate said as he brought her hand to his lips once more. "Until I return, *señora,* until I return."

# Chapter 29

Harvest was over when Oñate rode back into San Gabriel. There was no rejoicing this time, and the governor sat stooped on his horse as he rode into his little capital. She heard the whispers long before he came to her house: "The Viceroy ordered the governor back to New Mexico. He refuses to see him."

There were no gallantries when he appeared at her door. "May I come in?" he asked simply.

"Please," she said.

He sat staring at the floor as he spoke. "He called them pebbles—he called the four samples of stones I sent to him '*pebbles*.' He said the land has nothing but naked Indians."

Oñate looked up at her. "Has your husband returned?" he asked expectantly, but she shook her head. "I should never have even begun this conquest," he muttered.

"Oh, Governor, you are wrong. Do not think such a thing. Look at your accomplishments. Look at the vast territory you have conquered and given to the King—it is a new realm, larger than Mexico itself. Think of the souls that have been saved for the glory of God. God is most certainly pleased."

"It's not God I worry about," he said with dejection, "it's the Viceroy. He is the one who determines our fate."

"But he has sent us two new friars and the Sergeant Major is back after his voyage to Spain," she said.

"Ha!" Oñate laughed bitterly. "Two new friars. Where are the soldiers, the reinforcements with which I could make truly grand discoveries? Where are the new colonists to work the soil and build an empire? The Sergeant Major won no concessions for us—nothing, *nothing* from the

King, *nothing* from the Viceroy. Ask him and he will tell you the picture for the future is as bleak as I paint it. It is obvious the court in Mexico City has no intention of reoutfitting this expedition."

"God save us," she whispered softly. "Is it truly over?"

In the spring they planted their crops and saw the meager harvest completed, but Vicente did not return nor had there been any word from Mexico City about their fate. But María Angélica began to feel a spark of optimism in spite of all.

On the few occasions when Fray Ordóñez returned to San Gabriel from his missionary work in the outlying pueblos, he would pay a visit to her house. She did not know what it was about the priest that made her quite so uneasy in his presence, and she wondered why he always chose to come to her house. She did know she hated the way his eyes seemed always to be trying to read her thoughts, but he seemed to be a successful priest, for his baptisms far outnumbered those of any other friar there, and he did seem to like children. He always asked after hers when he visited, and he seemed taken with Alejandro.

María Angélica smiled when she thought about her son. He was such a handsome child, such a good boy, and so polite. He filled her with tremendous pride, but her daughter's behavior occasionally caused her some degree of embarrassment. Alegría was such a free, untamed little thing with her bright red curls, María Angélica was at a loss as to how to handle her.

Once when Fray Ordóñez came to visit, Alegría had caused such a scene. Alejandro greeted the priest and kissed his hand as the children were taught to do. Fray Ordóñez took the boy's face in his hands and kissed him on the forehead in a blessing.

"Now you give *Padre* Ordóñez a nice greeting, *hija,*" she said to Alegría and gave her a little nudge toward the priest.

"No!" Alegría shouted, grabbing her mother's skirt as she always did. In spite of her mother's urgings she would never greet the *padre*. "No!" she shouted. "I don't want him to kiss me. He looks like a bird!"

*"Hija!"* María Angélica gasped. "Mind your tongue! That isn't nice to say."

"But he does!" she reiterated. "And he likes Alejandro!"

María Angélica glanced with embarrassment at the friar. She saw some emotion in the priest's glittery black eyes before he concealed it, but she would not have been able to say what it was.

"Of course *Padre* Ordóñez likes Alejandro," she said, trying to smooth over her daughter's rudeness. "He is a very polite little boy. You must learn to be polite like Alejandro, also." And then she changed the subject, and the children, sensing their opportunity, escaped from the *sala*.

"How is the conversion going, *padre?*" she asked. "We have heard wonderful things about your success."

"I am most pleased," the friar said, clasping his long, bony fingers together, "but I am awaiting some communication from the Viceroy acknowledging it. However, so far none has arrived, and my patience is growing thin."

She saw the fire in the *padre*'s eyes and didn't know whether it was zeal or anger, but it was this very lack of news from the Viceroy that kept her hopes alive, and she did everything in her power as the weeks turned into months to convince the governor of the same.

"With each year that passes, our situation is more secure," she said to Oñate. "The King is not going to give up *Nuevo México*. Have you ever known a monarch of his own free will to give up *any* conquered land? Don't you think that the Viceroy would have recalled all of us, soldiers and settlers, long before now had that been his intention? The lack of news from Mexico City can only mean one thing—that this colony is to remain."

"I can only pray that you are right," Oñate said with a sigh, but his shoulders remained sagged. He looked at her, his eyes appraising.

"Why are you, *señora,* so desirous of staying in this godforsaken land? There is nothing here for you. Your husband is surely mad, and he is undoubtedly dead or else he would have returned by now. What makes you want to remain here?"

She felt prickles of fear crawl up her back, but she kept her voice even and looked levelly at him. "I have nothing in Mexico. All I have in the world is here. I have made a home in this land; my children were born here. I do not wish to leave my only home."

"I pray you will not have to, *señora,*" he said quietly, "but I fear you may have no other choice."

Unseen from the *sala,* Rohona stood in the hall, his face a mask.

That night he asked her, "And if the colony is ordered back to Mexico, what then?"

"I will not think about that," she said, "until it happens."

The snow came earlier than usual that winter and buried the little capital in a deep layer of white. Those who watched the weather predicted a hard winter, and when Fabia said their wheat and corn were diminishing at an alarming rate, María Angélica became truly worried, and Rohona began to spend more and more time away from the dwelling hunting game that was getting increasingly more difficult to find.

"I do not understand it," Fabia said one evening as they all sat near the fire trying to absorb its warmth. "Never have we used our wheat and corn so quickly. I know my old eyes do not see so well, but every time I enter the storeroom, it seems as if the grain has diminished."

"The children are growing rapidly and eating more all the time," María Angélica responded. "That surely must account for it."

Fabia frowned. "The poor little things don't eat that much. It must just be my eyes are getting old."

Rohona looked at the old woman. "Show me the storeroom," he said quietly.

Fabia put two tallow candles in tin *candelabros* and lit them. Rohona took one and followed the old woman to the storeroom. The door creaked open as she lifted the latch and pushed the rough planks open. A heady, musty smell of dried vegetables and grain filled Rohona's nostrils as he stepped into the room, lifting the *candelabro* high to spread its light into the shadowy corners. He went to the bin that held the wheat. A tiny mouse scampered into the corner and disappeared.

"Your eyes are not deceiving you," he said quietly. "I know how much wheat was put here at harvest. We could not have used as much as is gone from this bin." He lifted the *candelabro* again and turned to survey the rest of the room. "Did you and Mía not hang the dried squash from the *vigas* all the way to the corner?" he asked.

"We began in the corners," Fabia said as she held her *candelabro* and peered into a dark corner of the room.

"There is no squash there," she said with shock. "I know I have not used that squash. I use from the front and work my way to the back."

María Angélica, who had been standing in the doorway, hurried in and looked up at the empty *vigas* in the corners. "Someone is stealing our food! I hung squash in that corner myself."

"But how could that be?" Fabia asked. "Since it has gotten cold, there is always someone in the house, and the doors are bolted every night."

"Perhaps someone is lifting the bar from the outside," María Angélica offered, and they went to the front door to see if they could find any signs of tampering. Rohona looked carefully at the planking.

"No one is coming in this way," he said at length. "I want to look at the storeroom again," he added, and they all returned to the dark, musty room.

Rohona walked slowly around the room scrutinizing everything. He stopped at one spot several times and peered closely at the dirt-packed floor. He got down on his hands and knees and rubbed his fingers over the hard-packed dirt.

"Why is this spot damp?" he asked Fabia. "Has there been anything sitting here that would make it so?"

"Nothing," Fabia said, leaning over and rubbing her fingers on the spot. "Nothing."

Rohona rose and lifted the *candelabro* high as he looked up at the roof. Fabia's eyes followed his. "It's the old entrance. Someone is coming through the roof to steal our food," she said.

"But how do they get in and out without a ladder?" María Angélica asked.

"It could be done with a rope," Rohona said.

"But who would want to steal our grain?" she asked. "I have always been generous with our food. All the women know they can come here if they are in need. I'll admit I'm not as generous with food now that I have my own children, but I have never denied anyone who was truly hungry."

"Perhaps they do not steal from hunger," Rohona said, and Fabia nodded.

"Well, we should just seal the entrance," María Angélica said.

"I want to know who this person is," Rohona's voice had hardened. "One who steals will commit other crimes. We must discover who it is."

"Why?" María Angélica asked. "It could be dangerous."

"It is more dangerous not knowing who he is."

That night Rohona wrapped himself in a heavy buffalo robe and climbed to the uppermost roof where he could keep watch of the rooftop below and the old entranceway to the storeroom. He kept vigil throughout the long, cold night but no one appeared. For five nights he sat huddled in the heavy buffalo robe.

"Perhaps they have taken all they intend to," María Angélica offered. "Don't spend another night in the freezing cold. The clouds look like snow tonight."

"He will be back," Rohona said.

About midnight heavy white flakes began to fall and it was difficult to discern the roof below in the darkness. Suddenly Rohona was aware of movement, and he made out a strange form below that did not appear to have the shape of a man.

The form disappeared into the hole on the roof, and Rohona wondered briefly if it were a witch that was stealing their grain. Slowly and with great care so as not to slip on the new soft snow, he made his way down to the other rooftop and pressed himself against one of the walls, hoping the buffalo robe would blend into the mud-plastered wall and that the snowfall would blur the outlines. He did not have to wait long in that position. The hunchbacked form came up out of the hole in the roof by means of a rope, as Rohona had thought. Rohona knew immediately that it was not a witch.

Of course a man would need something in which to carry the grain he stole, Rohona thought as he clearly discerned the basket on the man's back.

The man put the cover back on the roof opening and with his hand spread the new-fallen snow around. He crossed the stairstep wall to the roof of the dwelling that joined that of Rohona and María Angélica. Rohona followed him across the rooftops until he came to the quarters of the muleteers and servants. The man descended through a roof entrance to one of the rooms.

*So that is where he lives,* Rohona said to himself. He turned to start back to his own dwelling thinking that on the morrow he would make certain which muleteer was the thief, but at that moment he heard a noise behind him and quickly moved back against a wall and stood motionless, holding his breath. The man emerged again onto the rooftop, basket on his back. Rohona followed him as he crossed the roofs again, but this time he stopped on the rooftop of a different dwelling, and Rohona watched as the scene he had witnessed on his own rooftop was repeated.

*We are not the only ones,* he thought.

After he had watched the scene repeated at four different dwellings, he returned home.

"I think that it is the Mexican *mestizo* Baltazar," he said to María Angélica, "the muleteer."

"But he has no family," she said. "Why would he steal food?"

"To sell it. Tomorrow I shall watch what he does."

"Don't you think we should tell Don Juan instead?" María Angélica asked, a crease of worry in her forehead.

"I wish to find out just what the *mestizo* is doing," Rohona said, "and besides, your governor rode to Picurís yesterday."

Early the next morning Rohona watched as the muleteer hitched his animals to a cart that was covered with a frieze tarp. A soldier came walking up. "Where are you going?" he asked the muleteer.

"Caypa," the *mestizo* said, "the Alcalde wants me to pick up some *mantas*."

"But why the tarp on an empty cart?" the soldier asked.

"To keep out the snow. The Alcalde doesn't want the cart to get wet inside. Might ruin the *mantas*, he said." The soldier nodded and walked away. The muleteer quickly finished hitching up his team and drove away hurriedly in the direction of Caypa.

There was a questioning look on María Angélica's face when Rohona entered.

"I looked into his room from the roof entrance," Rohona said. "It is stacked full of *mantas* and hides. He is stealing grain from everyone and selling it in the nearby pueblos for *mantas* and other goods."

"But what does he intend to do with them?"

"The governor sends carts south on occasion to trade for things in the mining outposts of northern Mexico, does he not? Perhaps the *mestizo* intends to join one of those cart trains. With the *mantas* he has stored in that room, he could buy many things."

"I wish the governor would return," she said.

Rohona walked around the village hoping to hear any conversation. He heard nothing, but he did see the Alcalde Ruíz. He hobbled over to him.

"*Perdón, Señor* Alcalde," he spoke, "do you know where the muleteer Baltazar is? Domingo wished to speak to him about some mules."

Rohona saw the man's pupils narrow, and he knew immediately the Alcalde was part of the plan also.

"Why, I sent him on an errand to Caypa," the Alcalde spoke, his voice unconcerned.

*"Gracias,"* Rohona mumbled in a servile tone. "I will tell Domingo."

Rohona started toward the stable knowing the Alcalde's eyes followed him. When he reached there he spoke to Domingo.

"Of course I will say I want to talk to the *mestizo* if anyone asks," the *caballerizo* said.

Rohona returned home, and María Angélica was waiting for him.

"The Alcalde is part of the plan, also," he said.

"I should have known the muleteer was not alone. He is not clever enough to have conceived this. I know the Alcalde is discontented. He was dismayed when he returned with the expedition and found so many had deserted—Don Juan told me so. That is why the governor made him Alcalde—to try to placate him because he was one of the ones who was most strongly urging him to abandon this colony, saying we must all return to Mexico in the face of the desertion. I would wager he has an account in Parral where he is keeping what he makes from selling the *mantas*. No doubt he thinks this conquest is doomed, and he wants to have something waiting for him when we all have to leave.

"You must take care," she said. "He is obviously dangerous and all the more so if he is desperate to leave this place. He may already be suspicious since you spoke to him."

That night Rohona wrapped himself again in a buffalo robe and went out onto the rooftop. The stars moved across the cold winter sky as he dozed, but then suddenly he was awake. He heard the faint but distinct creaking far in the distance. He rubbed his hands together to warm them as he waited. The creaking grew louder and he could hear the crunch of the frozen snow under the wheels. He made his way across the rooftops, but suddenly he stopped in his tracks and hunkered down. He was not the only man waiting in the cold darkness for the return of the muleteer.

Down below he saw a man emerge from the shadows and approach the cart as it pulled to a stop. The muleteer pulled back the tarp and the two men each grabbed a stack of *mantas* and quickly carried them into the muleteer's room.

*It is just as we thought,* Rohona said to himself as he recrossed the rooftops to his dwelling. He had not waited long enough to hear the words the Alcalde spoke to the muleteer.

"We can do nothing until the governor arrives," María Angélica said the next morning. "I would not know whom to trust, and we certainly do not want to give them time to hide the evidence. I wish I had paid more attention to how long Don Juan said he would be gone."

"I am going to go to the corral today," Rohona said, "and see if Domingo needs help. We have enough game for a while, and I do not wish to be too distant from the dwelling. That Alcalde is most certainly a dangerous man."

"I'm sure there is no need for concern," she said. "He cannot know we have discovered his secret."

Rohona stepped into the corral and started for the low barn where he heard Domingo whistling. He would never understand why the *españoles* liked to make that noise. His moccasins made the hard-crusted snow crunch under his feet. Then he heard a noise out of step with his own footsteps and knew immediately he was being stalked.

The person who followed him had never been taught to make his footsteps match that of his prey. Rohona whirled around pulling his knife from his belt, a steel-blade that, as a slave, he was not supposed to carry. Just as he whirled, the man following him lunged, his knife grazing Rohona's shoulder as Rohona's knife buried itself in the man's belly.

There was a look of shock on the muleteer's face as he pulled away, blood gushing out over his fingers as he held his wound. He took two steps backward, fell to his knees, wavered a moment, and pitched forward. Rohona took a step toward him.

"Drop the knife, you Indian bastard," a voice said.

Rohona saw the Alcalde standing some distance away, an arquebus leveled at him. Rohona dropped the knife.

The Alcalde shouted, "Come quickly! The Ácoma cripple has killed the muleteer Baltazar! The slave was carrying a Spanish knife! He killed the muleteer!"

Domingo rushed out of the barn as a few soldiers ran toward the corral. "What happened?" he asked Rohona.

"He jumped me," he said. "He lunged into my knife and . . ."

Domingo shouted to the Alcalde who still kept his distance. "The muleteer attacked the *indio*. It is not the Ácoma's fault."

"I saw the whole thing," the Alcalde shouted. "You were in the barn. The slave attacked the muleteer without provocation. He murdered him in cold blood."

Domingo glanced at Rohona's wound. "And what about the cut on the Ácoma's shoulder?"

"The muleteer did that in self-defense," the Alcalde answered.

By now a number of soldiers had gathered, and with them the Alcalde approached Rohona. He motioned with his gun. "We will have to put him in the jail until the governor returns, but we ought to shoot him now. That's what he deserves."

Rohona walked slowly to the cell that was used as the jail. The Alcalde prodded him into the one-room cubicle and slammed shut the double-planked door.

# Chapter 30

"No! Why have they put him in the *cárcel?*"

"They say he killed the muleteer in cold blood," Dorotea said.

"Oh, *Dios*," María Angélica said. "They know we know."

"Know what?"

"Rohona found out the muleteer Baltazar was stealing grain from everyone, little by little, entering through the roof entrances to the storerooms. He then would take the grain to the nearby pueblos and sell it for *mantas*. His room is stacked full of them, but as it turns out the Alcalde is in on it, too. We are sure he sends them to Parral to sell. I must get to Oñate. The governor must know what is happening. He is the only one who can save Rohona."

"But the governor is in Picurís," Dorotea said. "Let's just go tell everyone now what has happened. When they go to the muleteer's room, they will have the proof of it."

"No, don't you see?" María Angélica said. "We can't let on we know anything. The Alcalde will just deny any part in it. He will say the muleteer and Rohona were in it together and Rohona got greedy or something. And who are they going to believe—a slave or the Alcalde? Besides, Rohona will never live until the governor returns. The Alcalde will see to that."

Her voice under control, she asked, "Is your husband at home? I need his help."

Isidro Inojosa's black eyes appraised María Angélica. "You need my help?"

"Yes. They have put my slave in the *cárcel*. They say he killed the muleteer Baltazar in cold blood, but it was self-defense."

Inojosa's eyebrows lifted as if he found her hard to believe, but María Angélica did not waver as she continued, telling him what she and Rohona had discovered was happening.

"The Alcalde has put him in the *cárcel* until the governor returns, but you know as well as I do that the slave will not live to see the governor's return. He will be conveniently killed 'while trying to escape.' The Alcalde simply needs some time to find a place to put all his *mantas* before Don Juan gets back."

"And why do you need my help?"

"I need for you to ride immediately to Picurís and bring back the governor. If he returns before the Alcalde has had a chance to get rid of all his *mantas*, he can be caught. It is the only way to save the slave."

"You are that concerned about a slave?" Inojosa asked, his tone mocking.

"I am. That slave is the only reason my family does not starve to death. Without him we could not survive. You know as well as I do that my husband has been gone for over two years."

Inojosa's eyes were on her, appraising. She continued. "The governor told me that he is going to have to appoint a *guardián* for Vicente's—now my—*encomienda*. He feels certain Vicente is dead and since there are no male children of an age to take care of it and since I have not remarried, he must appoint someone else to look after it. Of course you know the *guardián* of an *encomienda* stands to profit from it. I like my life, Captain. I have a great deal of freedom, and I have grown to enjoy it. I have no desire to remarry—I do not wish to secure a husband just to have someone who can look after my *encomienda*. There is nothing I want or need from a man."

There was a smirk on Inojosa's face, but her voice remained business-like. "That Ácoma slave makes it possible for me to keep my freedom. If he dies I will be forced to remarry so my family will not starve to death.

"If you will ride to Picurís and bring back the governor before the Alcalde kills my slave, I will tell Don Juan that I want you to be named *guardián* of my *encomienda*."

Dorotea's eyes widened. Inojosa raised his eyebrow and stood still, then smiled and the scar on his face contorted it into an unpleasant grimace. María Angélica looked at him levelly, never dropping her eyes.

"It sounds like a reasonable bargain." He turned to Dorotea. "Go have my horse saddled."

María Angélica prepared to go. "Do not let the Alcalde see you leave, and, remember, the slave must not die."

Inojosa looked at her and nodded. "He won't."

As he headed toward the river where his servant had taken his horse, Dorotea walked with María Angélica back to her house.

Fabia put her wrinkled old arms around her. "Do not worry, Angelita, everything will be all right."

"Oh, Fabia, the Alcalde will kill him before the governor ever gets back."

"No he won't," Fabia said. "If he tries, he will try at night when no one is around, but I have spoken to Domingo and Cipriano. They are going to watch the *cárcel* all night, and if they see anyone approach, they are going to come out into the open and make a great deal of noise. It will be very difficult for the Alcalde to kill the *indio* and make it look like he was trying to escape."

María Angélica pushed her hair out of her face. "I will gather some food and blankets together, and this evening you must take them to the *cárcel*. Rohona will freeze in that unheated cell without something to cover him. Surely the guard will allow you to give him the things."

"I will make certain that I am not refused," Fabia said.

Through the interminable night María Angélica prayed, afraid to sleep, her nerves on edge.

When the dawn finally came sending its cold gray fingers over the eastern mountains, she went to Fabia's room. She touched the old woman on the shoulder, and Fabia was instantly awake. "Please," María Angélica said, "I can stand it no longer. Find out if Rohona is still alive."

Fabia dressed quickly, threw a heavy *rebozo* around herself, and scurried out the door.

María Angélica knelt and tried to pray but could not. When she heard the door open, she almost fainted from the tension.

"All is well, Angelita," Fabia spoke, "the *indio* still lives."

*"Alabado sea Dios,"* she whispered. "When, oh, when is the governor going to get here?"

"It is quite a ways to Picurís," Fabia said. "You will be lucky if Captain Inojosa got there by nightfall, and they probably won't start back in the dark."

"I don't know if I can make it through another night," María Angélica said, her forehead creased with worry. "What if the Alcalde has managed to get all the *mantas* out of the muleteer's room?"

"From what the *indio* told us, the room is stacked full with them. The Alcalde has to find somewhere else safe to put them. My guess is that it will take him several nights to move them all."

That day the slightest sound from outside brought María Angélica running to the door to see if the governor had returned, but each time she peered out, her hopes were dashed, and she would go back to waiting. Night fell and her face was white and pinched with worry.

"Let me make you something to let you sleep," Fabia said gently. "There is nothing more you can do to save the *indio* tonight."

"I won't sleep, Fabia," she said, "I can't."

* * *

At dawn Rohona walked into the *sala*. The governor and Inojosa were behind him. Fabia grabbed María Angélica to keep her from running to the Indian and throwing her arms around him.

"We caught that damned Alcalde red-handed," Oñate said as he walked over to her and took her hand. "Thank you, *señora*, for sending Captain Inojosa to me. We arrived shortly before dawn and slipped quietly into the village. We lay in wait near the muleteer's room and sure enough that son-of-a-bitch Ruíz came out carrying an armload of *mantas*. That bastard! And to do this after I had made him Alcalde! This conquest would have been a success had it not been for so many greedy, cowardly, and treacherous whores' sons among those who accompanied me."

"Governor," María Angélica said, "I cannot begin to tell you how grateful I am that you returned with such haste."

"And I, in turn, am grateful to your slave, *señora*. If it had not been for him discovering Ruíz's treachery, we might all have starved this winter."

"And you, Captain," she said to Inojosa, "you also have my gratitude, and you can be sure that I will not forget it."

"But of course," he said, his eyes glittery, his facial scar contorting his smile.

When Oñate and Isidro Inojosa had gone, María Angélica finally threw her arms around Rohona.

Everyone gathered in the plaza, and Oñate held a swift trial.

"I leave the verdict in the hands of the people," he shouted. "Let them choose the punishment that they see fit!"

A deafening roar rose in the plaza. "Guilty! *¡La muerte!* He deserves to die!"

The governor raised his hands and the noise quieted. "The people have spoken," he shouted, and he turned to the Alcalde Ruíz. "Do you have anything you wish to say before you receive your just reward?"

The Alcalde, unrepentant, looked at Oñate, a sneer on his face, and then he looked out at the people. "You are fools!" he shouted with contempt, "fools to stay in this good-for-nothing land and allow this braying mule of a governor to starve your families to death!"

Oñate slapped Ruíz viciously across the face. "You dare to accuse me of starving the people after what *you* have done?!" he shouted with rage. "Prepare the *garrote!*"

The iron collar was soon attached to an upright beam, and the Alcalde fought desperately against the three soldiers who led him to it. The soldiers held him securely while the iron was fastened around his neck. When the soldiers let go of him, he had to strain to stand on his tiptoes to keep the iron collar from strangling him.

A priest came forward. "Do you wish to confess your sins so that God may grant you mercy in the hereafter?"

The Alcalde looked at the blue-robed friar with venom, his eyes already beginning to bulge. "I will see you all in Hell!" he rasped.

"May God have mercy on your soul," the friar said, making the sign of the cross.

As the priest stepped down, the first stone was thrown. A hail followed, and Ruíz was quickly covered with blood. No longer able to stay on his toes, his body sank, and its weight strangled him on the iron collar. His eyes bulged grotesquely, and he was dead long before the last stone was thrown.

María Angélica thought she would be sick and hurried away from the gruesome sight. In the following few days she did not venture out of her house. She could not bear to pass the square and see the dead body still hanging there, the crows feasting on it. Oñate called it a salutary example; it only filled her with revulsion.

As winter wore on and the colonists felt hunger gnawing at them, they continued to curse the Alcalde. Oñate sent carts to the nearby pueblos, forcing them to give back much of the grain the Alcalde had sold to them, but he did not return the *mantas* and hides with which they had paid for the grain.

"They bought stolen goods," the governor said as his justification for keeping everything. He gave each household two *mantas*. "The rest I will send in carts to Parral to buy us necessities."

Planting time came, and still no communication had come from Mexico City. "Didn't I tell you?" María Angélica said to Oñate with a smile. "The longer we are here the more unlikely it is that the Viceroy is planning to abandon this conquest."

"I think you may be right, dear *señora*," Don Juan said with unusual enthusiasm. "I have decided to double the *fanegas* of corn we plant. We planted more wheat last fall, and our herds have increased—the roundup was good this year. Perhaps if we could make this colony truly self-sufficient—if we could raise more livestock and grain than we need—we could have an export that would bring us revenue. I could hire more soldiers to come here so that I would have the manpower to make truly important discoveries."

When the crops began to sprout in the late spring and showed their bright green stalks as summer approached, María Angélica was happier than she had been for years. Seven-year-old Alejandro and Alegría, now five, were growing rapidly and showed no signs of deprivation. Optimism took the place of constant worry, and even Rohona's words about the lack of rain could not dampen her spirits.

When he told her later the heads of wheat and the ears of corn held no grains because of the drought, she was forced to face reality.

"Please, *Dios*, don't do this to us," she begged, but the days grew hotter, scorching the land, and the rain did not come, and it became obvious the *fanegas* of grain the governor had planted would not even produce as much as they had harvested the previous year.

It was early for a visitor, but María Angélica opened the door to the quiet knock. When she saw the look on Oñate's face, she asked with concern, "Is something wrong, Governor?"

"Please," he said, "may I come in?"

"Of course." She opened the door wider and stepped aside. She tried to make her voice light. "And to what do I owe this early call?"

Oñate sat down heavily in the chair she offered him, and she sat opposite him, making an attempt to smile in spite of the bleakness she saw in his face.

"I wanted to be the one to tell you."

"Tell me what?"

"I am resigning as governor. I am going back to Mexico."

"No," she gasped, "you cannot."

"I must," he said. "There is nothing left to do."

She slid off her chair and knelt in front of him, grasping his hands in hers. "You cannot, Governor. You cannot!" There was desperation in her voice.

Oñate reached out and grasped her by the shoulders and pulled her to him. "Oh, my angel. Oh, my angel," he whispered as he covered her face with desperate kisses, "come with me to Zacatecas."

She pushed against his chest, trying to free herself from his embrace. "No, Governor, stop," she said, but Don Juan did not let her go.

"Vicente is dead. You know it. He has been gone for how many years now? Come with me to Zacatecas. You are so beautiful, *Dios*, how I have hungered for you all these years."

His voice broke suddenly. "How I wanted this conquest to be a success, how I wanted to be the founder of a new land." His shoulders began to shake, his arms fell away from her, and he began to sob.

"I have spent over four hundred thousand *pesos* of my own money, I am deeply in debt, I cannot go on. God damn the Viceroy. God damn this land."

María Angélica put her arms around him and smoothed his hair as if he were a child. "Do not give up, Don Juan," she whispered to him.

"The conquest is not a failure. We have been here for almost a decade. We have established a capital. The Viceroy cannot let this colony die, he can't, not after so many years. You must not give up, Don Juan, you must not, even in spite of the harvest."

"It is too late," Oñate said with defeat.

"No," she said, grasping him by the shoulders and looking him in the face. "No!"

"Yes, dearest lady," he answered with resignation, "it is too late. Fray Lázaro and Fray Ordóñez left at dawn this morning. They carry the paper with them. Montesclaros will have it before the new year is here."

She stood up, her face ashen. "No."

Oñate nodded his head sadly, and she sank down onto her chair. She looked at the once-vigorous, gray-haired leader who had brought the group of expectant soldiers and colonists north through terrible lands. Across from her sat an old man.

"Fray Lázaro has another letter, also," Oñate said, his voice hollow with defeat. "If the Viceroy does not appoint a new governor by June 30th of next year this entire colony will be abandoned. We will all pull up stakes and return to Mexico."

On August 24, 1607, the governor of *Nuevo México,* the *Adelantado* Don Juan de Oñate, resigned his position.

## Part Five

# LA VILLA

## Village, August 1610

# Chapter 31

Days on end of feverish work confronted them. Carts were loaded with all their worldly goods. Precious items brought north twelve long years ago from Mexico across arduously won country were packed with care so that they might survive the upcoming journey south. The raucous brays of mules mingled with the deep bellows of the oxen teams as the animals were yoked and hitched to the ungraceful, lumbering carts. The Indians of Yungue-Yungue and San Juan watched silently as the Spaniards prepared to leave their capital of San Gabriel.

No emotion showed on the natives' faces but relief might well have been one they felt—relief to see the strangers leaving their village at long last.

They finally finished packing their carts. As María Angélica leaned against the cool adobe wall of the dwelling she had called home for over a decade, tears rolled down her cheeks. It seemed she had lived there forever. It was the only home she knew. She suddenly wondered if Vicente were still alive. What would he do if he returned to their deserted village? She had not thought about him for years.

Shortly after he returned with the expedition that had discovered the South Sea, he went off again with his page to search for gold. After the third year and the next and the next had come and gone, everyone forgot about him and assumed him dead.

He did not know that Oñate had resigned three years ago and was in Mexico along with the Sergeant Major, Villagrá, Márquez, and others facing disgrace and very serious charges. He would be furious to know that the King had finally decided to retain *Nuevo México*—but only as a missionary province. No new *entradas*, no new expeditions, save those of friars going to convert natives, would be allowed.

He did not know that a new governor, Don Pedro Peralta, had been appointed and that there would be no more *adelantados*. The governors were now appointed by the Viceroy to four-year terms at a salary of two thousand *pesos*.

Vicente did not know that they were all moving, abandoning their capital of San Gabriel, moving over eight leagues to the south to a new capital city named *La Villa de Nuestra Señora de la Santa Fé*, located on a creek of the same name some leagues up from the *Río del Norte*.

Over a thousand Indian laborers in many shifts had toiled on the new capital city so that by the time they were ready to move, there was a central plaza about which government buildings and dwellings were constructed. On the north side of the square stood the long Palace of the Governor. Scarcely a palace by any standard anywhere in the world with its one-story mud brick walls but certainly palatial by any standards in *Nuevo México*, the building would house not only the governor in his private quarters, but also government offices.

The colonists were given two lots for house and garden, two contiguous fields for vegetable gardens, two others for vineyards and olive groves, and in addition four *caballerías* of land as well as irrigation rights. The Tlascalan Indians who had made up the infantry under Oñate and who worked as servants for the Spaniards built their quarters to the south of the governor's Palace across the creek in what was being called the Barrio de Analco.

Rohona was gone for days from San Gabriel helping with and overseeing the building of María Angélica's house and that of Dorotea, which stood next to it.

María Angélica was considered a widow by everyone, and Oñate, upon leaving for Mexico, had begged her again to go with him back to Zacatecas. Once, she had feared him, and Dorotea had even told her that Vicente was going to give her to Don Juan in return for favors the governor might do him, but now she just pitied the gray-haired *adelantado*. He was a broken, old man. There was left in him none of the vigorous leader that had brought them north.

"Accept the fact that you are a widow, that Vicente is dead," Oñate had said to her, but she chose to act as if she fully believed her husband would return. It was a convenient excuse to keep her life as she wanted it. It kept the suitors at bay and gave her a reason to stay in *Nuevo México*.

Isidro Inojosa had been named *guardián* of Vicente's *encomienda* as she had requested of Oñate. She despised the man but felt a debt toward him for having brought the governor back to San Gabriel when Rohona was accused of murder.

It worked to her advantage that Isidro Inojosa was zealous of her *encomienda*. He made her life easier to an extent that he did not fully realize.

If she were to marry, her husband would become the *guardián* of the *encomienda*, and Isidro Inojosa would lose a tidy sum of revenue, so it was to his advantage that she not take a husband. He did not know how big a favor he was doing her when he threatened those who looked eagerly at the young, beautiful widow and warned them to stay away.

María Angélica was glad Isidro Inojosa had seen to it that their houses were next to each other, and she was very pleased to have her best friend near. She was also glad for the proximity because Isidro was gone frequently, and if Dorotea and Siya ever needed anything, she or Rohona could help them in turn.

The nomadic, hostile Indians known as Querechos or Apaches had begun to menace the more distant pueblo villages to steal their corn. The Spaniards might not have cared whether a few natives were killed, but they saw the corn the natives raised as partly theirs, and that they would protect. As a result, it became a frequent occurrence for a detail of well-armed soldiers to go out on punitive expeditions against the raiding Apaches.

It was quickly learned that there was a remunerative value in the raids also. The laws of the Indies did not allow Spaniards to make slaves of the pueblo Indians unless as sentence for some grave offense. Nomadic Indians, however, were fair game and those taken prisoner on punitive expeditions had a good market value.

The mines in northern Mexico were always in need of slaves and the soldiers in *Nuevo México* were quick to realize the worth of an export in a region that produced so little of anything that could be sold or traded for things from the outside world.

Isidro Inojosa was almost always a member of any punitive detail sent out. Indeed, many of the expeditions were scarcely veiled as to their purpose and were being called by some by their real name—slave raids. Almost always the prisoners they took were children old enough to work but too young to be able to fight back or to run away.

At the moment, there were three such slaves in the Inojosa household. Two were young girls about ten or twelve years old. Dorotea had confided to María Angélica that in spite of their tender age, Isidro used them as he had used Siya when she was younger. He no longer bothered Siya or her, scorning them as being too old and barren.

"What he wants is a son," Dorotea said. "You cannot imagine how desperately he wants an heir. Knowing Isidro, you would never think he cared, but he does, and he uses the young Apache girls that come through our house. The older one of these two is stoic, and I do not hear her cries, but the younger one is still just a babe. I have to cover my ears to shut out the cries of pain and terror I hear at night. If after a couple of months the girls haven't become pregnant, Isidro will take them south and sell them like he has done with all the others."

* * *

María Angélica pushed herself away from the adobe wall and pushed the thoughts of Isidro Inojosa from her mind. She walked to the cart that was ready to pull out, and she glanced back at the dwelling where she had lived the previous ten years. She could not believe it had been so long and yet so short at the same time. It seemed only yesterday and yet an eternity ago that they had come to that far, north country. She had grown to love the land, and it did seem like home. She could scarcely remember the large *hacienda* in Mexico where she had grown up and had been married. It seemed lifetimes ago.

She turned her eyes away from the adobe building and looked south. What kind of life was in store for them in the new *villa?* Up ahead of the carts she saw her son and daughter mounted on horses.

No one had ever said anything about Domingo teaching the half-breed boy to ride. He was a handsome, well-mannered boy and spoke fluent Castilian; no one questioned his right to ride a horse. Pride filled her eyes as she watched her ten-year-old son sitting tall, straight-backed, and perfectly at ease on the bay horse. His hair was dark but had a very slight wave that showed his mixed ancestry, as did the bronze color of his skin, which was several shades lighter than that of the other natives of the village. His dark eyes, too, gave evidence of his Spanish parentage for although they appeared dark, near the pupil was a ring of gray. He was a handsome boy and many remarked upon it.

Sitting on a spotted mare next to him was her daughter. She could not love her daughter with the fierceness she loved Alejandro, but everyone seemed to delight in the laughing eight-year-old Alegría whose name, all remarked, had been so well chosen. But now and then María Angélica saw fleeting emotions cross Alegría's face that reminded her of Vicente, and she would shudder at the sight. She looked back at Alegría. Her bright red curls were flying, as always, in careless abandon. Try as she or Fabia might, they could never control the flame-colored hair that was just as unrestrained as its possessor was.

María Angélica could not hear her, but she could see that Alegría was chattering away to Alejandro, filled with excitement, delighted at the thought of the journey on which she would be allowed to ride as if she might have been a grown-up. She adored horses and was becoming almost as good a rider as her brother, who was a fine one, according to Domingo. She pestered the old horse trainer constantly, and he usually indulged her in her wish to ride. The old man predicted she would be a fine horseman just like her grandfather, María Angélica's father, had been. Alegría was an oddly beautiful little girl, rather tall for her age and skinny, but she had her mother's large grey eyes fringed with black lashes, and she had that amazing, unruly red hair that drew the comments of all.

She and Alejandro were constant companions when he was not helping Rohona in the fields or hunting game. They loved to ride and explore, and Alejandro, after much begging on her part, had even taught her how to use the bow and arrows Rohona had made for him. They were best of friends, and Alegría spoke Queres just as well as Alejandro did. In fact, they used it frequently if they did not want María Angélica to know what they were planning. Both children called her *mamá* or *mamacita,* for she had insisted upon it despite the fact that many of the Spaniards had been disapproving of the half-breed bastard boy calling a Spanish lady Mamá.

Although Alejandro called her Mamá, he believed the story that everyone else believed: that he was the son of an Indian woman and a Spanish soldier and that María Angélica had taken him in when her own child died. He loved her as a mother, and he loved Rohona as a father although he had begun to call him Uncle, and Alegría had copied him. Had Alejandro known that they truly were his mother and father, he might not have had the sadness around his eyes that sometimes showed through. But usually Alegría was there and took the sadness away.

When she was born, Alejandro could not pronounce the four syllables of her name and shortened it to Aley. The same either happened when she began talking, or else she copied him, shortening his name to the first two syllables also, making their names identical—Aley and Aley. They liked having the same name.

The trip south was difficult, but María Angélica did not mind; she was looking forward to her new home. She was glad the indecision of the last few years of Oñate's rule was finally over. They at least now knew their status and would not be constantly concerned about the fate of the colony.

The King had taken *Nuevo México* under his patronage and it would be supported by the royal treasury as a missionary province. She was happy that the purpose of the colony now was solely for the conversion of the natives. Perhaps they would no longer be exploited as they had been in the past.

Alejandro and Alegría thought of the journey to their new home as a wonderful adventure. Because of the requirements of travel, adult supervision was at a minimum, and the two children felt a tremendous sense of freedom. They did not want to ride with the slow-moving *carretas,* so they would urge their horses forward and gallop on ahead and lie in wait for the carts, ambushing them like the Apache de Navajo, swooping down on the lumbering vehicles with wild yells, brandishing bows Rohona had made. Then Alegría would ride her horse close and would leap off and into the *carreta* in which Fabia rode.

Fabia laughed and crossed herself and said with mock fear, "Save me, *Dios,* from this red devil."

Alegría laughed with delight and threw her arms around her old nursemaid's neck and kissed her weathered cheek.

In spite of the children's excitement, the trip was not an adventure for Fabia, however. She was getting older and was unable to walk the great distance over the rough terrain and found herself consigned to ride in one of the jostling carts.

"At times I think these old bones will never make it to the new *villa,*" she said to María Angélica who rode beside the cart while the children were off on another adventure. "In spite of this mattress, I feel as if I am being beaten and bruised to death."

María Angélica called to the muleteer. "Stop the cart, please."

"No, no," the old woman said, "that's not necessary. This wretched *carreta* is not going to conquer me. Old Fabia is not yet ready to die. I want a chance to live in a new house."

María Angélica tried to smile. She did not like to think of Fabia as growing old.

It took them over a week to go the eight or so leagues to the new village, and once there, no one had time to relax from the journey, for the carts had to be unpacked and the new homes put in order. María Angélica loved her new adobe house. It was built around a courtyard, and she was anxious to plant flowers in the small patio.

Sleeping arrangements would be the same in the new *villa* as they had been in San Gabriel. Fabia and Alegría shared a room, Alejandro had his small bed in Rohona's room, and she had a bedroom to herself that was shared at night by Rohona who left his room after Alejandro was asleep. Rohona always rose early, returned to his room, changed clothes, and went out to work.

She still marveled that no one save Fabia, Dorotea, and Siya knew of her relationship with the Indian. In such a small community in which everyone knew what everyone else did, it was a miracle no one had realized the secret in the Vizcarra household.

Now that the King supported *Nuevo México* as a missionary province, it appeared that the conversion of the natives to the Spaniards' religion would proceed much more quickly. There were new priests who had come with the new governor, Don Pedro Peralta, and they were busy at the different pueblos evangelizing.

Santo Domingo had been made the ecclesiastical capital when the seat of civil government was moved to Santa Fé, and Father Alonso Peinado, a kind and saintly man, was made prelate. Some credit had to be given the piercing-eyed Fray Isidro Ordóñez, for it had been his dispatches carried to the Viceroy that helped bring about the decision not to abandon *Nuevo México*.

There were few, however, who liked the zealous *padre* and many in whom he inspired varying degrees of fear. He had returned with the cart train and the new governor, and upon reaching *Nuevo México* he was constantly urging greater authority for the Church since it was the sole reason for the Spaniards remaining in that land. He was an abrasive man, and it was clear that enmity existed between Governor Peralta and the priest from the very beginning. There were some who said the friar had wanted to be named prelate instead of Padre Peinado.

Agitating for more priests to bring about the conversion of *Nuevo México,* Ordóñez, with the blessing of both the Father Commissary, Peinado, and Governor Peralta who were equally glad to see him go, was to return to Mexico the following year to seek further commitments from the Viceroy and the Franciscan Order.

Before he had finally gotten permission to return to Mexico, Fray Ordóñez traveled incessantly between the new ecclesiastical capital of Santo Domingo where the prelate had his headquarters and the *villa de Santa Fé* where the governor held his power. It was a long, hard ride up the *bajada* to the *villa,* but Ordóñez seemed intent on pressuring both the governor and the prelate until they granted his request.

He had another request he was pressing for in the new capital city, and it took him on most of his trips to María Angélica's house. The first mention had been almost in passing, and she had thought nothing of it, but then he mentioned it again the next time, and she saw from the look in his eyes that he was very serious.

"Perhaps the boy could travel to Mexico City with me."

The words were smooth, but they sent a shiver of alarm through her, which she tried to hide. Ordóñez's eyes told her he saw it, but he continued smoothly.

"Your ward, Alejandro, is a very bright boy. There is a keen intelligence in those big dark eyes of his. How old is he now? Ten?" She nodded.

"I could well use an intelligent young man to help me in my work. There are so many duties required of a missionary. But, *señora,* there are very few children I would accept as my acolyte—they could not meet my high standards for intelligence and correctitude. Your ward, however, shows such extraordinary promise." Ordóñez saw the pride in her face and he smiled warmly.

"You have every right to be proud of him, *señora.* You have done a wonderful job in raising such a fine child. The former governor spoke on many occasions of the Christian charity you possess, and I must say that he did not exaggerate. It is an example for all of us—myself included."

His words purred, warm and rich. He glimpsed the look on her face he had been awaiting and knew flattery was a powerful trap. He paused significantly.

"It is because I have learned from you that I make an exception to my rule. I would be proud to accept your ward as my personal acolyte."

He sat back as if awaiting her response of gratitude and thanks for having granted a request *she* might have made.

She felt suddenly flustered and did not know how to respond. Fear rippled through her. The priest wanted to take Alejandro? She suddenly had the sensation of being dragged away on some current over which she had no control.

"There, there," *Padre* Ordóñez said calmly as if he understood her feelings. "You are an intelligent woman," he said matter-of-factly, and his tone allowed her to regain her composure. "Let's consider your ward from an entirely objective point of view. It is obvious that you care for him deeply and love him like a son. That is perfectly understandable. Having raised him from the time he was just a babe in arms, it is right that you should love him thus."

He looked at her levelly. "It is this very love that causes your present turmoil. Because your love is a mother's love, you also have a mother's fear. If he were injured or if he died—God forbid it—your grief would seem insurmountable. You would feel that you could truly not endure it. Am I not right?"

She swallowed and looked at him. "Yes, *Padre*," she said, "I could not endure it."

"But by the same token," Ordóñez continued, "you would wish for him to have the greatest opportunity, the best of chances in this life, would you not?" She nodded, understanding fully the skill of the *padre*'s words as he continued.

"Life is never certain. God guarantees to no one a specified length of time on earth. We may both die tomorrow or we may live to a ripe old age. The same is true of your ward. May God grant him many years, but who is to say whether *la viruela* will strike him down in youth, or if a desert rattler may strike him unsuspecting? We know not. We can only trust in God's wisdom and exercise loving care."

The friar paused and María Angélica looked at him. "Go on, *Padre*," she said quietly.

Ordóñez smiled. "I did not underestimate your intelligence, *señora*, did I?" He made a tent with his bony fingers and rested his chin on it as his eyes appraised her. "You know where I am leading."

It was not a question, but she answered anyway. "I think so."

"Good," he said with satisfaction. "I am glad you understand because it means that you will understand my point. Have you taught your son to read?"

The question caught her by surprise, and she answered with some embarrassment. "No, not yet."

"But you do read, do you not?" he asked, and she nodded. He motioned to the books in the bookcases in the *sala*. "I assumed you did, and yet your ward, whom you consider as a son, is already ten years old and is illiterate."

Her cheeks colored as she said quietly, "Life here, unfortunately, does not lend itself to intellectual pursuits."

"You are quite right," Ordóñez replied, "but I am speaking only of literacy, not intellectual pursuits. Do you wish your ward to grow to manhood and be able only to mark an X on some document he cannot even read—a document whose contents he must rely on others to tell him?"

"Of course not," she said. "I must begin tomorrow to teach him."

*"Señora,"* Ordóñez said, "what I am offering you is an education for your ward—not just the ability to read. If he were to become my acolyte I would begin his education at once, and when he is grown he will be able to take an important position in the governing of this province. The Lord knows the civil government here needs competent men."

"I can only agree with you on that, *Padre*," she said.

"And so?"

María Angélica looked at him and tried to keep her eyes level, but it was difficult to do so.

"Because my husband has been gone for so long now, I am afraid he is dead, but I still pray for his return. If he does not, however, then I must count on Alejandro. He already is of tremendous help to me. He assists Domingo with the horses, he helps with the planting, and my Indian has taught him how to hunt. I am afraid I cannot do without his help."

"I'm so sorry, *señora*," Ordóñez said, his voice suddenly chilled. "I misread the situation. I thought you loved the boy like a son. I did not realize you saw him as only a servant to work for you."

María Angélica could not smother her gasp. "That is not so," she managed to say. "I truly love him like my son."

"Then why don't you do right by him?" the priest asked bluntly. "Allow him to go to Mexico with me. I can begin his education immediately. Allow him to see part of the rest of the world. Why do you want to keep him shackled in this isolated province? If he is going to take an important part in the governing of this land, he must know more about the rest of the world. One day this province will take its rightful place as part of New Spain, and when it does, your ward should be there guiding it."

He saw her thoughts on her face and smiled. He was right. She did have ambitions for the boy.

"You know how I feel toward your ward. I, too, have begun to love him like a son. You can rest assured that I will do absolutely everything in my power to watch over his safety, and I do have the Church behind me as added protection."

He reached across the space separating them and took her hand. "He will be back within a year. I do not intend to tarry in Mexico City—I shall have my supplies and reinforcements quickly. Before you know it, he will be back with you. He will know how to read and . . ." He paused and played his trump card. "He will have met the Viceroy—the Viceroy, *señora,* and he will have seen the great civilization of the City of Mexico, and it will be his desire to see such a civilization flourishing here."

The priest smiled again at her, his eyes bright, and he was certain of his success.

# Chapter 32

She saw the look of triumph in his eyes. He was much too clever, and she was aware of how he had manipulated her emotions. Still, he could give the boy advantages she could never hope to give. What an opportunity for Alejandro—to see Mexico City, to meet the Viceroy—those were things that she had never even imagined for him. He might well be the governor of the province someday—her Alejandro.

What would Fabia say? And Rohona? She would have to weather their disapproval as best she could, but she must think of Alejandro.

She looked back at Fray Ordóñez. She would not let him have the satisfaction of having persuaded her so quickly.

"Thank you, *Padre*," she said. "Your offer to see to my ward's education is very generous, indeed. However, it is a very difficult decision I must make. I must think very carefully about this."

Fray Ordóñez smiled, his eyes hooded.

"I shall ask God's guidance in this matter and I will let you know when I have made my decision." She rose.

Ordóñez came to his feet and his voice had a brittle edge to it. "You must decide quickly, I'm afraid, *señora*. I leave for Mexico City soon."

"If I have been unable to make a decision by that time it will undoubtedly mean it is God's will that he not go." She saw a flash of anger in the priest's eyes as he turned to leave.

"Angelita! You have lost your mind!" Fabia said, horrified. "How can you even think of sending our poor little thing with that scheming *padre?*"

"Dear Fabia," María Angélica said, taking her hand, "I know that Fray Ordóñez is a clever and scheming man, and I know also that Alejandro is not a poor little thing. He is ten; he is growing up. What Fray Ordóñez is offering him is an opportunity that will not come again. He recognizes Alejandro's intelligence—he can give the boy a far better education than I ever could. Someday my son will be an important man."

"I don't trust that *padre*," Fabia said. "Don't entrust your little son to him, even if he can make him viceroy!"

María Angélica laughed. "Fray Ordóñez is a zealous priest and probably a little ruthless when it comes to the Church's interests, but he will be looking out for Alejandro's interests, so he will undoubtedly guard those as well as he does the Church's."

"Don't do this, Angelita," Fabia said, her face somber. "Don't do this."

"I'm afraid my mind is made up," she said gently.

"What about the *indio?* Doesn't he have a say in this, too?"

"Rohona is not a Spaniard. He cannot be expected to understand the need for education and the opportunity this presents."

Fabia started to protest but knew she had lost.

"If you think it is best, Mía, then send him," Rohona finally answered, because he, too, knew his words had not been able to persuade the boy's mother. He did not want to see the boy sent away, but he knew also that his son was a Spaniard and would live his life as a pale one, just as the mother argued.

Alejandro stood in front of her, his eyes wide and filled with tears. "I do not want to go, Mamá," he whispered, "I do not want to go."

María Angélica hugged him to her. "Oh, *hijo*," she said as she stroked his hair, "I know you don't want to leave us. I know you are a little afraid, but this is a wonderful opportunity—think of it as a grand adventure. Remember how you said when you grew up you wanted to go on a great adventure? How many young boys get to travel all the way to New Spain, see the beautiful city of Mexico, and meet the Viceroy? You are a lucky boy that *Padre* Ordóñez will take you, and he is going to teach you to read, too. That is a wonderful thing. You have seen me read my *libros*—now you will be able to read them, too."

"I don't want to go," he whispered again. "I don't want to learn how to read. I want to ride and to hunt like Uncle."

Rohona had stood by silently while María Angélica told Alejandro of her plans for him, but then Rohona spoke, hoping to make the decision easier for his son to accept.

"Alejandro," he said, putting his hand on the boy's shoulder, "I wish very much that I could read. There are many things in the leaves with marks—there is much that can be learned there."

María Angélica looked up at Rohona with surprise. "You never told me that you would like to know how to read."

Rohona smiled at her. "I have seen you look at the leaves with marks—sometimes they make you laugh, sometimes they make you cry. I am very curious about these leaves that talk to you."

"Then I will teach you how to read them."

"Teach me, too, Mamá. Don't make me go with the *padre*," Alejandro said poignantly.

María Angélica took his face in her hands. "*Hijo, Padre* Ordóñez can teach you much more than I. The decision has already been made. The *padre* is coming up from Santo Domingo within a few weeks to fetch you." Tears rolled down Alejandro's cheeks, and María Angélica hugged him as he cried softly.

Fray Ordóñez stepped into the *sala*. There was a look of satisfaction on his face and his black eyes glittered like coals.

"You are early, *padre*," María Angélica said. "I did not expect you so soon."

The priest clasped his hands together. "I am anxious to be on my way to Mexico. Is the boy ready?"

She nodded and called Alejandro's name. He came running, but when he saw the priest, he stopped and walked slowly to his mother's side.

"*Padre* Ordóñez has come for you," she said brightly, but Alejandro's face was somber.

The priest walked over to Alejandro and placed his bony hand on the boy's shoulder. "You and I are going to be good friends, Alejandro," he said. "Our journey to Mexico City will be an exciting one, you will see."

María Angélica wondered why there was such an intensity in the priest's eyes and why his hands appeared so nervous.

"Rest assured you have made the right decision, *señora*. I am grateful to you."

"It is I who am grateful for this opportunity you have given my ward," she said. A curious look crossed Fray Ordóñez's face but he only smiled his tight smile.

As Alejandro walked to his horse to mount, Alegría pulled her hand out of Fabia's and ran to her brother. "No!" she shrieked. "No!" She grabbed his hand and clung wildly to him.

She had been distraught for days after she heard that Alejandro was going with Fray Ordóñez. "I hate that *padre!*" she had shrieked. "He can't take Aley! Who will I play with?" Nothing María Angélica said could console her daughter, and the little girl was so overwrought that Fabia had finally made an herb tea to calm her down.

Alegría seemed oddly remote that morning as Alejandro had prepared to leave, and when he went to hug her good-bye, she would not hug him back nor speak to him. María Angélica saw the hurt in his eyes as he turned to go, and Alegría stood, dry-eyed, with her hand in Fabia's as if she did not care that her constant companion was leaving—until he started to mount his horse.

She ran to him and threw her arms around him in a vise-like grip and shrieked wildly as if she had lost her senses. María Angélica ran to her, but Fray Ordóñez reached the girl first.

"Let go, child," he said as he grasped her arms and tried to pull her away. She kicked blindly at him, landing a solid blow on his shin.

María Angélica stood aghast. The priest blanched but did not let go of the girl, and with his back to María Angélica, he roughly pried the little girl's fingers away from Alejandro.

"You vicious little bitch," he hissed under his breath as he slapped her sharply across the face. The blow made Alegría go limp, and she sobbed pitifully. Fabia reached her and gathered her into her arms.

*"Pobrecita,"* Fabia cooed to her, "come with old Fabia."

As the old woman stood up, she threw a withering look at the priest, but he only stared back at her with a kind of grim satisfaction.

He turned to María Angélica who stood motionless. "The girl was hysterical. She would only have upset the boy with such behavior."

He did not wait for a response. "We must delay no longer," he said coldly. "Let us go, my son."

Alejandro hesitated just a moment and glanced pleadingly at María Angélica. Ordóñez stepped between them. "Mount your horse," he said, his voice steely.

The boy turned quickly to mount before he could see his mother take a step toward him. The priest saw it, though, from the corner of his eye and turned to face her.

"He is in my care now, *señora*. You need not worry." His gaze was riveted on her imperiously, and then he quickly mounted and put his heels to the horse's sides.

What was it she saw in those black, penetrating eyes of his? She shuddered. Why did she suddenly feel that he was evil? *I am just foolish,* she said to herself. *He is a man of God.* But still she had the urge to run after Alejandro and grab him from his horse.

She bit her lip to keep from crying as she watched her son ride off into the distance with the priest.

Alejandro turned and lifted his hand in a pitiful good-bye. A sob caught in her throat.

"Keep my little boy safe," she whispered as she crossed herself.

She was no longer able to stand there and watch him ride away. She ran to the house and to her room and fell across her bed, unable to control the sobs that shook her shoulders.

* * *

"This is your bed, Alejandro," Fray Ordóñez said as he lit the tallow candle and pointed to a low cot that sat in a corner of the small cell that was the priest's room. He put his hand on the boy's shoulder and Alejandro flinched.

"My son," Fray Ordóñez said, "you have no need to be afraid of me. I want us to be friends."

He took the boy's face in his hands and kissed him on the forehead. "I love you, my son, just as the *señora* loves you."

Alejandro did not move nor did he speak just as he had not spoken a word on the journey to Santo Domingo.

"You are such a good boy," Fray Ordóñez said, smiling at him. "You are so obedient. I know we will be good friends, and you will learn to love me like you love the *señora*."

His hand sat like a claw on the boy's shoulder and then he caressed the boy's cheek. "I am your father now. I am not just a priest but your father. You must call me *'Papacito'* when we are alone together. You will call me *'Padre'* when others are around but when we are alone you will call me *'Papacito'* and you will kiss my hand and say to me, 'I love you, *Papacito*.' " He took Alejandro's face in his hands again. "Say it to me now. Say 'I love you, *Papacito*.' "

Alejandro hesitated and Fray Ordóñez tightened his hands on the boy's face.

Alejandro's voice shook and his words were scarcely audible. "I, I love you, *Papacito*."

Ordóñez bent forward and kissed him on both cheeks. "You are such a good boy, Alejandro, such a good boy, and your *papacito* loves you, too."

The priest walked over to his own bed. "Come," he said, "come sit on my lap like a son sits on his father's lap." Alejandro walked hesitantly to where the priest stood. Ordóñez sat down on the edge of the bed and pulled the boy onto his lap.

"You are such a good boy," he said, "and you must know that whatever I say to you is good, and whatever I ask you to do is good. Do you understand?"

Alejandro's eyes were wide, but he did not answer. The priest pulled him against his bony chest and held him there, stroking his hair. "Oh, my sweet boy, how glorious our journey to Mexico City will be. What a comfort you will be to me. I loved you the moment I saw you—your big dark eyes, your golden skin, your timidity and politeness. And you will love your *papacito* and you will make him happy."

The priest lifted him off his lap and set him on the floor. "Now you must learn how to take care of your *papacito*. At the end of the day your *papacito* is tired with all the work he must do, and you must help him prepare for bed. First you must remove his sandals."

Ordóñez motioned to his feet. Alejandro hesitated and the priest spoke.

"Yes, take them off, my son." Alejandro knelt and fumbled with the sandals but managed to remove them.

"Now you must remove my belt."

Likewise Alejandro fumbled with the rope but succeeded in removing it. The priest pulled his habit from where he sat on it and motioned for Alejandro to pull it over his head. When the habit was removed, leaving him in his rough shirt and undertrousers, Ordóñez smiled.

"Now lay the habit neatly over that trunk, lay the belt on top, and place my sandals over there."

Alejandro did as he was told, scarcely looking at the priest. "Now you must wash my feet," the priest said with a smile. "Pour some water from that jug into the basin and bring the cloth and towel with you."

Alejandro followed the directions, but his hands trembled as he carried the basin of water to where the *padre* sat. He knelt and the friar put one of his feet in the basin. Alejandro washed it with the cloth.

"Now dry it with the towel."

When Alejandro had finished the other foot, the priest spoke again. "Now kiss your *papacito*'s feet and thank him for being good to you."

Alejandro did not look up and when he hesitated, the friar pushed his head down toward his feet. Alejandro leaned down and quickly touched his lips to Fray Ordóñez's feet. "Thank you for being good to me," he whispered.

"Thank you for being good to me, *Papacito,*" the priest corrected, and Alejandro repeated the words.

"Take the water outside and pour it on the vegetable garden."

When the boy returned, the *padre* took the basin and poured more water into it.

"Now it is my turn to bathe you," he said. "Cleanliness is to be prized—the soul cannot be clean if the body is not clean also." He spread the towel on the floor as he continued. "Take your clothes off."

Alejandro shook his head no. Fray Ordóñez rose and grasped him painfully by the shoulder. "When your *papacito* tells you to do something, you do it. Now, take your clothes off."

Alejandro shuddered slightly and slowly pulled his clothes off.

"Stand on the towel," he admonished and Alejandro stepped tremblingly onto it. The priest's voice became soft and soothing. "I am just going to wash you like the *señora* washed you when you were a child."

"I can wash myself, please," Alejandro whispered, his voice catching.

Ordóñez smiled at him. "But I am your *papacito* now and I want to see that you get really clean."

He knelt, dipped the cloth in the basin, and began to rub it over Alejandro's trembling body. "Such a good boy," he cooed, "such a beautiful boy." He washed his arms and back and legs and genitals. Then he dried him briskly.

"That wasn't so bad now, was it?" he laughed and picked up the basin and set it on a small chest.

"May I get dressed?" Alejandro whispered.

"May I get dressed, *Papacito*," the priest corrected, adding quickly, "no, you may not get dressed, not yet. We must say our prayers and then do our penance."

Ordóñez pulled off the shirt he had worn under his habit, leaving only his loose priest's trousers.

"Come," he said as he knelt beside his bed. He motioned and Alejandro, still naked, knelt also. The priest intoned long prayers and recited the rosary.

When he was done, his head dropped onto his bed and he began to sob. Alejandro looked at him with shock. The priest reached under his bed and brought out a slender switch. He began the Act of Contrition as he brought the switch down across his shoulders again and again.

He continued to sob and whisper, "Lord, I am unworthy, punish me, give me the tortures of Hell, but thank you for giving me this boy."

Alejandro was aghast, his eyes wide with horror, but he could not take them from the priest who switched himself unmercifully, raising ugly red welts on his own back. Then the friar collapsed forward onto the bed and lay unmoving for long moments. Slowly he pushed himself up and peered at Alejandro, who dropped his eyes quickly.

"I am forgiven, my son," he whispered. "It feels so good to have my sins lifted."

He placed his hand on Alejandro's shoulder and the boy jumped involuntarily. "Now," the priest said, "we must get rid of your sins, too."

Alejandro looked up with fear. "I have done nothing wrong, *Padre*, I swear."

"Young boys are full of sin," Fray Ordóñez said as he rose. "They make others sin. We are going to take your sins away."

"No, please, *Papacito*," Alejandro whispered, but just then the switch came sharply down across his bare buttocks, and he flinched against the pain. He bit his lip to keep from crying as the switch came down again and again across his buttocks until they burned like fire.

He heard the priest crying again and realized the switching had stopped. The *padre* was kneeling beside him, embracing him, babbling, "Oh, my dear boy, oh my sweet boy, I did not want to hurt you, but I had to get rid of the sin."

Ordóñez rose and pulled Alejandro to his feet. "Here," he said, "lie down on your bed and let me rub some salve into those cruel welts."

Alejandro sank onto his bed, unable to move as the priest fetched something from the chest. He began to rub a heavy, sweet-smelling ointment onto the lacerated skin and Alejandro winced at the pain and felt sick at the smell.

The priest finished and kissed the back of Alejandro's head. "Sleep well, my beautiful boy." He blew out the candle, and Alejandro heard him get into bed. The tears Alejandro had not shed earlier rolled now from his eyes, and he tried to smother his sobs, but he was unsuccessful because suddenly the friar was beside his bed.

"Don't cry, my son," he whispered, "you will get used to it and then you will welcome the wonderfulness of the pain." He was pulling Alejandro up. "Come," he said, "come to my bed. *Papacito* will comfort you."

Alejandro tried to resist, but the *padre* yanked him roughly to the other bed. Alejandro lay completely stiff, trying to keep his body from shaking as the priest embraced him. "Do not be afraid, my son," he whispered.

Alejandro smelled the man's fetid breath and thought he would be sick. He shuddered with revulsion and wanted to cry again but could not.

After some minutes had passed, he felt the priest relax and then heard the deep breathing and the quiet snores. He waited, and as slowly as he could, he slid out of the friar's bed. With complete silence he found his clothes in the dark, pulled them on, and crept across the room. Fray Ordóñez snorted and turned heavily in bed and Alejandro stopped, frozen with fear.

He waited long, agonizing moments before he slowly opened the door and slid outside. He ran quietly to the horse corral and entered it stealthily as Rohona had taught him. He groped in the darkness of the small barn-like tackroom and found a bridle and some rope. It did not take him long to find his horse. He winced with pain as he mounted and rode quietly out of the pueblo.

When he was some distance from the village, he put his heels to his horse's flanks and galloped in the direction in which the stars told him was the *villa*.

When daylight came, he hid himself and his horse in a small narrow canyon that was filled with brush, boulders, and small trees. He could not take a chance on being seen in daylight. He took a large branch and backtracked out of the canyon, brushing away the horse's hoofprints back to a gravelly area he had crossed then brushed away his own tracks as he hurried back to the canyon where he had left his horse.

The sun rose overhead and it grew hot, and his sweat and the sticky ointment made his trousers stick painfully to his skin. He prayed for darkness and that the horse would make no noise if someone came near.

As the sun began to fall lower in the sky he was afraid he could not keep himself from starting out before it was safe. He thought the day would never end. His stomach growled with hunger and his mouth was dry from thirst. He prayed he would find water in a *cañada* on the way back.

At last darkness fell and he cautiously made his way out of the canyon. He urged his mount as fast as it would go, tears blinding him from the pain he felt at riding. He tried to ride lying forward as much as possible, but nothing eased the burning torture.

At dawn he reached the *villa*. He took the horse quickly into the corral and ran to the window of his mother's room and pounded on the wooden grate that covered it. At length she opened the inside shutters and peered out.

*"Mamá,"* he wept, *"mamá,* let me in."

*"Hijo!* Oh, my god, what has happened?" She ran to the *sala,* threw up the bar that bolted the door and pulled it open. The boy ran into her arms, weeping.

*"Hijo, hijo,"* she whispered, "what has happened?"

At that moment Fabia, who had waked at the commotion, came into the room, pulling her *rebozo* around her. "What is it?" she asked.

"Alejandro has come back," María Angélica said as the old woman came running to hug him.

"What happened, *hijo?"* María Angélica asked as she grasped him by the shoulders. She saw the unquenched fear in his eyes and pulled him to her again. "Oh, *hijo, hijo,* everything is all right now."

Fabia saw then the trousers stuck to Alejandro's skin. *"Madre de Dios,* what is this?"

She started to pull the fabric away from him, but he cried, "No, no, don't look!"

*"Hijo,"* María Angélica gasped as she turned him around in her arms and saw the encrusted fabric stuck to him. "My God in Heaven, did *Padre* Ordóñez do this to you?" Alejandro nodded his head as he hid his face in his hands.

Nahuatl curses hissed from Fabia's mouth. "I knew that friar was the Devil's own work! Come, Angelita, bring Alejandro to the kitchen. We must get those trousers off of him."

"Climb up on the table, *hijo."*

María Angélica held Alejandro's hand as Fabia dipped a rag in a bowl of tepid water and applied it to the trousers to soften the crusted fabric so she could remove it from him.

*"Hijo,"* María Angélica said gently, "tell me what happened. Did you do something to make Fray Ordóñez mad?"

"Of course he didn't," Fabia snapped. "That *padre* is simply an evil man."

"What happened, Alejandro?"

Alejandro hiccupped and whispered hesitantly, his face hidden in his arms. "The *padre* said he must take away my sins so he started whipping me. I swear I did everything he asked me to, but he whipped me anyway."

"I know, I know," María Angélica said softly, "I know you would have done everything he asked. Was that all?"

Alejandro spoke so softly she had to lean forward to hear him. "He made me get in bed with him."

Her face turned ashen and a look of deadly fury covered Fabia's. "Is that all?" María Angélica asked, her words choked.

The boy nodded his head. "When I heard him snoring, I slipped out and ran away."

"Oh, *hijo*," María Angélica gasped and laid her head down on her hands and sobbed in horror.

Alejandro touched her hair. "Don't cry, *mamá*, please."

She wept more bitterly still. "Oh, *hijo*, I'm so sorry, so sorry."

"It's all right now, *mamá*."

Fabia had finished her ministrations and went to his room and brought back another pair of trousers. "Put these on, *hijo*," she said and Alejandro slipped off the table and pulled the pants on.

"Where is Uncle?" he asked.

María Angélica's head flew up. "Uncle has gone hunting," she said. "He won't be back for several days."

Fabia took Alejandro by the shoulders and looked directly at him. "Don't ever, ever, tell Uncle what happened. Do you understand?" Her voice had an edge to it Alejandro had never heard before and he nodded, his eyes wide. "Don't ever tell Uncle what has happened," she said again. "He might do something to the *padre*, and they would punish Uncle very severely. Do you understand?"

"Yes," the boy said, "I will never tell Uncle anything—I will never tell anyone."

Fabia hugged him, and María Angélica spoke. "We will say simply that you ran away from the *padre* because you were homesick, and we couldn't bear to send you back."

A week later they heard that Fray Ordóñez had already departed for New Spain and breathed a sigh of relief. Thank God they would not have to face him.

But a year later, in August of 1612, Fray Isidro Ordóñez arrived in the ecclesiastical capital of Santo Domingo, bringing with him a caravan of twenty wagons, a military escort of soldiers paid for one year's duty in the province, eight new clergy, servants, teamsters, and livestock.

He entered grandly and importantly, and the news quickly reached Santa Fé that he carried a letter that removed Peinado as prelate and named Ordóñez as the new Father Commissary.

Governor Peralta received that news with the unpleasant comment, "I would to God the Devil were coming instead of *that* friar!"

Within a year Peralta was to realize how apt his assessment of Ordóñez was. Fabia already knew she was right.

# Chapter 33

Slightly less than a year had passed since Fray Ordóñez returned to *Nuevo México* from his mission to Mexico City. Now, in May of 1613, Governor Peralta sent a detail of soldiers north to the village of Taos to collect the tribute of *mantas* that was due from the pueblo. He spoke earnestly to the soldiers he had summoned to the Governor's Palace.

"The first attempt to collect the tribute was unsuccessful. You know that, as you also know there are whispers that Taos is in revolt or close to it. I just received word this morning from the pueblo that the tribute is ready. You know the seriousness of this matter. We cannot let that village start a precedent; I want that tribute collected before they change their minds again."

With all haste the soldiers rode out of Santa Fé, the hooves of their horses raising a cloud of dust in the plaza. They rode north across the juniper and piñon-studded terrain, pushing their horses as much as they felt they could. They rode into Nambé pueblo to water and rest their horses and themselves before they continued on.

"Father," one of the soldiers said as he saw Fray Ordóñez approaching them, "what brings you to Nambé?"

"I might ask the same of you," the priest said. "Where do you think you are going?"

"Taos," one of the soldiers answered, "governor's orders. The tribute's ready and what with all the whispers of revolt, Don Pedro wants us to collect it immediately."

"But don't you realize," the friar said, his eyes hard, "what the day after tomorrow is?"

"Saturday, sir," one soldier said.

"Just like I thought," the priest replied, his fists clenched at his sides.

"Sinners!" he shouted. "You are all sinners! I have never seen more iniquity in my life than I have seen in this godforsaken province!"

The soldiers stood in shocked silence at the *padre*'s outburst.

"We have come here to do a holy duty!" he continued. "And I am undermined at every turn. How can we evangelize the heathen when all they see is the execrable example set by their overlords." His voice rose higher.

"Day after tomorrow is the Eve of Pentecost! The eve of that most holy day on which the Lord sent the Holy Spirit down upon the Apostles, a day to offer humble prayer and thanks for so great a gift—and you did not know it!"

He seemed to become more calm. "I order you to return to the *villa*, now. I command you to hear Mass on Pentecost at the Santa Fé church."

"But, *Padre*," one of the soldiers said, "we have strict orders from the governor to go to Taos immediately. He is very concerned about the possibility of revolt."

"Damn the governor!" Ordóñez shouted. "I hold the highest authority in this province. I order you to return to Santa Fé or be excommunicated. You will not shirk your holy duty for some errand of the governor!"

Another soldier started to open his mouth to protest, but the friar silenced him with his shrill voice.

"You are excommunicated if you do not mount your horses this moment and ride to Santa Fé!"

"What?!" Peralta shouted, a vein throbbing in his forehead. "How dare he countermand my order! I am the governor of this province. Who the hell does that *padre* think he is anyway, *Jesús Cristo?!*"

He slammed his fist down on his desk, and spoke to the soldiers who stood at attention in front of him. "I, Don Pedro Peralta, governor of this province by appointment of the Viceroy himself, as civil authority of this land and in the name of the King, order you to return to Taos to collect the tribute." He paused, and his voice returned to a more normal tone.

"But to satisfy the Father Commissary that you will not shirk your religious duty in the execution of your public one, I order you to hear the Mass of Pentecost at the mission in San Ildefonso. Do you understand?"

"Yes, sir," the soldiers responded.

Ordóñez came riding into Santa Fé somewhat later and went immediately to the *convento* at the Santa Fé church. He seemed in good spirits as he walked in.

"Fray Luís," he spoke to the priest of the Santa Fé church, "you are well, I judge. I just stopped on my way back to Santo Domingo. I ordered some of the governor's soldiers who were on their way to Taos to come back to Santa Fé to hear the Mass of Pentecost. I want you to make sure they do."

Father Tirado paled slightly. He had already heard the story. His voice was weak when he spoke. "But the governor ordered them back to Taos."

"You mean he overrode *my* order?"

"Yes," Fray Tirado answered apologetically, "but he did command them to hear the Mass of Pentecost at San Ildefonso."

"That makes no difference. The important thing is that he dared overrule me. I am the supreme authority in this land. I will show him who rules in *Nuevo México*. Call your scribe. I'm going to draft a letter to that accursed apostate."

When the scribe was seated at a desk, Ordóñez began. "By the authority of the Holy Office invested in me, I order you in the name of the Inquisition to recall within two hours the soldiers you sent to Taos or face the consequence that is perpetual excommunication and the damnation of your immortal soul."

"Why, the nerve of that bastard!" Peralta growled upon reading the order. "The Inquisition! He has no authority to invoke the Inquisition on this or any other matter! He has no official appointment from the Holy Office that I know of!"

Peralta called to his notary, and immediately drafted a reply to Fray Ordóñez. "If the Father Commissary has brought a commission from the Holy Office of the Inquisition, he should be pleased to present the patent of appointment to me formally as is required by law. When I have been presented with the said patent, the Father Commissary can be sure that I will obey it in all haste."

The governor sent the message immediately to the Santa Fé convent, and the presumptuous reply caused Ordóñez to turn crimson with rage.

"He will rue the day he ever questioned my authority!" he shouted. Although the two hours had not yet passed, he made his promised pronouncement. "By the holy authority vested in me, I pronounce the governor excommunicated."

He had the scribe draw up the formal declaration of excommunication, and when it was finished, Ordóñez rushed outside the church where, with his own hands, he nailed it to the door.

When he reentered the church, he spoke to the priest. "Fray Tirado, these are your instructions. If the governor seeks absolution, he is to pay a fine of fifty pesos to me, the Father Commissary; he must swear to be obedient to me; and he must hear Mass in public in this church like a penitent, barefoot and a candle in his hand. Do you understand?"

"Yes, Your Grace," Father Tirado said.

"I must get back to Santo Domingo. I expect to see my orders carried out to the letter."

The following day, the Eve of Pentecost, the Santa Fé church was filled with people to observe the Holy Day. The church buzzed with talk about the governor's excommunication, and the governor's chair, in its place of honor near the front, sat empty. Father Tirado entered, and a shocked silence fell over the congregation as he spoke.

"It is decreed that anyone whosoever shall as much as speak to the governor shall suffer excommunication. Be ye warned."

"My Lord," María Angélica whispered, "what is going on?"

"Lunacy," Dorotea answered, "sheer lunacy. It's that friar again. Ordóñez is stirring up trouble again, and we haven't seen the end of it yet." María Angélica clasped her hands together as Dorotea continued. "Fray Tirado secretly gave Isidro a message to take to the governor. If Peralta will come to the church at dawn with three or four friends, Fray Tirado will say the Mass of Penance and thus the governor can avoid a public spectacle. Isidro told me Peralta has refused. 'Why should I do penance when I have done nothing wrong?' the governor demanded, or so Isidro said."

"What has gotten into the authorities of this province?" María Angélica asked with anxiety.

"Nothing new," Dorotea answered disgustedly, "they are each after as much power as they can grab."

María Angélica had hoped that Fray Ordóñez, now that he was prelate, would spend all his time in Santo Domingo. She had no desire to have to face him again.

When the news had reached Santa Fé that Ordóñez had returned from Mexico City, she almost collapsed. Fabia took her by the shoulders and seated her in a chair and then sat down in front of her and took her by the hands.

"There is no way you can avoid that man. He will come to Santa Fé one of these days, and you will meet him face to face no matter how much you try to avoid it. You must be prepared."

María Angélica nodded, knowing that it was true, and Fabia continued. "One look at your face and that friar will know that you know. There is no way you can hide it from your face—but it does not matter. You must meet his gaze, and you must not show shame on your face. It is his shame not yours, although you can be assured that evil man feels no shame."

María Angélica straightened up, sat back, and took a deep breath. "You are absolutely right, I must not show him fear—that will give him more confidence in his invulnerability."

"You must talk to the boy and tell him these things also."

* * *

Alejandro walked into the room and knew instantly what the topic of conversation was going to be about when he saw Fabia and his mother's faces. He, too, had heard that Fray Ordóñez had returned.

María Angélica looked at her son. In two more months he would be twelve. He no longer looked like a child; he was taller than most his age and almost as tall as she. Already his shoulders gave evidence of the breadth they would have when he was a man. He held himself erect like the man who was his father, and he had learned also to keep his face a mask so that others could not tell what were his thoughts. She knew his strength and endurance, for he had labored and hunted alongside Rohona, and he could do the work of a man. He would no longer be prey for that hawk-faced priest, but that did not mean that Fray Ordóñez could not harm him—or the family, for that matter.

"Sit down, *hijo,*" she said. She reached out and lifted his chin.

"You know what this conversation is about," she said gently, "but you have nothing to be ashamed of."

She clasped her hands in her lap, and Alejandro continued to look at her, but she saw the shame in his eyes. She continued evenly. "You will undoubtedly come face to face with Fray Ordóñez on some occasion. It will be impossible to avoid, but you are a man now and you must not have fear of him. Rohona has taught you well to keep your thoughts hidden from your face. If you meet that friar, look levelly at him as if nothing ever happened."

She glanced at her hands and back up. "Fray Ordóñez will be able to tell from my face that I know what he did. There is nothing I can do to conceal it because I never learned to keep my thoughts completely hidden, but I, too, must make every effort. We must not show fear to that man." Alejandro nodded solemnly.

Fabia spoke up. "That friar is evil, *hijito,* but your *mamá* is right. If he knows we are not afraid and we keep to ourselves and do not involve ourselves in any of the things he may do, I don't think he will bother us. If he tries to, well, there are things that happen in this province that are sometimes never explained. That *padre* is not invincible."

The look on Alejandro's face changed. He straightened his shoulders. "*Sí,* Fabia," he said, "no one is invincible."

Weeks of turmoil continued in the *villa* between the new prelate and the governor. Peralta arrested Asencio Archuleta, the ecclesiastical notary, for refusing to give him a written statement of Father Tirado's order that anyone who talked to him would suffer excommunication.

Furious that the governor had arrested the Church's notary, even though he was only a layman, Fray Ordóñez gathered together all of the citizens of the *villa* who had had differences in the past with the present governor.

When he spoke, his eyes flashed with anger and his words inflamed.

"How can you sit there and allow your governor to use you so? He rules like a tyrant. He can have any one of you arrested tomorrow and hanged if it is his whim, and you know it! This province was kept by the King as a missionary field. The governor is here only to protect the Church, and yet he rules all of you as if he had the power of a king. What are you? His spineless puppets here to do his bidding?"

He saw anger suffuse the faces of the men there, and he smiled to himself. Of course they were still Spaniards—one didn't wound the pride of a Spaniard without expecting retribution. He saw them dredging up in their minds any slight to their pride that, no matter how small, the present governor might have committed. He knew they would soon be his, and he continued, his voice more soothing.

"If the governor will not protect the Church in this province, I must ask you men of valor to do it for me. We cannot allow that man to subject this land to his will. He cannot be allowed to make slaves of Spanish citizens. And I can guarantee you," he continued, "that you will be amply rewarded for your efforts. The Viceroy will see to it that all *encomiendas* are taken out of the hands of the enemies of the Church and distributed to its loyal supporters, and in addition, the powerful Inquisition stands ready to remunerate handsomely those who help preserve the rightful place of the Church here in *Nuevo México*."

Ordóñez saw greed light the eyes of those who listened to him, and when they realized he had finished speaking, they let out a roar of approval because they knew the wealth of the Holy Office and wished for some of it for themselves.

The village was soon divided into two factions, those siding with the governor and those with the Father Commissary, and a bitterness between civil and ecclesiastical authority developed that was to undermine life in *Nuevo México* for many years to come.

The war between the authorities was to become even worse. Father Tirado of the Santa Fé church threw the governor's chair into the street, and Fray Ordóñez along with the soldiers of his faction seized Peralta as he was on his way to Mexico City with dispatches for the Viceroy about conditions in *Nuevo México* and the actions of the new prelate.

Ordóñez arrested him in the name of the Inquisition, and for nine months Peralta was held prisoner while the priest was the virtual ruler of *Nuevo México*. Excommunications were handed down or threatened if anyone so much as dared question the Father Commissary's right to do whatever was his whim. Even a number of priests were appalled at Ordóñez's arbitrary actions and were thrown in jail when they voiced their opposition to his behavior.

María Angélica had seen the friar on two occasions after his return from Mexico, but both times it had been in the Santa Fé church when he had preached a sermon—more nearly a tirade—to the townspeople concerning the governor. She was thankful the church was filled with people, but nevertheless Ordóñez had made a point to fix his small black eyes on her.

She tried to gaze back placidly at him. The people around her gave her strength as did the distance between her and the pulpit, and she decided to look directly at him and focus on the center of the cross on the chasuble he wore. It was convenient because she could appear to be paying attention, but she did not have to meet his eyes. When Mass was over she left quickly and hurried home, not stopping to engage in the conversations that buzzed amongst the people.

Toward the first of December, however, she came face to face with him. It was late afternoon and the sky was leaden with dark, low-hanging clouds. There would surely be snow by morning, and she wanted to get Fabia's herbs to the Palace of the Governor before the snow began in earnest. Fabia had intended to take the herbs herself to the servant whose little daughter was suffering from croup, but María Angélica insisted that she would do it. Fabia herself had a cough, and María Angélica did not want her out in the cold air. She had seen Fabia grow frail with a cough the previous winter and did not want it to happen again.

As she started back home across the deserted plaza, she bent her head against the cold wind and clutched her *rebozo* tightly around her face. She was not halfway across the plaza when the wind-driven snow began slashing at her. She increased her pace and bent her head lower, hurrying to get home. He must have placed himself in her path because he was standing still when she ran directly into him. The first thing she saw was the bottom of his blue habit, and she knew who he was before she heard his mirthless laugh and looked up and saw his piercing black eyes.

"So, *Señora* de Vizcarra," he said in an inquisitorial tone, "what takes you to the governor's quarters on such an inclement night?"

She would not let him make her afraid. She looked up at him and said evenly, "I was taking medicine to Josefita's little girl who has the croup."

"Are you not aware that anyone who has dealings with the governor is under pain of excommunication?" he asked menacingly.

She looked directly at him. "Why, I did not know you had let Don Pedro out of jail. I assumed he was still incarcerated at Sandía."

She saw Ordóñez's eyes go opaque and saw a muscle twitch in his jaw, and she knew he had felt the barb of her words. Instantly she regretted her remark and knew how stupid it had been, but the priest appeared to ignore it for the moment as he changed the subject.

"I have not had the pleasure of the hospitality of your home since my return from Mexico," he said pointedly.

The last thing on earth she wanted was to have that friar under her roof, but there was nothing else to do. "Please, then," she said smoothly, "won't you come and have a cup of hot chocolate? Fabia hasn't been feeling well so I can't offer you any of her specialties, unfortunately."

"That's quite all right," he said as he turned and walked with her to her house.

When María Angélica stepped through the door with the friar behind her, Fabia gasped, but it was smothered in a fit of coughing and she left the room quickly.

"Please be seated," she said, motioning to a chair. "I will get the chocolate."

She hurried to the kitchen where Fabia sipped a glass of water. The old woman looked at her, scowling.

"I could do nothing else."

"It had to happen, I suppose."

"What had to happen?" Alejandro and Alegría said in unison. They had both been sitting in the kitchen next to the fire when she had entered.

"Fray Ordóñez has come for a cup of hot chocolate," María Angélica said.

"Why did you invite *el diablo* to our house?" Alegría asked.

"Shush," María Angélica said with annoyance. "I could do nothing about it. But I want you *both* to come in, have chocolate with us, and be polite."

"I don't want to," Alegría pouted.

"I'm sorry, but you must," María Angélica answered. Alegría started to protest again, but Alejandro stopped her.

María Angélica saw Fray Ordóñez's eyes widen in surprise as he saw Alejandro. It was obvious the priest hadn't expected her to bring him in. She also saw the man take in Alejandro's stature. Gone was the young boy he had once hoped to take to Mexico with him. In his place was a tall, broad-shouldered young half-breed whose chiseled features showed nothing to indicate his thoughts.

*"Buenas tardes, Padre,"* Alejandro said emotionlessly as he made a slight bow from the waist and sat down in a chair next to María Angélica. Alegría echoed her brother, but there was distaste in her tone.

María Angélica saw the look of a hawk return to the friar's face.

"The children have certainly grown since I last saw them. What has it been? Two, three years?" he said and smiled tightly.

"Three," she said.

Alejandro and Alegría sat watching the priest.

María Angélica bent her head to her cup of chocolate, took a sip, and set the cup down. She drew her *rebozo* closer around her shoulders, smoothed a wrinkle in her skirt, and looked up blankly at Fray Ordóñez.

She would take another sip of chocolate and repeat her little ritual if he did not speak. She was reaching for her cup when he broke the silence.

"Did you know that your guardian has been excommunicated?"

His words were quiet but they were spoken to be like small cutting knives. It was the tone of them more than the content of the words that made her hand tremble briefly as she picked up her cup. Who on earth did he mean? She looked up at him. "My guardian?" she asked evenly as she took a sip of her chocolate.

"Yes," he said, his tone menacing.

She looked up at him quizzically over her cup. She couldn't imagine who he meant, but she would not let him frighten her with his tone nor would she ask him the name of this person he thought was her protector. He would have to tell her.

She took another sip of chocolate to stall a moment longer, set her cup down, and looked at him as if she was expecting him to continue. She could see the anger growing in his eyes.

"I hope you and your children are not left destitute."

She struggled to remain expressionless but she would not ask him any questions.

"You realize I have the authority to seize the *encomienda* of anyone who is excommunicated?"

So, that was it. He was talking about Isidro Inojosa—the *guardián* of her *encomienda*. She wanted to laugh. Isidro Inojosa excommunicated? He had already been in a league with the devil for years. Excommunication couldn't possibly mean a thing to him. And her *encomienda?* She had never seen the share of the revenue that she was entitled to. Isidro Inojosa kept that for her since she was a woman and "knew nothing about accounting." He told her he was keeping it in trust for her.

Ordóñez was trying to threaten her with the loss of revenue from her *encomienda?* She wanted to laugh in his face, but she knew there were any number of ways that particular friar could find to bring harm to her or her children. She tried to make her voice sound grave.

"Isidro Inojosa should have been excommunicated years ago," she said. "I know it must have been painful for you to have to issue such a harsh decree, but he is truly a godless man. We can only hope your action will cause him to review his life and realize how important the Church truly is in our lives."

She looked down at her hands as she continued. "We, of course, will find some way to manage without the *encomienda* of which he is *guardián*."

She looked up at Fray Ordóñez and tried to make it appear that she was concerned at the possible loss. She saw the friar fighting his anger. This was not what he had expected from the conversation. He took a sip of his chocolate, and his bony knuckles were white around the cup.

"God willing, it won't come to this, we should hope." He rose, and his voice was cold. "I must go, *señora*. Thank you for the chocolate."

"Please," she said, trying to make her voice pleasant, "do drop by again when you are in the *villa*." The friar had said not one word about Alejandro running away from him at Santo Domingo.

He gave her a hard, appraising look as he set his cup down.

*"Buenas tardes, Padre,"* Alejandro said evenly, and Alegría echoed him as she dropped a brief curtsy.

The priest turned on his heel and María Angélica escorted him to the door. She could not believe he had made no mention of Alejandro's flight from Santo Domingo. It was certainly better that he hadn't, for she didn't know what she might have said or done. Had he been waiting for her to say something? She closed the door quickly after him against the cold, harsh wind that carried a flurry of snowflakes into the room. She let the bolt down and turned to her children.

"We are really in for a snow tonight," she said. "It would be such a shame if Padre Ordóñez were caught in a drift and couldn't get out."

Alegría let out a peal of laughter. "Oh, *mamá*, I hope he does!"

María Angélica took their hands and they started back toward the kitchen.

"I love you, *mamá*," Alejandro said quietly.

She turned and patted his cheek. "I love you, too, *hijo*, and I am very proud of you."

It was Ordóñez who ruled the province when the next governor, Bernardino de Ceballos, reached Santa Fé in May of 1614. The influence of the Father Commissary and his followers had grown so great that when the new governor arrived, he sided with them out of either fear or necessity.

The hawk-faced friar's power was such that he still held the former governor incarcerated and would not allow his return to Mexico with the outbound cart train. But in October of that year Peralta managed to send Isidro Inojosa to Mexico City to tell of what was happening in the province. When the priest found out the captain was gone, he sent men to stop him, but Inojosa escaped and finally in November, Peralta was allowed to depart.

"God forgive me," Dorotea said as they walked home from Mass. "I have never wished my husband well, but I am praying fervently that he succeeds in his mission. Someone must stop that friar."

"I can't tell you how many times I have prayed for someone to," María Angélica said. "Surely Isidro or Governor Peralta will get through, but in the meantime we must persevere."

"That will be easier, of course, without Isidro here. As long as Ordóñez is in control, the situation is always dangerous for us. Isidro has always supported the governors against the *padres*. That's why Peralta trusted him to go to Mexico City. So many of the men in this province bend with the prevailing wind. If they think it's to their benefit, they side with the civil authority, if not, they back the Church's leadership. It's hard to trust anyone, but Peralta well knows my husband's hatred of the priests and that friar in particular."

"There are many of us who must worry about our immortal souls for the thoughts we have had about that unholy man," María Angélica said.

She tried to stay out of the imbroglio between the factions and mostly succeeded because she had no husband who would have had to take sides in the dispute. As well, in the eyes of Fray Ordóñez she must have successfully distanced herself from Isidro Inojosa because the priest did not threaten her again. In fact, he left her alone. She assumed he had decided she was no threat to him, and he was more concerned with securing dominance over the important citizens of the province than he was with wasting his time on a poor widow.

She spent many hours that winter, as she had the previous ones, embroidering the cloth that Rohona wove. No money circulated in the province and embroidered goods were a profitable item of exchange for such things as sugar or raisins or cinnamon.

After Ordóñez had gone to Mexico City three years previously, she had begun to teach her children and their father the rudiments of reading. There were few books in the land, and only the clergy and governor had any paper on which to write, but she managed to get some slates from a priest who had just arrived in the province in exchange for embroidering altar cloths and vestments for him.

At first Alejandro was reluctant to sit through the tedium of learning to read and write, but Rohona was fascinated that one could make marks on paper that said words. When Alejandro saw the man he admired most working diligently at learning the strange lines and circles, he, too, became interested, and a sort of competition developed between father and son to see who could learn the most new words.

Alegría went along with them. Anything they did, she was determined to do also, and as a result she learned to read rapidly.

The struggle was by far more difficult for Rohona than for either of the two children. They were completely fluent in Castilian whereas, although by that time he spoke well, he still did not have their mastery of the language. He had another motivation, however, that pushed him to learn the strange skill of reading: a long-held desire to understand the pale strangers.

He could scarcely call the Spaniards strangers after having lived among them for a decade and a half, but there were still many things he did not understand. He had long hungered for them to go back from whence they came, despite the fact that he loved one of them.

Many of the Ácoma slaves had run away over the years and there were reports that the village on the rock citadel was being rebuilt and now had a fair number of inhabitants. He longed to return, longed to stand on the high cliffs and look out over the valley floor, longed to see the places where he had played as a child, longed to talk to his kinsmen and dance for the K'atsina to bring rain although he knew that he could never again dance beautifully.

How good it would be to sit in the *kiva* with the other men. His son was of the age to be initiated into the K'atsina society; how he wished he could help prepare him for that sacred ceremony. He had taught his son many things of Áco, but, sadly, he knew his son was more Castilian than Ácoma, and it grieved him deeply.

He longed to return, but he was realistic enough to know he could not take her with him, and he knew also that he could not desert his family. And so he stayed and learned how to read, thinking always about Áco and about the strangers, and knowing, feeling deep within him that there was something he needed to understand but did not.

Reading held him fascinated. He could never have imagined that so many things could be told by small marks on paper. The most astonishing result of reading was to learn how immense the world really was. At first the concept of huge oceans separating them from land where many other people lived was totally incomprehensible. Gradually, however, the vastness of the world began to sink into his mind and made him feel that strange sensation of needing to know something, of needing to come to a conclusion about something, but he was never able to grasp what it was he sought. He thought perhaps by understanding the strangers better that he would eventually discover what disturbed him.

# Chapter 34

For the next two years Fray Ordóñez ruled the province, although Governor Ceballos tried at times to assert his authority. Gradually the Father Commissary alienated the remainder of the clergy by his dictatorial actions and several sent letters of complaint to the Provincial of the Franciscan Order in Mexico. In spite of Ordóñez's efforts to stop all communication with the viceregal capital, some of the letters managed to get through, and in January of 1617 the mission supply caravan reached Santa Fé with more clergy and supplies for the missions as well as a harsh summons that ordered Ordóñez to return to Mexico City. He never returned to *Nuevo México*.

The mission supply caravan brought the appointment to Father Commissary of Father Estéban de Perea who had built the mission among the Río Grande Tigua at Sandía pueblo. Not only was Perea named successor to Ordóñez, he was also given the title of Father Custodian of the province, which indicated that the church officials in Mexico City regarded the missionary work as progressing well. Giving New Mexico the status of a Custodia meant the missions under the Father Custodian were a semiautonomous unit and gave the Father Custodian close to the power of a bishop.

Perea was a champion of Indian rights, but he had never been in agreement with Ordóñez's usurpation of power and had stayed away from the intrigue in Santa Fé, devoting his efforts to building the mission church and convent in Sandía and to bringing the faith to the Indians there. He was a zealous friar and believed totally that the sole purpose of the Spaniards in Nuevo México was for the conversion of souls. In that, he was like Ordóñez.

Fray Perea was a mature man of fifty years, gray-headed and even-tempered, but he was also as hard as steel when it came to the rights of the Church. One of his first acts as Custodian was to gather evidence against a colonist who was in the habit of making disrespectful remarks about the clergy. The Father Custodian had him arrested, tried, and made to walk through the streets to church gagged and chained where he heard Mass, admitted his guilt, and retracted his statements.

Indian labor was another area about which Fray Perea showed great concern, for the Spanish colonists exploited the natives, using many of them as unpaid laborers.

Seeking better, more abundant land and a nearby supply of labor, some colonists had begun, even during Oñate's time, to move away from the capital village to build haciendas with the help of Indian labor in order to cultivate more land and raise sizeable herds of livestock. Not only did they impress the natives as unpaid workers, they encroached upon the good growing land the Indians had tilled for centuries.

Father Perea was adamant about this issue and denounced it to his superiors in Mexico City. Nothing was said, however, about the mission friars themselves who used unpaid Indian labor to build their mission church, build their dwellings, called *conventos*, till acres of land for them as well as herd the ever-increasing mission flocks.

The friars justified their use of the Indians as being necessary for the advancement of the Church. In times of hunger, the friars said beneficently, they could supply grain to the starving natives from the missions' large stores. It did not occur to them that had they allowed the worker to spend his time in his own fields, he would have had his own grain to store for years of famine as had been the case before the Spaniards arrived.

The ill will that arose between the colonists and friars over Indian labor seethed beneath the surface of colony life. It incensed the colonists to have the prelates preach against the exploitation of the Indians and to bring all their power to bear in order that the colonists not be allowed to use native labor. They saw the friars' large tracts of the best pueblo land under cultivation by scores of natives and saw the missions' ever-growing herds of cattle, horses, sheep, goats, pigs, and chickens tended by Indians.

As a result, the province continued in a state of turmoil. The new procedure of sending appointed governors to *Nuevo México* had not made the land any more peaceful than during Oñate's time.

María Angélica's only involvement in these disputes was that Isidro Inojosa was *guardián* of her *encomienda*. Fray Ordóñez's threat to seize her *encomienda* and that of Inojosa's had been a hollow one. *Encomiendas* could only be removed with the approval of the Viceroy, and although Ordóñez had essentially ruled the province, he did not have the power he had led everyone to believe. In the end even he realized that he dare not usurp the Viceroy's power in the matter although he allowed the threat to always hang there.

With the departure of Fray Ordóñez and the danger he embodied, life in the new *villa* was relatively pleasant for María Angélica. No longer did starvation prowl about their door like a hungry wolf, and with the coming of the mission supply caravans every three years, they could expect a few amenities from civilization such as chocolate or Campeche honey or a bright piece of cloth.

Alejandro had turned seventeen and had grown into a tall, broad-shouldered man. He was as skillful with Castilian weapons as he was with Indian ones, and he rode better than anyone, much to old Domingo's great satisfaction.

He had even gone on punitive raids against the Apache who were becoming bolder in their attacks on native villages. He found the forays and hand-to-hand fighting exhilarating but confessed to his mother one night, "It was a massacre, *mamá*. There is no other word for it. The soldiers were unnecessarily brutal. You would not believe it, but they hacked a baby to pieces because it was crying. It made me sick, and I rode away. I will not go on another raid. I intend to spend my time hunting game and helping to oversee the animals, now that Domingo is getting old."

Alejandro made both his mother and father proud of him, and his good looks had not gone unnoticed by eligible girls, Spanish and Indian. The fact that he could read and write gave him status in a land where nearly all, save the priests, were illiterate. When the time came, his mother knew he would make a good marriage.

Fifteen-year-old Alegría did not lack for admirers either, but she was even more unaware of them than her brother. María Angélica had indulged her as a child and allowed her to do whatever she pleased, and as a result, she was like a wild colt. María Angélica knew that out of guilt she had allowed Alegría to grow up learning no self-restraint. She was never able to love her daughter as she did her son. If she would catch a glimpse of Vicente in the little girl, she would tremble. Sometimes Alegría's eyes would stare blankly into the distance and evoke the unpleasant memory of her father, and María Angélica would cross herself.

If Alegría did not get her way when she was little, she would throw tantrums that scared María Angélica with their intensity. Once she slapped Alegría across the face when she was being particularly ugly and said angrily to her, "You're just like your father, you little beast!" Horrified at her words María Angélica had backed away. She could not believe she had struck her child. She was overcome with guilt and from that time on, she allowed Alegría to have her own way—and that usually meant playing outside and tagging after her brother and not doing anything unpleasant she might be asked to do. If Alegría got her own way, she was a happy child.

Alegría was compulsive and loved to ride, particularly with her brother along for company. She constantly nagged and cajoled him to leave his work and go riding with her.

"Aley, I am no longer a child," he would say. "I'm a man and I am expected to work."

She would pout and make fun of him. "So you are a big man now—a big *hombre* and you have no time for foolish child's play."

"That's not true," he said helplessly. "You know *mamá* has no husband, and I must help support the household."

"My father's been gone since you were a little boy. How did she manage then?" she asked with a taunt.

"Fabia was stronger, for one thing," Alejandro said and went to do his work, but at times her cajoling would be successful, and acting as if he were indulging a child, he would go with her and they would ride together in the mountains or down to the *Río del Norte* as they had when they were children.

Alegría had grown into a tall, graceful girl, but her flame-colored hair remained untamed. She tried to do nothing with it and her appearance did not seem to bother her. Her only attire was a loose skirt that came scarcely to her ankles and a cotton *huipil,* a blouse like the peasants in Mexico wore. In summer she went barefoot, even for riding, and in winter she wore the rabbit fur moccasins Rohona made for her.

In spite of her mother's belated efforts to get her to dress more befitting a young lady, Alegría continued to wear what she wanted. The young men, and the not so young, could not keep their eyes off the free young thing who was quickly becoming a woman. Her large, dark-fringed gray eyes looked through them, or at them levelly or sometimes laughingly, if they amused her. She was disarmingly unrestrained, and people were intrigued with her unusual laughter and her strange, restless joy. She was like an iridescent bird that delighted the eye but inspired many to want to capture it for themselves.

When the mission supply caravan arrived that year, it was obvious in the eyes of the soldiers who had come as the military escort that the young girl with the flame-colored hair was every bit a woman. María Angélica was disturbed by some of the looks she saw and realized that whether she liked it or not, Alegría was of an age to be married. But she had none of the skills required of a mistress of a house, and it was too late when María Angélica began to try to remedy the situation.

"You need to learn these things," she would say to her daughter in a reasonable voice.

Alegría would have none of it. She laughed a high, flippant laugh and said as she danced out of the room, "Not me! I would rather ride, *mamá,* ride forever!"

María Angélica knew there were several men who would leap at the chance to marry her daughter, but she was well aware of Alegría's lack of skills. What would happen to her as a wife when it became apparent she could do nothing? And, Heaven help her, what would Alegría do herself when placed in that situation? Where could she find someone who would accept her free-spirited, unusual daughter as she was?

"Perhaps a Queres-speaking Indian would make a good husband for her since she speaks that language fluently," María Angélica said to Rohona.

"Mía, she has no skills for an Indian wife," he said, touching her hand. "No Indian husband would understand or appreciate her. You know she is not like most girls."

She nodded sadly. "I just pray there will be some nice young man with the next caravan who may prove a suitable husband for my beautiful, carefree, unskilled daughter."

Perhaps she should not have allowed Alegría to have her own way all the time when she was younger. Perhaps she should have demanded more of her. It was too late now, though, to impose her will on her headstrong daughter.

The household had been in Santa Fé eight years and each winter had seen old Fabia become more frail. She was nearly toothless and reduced to subsisting on gruel and mashed food. During the first snow of winter, she caught a chill and developed a deep, rattling cough. She was so weak she could not get out of bed although she protested she had work to do. Alegría fed her all her meals and entertained her with lively chatter. She would not let herself believe her old nursemaid would not recover.

Fabia smiled weakly and patted Alegría's hand. "You are my best medicine, *niña,*" the old woman said. "Your beauty is good for these old eyes."

Alegría made a silly face.

One evening when the girl brought her supper to her, Fabia refused it. "No, *niña,*" the old woman whispered, "I need no food, for tonight I am going to die."

"No!"

"I'm sorry, but yes. I am old and tired."

Alegría ran from the room to find her mother, tears streaming down her cheeks. *"Mamá, mamá,"* she wailed, "Fabia is dying."

María Angélica had not seen her daughter cry in years and knew that what she said must be true. Alejandro, who had heard his sister's cry, came to see what was the matter.

"Oh, Aley," Alegría said, running to him and burying her head against his chest, "Fabia says she is dying!"

Alejandro patted his sister gently and together they walked back to the room the old woman shared with Alegría.

They knelt at her bedside. Fabia opened her eyes and smiled, first at María Angélica, who stood behind them, and then at the brother and sister with their tear-filled eyes. She reached out her wrinkled old hand and grasped theirs.

"How I love you both," she said in a rasping whisper. "I do not mind dying; I have had a good life. I have had you and your *mamá* to love. Who could want more?"

Tears streamed down Alegría's cheeks. The old woman tried to reach and wipe them away. "Oh my joy, oh my happiness," she said gently, "do not cry. An old woman is not worth it."

Her hand fell and her eyes closed as if the words had exhausted her.

Alegría turned and buried her face against Alejandro's chest, and he put a comforting arm around her shoulders.

Fabia opened her eyes once more. "No!" she rasped, looked toward María Angélica, and held out her hand. "No! Angelita, no!"

María Angélica knelt and took the old woman's hand. "What is it, Fabia?"

The old woman clutched her hand. "You must stop them! You must tell them!"

Another sentence rattled in her throat, but María Angélica could not understand the words. The old woman's eyes closed.

"What?" María Angélica asked. "Whom must I stop?" But Fabia's lips did not move, and from the stillness of her hand, María Angélica knew she was dead.

María Angélica laid her head on the edge of the bed and cried softly. The rock of her life was gone. She owed the happiness of her life to that frail, wrinkled old woman who lay now so still in death.

"Oh, Fabia," she sobbed, "I never thanked you for all that you did for me."

Alegría wept uncontrollably and pounded her knees with her fists. She had known the old woman loved her totally, without reservation, as children know such things. Nor was Alejandro able to keep back the tears; he, too, knew he had been loved by the old woman. He felt an arm go across his shoulders. He did not know how long Rohona had been kneeling at his side.

"She was a good woman," Rohona said softly, "she made this family happy. We owe much to her."

As the coffin was carried from the church to the small *campo santo* for burial, María Angélica and Alegría followed, dressed in deep mourning as when any member of a family has died. They laid the old woman to rest in the hard ground, and María Angélica felt as if a heavy weight had been put on her heart. She felt a sudden apprehension and crossed herself quickly, but the sense of dread and foreboding that had seized her remained.

She could not know that to the north, near the old capital of San Gabriel, an emaciated man stumbled toward the dwellings, his pale eyes wild and crazed. His graying hair was so filthy and matted that the red still in it could not be seen. The man fell several times, always dragging himself up and continuing on.

"Governor, Governor!" he shouted as he neared the buildings, but all he saw were the closed bronze faces of natives who watched him as if he might have been a witch. They backed away when he approached.

He turned and entered some of the buildings, always calling, "Governor, Governor!" When he stumbled out, he ran to a group of Indians who again backed away at his approach.

"Where are they?" he shouted crazily. "Where are they? Where is the governor?"

He looked from one to another as they rubbed ashes on themselves.

"What the hell are you doing?" he yelled shrilly, not knowing ashes were used against witches. He whirled in circles looking frantically for a light-colored face but saw none.

"Where are they?" he roared, running from side to side.

A native stepped forward, hoping to get the witch to leave their village. He spoke in broken Castilian. "Pale ones go away, go south, many, many moons ago."

"No!" the crazy man screamed. "No!" He dug into a pouch around his neck and pulled out three nuggets. He thrust his hand toward the stony-faced Indians. They saw the shiny, yellow rocks and were afraid they were witches' magic.

"I found it. I found it!" The crazy man laughed hysterically.

"Go with them," the Indian spokesman said, pointing south. "Pale ones go that way."

The wild-eyed man shoved the nuggets back into the pouch, whirled and started to run.

"Wait!" he yelled as if to someone just ahead of him. "Wait! Wait for me! I have found it! I have gold!" The man ran, stumbling until he was out of sight.

The Indian spokesman nodded to a few men who went to their houses and came back with bows and quivers of arrows. Without a word they followed the witch who ran, stumbling, yelling, and shouting for the governor to wait. When he was some distance from the village, one of the men gave a signal and when the witch climbed down the side of an arroyo, arrows flew, thudding into his back. He pitched forward, and blood gushed from his mouth onto the hard ground. His lips moved silently for a moment and then were still. The Indians piled rocks and sifted dirt over the lifeless body.

María Angélica was never to know that her husband had been buried the same day as old Fabia. She did not know that her black dress of mourning had served for two deaths. Vicente had, for her, died many years before.

# Chapter 35

On December 21, 1618, a new governor and military escort arrived in the little capital of Santa Fé. Don Juan de Eulate was a presumptuous, self-important, profit-minded man. He was a poor choice for *Nuevo México* but that was unknown during the many parties given in the capital city to welcome him and to celebrate the Christmas season.

A ball was held in the Casa Real and everyone invited wore his or her finest apparel to meet the new head of government.

Despite the fact that she would be required to dress in something other than her usual peasant attire, Alegría was delighted at the prospect of the party. She loved the fast, lively folk dances of *Nuevo México,* but she had never been to a ball before.

María Angélica worked feverishly preparing the clothes for her children. She wanted them to create a good impression on the new arrivals. From an old trunk she took the mulberry silk dress she had worn long years ago during the Act of Possession when Oñate had laid claim to *Nuevo México*. How the time had flown.

For some reason she remembered that terrible night when Vicente had forced Fabia to tell their fortunes. The old woman had been all too accurate. It was twenty years ago to the month that the Maese had died at Ácoma. Oñate was in disgrace. And Vicente? Fabia had said he would discover gold, but no one would believe him and he would die insane. That part of the fortune was surely wrong for Vicente had never returned.

María Angélica smoothed the wrinkles in the mulberry silk with her hands, and the musty smell of age drifted up, enveloping her. She was thirty-eight. She could be a grandmother although no gray had yet come to her dark hair and her skin was still relatively smooth thanks to Fabia's recipe for herb cream. Hands calloused from work and fine lines at the corners of her eyes were the only signs of age. She was content with her life; she had had her share of happiness, of blessings. If she could see her children married and settled, she could ask no more.

She shook out the mulberry silk and hung it in the courtyard to air before she would iron it and fit it to Alegría. Unfortunately she didn't have the necessary accoutrements for Alegría to wear under the gown. A scarcity of linen made for a scarcity of underclothes and there were few women in *Nuevo México* who wore anything beneath their clothes. But it didn't matter. Her daughter would have an elegant dress to wear to meet the new governor.

She went through Vicente's old clothes and found a rich velvet doublet in addition to a pair of silk hose that needed just a spot of mending. By the time she was through, she had an outfit for Alejandro that would be appropriately distinguished-looking. She had no doubts that he would be the most handsome man there. He would turn the heads of all the girls, and she knew he already inspired respect among the soldiers for his riding skill and ability with any sort of weapon.

She hoped that he would make a good impression upon the new governor, for Eulate would be in a position to aid the young man so that he might later assume an important role in the province. She was certain that Alejandro's ability to read and write would be an advantage over the illiterate, if pureblood, Spanish young men who might seek the governor's favor.

The mulberry silk fit Alegría well except that it was a bit short. The girl, who had just passed her seventeenth birthday, was slightly taller than her mother. Alejandro looked stunning in his Castilian clothes and much taller and broader-shouldered than in the simple loose trousers and shirt he usually wore. His bearing was dignified, and he looked much older than his eighteen and a half years. When his mother saw him, she had to wipe away the tears because he filled her with so much pride.

When Alegría entered the room, Alejandro gasped to see his sister in such finery. The contrast was so great from the unkempt way in which he usually saw her, that he broke out laughing. Alegría, who felt uncomfortable anyway, fled from the room in embarrassment. María Angélica went after her and, with much cajoling, brought her back.

"Say you're sorry," his mother said to him.

Alejandro looked contrite. "I really am sorry, Aley. You look beautiful. Do you want to laugh at me in this getup?" He motioned to his clothes and did a silly little dance.

The pout left Alegría's lips, but she said petulantly, "I'll forgive you, Aley, only if you promise to punch anyone at the ball who laughs at me."

Alejandro smiled but said with seriousness, "No one will laugh at you, Aley. I can promise you that."

* * *

He was right. No one at the ball laughed at the beautiful flame-haired young woman. Her mother had pinned Alegría's mop of red hair in a mass of curls on top of her head. By having her unruly hair up out of her face, the young woman's gray eyes appeared even larger, her eyelashes even longer. But without the fringe of disheveled hair covering them, the gray eyes revealed brief moments of something undefinable.

The mulberry silk was still beautiful and more sumptuous than anything to be found in the province. She was a tall girl and stood very straight, and that night she looked as indulged as the daughter of a viceroy.

Silence fell over the Casa Real when she entered, and her mother could see her daughter's nervousness as all eyes fell on her, but quickly the buzz of voices and the music began again. María Angélica saw appear on her daughter's lips that unrestrained and incautious smile that was so typical of Alegría's face and hoped she would do nothing that would show her sometimes poor judgment.

Alegría was quickly surrounded by a bevy of men hoping for a dance with her, and occasionally María Angélica heard the laugh that was so characteristic of her willful daughter. She wished Alegría would act just a bit more reserved around the young men.

In the beginning Alejandro did not dance and tried to hide his nervousness, but his mother saw it and whispered to Dorotea who nodded and smiled.

"Well," Dorotea said as she walked up to Alejandro, "aren't you going to ask your Auntie to dance? After all, I want to be able to say that I danced with the most handsome man here."

He turned red and stammered something unintelligible, but Dorotea ignored his discomfort and took his arm.

"Just think how jealous I am going to make all those pretty young things out there." She led Alejandro out amongst the dancers and they joined the others and were quickly moving with the music.

Afterward, Alejandro bowed deeply to his mother. "Care to take your chances with me, *mamá?*"

"But of course, kind sir," she said with a laugh and a little curtsy.

She leaned forward at one point and whispered to him, "I think there is a certain little dark-eyed girl in a crimson dress who would not refuse an offer to dance."

Alejandro turned his head slightly and followed the direction of his mother's eyes. He saw the girl in the crimson dress, now shyly looking at her clasped hands. When the dance was over they returned to where Dorotea was standing.

"Seize the moment, *hijito,*" María Angélica said lightly.

Alejandro smiled and bowed. "If you two ladies will excuse me," he said.

Alejandro danced with the girl in the crimson dress and with another and another. Clearly he was not scorned as a half-breed by the New Mexicans there. His kind was increasing rapidly in the isolated province. Some of the soldiers of the newly arrived military detail, however, looked disdainfully at the tall, good-looking half-breed who spoke better Castilian than they did.

The new governor took a great interest in the beautiful gray-eyed woman, her lovely daughter, and the handsome young half-Indian who accompanied them, and before he greeted them in the receiving line, he had heard their story.

"*Doña* María Angélica de Vizcarra and her daughter the *Señorita* Alegría," the royal notary had announced when they arrived at the head of the reception line, "and her ward, the young man, Alejandro."

María Angélica curtsied to the governor, and he took her hand and brought it to his lips for too long a time, paying her an honor she was not sure she wanted, but she murmured politely, "May your stay in *Nuevo México* be a pleasant one, Governor."

"Indeed I hope so," Eulate answered, smiling broadly at her before he turned and took Alegría's hand and then greeted the young man who had accompanied them.

As the next couple were announced, Eulate thought it fortunate that the woman with gray eyes was a widow, despite the fact that it seemed she still believed her husband would return after an absence of almost fourteen years.

He appraised the daughter. She was a gorgeous thing, and he knew he would like to be the one to tame her. Both women tempted him, and he thought that his stay in *Nuevo México* might be much more pleasant than he had imagined. The young half-breed interested him, too.

"He might be of use in dealing with the natives," Eulate said later to the former governor who stood beside him and who had supplied interesting details of the inhabitants of the province.

"Not only does he speak one of the native languages," the former governor commented, "but he can actually read and write Castilian as well."

Eulate's eyebrows raised and he smiled. "He may indeed prove an asset to me, but," he paused, "for the moment, I intend to see that young, red-haired thing up close again."

The governor walked to where Alegría stood surrounded by young men. "If you will excuse me, gentlemen," he said, and immediately they backed away, making a corridor.

"Señorita, may I have the honor?"

"Of course you can," Alegría said as if he might have been just one of the others who had crowded around her.

He danced one dance with her, and the blood pounded through his veins as it had when he was younger. She was not demure like so many young women. She laughed with no embarrassment, and she looked directly at him, uninhibited, an unusual light in her eyes. There was something untamed about her, something unsettling. Perhaps it was the curious way her eyes seemed to smile and then turn momentarily vacant. Eulate knew she must drive the young men wild, for she did the older men, as he could attest. But he would be careful. He would dance with her only once. When the music ended, he thanked her for the dance, returned her to her admirers, and started across the floor to her mother.

María Angélica was flattered that the new governor was taking such an obvious interest in her children. She did not particularly like the way his eyes rested upon her as he crossed the room, but she would not jeopardize her children's future by appearing cold and aloof as she usually did around men who might be inclined to ease the loneliness of a widow.

"Doña María Angélica," Eulate said with a bow, "I had the honor to dance with your lovely daughter, and now I would like the honor of dancing with her equally beautiful mother."

Eulate did not limit himself to just one dance with her. He felt no need to be careful, and he was enjoying comparing mother and daughter and considering the possibilities of his tenure as governor.

The daughter had inherited her mother's incredible, large gray eyes with their thick dark lashes, but there was a serenity in the mother's eyes—a calm intelligence that spoke more of deep, sustaining passion than of the abandon of youth. She did not look like a woman who had been waiting fourteen years for the man she loved to return. She seemed to possess a deep contentment and a satisfaction that only a man or deep religious faith could give a woman. She intrigued him and aroused his passion as much as the daughter had. The daughter he would take in a meadow quickly and overpoweringly like a stallion. The mother he would take slowly, deeply, and satisfyingly between the silk sheets he had brought to *Nuevo México*.

Although María Angélica tried to be attentive to the new governor, she nonetheless had ample opportunity to survey the young men. It might have been better to look for a husband for her daughter among the older men, perhaps a widower, who had land and cattle and stable roots in *Nuevo México*, but first she would look among the young men, men whose vitality could match that of her frequently intemperate daughter.

There were several prospects who had come with the governor's retinue. The governor's secretary, although not handsome, seemed like a well-mannered and educated man. She guessed he was about twenty-six. There were a few others—an arrogant, good-looking lieutenant of about twenty-three or so, a dark-eyed captain who exuded confidence, and several others who also bore watching. She would have to mingle more with the community than she had in the past in order to learn something of the men who had recently come north.

She knew the ball was a success as far as her children were concerned, and she was exceedingly happy as she walked home, her arms linked in theirs. They laughed gaily about different things that had happened at the ball. A soft snow began to fall, and they turned their faces up to it, laughing as the huge flakes landed on their skin, tickling them. Snow dusted the ground, and it was as if they were walking on a lamb's wool carpet toward their home.

They did not see the man standing on the roof of their house looking at them, a buffalo robe thrown over his shoulders.

Rohona watched them, proud of his beautiful family, but there was a sadness in his eyes that was hidden by the night. His son was of two bloods, and although he spoke the language of Áco, and Rohona had told him much about the old life, he knew Alejandro had been raised as a Spanish youth, and it left a heaviness in his heart. Their customs were his son's customs, and his son's children would never know Áco. They would not know how to make a prayer stick to send to the K'atsina for rain; they would not know the sacredness of corn; they would not know about Iyatiku, the mother of them all.

Within two months he would be free. In February he would have been a slave for twenty years. When he first heard the sentence the gray-haired leader pronounced, twenty years seemed a lifetime. He thought his servitude would have no end. But it would.

He wanted to feel his freedom standing on the high rock of Áco. He wanted to dance for the K'atsina, although he knew he could not dance beautifully for them with his lameness. He wanted to sit in the *kiva* with its intoxicating aroma of piñon wood listening to a prayer sung by a medicine man.

Yet, how could he leave the woman with hair the color of wet pine bark and with the soft gray eyes he loved to have look at him? How could he leave the woman who had given him two beautiful children, the woman who filled his days with contentment and gave him so much pleasure at night in the bed he had come to like better than pelts on a hard floor? How could he leave them, knowing that they would have no one to provide for them? He knew he could not.

Áco had been rebuilt. He had heard that the village was almost as large as it once had been. Almost all the Ácoma slaves had eventually run away, save he and Siya and perhaps a few others. They had gone back to the high sandstone mesa to live and with them had gone not a small number of Queres-speaking natives from Santo Domingo, San Felipe, Cochiti—natives who disliked the Spaniards and disliked the forced labor they had to do for either the long-robes at the missions or the horseback-riding *encomenderos*.

Not only had the disaffected Queres-speaking sought refuge at Áco, but natives from other villages had also helped swell the population atop the White Rock. Rohona was glad the mesa was no longer uninhabited. Áco had not died.

He descended from the roof, shook off the snow, and entered the house. He went into the *sala* where he heard them laughing. Alegría ran to him and took his arm.

"Oh, uncle," she laughed, "you should have seen me dance!" She recounted in a babbling rush of words and gestures all that had happened at the ball.

At length María Angélica took advantage of a lull in the talk. "It is late. We must get some sleep."

Reluctantly, they all retired to their rooms, and when he thought Alejandro was asleep, Rohona rose and went to join María Angélica.

She was awake and waiting for him. A tallow candle flickered in the room, filling it with a soft glow. She held out her arms to him, and he came to her filled with passion. She slipped her gown off and her naked body arched against him. There was a different intensity to his lovemaking that night.

Afterwards she lay in his arms, her face resting against his chest. She knew something was wrong. She lifted her face and looked at him, running her fingers over his cheeks and mouth and down his arm.

"I love you," she whispered.

He crushed her to him tightly and murmured, "And how much love I have for you, Mía."

"What is it?" she whispered. "What makes you sad?"

For a long moment he did not speak, but then he said quietly, "The twenty years are almost gone."

She was suddenly very cold. The years had disappeared almost without her notice. She had raised her children and loved the man she considered her husband. The length of the servitude was meaningless to her and she had never really contemplated the term of it. He obviously had. She had never thought of him as a slave. It had always been to her as if they were man and wife. Had he lived all these years feeling that he was an *esclavo?* The thought cut like a knife when she considered that perhaps he had.

It was several moments before she could speak. "In all these years I have never thought of you as a slave," she said. Her voice caught. "I have just wanted you near, as my husband."

"I do not feel like a slave, Mía. I, too, have wanted to be as your husband and to live with you and our children. I love you more than words can express, here," he said as he tapped his chest. "I have always had much need of you. I will always have much need of you."

He said quietly, "Mía, I am not returning to Áco."

She trembled with relief. "I do not think that I could live without you."

He tasted her salty tears as he kissed her, and she pressed her hips against him, needing him, wanting him again. This time he took her slowly, gently and he gloried in her need, knowing that he needed her just as much.

The idea did not come to her immediately. One day it just appeared in her mind, and it made her happy to think about it. He had chosen to stay with her where he would still be no more than a slave in the eyes of everyone. He could have returned to Áco and could have lived in total freedom, but he had chosen not to. Why could he not, however, return to Áco to visit, to see his home, to talk to friends?

On the anniversary of his servitude, she asked him. At first he said that he could not, for there were many things to be done, and he did not want to leave her alone.

"It would make me very happy if you were to go," she said. "Please, go for me." She touched his hand. "Take Alejandro with you. Show him Áco—he should see it."

A smile came to Rohona's lips as he thought about his son seeing his homeland. He tried to hide his emotion. "Yes," he said to her, "I like your idea. I would like to go and take the boy. It will be good, but we shall return before planting time."

For several days Rohona worked feverishly, preparing. He hunted game to leave with them. Alejandro was filled with excitement about the trip and helped with the preparations.

Alegría was distraught. She, too, wanted to go to the fabled village. "Why should Alejandro get to go when I cannot?" she demanded angrily. "I speak Queres just as well as he does."

Her mother patted her hand. "You are a girl, *hija*. It wouldn't be proper."

"Proper?" Alegría snapped. She jerked her head around and stared into the distance. When she spoke her words were hard. "I'll go one of these days whether you like it or not. You'll see."

Rohona and Alejandro left for Áco near the first of March. They rode horses and with them they carried a note written by María Angélica that said the horses were hers and the two men had her permission to use them.

It had not occurred to her, however, to inform the governor that they were making the journey. It did not seem his business. She was surprised and flustered when he appeared at her door and evidenced his displeasure at having learned they were gone. She stammered momentarily, thinking furiously what she should say.

"The boy grew up speaking Queres. He has wished to see Áco for years—that is where the Indian is from."

It seemed her answer was satisfactory, for the governor appeared mollified and said thoughtfully, "Yes, I suppose that might be a good idea. I have heard there are some renegade Indians living there—it might not be a bad idea to see what they are up to. As soon as the boy gets back, send him to me. I want to talk to him. But what about the cripple?" he asked. "Are you sure he will come back?"

María Angélica cringed at the word, but she managed to keep her voice even. "Yes, he will return. He has converted to Christianity. Áco has no mission."

Alegría was not her usual happy, carefree self after Alejandro and Rohona left. The house was strangely silent.

"I am lonely," she would complain as she stared vacantly into space, doing nothing.

María Angélica smiled sadly and answered her, "I, too, miss them, *hijita*." But a faint worry began to tug at her.

Once when she passed the *sala* she saw Alegría sitting slumped in a chair, brooding. A vision from the past swept over her, and she was suddenly reminded of Vicente and how he would sit, staring into space. She crossed herself quickly and tried to push the thoughts from her mind.

She sighed a deep sigh of relief when Alegría's spirits rose. They began to have frequent visitors, and the heavy silence left the house. At least one young man came calling every night and sometimes more than one appeared at the door. The governor, too, became a frequent visitor.

She welcomed the young men eagerly while studying them carefully. But Alegría did not seem to develop a serious feeling for any of them, and María Angélica was sure they represented nothing more than a respite from boredom for her daughter.

Against her better judgment, but wanting only to keep Alegría occupied, she allowed her to go riding alone with the dark-eyed captain.

"When he suggested we dismount and rest for a moment," Alegría reported later, "I just laughed and raced off, yelling back, 'I'm not tired!' You should have seen his face, *mamá*, but, truly, I am a better rider than he will ever be."

Lieutenant Reinaldo de la Torre, an arrogant, good-looking young man, was one of the most persistent suitors. He had done nothing untoward, but there was something about him that María Angélica did not like. Perhaps it was a coldness to his eyes that reminded her of Vicente, and she felt a measure of relief when near the end of April Rohona and Alejandro returned.

Alejandro delighted Alegría and his mother with his tales of the White Rock. "I had no idea how immense the mesa is, and the view from the top is magnificent, *mamá*. You must see it sometime."

"And what about me?" Alegría asked with a pout.

"You would love it, Aley," he said. "It gives you the feeling that you are a hawk soaring high in the air surveying the ground below. I am amazed that the Spaniards ever conquered the place, perched as it is on what seems to me an impregnable citadel."

"Had they not had their cannon," Rohona said, "they would never have breached the mesa, but the Spaniards' knowledge gave them victory. That is a good lesson, Alejandro.

"Victory comes with knowledge. The Spaniards have the knowledge of guns and horses—that makes them very powerful against those who do not have that knowledge. One should learn all that is possible to learn."

"One aspect of the journey to Áco saddened me, though," Alejandro said with disappointment. "I don't think they liked me very well. They are distrustful of strangers, and although I spoke their language well, I think they hated me because I have the blood of the Spaniards in me."

That very thing was acutely painful to Rohona. He loved his son so deeply it had not occurred to him how the people would react to the boy. He should have known, however.

He wanted to shout, "He's my son! He's my son!" But he did not. He, more than anyone, had reason to know why they would hate Spaniards, but he also knew that there were those who were good among the Spaniards just as there were good, as well as bad, among the Ácoma.

He wished he could have told his people that, but they would not have listened to him.

# Chapter 36

"Yes, sir," Alejandro responded to the governor's questions about Áco. "Yes, I was there for almost two months, and I lived among them on the top of the mesa."

"Is the village rebuilt?" Eulate asked him.

"Yes, completely. One would never know the Spaniards had burned it."

"It's true you speak their language? Would you say they accepted you as one of them?"

"Yes, I speak Queres, but no, they do not accept me, sir," Alejandro said, trying to hide his disappointment. "Excuse me, sir, but they hate the Spanish, and I have the blood of Spaniards in me; therefore, they distrust and dislike me."

"In your opinion, what do you think we, the civil government, could do that would please the natives most?"

Alejandro thought for some moments. "Allow them to keep their old customs—to dance their dances, to have their native healers in addition to the Spanish friars."

Eulate said nothing as he sat thoughtfully. "Thank you," he said, rising and putting out his hand to Alejandro, "you are probably right. You have a good head on your shoulders. *Nuevo México* has need of men like you."

In May, the month of the last frost, the planting of the corn began and the *rodeo* of horses and cattle that had ranged free throughout the winter occupied all the men. The livestock Vicente brought north had thrived and multiplied under the care of such good men as Domingo and Cipriano. María Angélica's herds were now a source of some wealth, and existence in *Nuevo México* was not as precarious as it once had been. Others had also built up herds, and the colony seemed that it would finally survive.

Alejandro loved animals, and under the tutelage of Domingo and Cipriano, it would not be very many years before he would have enough skill and knowledge to be entrusted with the entire operation of his mother's holdings.

Branding had been going on for several days, and Alejandro had been up before dawn every day, not returning home until after sunset, hot, dirty, and tired.

Alegría chided him that he never had time to ride with her anymore. "All you do is work, work, work," she complained as they sat in the courtyard after supper. The night air was cool and soft, and a few stars had become visible as the twilight disappeared into darkness.

"But there is work to do," Alejandro said apologetically. "I am a man now, I cannot spend my time riding all over everywhere with you."

"So you're a man now and have no more time for me," Alegría laughed bitterly, and he heard the hurt in her voice.

"That's not true, Aley."

"Then promise you'll ride with me tomorrow," she said quickly.

There was a short pause. "*Muy bien*, a short ride tomorrow afternoon."

"Oh, thank you, Aley," she said gaily. "It was so lonesome around here when you and Uncle were gone, and since you've been back all you have done is work." Her voice had an unusual edge to it. "You know I can't stand being lonely."

Alejandro laughed. "It didn't sound lonely around here to me what with all the soldiers coming around and howling at your window!"

Alegría intended to make him keep his promise, and when he hadn't returned by mid-afternoon the following day, she rode out looking for him. He was still branding cattle.

"You promised," she said, when he protested that he had too much to do, and tears welled in her eyes.

"All right," he said, unable to bear her tears, "just let me finish up those two calves and then wash off a little. The *herradero* is a dirty job."

"Why don't you just wash off in the spring?" she asked. "That's where I wanted to ride anyway—down to that little one we found years ago where the trees hang over."

*"Bueno,"* he answered, "you go on. I'll catch you."

She turned and rode off at a gallop. Alejandro smiled as he watched her unruly red hair glinting in the sunlight like sparks flying from a blacksmith's hammer.

He would not have smiled had he seen the soldier who also watched Alegría ride off alone.

Alegría liked to ride at a breakneck gallop but usually restrained herself because of the many lectures Domingo had given her about taking care of one's horses. That afternoon she started at a fast run to feel the wind in her face but then slowed her pace and savored the warm May afternoon. Here and there a few low-growing white and lavender flowers sprouted valiantly out of the dry, rocky dirt among the piñon and juniper.

At length she reached the hidden spring, which was announced by a few overhanging cottonwoods and willow. She rode under the trees and into the shaded opening. The cottonwoods' new leaves were bright and shimmery. She dismounted and tethered the horse to a willow branch and then went to sit on some lichen-covered rocks above where the water bubbled up. It was one of their favorite spots. She and Alejandro had found it when they were young, and they had considered it their secret place where no grown-up could find them.

That, a moment later, turned out to be just a foolish childhood belief.

"Lieutenant de la Torre," she said, looking up, as the soldier rode into the small clearing.

*"Buenas tardes, señorita,"* he said, smiling as he dismounted. "I did not know this godforsaken land had such an enchanting spot."

She lifted her arms exuberantly toward the canopy of branches. "It's beautiful, isn't it? I love to come here, but there are other pretty spots in *Nuevo México,* Lieutenant, you just haven't been here long enough to find them."

"Oh, but I think I have," he said as he approached her. She smiled at him, not realizing the intent of his words. He sat down on the ground near her. "Your *mamá* lets you come out here alone?"

"She lets me go wherever I want," Alegría said with a toss of her head. "I'm a very good rider—she doesn't worry."

"What about wild animals?"

She laughed. "Perhaps in the mountains you will find bears and mountain lions, but here there are just rabbits and maybe a coyote."

"You are a wild little creature too, aren't you?" he asked with a lazy grin as he reached out and ran his fingers down her bare arm.

She jerked her arm away and started to rise. "I think perhaps I should be going back."

"Not so soon, *niña,*" he said as he grasped her wrist and pulled her back down next to him.

"Let go of me," she yelped as she tried to scramble away, but he yanked her back and pawed at her clothing.

"Let go!" she said angrily—but he did not let go, and her blouse ripped as she tried to jerk away. He grabbed her and pinned her to the ground.

"Now I shall see what I have hungered for night after night since I arrived in this damnable province," he said as he pulled at her skirt.

She struggled madly and hit him with her fists, but he managed to get her skirt off and whistled when he saw she wore nothing else underneath.

He grunted as he threw his leg over her and sat on her, pinning her to the ground. "Now, let's get the rest of that *camisa* off," he said and pulled the torn blouse from her.

She bit deeply into his hand and he let out an oath, then laughed, "*Dios*, you are a *fiera!*"

He stood up and for a moment she was motionless, surprised at his action.

"Now I want to see you in all your glory before I tame you," he said with a crude laugh.

She scrambled to her feet and started to run for her horse, but he yanked her back and slapped her across the face.

"Stand still," he growled, "I want to look at you." She stood there trembling, her eyes downcast as tears rolled down her cheeks.

"Jesus, Mary, Joseph," he whistled as he looked at her. "What a body."

There was a strangled noise, and Alegría looked up in shock to see a man's arm around the soldier's throat and a knife pressed against his neck.

"Aley!" she gasped. She had not heard him approach, nor, obviously, had the soldier. Rohona had taught him well.

"Now let's see *you* disrobe, *soldado*," Alejandro said between his teeth.

Alegría would not have recognized his voice, it sounded so cold and murderous. She grabbed for her clothes, yanking on her skirt.

The soldier tried to speak, but Alejandro tightened his arm around the man's neck with a jerk and the soldier gasped for air. "Take your breeches off," he ordered.

Alegría stood in shocked silence as she watched the man fumble with his clothing. "Everything, *soldado*," Alejandro said, and the man struggled but finally stood naked, his breeches around his ankles. Alejandro gave him a shove and the soldier tripped and fell. Alejandro held the knife blade poised between his fingers.

"Take your boots off, and if you make one move, I'll send this knife through your heart as if you were a toad."

The lieutenant did as he was told. Keeping his eye on him, Alejandro backed to the man's horse, pulled the sword out of its scabbard, and removed a dagger and a matchlock pistol. He took a rope and quickly looped it with his teeth and free hand. At that moment the soldier thought he saw his chance and leaped up and ran at Alejandro.

Like an arrow, the knife flew out of Alejandro's hand, and with a thunk, impaled the lieutenant's forearm. The soldier grabbed at his arm, crying out in pain. As soon as the knife left Alejandro's hand, the rope was stretched taut in both and he leaped forward, twisting the rope around de la Torre's neck, yanking him to the ground. With his knee on his back, Alejandro pulled the knife from the soldier's arm.

"Get on your horse," Alejandro growled, dragging the man to his feet.

Stripes of bright red blood were swiped across the horse's neck as the man mounted with a shove from Alejandro who wrapped the rope that hung from the man's neck around his wrists then down around one foot. He tossed the end under the horse's belly and walked around to the other side and tied the rope around the other foot and back up around the wrists.

The man looked in pain. "Are you going to let me bleed to death up here, you heathen bastard?"

"I ought to, you son of a whore," Alejandro said as he walked over and picked up the man's shirt and ripped it up. With the strips he bound the man's wounded forearm, none too gently. Then he led the horse through the trees, gave it a wallop on the rump, and sent it headlong over the rough terrain in the direction of the *villa*.

"Pray that it's dark by the time you get back!" Alejandro yelled after the man.

When he returned to her, Alegría was lying, head on her arm, sobbing uncontrollably. She had pulled on her skirt but the remnants of the blouse did not cover her breasts. Alejandro sat down beside her, and she threw herself into his arms.

"Aley, Aley," he said gently, smoothing her hair, "everything is all right. Don't cry." She trembled and he felt the heat of her bare breasts against his chest.

She raised her head and looked at him, her cheeks tear-stained and dirty. Her gray eyes were unwavering.

"Oh, Aley," she whispered, and kissed him roughly on the mouth.

Before he knew it, she was pushing him back on the ground. Her arms were around him, crushing herself against him, and she clung to him as she kissed him fiercely and passionately. She pressed her body against him in a wanting she did nothing to control.

"Aley," he said with shock. "What are you doing?"

She pulled off her skirt and leaned forward so her breasts touched his face, and she pulled his hand over her belly and between her legs. She made sounds in her throat.

"Aley, my God," he started to say but she clamped her hand over his mouth so he could not continue. An unusual look filled her gray eyes and she began to pull at his clothes.

"No, Aley," he whispered, "no," as he took hold of her hands.

"Yes," she said with vehemence, as she pulled his hands to her breasts and rubbed them against her small nipples that were already taut and hard.

She made sounds in her throat again as her hands began to run over his body, and he seemed unable to move. She sat up and pulled his shirt from him and he protested, but she ran her hands over his naked chest and her hand slid down to grasp him intimately.

"Oh, God, no," he groaned. He took her by the shoulders to push her away, but instead she pushed his loose trousers down and slithered her body along the length of his. Her weight pressed him against the damp ground, and with her feet she shoved the trousers farther down and straddled him, guiding herself onto him. He closed his eyes and the weight of her body slid fully on him.

She cried out with the pain, and he withdrew quickly, whispering, "Oh my God, Aley, I'm so sorry."

She clutched at him, moving her hips against him. "You can't stop now. Love me, love me."

"Aley, Aley, no," he rasped hoarsely.

"Don't stop," she cried as she wound her fingers in his hair and pulled her face toward his and kissed him voraciously, thrusting her tongue into his mouth, thrusting her hips against him, and then he was inside her and she was making tiny animal sounds as her legs grasped his body. A loud roar exploded from his chest, and his body shook in spasms, and then he lay still as she made small, mewling sounds.

He rolled her to the side and lay back, silent and unmoving, his forearm across his eyes. She rolled onto her side toward him and laid her head on his damp chest.

"I love you, Aley," she whispered. "Please love me. You *have* to love me!"

She lifted her head, and he felt her eyes on him, and he opened his own. Her eyes burned into him with their intensity, and her tousled hair framed her face like a halo of fire.

She bent and put her mouth on his, and he closed his eyes, glad to shut out the look in hers that he was unable to bear. He felt her tears on his own cheeks, and he pulled his mouth from hers, a puzzled look on his face.

"Oh, Aley," she said, smiling strangely through her tears, "how I have loved you! I have always loved you, idolized you since I was tiny. How I wanted you then to be my real brother! You were always so handsome and good to me—and I loved you so much, but now I am glad you are not my brother, for I want you to love me like a woman."

She sat up, arching her back and running her hands down her body, swaying gently, cupping her breasts with her hands as she looked at him.

"Possess me, consume me. You are the person I love most in this world."

Alejandro looked at her. The companion of his childhood, the girl he had loved like a sister, he now had loved like a woman. She laid her head down on his chest again, and he could feel her lips pressed to his skin.

He could feel her teeth against his skin, biting him, and her hands ran over his body.

"Aley, no. We must get back," he said hoarsely. He pushed her head off him, rose, and pulled her to her feet. "Come, let's try to clean ourselves up a little."

They scooped up handfuls of water from the spring and bathed themselves as best they could. He could not meet her gaze and looked down as he washed himself. She picked up her skirt and brushed the dirt from it before she pulled it on. She tried to pull the remnants of her blouse together but Alejandro spoke, handing her his shirt.

"Here, you'd better wear this."

They mounted their horses and without speaking started back toward Santa Fé. Before they reached the *villa,* Alegría stopped her horse and faced him. Her eyes were bright.

"I want you again." Her voice had a hoarse quality to it. "Tonight."

"Aley," he said, looking away from her, "we can't."

She reached out and grasped his arm. "Please."

He shook his head. "We shouldn't." He turned back and saw her eyes. He hesitated and looked away again. "Tonight. Just tonight. I will come to your room after Uncle has gone to *mamá*'s room."

Her eyes widened in surprise. "After he goes to *mamá*'s room?" she asked in a shocked voice. "What do you mean?"

Alejandro looked back at her. "After all these years you don't know?"

"Know what?" she asked.

"That they are lovers."

Her shock was genuine. "No, no . . . " she stammered, "I, I didn't know. How, how long have they . . . " Her question trailed off.

"I suppose since your father went away for the last time. *Mamá* was undoubtedly lonely and still very beautiful as she is today. Uncle is a good man, he cares for the family, he lives in the house—they were always near each other. I suppose it was natural. I first found out when I was about eight or so. One night I was still awake when he got out of bed. I got up to see where he was going, and I saw him go into *mamá*'s room. I knew why he had gone there. I ran back and jumped in my bed. I was so happy they loved each other. I used to daydream that he was my father and *mamá* my real mother, and you my sister, and we all loved each other and lived as a real family far, far away from here."

Alegría looked at him. "It seems we had the same dream." They rode the rest of the way in silence.

María Angélica's face drained of color as she listened to Alejandro tell the story of what had happened to Alegría with the soldier. He did not tell her what had happened between the two of them.

"Are you sure he did nothing?" María Angélica pressed him as she looked at Alegría's filthy, crumpled skirt, the shirt of Alejandro's she wore, her tangled hair, and the unusual look on her face.

"He did not touch her, I swear, *mamá,*" Alejandro said.

María Angélica walked over to Alegría and took her in her arms to comfort her, but Alegría pushed her away. "I'm all right, *mamá,*" she said.

"I'm going to tell the governor what has happened," Alejandro said, "in case de la Torre has not returned or if he has and has told a different story."

"Yes, do," she replied. "From now on, Alegría," she added, "you are never to go riding alone. You must always go with Alejandro."

De la Torre had not returned by the time Alejandro spoke to the governor about the incident. Eulate evinced anger at the assault on Alegría, but he laughed heartily at the manner in which Alejandro had handled the affair.

"I would say," the governor laughed, "that the punishment was appropriate." But then he added seriously, "De la Torre will not forget this blow to his pride, you can be sure of that."

"I know, he will be fit to be tied."

Eulate laughed at the joke. "He is tied already—trussed up like a chicken so it sounds, but have a care when your back is turned." The governor said matter-of-factly, "You probably should have killed the bastard."

"I would have done it with pleasure, sir, but—he is one of your soldiers."

"If he tries to kill you—which he will certainly do," the governor said, "soldier of mine or not, you have every right to protect yourself even if it means that one of you dies."

By nightfall word had spread and the entire *villa* knew what had happened, for Eulate had sent out a small group to look for the naked soldier, trussed to his horse.

De la Torre was found in a clump of juniper near the *villa*. He had managed to stop the horse and was evidently awaiting darkness to make his ignominious entrance. His fury far surpassed his humiliation, and there were many who heard him swear he would kill the half-breed at the next opportunity.

When the oath filtered back to María Angélica, she was terrified. But Alejandro had friends and people who would be alert. No one would have any qualms about dispatching the soldier who had attacked Alegría and threatened Alejandro.

For his own part Alejandro was not afraid. Rohona had taught him valuable lessons in silence and being alert to what was near. And Alejandro knew the Castilians, knew their weapons, their treachery, and the ways their minds worked. He would not be an easy victim.

The night Alejandro and Alegría returned from the spring, he went to her room as he said he would, and in spite of his protests that they should not, from that night on, they were constant lovers.

She was always naked, waiting for him. When he opened the door softly, she ran to him, and sometimes she would free him from his clothes so that he could enter her while they stood there embracing. Then they would go to the bed, and she would urge him to take her again.

Sometimes afterwards she would sit on the bed looking at him. "I could spend every hour with you," she would say as she ran her hands over his chest and down across his belly. She would reach out and take his hands and place them on her breasts to caress her, and her nipples always peaked under his touch. She would let her flaming hair cascade around his face and would pull his face close to kiss his eyes and kiss away the look in them. She would take his hands and run them along her legs until they reached her most sensitive part, and she would throw her head back, moaning softly, biting her lips, begging him.

Alegría and Alejandro scarcely looked at each other at home. María Angélica assumed it was from embarrassment at what had happened, although they still went riding frequently. When they returned, however, Alegría did not look at her brother, and she rarely laughed. That had been the most common sound in the household. The rooms now seemed strangely silent.

Again María Angélica had an unpleasant sensation as Vicente flashed through her mind. Although Alegría was pleasant, unlike her father, she had become unusually quiet and withdrawn. She refused to see any young men, and she would not attend parties or social gatherings.

Alejandro, too, had changed. His mother knew it was not because he was afraid of the threat against his life; she knew he was fearless as well as totally confident in his abilities. He worked hard. Domingo and Cipriano had even said he was driving himself too much, and they were worried.

What had happened that afternoon that had affected her children so? She prayed for guidance from God and that soon things would be back to normal in the household.

She voiced her concerns to Rohona, but what she said sounded trivial and unimportant although he, too, had felt a change. But he was busy with the planting, leaving before dawn and not returning until dark, and neither was aware of standing on the edge of an abyss.

# Chapter 37

Eulate was becoming the most popular governor with the natives that *Nuevo México* had yet had. He had given orders to the *alcaldes*, Spaniards who served in a petty judicial capacity in the pueblos, to inform the natives that they would be allowed to perform their ceremonial dances using whatever traditional accoutrements they desired.

His decree was of major significance. Of all the demands the Spaniards had made on the Indians, prohibiting dances and rituals had been one of the most onerous. The very fabric and continuity of Pueblo society was based upon such ceremonials and to prohibit them meant to eventually extinguish their identity as a people.

Many objects used in the ceremonials held special significance and were sacred to the natives. Pine boughs were not merely for decoration; they symbolized the everlasting, the perpetual birth. Corn was the most sacred, central item of their lives and prayers. K'atsina masks were not merely masks that hid the identity of the wearer; they were a vehicle for transubstantiation, a concept any Catholic would understand. The masks were considered alive and were regularly "fed" and had the power to make the person who wore the mask the real native deity. The person was merely the vehicle through which the K'atsina worked. Thus, when the priest destroyed the sacred masks, it was tantamount to destroying the K'atsina themselves. Eulate's decree that the Indians could use such things was a reversal of one aspect of Spanish oppression that had caused much bitterness and resentment among the pueblo dwellers.

In the place of the Indians' brightly colored, dance and music-filled religion in which all could participate, the natives were told they must accept a religion in which only one man, dressed in sumptuously brocaded and embroidered vestments, was allowed to participate. They felt scarce involvement in a religion that required them to kneel on hard dirt and watch a stranger intoning unintelligible words to some god they could not visualize who was to bring them some good, no evidence of which they had yet seen.

The decree of the governor, allowing practice of Pueblo ceremonials, had as profound an impact on the clergy as it did on the natives.

The friars had fought vigorously to destroy any and all elements of Pueblo religion. Absolute believers in the exclusivity of the Church, its evangelizers in *Nuevo México*, considered any Indian ritual devil worship, and the friars, therefore, had destroyed as many of the devil-inspired masks as they could.

For the governor to permit, let alone sanction, the Indian rituals and ceremonies undermined all that the priests had been working toward. Moreover, the decree was a blatant affront to the Church, which was the sole ostensible reason for the Spaniards to be in *Nuevo México*. The King had retained the province only because of Holy Mother Church. The friars, therefore, saw the civil government as subservient to them, its existence a mere protection for the friars as they carried on their work.

Eulate's decree meant only one thing to the priests: he had no regard whatsoever for their holy work and, as such, was an enemy of the Church and its sovereignty in *Nuevo México*. The Father Custodian, Fray Perea, was livid. A devout, dedicated messenger of the Word, Fray Perea vented the intensity of his anger at having his holy work undermined. He was an absolute believer in the supremacy of Church authority over that of civil authority and felt therefore that Eulate had no right nor jurisdiction in such a matter. Thus, the enmity between Church officers and civil officials over the question of power and authority in *Nuevo México* was continued and would continue as bitter as it had been between Governor Peralta and Fray Ordóñez.

Because of his decree Eulate became the friend of the Indians, but he had an underlying motive of which the natives were at first unaware. If there were any profit to be made in *Nuevo México*, it had to be made by means of Indian labor. The governors of the province were compensated by a salary for their four years' appointment, but few were willing to undertake such a venture for salary alone and looked for other means of revenue. As there was apparently no gold or silver in the province, other exports were sought. These, the governors as well as the friars and colonists learned, were products the natives made or were forced to produce. The cotton *mantas* the Indians wove and embroidered had market value in Mexico as did Indian slaves, tanned deer hides, buffalo or cattle hides, any type of livestock, piñon nuts, and salt. Indians worked as livestock herders, hide tanners, salt and piñon gatherers. The more Indians one had working for him, the more money could be made.

Eulate reasoned that with the Indians' goodwill it would be much easier to get them to work for him. He was right. Not only did he have Indian laborers gathering salt from the lakes east of the *Río del Norte,* they also acted as burden-bearers carrying the heavy salt all the way to the *Río* where the carts bound for the south could pick it up. The Indians were the gatherers and burden-bearers for piñon nuts that were a great delicacy in Mexico where they fetched many times their value in *Nuevo México.*

Eulate took over a large area in the Governor's Palace and converted it into a *manta* factory where many natives sat weaving ten to twelve hours a day for no compensation save perhaps a little toasted corn for a midday meal. The Indians paid a steep price in labor for the privilege of practicing their ceremonies and rituals.

To his mother's dismay, Alejandro began to avoid the company of the governor. He was no longer flattered by Eulate's attention because it frequently involved doing some distasteful assignment. He did not like to be the messenger to the Queres-speaking villages who came to inform them they were to supply forty or fifty or a hundred workers for a job the governor wanted done. It did not take Alejandro or others long to perceive Eulate's motivation in allowing the natives to practice their ceremonies.

Three months had passed since the episode at the spring and Alegría was still driven and consumed by her passion. If something came up that made it impossible for them to find a few moments alone, she felt as if she were being driven crazy with longing, for she had told him so again and again.

"All I can think about is the next time you will possess me," she would say, grasping his arm, her fingers biting into his skin.

Hers was an insatiability that he seemed unable to satisfy. She wanted him constantly and had devised signals to tell him so. Then, no matter the time or place, he would try to arrange to come to her because of her need and because of his fear that she would do something reckless that would cause them to be discovered.

Although they were faintly tinged with color, her cheeks developed hollows in them. She seemed remote and completely absorbed in herself. She was no longer gay and laughing, though at times she did smile to herself—a faint, enigmatic smile.

María Angélica told herself again and again that it was just a stage Alegría was going through. When she witnessed the girl becoming more remote and withdrawn from the family and self-absorbed in her own thoughts, María Angélica could not face the very real possibility that her daughter was becoming every day more and more like her father.

* * *

Alegría had known from the first month. Her mother had never told her anything about the workings of a woman's body, but old Fabia had explained everything when her first *regla* came when she was twelve.

When her *regla* had not come for the first time after she and Alejandro had become lovers, she knew. The *regla* did not come a second time nor a third, and she knew the tingling feeling in her breasts was not due solely to Alejandro's caresses. She was consumed with joy as she stood in front of the polished metal mirror and ran her hand lovingly over her belly.

"He planted himself in me the first time," she whispered to herself, smiling faintly. "I wanted to become a part of him. I wanted him to consume me, but he became a part of me. I know I will never have more happiness than at this moment while a part of him grows inside me. I have stolen a piece of him for my very own."

She did not tell Alejandro and was careful not to let her mother see her if she were sick.

The fourth *regla* did not come and she no longer felt any sickness. A very slight rounding in her abdomen became evident and once or twice she felt a faint fluttering there, almost like a butterfly.

At night he ran his hands all over her body, but he had not yet noticed the slight swelling of her abdomen. When he kissed her belly, she pressed his head closer, delighting in the fact that under his lips, his child grew.

In the early fall Rohona thought about returning to Áco. There was a note of hesitation in his voice. "I would like to make the trip again in order to attend the ceremonies of harvest."

"Go," María Angélica urged him with a smile. "I think Alejandro should stay, though," she added, a note of worry in her voice. "I fear that if both you and he are gone, the soldier who tried to force himself on Alegría may do so again. So far he has not attempted to take any revenge, but with both men gone from the household . . ."

"If you are concerned, I will stay," Rohona said.

"No, go to Áco. Alejandro is a man. He can take care of himself and us, too."

When Alegría heard that Rohona was going to Áco again, she immediately assumed Alejandro would go with him and was distraught with anxiety. That night when he came to her room, she was lying curled up on the bed, holding her head in her hands.

"I can't survive if you are gone," she cried as she lay shaking, pulling at her hair.

He came to the bed and sat down. "Aley, Aley, don't cry. Please don't cry. I am not going. It has been decided that I am to stay." He was disturbed by her despondency.

She sat up and threw her arms around his neck and kissed him all over the face.

He worried constantly about what they were doing, but he could not bear to be without her joy. It had fed him as a boy, and it fed him now as a man. It was as if she were a part of him that had always been missing, a need for love that he had always felt as a child but could never satisfy, knowing that he was only detritus, leavings from a nameless mother raped by a nameless father.

Alegría was like a young animal in estrus. Her driving necessity had become his necessity, and he could not have stayed away from her even if his desire were leading him to the edge of a precipice, just as a male animal driven mad by the mating scent of a female ignores all danger for one purpose and one purpose alone: to satisfy the urge she created in him.

"I would die if you were going to Áco," she said.

Alejandro had stood to remove his shirt when a loud banging came at the front door of the house, followed by shouting.

"*¡Jesús!* What is that?" he said with horror, pulling down his shirt and sprinting to the door of the bedroom.

"Don't go!" Alegría said with urgency. "Stay with *me!*"

"God, Aley, I've got to see what it is." He slipped out the door and reached the *sala* just as his mother and Rohona did.

"*¡Incendio en la casa real!*" someone shouted outside.

"Not the governor's palace!" María Angélica said, pulling her *rebozo* more tightly around her to cover her nightgown as Alejandro threw up the bar that bolted the door.

"Come quickly!" the soldier standing there said. "Fire has broken out in the *manta* factory. Bring buckets!"

"Take a bucket with you, *hijo,*" María Angélica said. "I'll get dressed and bring more. *¡Ándale!*"

It was not necessary to tell Alejandro to hurry, for he was already racing to the kitchen and Rohona followed with his uneven gait.

María Angélica pulled on an old dress and ran to Alegría's room. "*Hija,* throw on some clothes! The governor's house is on fire. They'll need everyone's help."

María Angélica grabbed a leather bucket and a *tinaja* and started for the governor's palace. A halo of light above the *casas reales* illuminated the people scurrying across the plaza and rushing into the compound while a cacophony of strident, shouting voices and the crackling of fire filled the normally still village night.

"Here," María Angélica said, as she shoved the bucket and the *tinaja* into the hands of a boy. "Run these to the *acequia* so they can be filled with water."

Smoke poured into the courtyard from the doorway of the large room that the governor used as the *manta* factory, and she coughed as she entered the patio to join the bucket brigade that was conveying water to the burning room from small *acequia* that supplied the palace's needs.

Through the smoky haze she saw Alejandro and Rohona along with the governor, some of his soldiers, and other men near the door, throwing in bucket after bucket of water, trying to quench the fire before it spread to other areas of the compound. Their faces were blackened by the smoke; their clothes soaked from the slopping water. People yelled instructions while others prayed loudly for higher powers to lend a hand.

Smoke, noise, and confusion filled the back courtyard of the compound as more people arrived to help.

"Your Excellency!" Rohona shouted and the governor turned with a harsh look to face the *indio*. "*Perdón*, Excellency," Rohona shouted above the din, "but the fire is gaining. We must starve it or it will consume more of the *casa*."

Alejandro interjected quickly, "He is right, *Gobernador*. We should try to seal the door!"

A fit of coughing seized the governor as he inhaled smoke. "Do it!" he managed to say. "Take the slave and figure out something while we keep the water going!"

Alejandro saw the carpenter Jacobo. "*¡Ven con nosotros! ¡Rápido!*" he yelled to him. "Help us get a door off to try to seal the entrance of the room!"

Jacobo nodded and left the bucket brigade. They found a hammer and removed a heavy planked door from another room in the casa real. "Find us some more wood and nails," Alejandro said, "and *jerga*, if you can."

When other men saw Alejandro and Rohona shouldering the heavy wooden door, they joined them and rushed the planking toward the burning room.

"*Mojen la puerta,*" Rohona instructed, and the men grabbed buckets from the brigade and slopped water on the door to wet it down.

They shoved the door up against the entrance and Jacobo arrived with boards and nails to hold the door against the opening. They soaked large pieces of frieze with water and likewise nailed the rough, wet fabric over the planking.

When that was done, the men took a moment to relax and catch their breath. They wiped their faces with their sleeves, smearing the soot and sweat.

"Lieutenant, keep the water going," the governor shouted to Reinaldo de la Torre who stood near the boarded doorway. "We've got to keep the covering wet so it cannot catch fire. Thank God there are no windows in the room. Maybe we have a chance to kill the fire."

María Angélica stepped out of the brigade with a leather bucket full of water and brought it to the men who rested briefly. "Here, drink this while you catch your breath," she said.

"*Gracias, señora,*" they all murmured and passed the bucket around.

She walked to where Alejandro stood. "Have you seen Alegría?" she asked. "I told her to come help, but I haven't caught a glimpse of her."

"Alejandro, go up on the roof," the governor spoke. "The dirt covering up there is a good two feet thick and is good protection, but check to make sure the fire is not starting to burn through anywhere. Take several men with you. We'll hand up some buckets for you to water it down, just to be on the safe side."

*"Sí, Gobernador."*

Alejandro picked some men and they climbed the pine ladder that was brought for them. The bucket brigade was no longer as frantic trying to deliver water, and while the men looked for hot spots, María Angélica walked around the compound looking for Alegría. Rohona had not seen her either, and her mother began to feel a prick of worry.

"Everything seems all right," Alejandro said to the governor when he descended. "It might be wise, though, to keep a watch up there."

"Yes," Eulate said, "we'll have to keep a vigil through the night down here, too. *Incendios* have the damnedest way of restarting themselves. But at least we have a little breather now." The governor ran both hands through his hair. "That slave of yours has a good head on his shoulders."

"You're right about that, sir, but I have never thought of him as a slave."

*"Señora,"* Eulate said and made a small bow as María Angélica walked up, "thank you for your help. All the citizens of this *villa* have aided me in putting out the fire in my dwelling."

"You would do the same for us, governor," she said. "May I borrow Alejandro for a few moments, please?"

"Certainly."

She took Alejandro by the arm and led him out of earshot of others in the courtyard. "I have looked but can't find Alegría."

"Do you think she came?" he asked, glancing around.

"She must have."

"I don't see de la Torre," Alejandro said as he looked around the patio. "He was just here, up by the door."

The worry on his mother's face turned to fear.

*"No te preocupa, mamá,"* Alejandro said, "I'll find her. You run home and make sure she's not still there. I'll have Uncle look through all the rooms here, and I'll check outside."

María Angélica hurried in the front door of her house, calling, "Alegría! Are you here? *Hija*, are you here?" She ran to the girl's room and opened the door.

Alegría sat up and pulled the covers under her chin.

*"¡Hija!"* María Angélica said. "What are you doing? Why didn't you come to help? I was worried sick when I couldn't find you!"

"I didn't think they'd need me," she said.

*"Hija,"* María Angélica said with a scold in her voice, "everyone is needed at a fire."

"Did they get it put out?" the girl asked.

*"Gracias a Dios,"* her mother answered, "but I'm really upset at you, *hija*. I've worried Alejandro and Uncle for nothing. Now, I've got to go find them and tell them you're here."

Alejandro walked a circuit around the governor's compound. A few people milled around out in front resting and discussing the fire. He thought he saw something move back near the larger *acequia*.

"Aley," he called softly.

He saw a shadow move. It was just like her to entice him to follow her. He walked toward the *acequia*.

"Aley, let's not play games tonight. *Mamá*'s worried about you."

"She ought to be," the shadow growled as it came out of the darkness at him.

Alejandro felt the sharp, slicing pain of a knife embedded in his shoulder and then yanked out as he was knocked backwards into the *acequia*.

A heavy form crashed down on top of him, pushing him to the bottom of the irrigation ditch. Alejandro rolled and fought and managed to come to the surface, sucking in air and pain as he did so.

"You should have killed me when you had the chance, you son of a bitch," Reinaldo de la Torre hissed as he came up out of the water and lunged at Alejandro with the knife he still held in his hand, "because I'm going to kill you first and then fuck that little red-haired whore you live with."

Fury welled in Alejandro and he tried to parry the blow with his forearm but lost his footing and slipped on the mud-slick bottom of the ditch and felt the knife blade graze his scalp. He grabbed a deep breath of air, sank under the water, and reached for his attacker's legs. He managed to grasp them and give a hard upwards yank, pulling the lieutenant off balance and dragging him under the water also.

Alejandro grabbed him around the neck. There was little strength left in the arm with the wounded shoulder, but he squeezed the man's neck, the thumb of his good hand pressing into the windpipe. They flailed to the surface and Alejandro gasped for air, pushing the lieutenant back under the water. De la Torre stabbed at him and Alejandro felt the tip prick his back and forearm and side, but the attacker's arms lost their coordination and then the body relaxed.

Alejandro felt other arms grasp him and he tried to fight, but his air was gone and he sucked in water and began to choke. Arms yanked him up, dragging him out of the water and onto the side of the ditch.

*"Cálmate, cálmate,"* a voice said. "We're not fighting you."

Alejandro coughed and gagged but was aware that others were pulling the other man out of the *acequia*.

"It's the lieutenant," someone said.

Alejandro lay on his side coughing weakly and saw men pounding on de la Torre's back. "It's no use," another voice said, "he's dead."

Alejandro felt himself being lifted to a sitting position and heard words in Queres saying a prayer of thanks to the K'atsina at Wenimats.

"Kakana," Rohona said softly, using a name Alejandro had not heard in years. "Are you hurt badly?"

"I don't think so, Uncle," he managed to whisper.

*"¡Hijo!"* his mother gasped as she saw him sitting slumped against Rohona. "Oh, my God. What has happened?"

"I went looking for Aley," he whispered. "The lieutenant jumped me."

"Come, we must get you home."

Alegría had gotten dressed and was standing, peering out the door as she saw him stagger toward the house supported by Rohona on one side and her mother on the other.

She shrieked and backed away as they came into the *sala*. Red stains streaked his clothes that dripped pale droplets of bloody water onto the Mexican rug that covered the floor.

"Aley, Aley, I'm okay," he said weakly. "I'm okay."

Alegría gulped air as if she could not breathe and then ran to Alejandro, throwing her arms around him.

*"¡Cuidado, hija!"* María Angélica said impatiently. "We've got to get his wounds cleaned."

As María Angélica and Rohona turned toward the kitchen with Alejandro, Alegría whirled and ran to her room.

After his wounds were cleaned and bandaged, his mother and father helped him to his room and put him to bed. They left the room together and after some minutes, Alejandro rose quietly and went to the door. He peered out and when he saw no one, he walked softly to Alegría's room. The tallow candle still burned by her bedside, but when he approached he saw that she was sleeping. He turned to leave, but she came awake.

"Oh, Aley," she said, reaching out to him.

He sat down on the edge of the bed and she threw her arms around his neck. He grimaced with pain, but she hugged him tightly. "Make love to me," she whispered.

He tried to laugh. "Aley, I don't think I can. I hurt too much tonight."

"If you had stayed with me when I wanted, this wouldn't have happened," she said.

# Chapter 38

The governor convened a court of inquiry, and after hearing the testimony by numerous villagers and soldiers of the threats to Alejandro's life that the lieutenant had made, and after it was determined that Alejandro had been unarmed during the fight, Eulate quickly decreed that the killing had been in self-defense.

Although the threat of de la Torre had been removed with his death, Alejandro did not make the journey to Áco with Rohona. He stayed in the *villa* to recuperate from his wounds to Alegría's delight.

The wide skirts and loose blouses she wore effectively hid her thickening waistline from her mother's eyes, but she had never decided upon the right moment to tell Alejandro that she was carrying his child. One night as he sat on the bed watching her disrobe, he saw her profile outlined by the flickering light of the tallow candle.

He gasped. How could he not have noticed such a thing?

Alegría turned toward him and held her rounding belly. Her mass of flame-colored hair seemed to frame her face in firelight. She smiled a slow lynx-like smile, walked toward him with feline steps, and knelt on the bed beside him. She took his hands and placed them on her stomach.

"Yes," she whispered gleefully, "oh, yes, yes! I have you inside me."

"How long?"

"You gave it to me the very first time," she laughed melodiously. "I wanted to be a part of you, and you became a part of me."

Alejandro asked the question she had not asked herself, "What are we going to do?"

She smiled at him, still thinking no further than the joy she knew. "Are you happy?"

"Yes," he said, but he had still not smiled. "But what are we going to do about it?" he reiterated.

"What are we going to do?" She lay back on the bed. "Of course, we will be married. We will be so happy; we will never be separated; we will . . ."

"Where will we live? We will need a home."

"Why, we'll live here with *mamá*. She will take care of us," Alegría said happily, sitting up again. She seemed unaware of the solemn look on Alejandro's face.

"We must tell her," he said. "But what is she going to think about you marrying a penniless, half-breed bastard? You are Castilian; you could marry well."

She laughed and kissed him, her tongue darting into his mouth, her hands grasping his arms.

"Weren't you the one who told me Uncle was her lover?"

For the first time, the smile left her face, and he heard bitterness in her voice. "She has always loved you more than me anyway."

"That is not true," Alejandro said, taking her in his arms, not wanting to see the look in her eyes. Any unhappiness she had vanished and she rubbed up against him like a purring cat. She sat away from him and smiled.

"Let's go tell her now."

"Don't you think it might be better to wait until morning?"

"No," she said excitedly, climbing off the bed, "let's go tell her now."

A light shone under the door. Alejandro knocked softly.

"Come in," María Angélica said.

Alegría was smiling broadly as they entered; Alejandro's face remained expressionless as he had learned from Rohona. María Angélica laid aside her well-worn book and patted the edge of her bed for them to sit.

"Yes, what is it?" she asked, smiling.

Alegría sat down on the bed and Alejandro pulled a chair close. Alegría flashed a look at him and then turned toward María Angélica.

"We're in love, *mamá*," she said with joy in her voice.

"You're both in love?" her mother asked naively. "With whom?"

Alegría laughed. "With each other, of course!"

María Angélica froze, and her face turned ashen. Her breath caught in her throat and her eyes widened in horror. Fabia's dying words returned to her, and she finally understood what the old woman had meant. "Stop them. You must tell them!" Fabia must have seen it coming.

"Oh my God," María Angélica whispered, covering her mouth with her hands.

The smile was frozen on Alegría's face; Alejandro seemed to have stopped breathing.

*"Mamá,"* Alegría said, taking her mother's hand. *"Mamá,* we love each other. What is wrong with that?"

*"No! It isn't right, it isn't right!"* María Angélica said, choked with the terrible thought of it.

Alejandro looked as if he would have preferred death than to have had to sit there.

"How can you say it isn't right?" Alegría demanded. "You and Uncle—he is Indian!"

"No," she said, "it is not because Alejandro is part Indian—I would never object to that. I love Uncle, I have loved him for years. How could I ever object to Alejandro being part Indian when *he is my own son!"*

Alejandro's eyes widened in disbelief.

"Yes, *hijo,* it is true," she said softly, putting her hand out to him. "I am your real mother and Uncle is your father. You are our true son."

Alejandro slid off the chair onto his knees at the bedside and his head dropped down onto the bed to hide the tears he could not control.

*"Hijo, hijo,"* she whispered as she stroked his hair. "How I have loved you all these years. So many times I wanted to tell you. Oh, how I wish I had, and this would never have happened."

"But we love each other," Alegría wailed pitifully.

María Angélica turned toward her. "But you cannot. You are brother and sister. It is not permitted. It is wrong. It is sinful. The Church does not allow it even if you are only half-brother and sister."

Alegría's hand flew to her mouth, and she ran from the room. María Angélica started to rise.

"No, *mamá,* let me go to her. It is best," Alejandro said.

She looked at him and cupped his face between her hands. "Oh, *hijo,* how much I have loved you all these years."

*"Mamá,"* Alejandro whispered, "I have always loved you as my mother. How I wanted you to be my real mother and Uncle my father—and to know that you truly are, it is like a dream."

Tears spilled down her cheeks. "Go to your sister now," she said, "I will pray for God's guidance."

Alegría lay on the bed sobbing hysterically and he sat down beside her.

She turned her tear-ravaged face up to him. "Oh, Aley," she cried despondently, throwing her arms around him. "I always knew she loved you better than me. Now I know why!"

"She loves us both, Aley," Alejandro said to her gently. "We must decide what to do."

"I can't lose you, I can't lose you!" she moaned as she clutched at him, her fingernails making marks on his skin. "I need you. You are part of me. I would die without you."

He took her hands and repeated the statement that she did not seem to want to hear. "We must decide what to do."

"We will get married. We love each other, and *mamá* cannot stop us."

He took her roughly by the shoulders. "Alegría, don't you understand? *Mamá can* stop us! Don't you see? We are brother and sister. *We are committing incest!* That is an unspeakable sin. The Church would never marry us. What will the priests do when they find out? What will the people of the *villa* do? What do you think will happen to us and the baby?"

Suddenly the desperation of their situation dawned in Alegría's eyes, and her face was contorted with horror and fear. She began to sob again.

Alejandro clapped a hand over her mouth. "Be quiet!" he said in a harsh whisper. "Or you'll bring *mamá*, and she will learn the full extent of our love."

His eyes moved to her rounded naked belly. Suddenly she became very still, then trembled violently. Alejandro could not bear the look in her eyes. He gathered her into his arms and smoothed her hair.

"We must leave," he said, making the decision for them. "*Mamá* will try to separate us. I would guess she will want to send you away—to Mexico to have the baby."

"No!" Alegría broke in, her voice a ragged whisper, her eyes crazed.

"I will not let her," Alejandro reassured her. "Uncle is at Áco," he said and then corrected himself. "Father is at Áco. We will go to Áco first. I will talk to him, and we will decide then what to do. But we must go tonight—tomorrow will be too late."

He took her by the shoulders, his look imperative. "Dress warmly—take anything buckskin you have. Wear your rabbit-fur moccasins. Take a couple of wool shawls. I am going now to get the horses ready. We must not alert *mamá* to what we are doing or we are lost. Do you understand? *Do you understand?*" he demanded, his grasp rough.

She nodded mutely, her gray eyes filled with terror.

"Be ready when I return and do not make *any* noise."

He closed the door behind him and went to his mother's room. She was kneeling in front of the statue of the Virgin and he knelt beside her. He saw the tears and anguish on his mother's face, her eyes so like her daughter's.

"She is sleeping," he said. "I left the tallow candle burning in her room, for she was afraid. Do not disturb her tonight—I think it best that she get some sleep. Tomorrow we will talk."

"Oh, *hijito*," María Angélica said as she embraced him, "I have caused you so much pain, so much hurt, and it was never my intention. Forgive me, please. I only wanted to be able to love you, to care for you as my child—that was why I never told you."

"*Mamá,* I do not blame you," Alejandro said. "I have loved you as my mother for my entire life. I love you still. I will always love you."

He kissed her on the cheek and through her sobs she did not hear his words, "Good-bye, *mamá,* forgive *me.*"

Part Six

# LA HUIDA

## Flight, October 1619

# Chapter 39

"They're gone?!" Dorotea said with shock. "Gone where?"

"I don't know," María Angélica gasped, out of breath. "They came and told me last night they were in love with each other. I told them the truth about themselves—I think they must be lovers." Her eyes were red. There were no more tears.

Her friend led her to a bench in the entranceway. Dorotea had no words to say and could comfort only with her presence.

"I prayed for guidance last night," María Angélica said, "and hoped this morning would bring a solution, but when I went to Alejandro's room there was no answer nor was there any at Alegría's. Then I saw that they were gone. I cannot imagine where they would go. But I must tell Rohona, I must get to Áco—he will know what to do."

"Perhaps they have already gone there," Dorotea offered.

"Why would they go *there?* Rohona would tell them the same thing I did. I think they would go somewhere they weren't known and could keep their identity secret."

"And where in *Nuevo México* would that be possible?" Dorotea asked. "A beautiful young red-haired Castilian woman and a tall, handsome *mestizo?*"

"I don't know, I don't know, but I must get to Rohona. I must talk to him. He'll know what to do. Maybe they have gone to New Spain. Maybe he can go after them. He would know how to track them. Please, Dorotea, bring Siya here so I may get directions. I must get to Áco. It is the only thing I know to do."

Siya listened solemnly to María Angélica recount what had occurred.

"Please, Siya," she finished, "can you tell me how to get there?"

"I can go with you. It is a long journey."

"Take her with you," Dorotea said. "It is leagues to Ácoma. How on earth can you ever hope to find it in this godforsaken land?"

María Angélica started to object, but her friend was insistent. "You *must* go together."

"But what about Isidro?" María Angélica asked. "What will he do when he finds out?"

Dorotea said with reassurance, "Siya's twenty years of servitude are over. He no longer owns her. Besides, he has gone with the governor's cart train, taking slaves to Parral. You will be back long before he is."

Later, after making her preparations, she returned to Dorotea's house.

Siya was ready. "It has been twenty years since I saw Áco mesa, but I know I will be able to get us there. We will follow the *Río del Norte* south and then turn west. The route is longer but a little easier." Siya's voice was confident. "We will cross one bad-smelling stream that this time of year will have little water, and the next stream we will follow until North Mountain, very large, will be just ahead on our right. If we come to the place where black, hard, bubbly rock spreads across the land like it had been poured there, we have gone too far. Then we must go back and then go south. There is a creek to follow in between the mesa ridge, and then we will come into a big valley. We will see Katsimo, the enchanted mesa; beyond that is the high mesa of Áco. I assure you, we can do it."

"Do you have plenty of food?" Dorotea asked. "And water?"

"Yes," María Angélica said, "I am taking two good horses for us and another for provisions as well as blankets. We will be fine, and we'll stay at Áco until Rohona decides what should be done."

She took a paper from the stack she had brought and handed it to Dorotea. "I need to have this witnessed."

"It's a will?" Dorotea asked.

"Yes, I am leaving everything I own to you, Dorotea, in the event that something happens to me. I trust that if there is ever any need in which any of the people I love find themselves, and you are aware of it, you will aid them. Otherwise, I wish you to have it all."

"Don't go," Dorotea whispered.

"I must. Let us find two witnesses now."

Dorotea returned with an old woman and her husband who lived nearby. They were curious about the reason for the document, but Dorotea explained that the priest had suggested it to María Angélica since she was a widow. They accepted the explanation, as well as a glass of wine, and signed the document.

* * *

"Shouldn't you wait until morning to start?" Dorotea asked.

"No," María Angélica said, "we will not attract any attention during the dark, and we will be able to get away from the *villa* unseen, and tomorrow we won't have to worry about someone out riding early." She hugged her.

"Good-bye, and thank you, Doro. You have been a wonderful friend to me."

Siya hugged Dorotea also.

"Good-bye," Dorotea said, her voice choked with emotion. "Return quickly." She watched them walk toward María Angélica's house until the shadows hid them.

*"Vayan con Dios,"* Dorotea whispered in the darkness, but all she felt was a sense of imminent catastrophe, and she crossed herself at the thought of it.

María Angélica lost count of the days. Their monotony blurred them in her memory. In spite of Siya's presence, she felt incredibly alone in the vast emptiness of the land, and she prayed constantly as they rode. She prayed for deliverance, guidance, forgiveness; she prayed just to keep her mind occupied.

They rode each day as far as their endurance would take them. She knew it was foolhardy to ride when it was dark for it would be easy for the horse to make a misstep, but she wanted to exhaust herself so that each night as soon as she lay down, she would fall instantly asleep. She did not want the sound of a distant coyote or wind in the dry fall brush to wake her in terror.

They finally made the decision to turn south. "This *cañada* leads to Áco mesa," Siya assured her.

It seemed to María Angélica that they had ridden a hundred leagues although she knew that was not possible. Siya's landmarks had been relatively easy to follow, and the sun was ready to fall behind the mesa that stretched along the west when they entered the valley. María Angélica could scarcely contain her joy knowing she was finally so close to the fabled Áco, the place where the Maese had died—the place where the man she loved was born.

If they could not reach it that day, on the morrow they would. She knew the two horses were tired, but she could not refrain from putting her heels to her mare's sides. Her mount responded and raced across the flat valley land as Siya followed. In the distance she saw a sheer-walled mesa rising up from the valley floor. It was breathtaking in its beauty and majesty. She stopped her horse and looked at it.

"It is Katsimo," Siya said when she pulled up her horse beside María Angélica's.

"No wonder you call it enchanted," María Angélica said. "It is beautiful."

The setting sun turned the rock a vibrant rose red on its west face while the east was shadowed violet. It was dark by the time they reached the base of the towering rock. She knew Áco was beyond it, not too distant, but the light failed before she glimpsed it, yet they did not stop.

She was no longer tired. The fall night air blowing against her face was crisp and chill, but she did not mind that her cheeks and hands were numb.

A harvest moon rose above the line of east mesas like a fat Indian pumpkin, casting light across the valley floor. Then she saw it—massive and solitary, its crags etched by moonlight and night shadows. It was a stark and terrifyingly beautiful creation of God.

Had she not been so entranced at the sight of the breathtaking mesa, she might have seen the small arroyo. Only when she felt the mare's front feet glide into nothing and then frantically fight for balance did she know the danger of her carelessness. She pitched headlong over the mare's neck. It seemed an eternity passed as she waited for her body to strike the hard ground. As she hit, she heard a noise that sounded as if a twig had snapped.

She must have been knocked unconscious for she later came awake, aware that the moon was high overhead. She tried to move but could not.

"Siya," she whispered, "Siya." No one answered. María Angélica could not feel her limbs.

For an instant she thought perhaps she was dead, but the pain she felt at the base of her neck told her differently. In the pale moonlight she could, with excruciating effort, move her head just enough to see a blanket covering her twisted, inert body as it lay on the hard ground. She knew her back must be broken.

Throughout the rest of the night she came in and out of consciousness. In one of her lucid moments, she confessed her sins to the star-encrusted blackness, hoping God would hear her.

"I am not afraid to die, for I know your mercy," she whispered. "You have been good to me and my family, but if I may ask one more favor, guide and protect my children and watch over the man I truly loved as a husband."

She did not know whether she had slept or fallen unconscious the remainder of the night. She never expected to awake again to sunlight, but the warmth and brightness on her face told her day had finally come.

It seemed that far in the distance she heard someone saying, "Mía, Mía, Mía." She struggled to open her eyes and focus them. Gradually her vision cleared, and she saw his face bending over her.

"Oh, my love," she whispered as tears rolled freely down her face, "you came."

He started to say something, but she interrupted. "Please, let me talk, I have very little time left. Alejandro and Alegría have run away, and Siya was with me."

"I know," he said, "Siya came for me. The children are here."

*"Mamá,"* Alejandro said, leaning closer to his mother so that she could see him.

She managed to turn her head enough to also see Alegría and Siya kneeling near her. "Oh, thank God, thank God," María Angélica whispered to Rohona. "You will be able to help them now."

"Yes."

"You must tell them that their love cannot be. You must tell them that it is my fault, not theirs, that this thing has come to pass."

"I share the fault," Rohona said. "We must now worry about you. We must care for *you*."

"There is nothing to be done for me." She closed her eyes, tired from the effort of talking.

Rohona prayed silently to the Castilian god. "Don't let her die. You saved her once before, you can save her now. You must save her. I do not want her to die."

She opened her eyes once more. "I love you, dearest husband. Take care of our children. Touch my face; kiss me."

"You will not die," Rohona said hoarsely. "Your god will save you."

María Angélica smiled. "No, He cannot save me from this. Perhaps there is a reason for my death, and the understanding will come someday. Please, kiss me now."

"I need you. I want him to save you."

"He has," she whispered, as Rohona bent his head to kiss her. He held her face in his hands and kissed her long and deep.

For twenty years he had loved the woman with gray eyes and hair the color of wet pine bark. He had lived with her, and she had been his happiness. She had made him whole. He had never been a cripple to her. He remembered vividly the first time in the golden leaves that he had made her his and had known that she had wanted him as a man. It had been a glorious soaring as if on eagle wings.

He smoothed back her hair and waited for her god to act to save her. He had always provided. She smiled and closed her eyes. Rohona knew within seconds that she would never open them again.

# Chapter 40

Rohona stood on Áco mesa looking toward the west as the sun sank slowly, coloring the landscape with deep hues of rose-wine and violet. He could not be sure which stone tower it was or if he could even see it in the growing darkness, but he knew she was there, safe but not alone. Part of him would always be there with her. A part of him had died, too, when she had and lay with her beneath the rocks that made her grave.

He had taken her on horseback toward the west to the far stone towers that thrust up like fingers from the valley floor. He chose a rock pillar, the height of more than four men, chose it for its sheer, straight sides, the top inaccessible to all but the most proficient climbers. No wolf or coyote could ever reach the top; only an eagle or a hawk might perch there, and her body was covered by many stones. No bird of prey would ever touch her.

Alejandro helped him get her body to the top of the high rock, like Áco only in miniature. Together they made trip after trip down off the rock to get stones, carrying them to the top in baskets on their backs. Rohona wrapped her in an embroidered cotton *manta,* and they piled the stones on her, chinking them so they fitted well together.

When she was at last encased in her stone coffin, Rohona went down once more to the valley floor and cut two small piñon branches that he notched and crossed. He lashed them together with a piece of sinew and carried the symbol of her god back to the top of the rock where he planted it securely amongst the stones.

He and Alejandro knelt on the hard rock surface and prayed the Castilian prayers. Rohona's tears lay in the grave with her, but Alejandro's streamed down his cheeks. "Oh, *mamá,*" he wept, "it was so little time that I knew you were my mother, but I have loved you since I was born.

You asked my forgiveness, *mamá,* now I ask yours. You are dead because of me. On my life I never wished it. I have killed one I loved, God forgive me."

"You did not kill her, *hijo.*" Rohona put his hand on his son's shoulder. "She always said her god had a purpose, and one day we may know what that purpose is, but our job now is to live."

The sun slipped below the western horizon, wrapping Rohona in darkness and in the chill night air of fall as he stood looking out over the valley toward where she lay.

He thought at first he would take her body back to the *villa* of Santa Fé for burial in the special ground they used, but something told him not to. He did not know what the reaction of the Spaniards would be, but he did know there would be too many questions asked that he would not know how to answer, and he had a deep apprehension for the boy and girl.

He took the horses that Alejandro and Alegría as well as María Angélica and Siya had ridden to Áco and led them the long distance to the eastern side of the big river and let them loose. He would have liked to keep them but it would be dangerous if a Spaniard ever saw them at Áco mesa and recognized them. From the eastern side of the *río,* the animals might find their way back to the *villa.* If they did the Spaniards would probably assume that some unfortunate accident had befallen their riders and any questions they had would have to go unanswered.

Rohona, however, sent a runner with a message to tell Dorotea what had happened. He knew she would never breathe a word that she had any knowledge of what had become of Señora de Vizcarra nor that the half-breed boy and the woman's daughter were living at Áco. Nor did Rohona worry that any Ácoma would divulge the secret he wished kept.

Together he and Alejandro built a dwelling attached to the end of one of the house rows as all dwellings were built on the mesa top, and Siya worked diligently to provide the necessities of a home.

Alejandro and particularly Alegría were outcasts in the village at Áco. They were disliked intensely because of their Spanish blood and no one would have anything to do with them. But the Ácoma were a closed-mouth people, and they would never have revealed anything about themselves or their village, even the fact that a half-breed boy and an unusual flame-haired Spanish girl were living on their mesa.

It was a source of bitter sorrow to Rohona that his son and the girl he loved like a daughter were despised by his people. It did not matter that they both spoke the language of Áco. In fact, they were perhaps looked at with even more suspicion because of it. The Ácoma did not like strangers, and a stranger who could speak their language they regarded as more of a threat than one who could not.

In the village Rohona acknowledged Alejandro as his. It filled him with deep pride to be able to call the tall, handsome young man his son, but that held no weight with the Ácoma. Descent was by the mother, and if one's mother were Ácoma, one was Ácoma and belonged to her clan. If one's mother were not of the White Rock, one had no clanship and therefore could never be Ácoma.

Rohona was proud of his son, proud of his son's abilities. He was a fine marksman with a bow, and his stamina for running in pursuit of game was as good as anyone's in the village, for he had gone hunting for game alongside Rohona since before he was ten years old. They would sometimes range far into the mountains near the *villa* of Santa Fé with the result that their household never lacked for food.

Slowly the villagers at Áco began to afford him respect for his hunting abilities, but they would not accept him as one of them. From daybreak to dark, if he was not hunting, Alejandro worked feverishly building the dwelling, learning to make arrows, to sew moccasins, learning everything it would be necessary to know to live on Áco mesa. His thoughts and feelings, whatever they might have been, never showed on his face, and he scarcely spoke.

Alegría's face, so full of joy for many years, no longer showed the emotion whose name she carried. Even to Alejandro she no longer gave any evidence of happiness. She sat in their dwelling staring blankly, running her hands occasionally over her rapidly enlarging stomach.

The flight from the *villa* of Santa Fé to Áco had been difficult. She had thought it would be a great adventure because she loved to ride, and she had envisioned great freedom as they sought the fabled rock citadel she had so longed to see since she was young and heard the stories Uncle and Siya told of the village perched on the high mesa.

They had not taken enough food, the ground was cold and hard to sleep on, and the sounds of coyotes kept her awake well into the night. In the morning she arose cold and stiff with a full day of riding ahead. Finally when she was near despair and hysterics, they reached the mesa.

The stories about the high rock that delighted her before vanished from her mind, and all that filled her was terrifying awe when she looked up at the village. She did not think she could ever climb the precipitous wall, but fortunately Rohona heard of the arrival of a strange red-haired young woman and half-breed man and hurried down off the mesa, knowing it had to be his children, surprised and worried at their arrival. One look at them, however, told him why they had come. He had been gone from the *villa* for well over a month, and the wide loose skirt and blouse no longer hid the five months of Alegría's pregnancy.

Why had he been so blind? How could he not have noticed that they were lovers? He knew the taboo that brother and sister should not wed. Did the same apply to half-brother and sister? He did not know. He knew only that he loved them as his children and that they had joined together to make a child. That child would be his grandchild whether it was normal or whether it was like the Mud Heads of Zuñi that were said to be offspring of brother and sister.

He would not ponder what the gods, Indian or Christian, intended. He would let the Castilian god provide if he so chose. If the god had some purpose, it was too difficult for him to understand, and he was too tired to keep trying. It was to life that he would devote his energies.

In the days that followed, it was not the girl who had lost her laughter that concerned him. It was Alejandro. He toiled to the absolute limits of his physical endurance as if a demon gnawed within him. The Ácoma afforded him a degree of unspoken respect, but the boy would never be accepted by them. Rohona knew it, and the boy knew it. Alejandro was of two worlds and belonged to neither. His isolation was not only social but had also penetrated to his soul.

Perhaps they should have told him. Rohona had never seen his son's deep loneliness until he and the girl came to Áco. Perhaps they should have told the boy when he was small that the woman he wanted so desperately to be his mother indeed was. Perhaps they should have told him the man with whom he shared a room, the man whose footsteps he dogged, the man whom he idolized, was truly his father. Had they told him, perhaps the boy would not have had that loneliness of the soul that came from belonging to no one, to nothing.

Had they told him, he could have given his love to the girl as a sister not as a woman. Rohona and their mother had seen from the beginning the fondness the two children had for each other, and they were pleased. The little girl worshipped her older brother, and he in turn was protective of her, and they were constant companions when they were young. The girl's joy and her uninhibited nature, like that of a little animal, must have entranced the solemn boy.

Had her joy, however, been hiding something else within her? With the joy gone from her face there showed in the beautiful features something else that Rohona could not decipher.

She made no move whatever to help Siya on whose shoulders now weighed the responsibility of the household, but Siya did not mind, for she worried about both Alegría and Alejandro. She had gotten into the habit of praying to the Castilian god that Alegría would return to normal once the baby was born. It was obvious that the girl was not herself because she had not once acknowledged her mother's death.

If Alejandro spoke of their mother, Alegría simply looked at him as if she did not hear.

Although the Ácoma did not like to talk about the dead, Rohona made one attempt to talk to Alegría of her mother, thinking it might help her, but she shut her eyes and a shiver passed through her body, and he did not try again.

In the days that passed, her large gray eyes remained blank yet at times seemed to see something no one else did. Occasionally there were flickers of some emotion at the corners of her eyes and lips that left Rohona with an uneasy sensation.

He was just as glad she was content to stay in their dwelling most of the time, for if she did go out and wander over the mesa top of the village, the Ácoma watched her surreptitiously as if they thought the strange flame-haired girl with the gray eyes of a wolf might have been a witch. He had even seen one old woman rub a bit of ashes on herself to ward off a witch's influence.

Alegría seemed to have enmeshed Alejandro completely. It was as if she held him prisoner by her voracious need of him. When the boy came into the dwelling, her eyes fixed him with a gaze that smouldered.

Rohona and Siya, too, came to recognize the look or touch that signalled her wanting, and discreetly they would leave the dwelling so that Alejandro and Alegría might have the privacy they required, but at night when Rohona was awakened by the sounds of her passion, the only thing to do was feign sleep.

He was forty-six years of age as best he could reckon from the calendar of the Spaniards. He still desired a woman, but she no longer lived, and he knew deep within he would never again experience the life-making force. With her death the passion that was still within him had changed and had become the passion of the old, passion whose source was in the past, the passion that came from one's memories, not from expectations of the present or the future.

The twenty-odd years he had spent with the strangers had changed him more than he realized, but he had no regrets. When he thought of the woman who lay beneath the mound of stones on a high pinnacle, grief and pain no longer tore his insides. Her memory was stored warm and safe near his heart, and it afforded him a great measure of contentment. Frequently he stood on a western promontory of the mesa at sundown and spoke silently to her, telling her of the things he had done that day, or of his feelings or worries. In this he was not Indian.

It did not bother him that the girl and boy so frequently coupled. What did bother him was the girl's seeming insatiability. Her eyes no longer reminded him of her mother.

He felt uneasy, for he thought he glimpsed the seeds of madness in her vacant stare. Her desire seemed to be all-consuming, driving her and the boy somewhere, to something, in a constant spiral. But there was nothing he could do. So he chose simply to love them and await the birth of his grandchild. Perhaps that not too distant event would bring a change.

# Chapter 41

It was cold and bitter the night the baby came. A fierce, freezing wind blew from North Mountain, tearing at the village perched unprotected on the mesa top. The pains were sharp, and the girl had not had an Ácoma mother to teach her how to bear them without crying aloud. The only person who might have helped her endure the ordeal of birth—the only person who had foreseen what was coming—had been dead for more than a year. Only Fabia could have made her gain control.

The girl lay writhing on a buffalo hide, curled in a fetal position, her arms grasping at her distended belly. A tallow candle, brought months ago from the *villa* of the *españoles*, gave off a smoky light that cast disjointed, flickering shadows on the bare walls.

As the wind wreaked its winter vengeance on the naked, mud-plastered houses, the small dwelling was filled with cries of agony that fought for supremacy with the deafening tumult outside. Alejandro's face was deathly pale and his eyes stark with torment. He made several attempts to comfort her, but they were to no avail, and so he sat helpless and impotent. The girl shrieked and held her swollen belly as if she were trying to keep it from ripping apart or as if she were trying to keep the child within her.

For a long time Siya tried quietly to calm her. "Breathe deeply, Alegría," she spoke gently. "Do not cry out so—it makes the pains more difficult." But nothing she said would make the girl restrain her cries.

At last Siya spoke sharply. "Bear the pains like a woman! It is our duty. It is our strength. You dishonor yourself as a woman with your behavior!"

* * *

The labor was prolonged.

"She does not want the baby to come out," Siya muttered.

At length the girl's screams changed to long, deep grunts, and Siya smiled. "It won't be long now," she whispered to Rohona and Alejandro.

The lusty cry of the infant eased the tension in the room.

It was a son. Siya swaddled the crying baby and put it at its mother's breast, urging the tiny mouth to take the nipple, which it grasped hungrily. The girl's eyes were wide and vacant and she looked only at the father. It was as if the child did not exist. She did not utter a word.

"Oh, Alegría," Alejandro whispered to her in Castilian, "what a beautiful son you have given me." He bent forward and gently placed a kiss on her lips.

Alegría's eyes, which before had been vacant, burned now with an odd intensity. "Oh, Aley, you are no longer a part of me."

He averted his eyes from hers and nodded at the tiny baby. "Yes, I am," he said, "I will always be a part of you in this child. We can never be separated now."

The girl's eyes fluttered momentarily. "I feel faint," she whispered hoarsely, and her eyes closed.

Alejandro turned to see a great stain of blood spreading on the buffalo robe and Siya working feverishly. The look on the woman's face caused fear to clutch at him with sharp, icy claws. Siya was muttering in Queres, but Alejandro understood her words.

"She is bleeding too much."

Siya kneaded the girl's stomach again and again, and Rohona took the baby from its mother's breast and cradled it so it would not be in Siya's way. Alejandro tried to pray, but he could not. The sight of the blood made him reel.

"She will die if it does not stop," Siya mumbled as she worked frantically.

Alegría's eyes opened fitfully, and they were filled with terror. "Aley, am I dying?"

"No," he said, "you will not die. I will not let it happen." He smoothed her hair from her face, avoiding looking into her eyes. As he touched her hair, he remembered how the flame-colored curls used to fly in abandon when they rode. He had always thought her hair was the most beautiful thing in the world; to him the mass of sparkling fire was the visual definition of happiness. *Alegría, alegría.*

She clutched at his hand as if by holding onto it she would not sink away. There was terror in her eyes when she spoke. "Aley, don't let me die! Please don't let me die! I can't die without you! I cannot bear to be alone!"

"I will not let you die," Alejandro promised. But it was a promise he could not keep. Slowly her eyes dulled and then closed, and her hand fell limp in his.

"No, no," he sobbed, holding the limp, flame-haired girl to his chest. "God help me, I have killed two people I love," he whispered with anguish. He laid her back down on the fur hide and looked at her silently, his chest heaving, his face contorted in grief.

Rohona reached to touch him, but a deep, strangled sound tore forth in a paroxysm from his throat as he pushed himself from the floor and ripped aside the door covering, plunging into the violent night.

Rohona handed the baby to Siya and ran to grab the door covering to shut out the cold that blasted into the small room. Siya tucked the child to her, wrapping another blanket around it as Rohona ducked outside and secured the cover behind him. The cold wind sliced his face like a knife as he made his way to the roof edge and descended the ladder to the ground.

The black of the night and the howling wind obliterated any trace of his son, but Rohona ran down the house rows, looking, shouting Alejandro's name. But it was to no avail.

His hands and face were numb from the cold, his voice stolen by the freezing wind. At length he returned to the dwelling where the dead girl lay. Siya had cleaned the baby and wrapped it snugly. It was cradled in her arms for warmth, and she crooned softly to it.

Rohona made the death preparations as best he could. He knew that no medicine man would do them for Alegría. Gently he smeared corn pollen on her cheeks and eyelids and tied a short fluffy eagle feather into her hair at the crown of her head. Taking a pair of scissors he had brought from the *villa* of the *españoles*, he cut her brightly colored hair the way Iyatiku wore hers and the way they had been instructed to cut the hair of the dead so that Iyatiku would recognize them. Then he wrapped the girl in a cotton *manta* and chanted a prayer in Queres.

He sat back and slowly lifted his arm and made the sign of the cross over the inert body. He bowed his head and murmured the Castilian prayers he had once learned.

The wind howled around the dwelling, making the door covering snap. He turned away from the *manta*-wrapped body. Gently he took the tiny newborn from Siya and went to his knees, the baby securely in the crook of his arm. He prayed to the Spanish god a simple prayer.

"If you provide, provide for this child."

He turned to Siya. "There is nothing we can do now," he said. "The boy will return when his grief is spent."

He lay down on his bed of hides, tucking the baby close to him so that his body heat might keep it warm during the rest of the bitter night, and Siya lay down close by.

A loud cry woke Rohona, and he realized the gray of dawn had arrived. The wind had stopped. Siya sat up as he quieted the baby although he had no food to give it. When he glanced around the still dim room, he saw the *manta*-wrapped body of the baby's mother and saw, too, that his son had not returned. He hoped Alejandro had found some sheltered spot to weather the night, but worry plucked at him. He handed the baby to Siya.

"I must find him," he whispered.

Rohona stepped out into the brittle dawn air, and as he stood on the roof he looked in all directions, then made his way down the pine ladder.

It was midday when Rohona found him. Although the sun shone, it was still bitterly, bone-achingly cold. He had scoured the entire mesa top, searching everywhere for the boy, his son.

Although his fingers would scarcely bend because of it, Rohona did not physically feel the cold, but there was ice in his soul, freezing him from the inside out. When the mesa top yielded no evidence of his son, he began to walk its precipitous edge, peering down the craggy rock sides to the rough terrain below with its boulders and drifted, pulverized sandstone.

A wail of grief froze in his heart when he saw the body below, bent grotesquely on the rock on which it had fallen. Had the boy sought to end his life or had he in his grief not known the edge of the cliff was so near?

He descended the mesa as quickly as his crippled foot would allow and loped to the spot where his son lay dead and frozen. His tall, beautiful son—the son the woman with gray eyes and hair the color of wet pine bark had given him. The son whom her god had granted him to raise, her god had taken away.

Rohona stroked the boy's cold hair, and tears made icy rivulets down his face. "My son," he whispered, "Kakana, my son."

He turned his eyes to the brilliant blue vault of the sky. "I do not like you, *Dios*," he shouted with anger. "Why do you give me so much pain to bear? Why do you make my mind battle in my head, trying to know your purpose? I do not want to understand. Leave me alone."

He toiled the rest of the day and the two that followed. He had unlashed the rungs of a ladder, and using the two long poles, he made a travois on which he laid the body of Alejandro and that of the girl he had loved as a daughter. He grasped the poles of the travois and step by grueling step pulled it across the valley floor to the rock pinnacle on which their mother lay. The struggle to get the bodies to the top of the stone tower was arduous, and there were times he thought he would fail, but at last he reached the pinnacle.

Their graves of stone he made like their mother's, bringing the stones up from below in a basket on his back. At night he slept on the rock wrapped in a hide until the graves and their crude crosses were finished. When all was done, he knelt at the weathered cross wedged into the stones of the mother's grave.

"Oh, Mía," he whispered, tears coursing down his face, "your children are with you now. If the god you believed in is merciful, I pray he will take care of you and Alejandro and Alegría—for me."

There was a long pause. "I am alone, Mía," he said, his head bowed. "I am alone now. Your god has taken everything from me. Everything that was ever mine he has taken. I am alone."

He threw back his head and keened his grief. It rose in long wails into the empty sky. When the sound died away, his head slumped forward onto his breast, and the pain consumed him. The burden of his loneliness lay on his shoulders like the cold stones lay on the ones he loved.

He sat unmoving for so long he seemed to have become a part of the rock.

Abruptly his head came up, and his eyes flew toward the east. "Oh, Mía, no!" he cried exultantly. "I am not alone! I have forgotten the child!"

He was suddenly motionless. He turned to the west, toward Wenimats. His words to the K'atsina were soft and plaintive.

"Let the child live."

Quickly he rose and made his way to the ground. In his uneven gait he loped the entire distance across the valley floor, reaching the base of Áco as the sun made its vibrant preparation to fall below the black mesa that stretched across the west.

When the sun rose the following morning, the fourth day, it bathed a stark figure in its winter light.

"Behold, Sun, the child called Mastya."

Rohona's voice rose with pride into the cold, crystal air as he held the tiny bundle toward the east.

# Author's Note

*Ácoma* is a work of fiction. It is not meant as a work of history or anthropology. Based, however, upon extensive historical and anthropological research, the novel hopes to have allowed the reader a glimpse of life in seventeenth-century New Mexico. Although historical accuracy was a guiding principle, some of the author's decisions were arbitrary. For example, would the Franciscan friars wear their traditional gray habits, or would they wear blue habits to which they changed in the early 1600s in veneration of the Immaculate Conception of Mary? Although Don Juan de Oñate's *entrada* occurred in 1598, the author chose to attire the priests who accompanied him in blue. In the novel, would the mountains at Santa Fé be called the Sierra Madre as they were until the late eighteenth century or would they be referred to by the present-day name of Sangre de Cristo Mountains, which dates from the nineteenth century? The author chose the much more evocative and visual name, Sangre de Cristo ("Blood of Christ").

Certain decisions in terminology posed problems: should translations be literal or should the best English equivalent be used? At times, however, there wasn't a good equivalent in English from which to choose. For example, the army rank of *sargento mayor* translates literally as "sergeant major." The men under Oñate's command were not a regularly constituted army and rank was arbitrarily conferred. In the case of his nephews, the younger, Vicente de Zaldívar, was designated as *sargento mayor* and third in command of the conquest. His rank and responsibility were certainly higher than that of a sergeant major in the United States Army. However, rather than attempt to find an equivalent rank, the author chose to designate Vicente de Zaldívar simply as "sergeant major."

Cloth and furniture were always scarce in colonial New Mexico, and life was perhaps even more stark than the author has allowed. Native ceremonies, too, are used for artistic and novelistic purposes and should not be read as anthropological descriptions of Pueblo ceremonials. The timing and depiction of certain religious events do not necessarily correspond to present-day practices. It is hoped, however, that the sacredness of these ceremonies and the reverence with which they were and are performed has been rendered faithfully.

The author welcomes comments and inquiries about any historical aspects of the novel.

Los Llanos de Cíbola (Buffalo Plains)
Río Izama (Río Chama)
San Gabriel
Taos
Picuris
Santa Clara (Caypa)
San Juan (Okhé)
San Ildefonso
Nambé
Cochití
Tesuque
Santo Domingo
Santa Fé
Jemez
San Felipe
San Marcos
Zia
Santa Ana
Puaray
Galisteo
Moqui
Zuñi
Sandía
San Cristobal
Isleta
Ácoma
Los Pueblos de las Salinas
Las Humañas
Socorro
Qualacú
Río Gila
Jornada del Muerto
NUEVO MÉXICO
El Paso del Norte
Río Bravo del Norte (Río Grande)
NUEVA ESPAÑA